"Read... ...
to bring the heat, and more. Her characters are
multidimensional, tantalizing and charming."
—*RT Book Reviews* on *Texas Wild*,
4 ½ stars, Top Pick

"Brenda Jackson is the queen of newly discovered
love… If there's one thing Jackson knows how to do,
it's how to pluck those heartstrings
and stir up some seriously saucy drama."
—*BookPage* on *Inseparable*

"This deliciously sensual romance
ramps up the emotional stakes and the action
with a bit of deception and corporate espionage....
[S]exy and sizzling."
—*Library Journal* on *Intimate Seduction*

"Jackson does not disappoint…
first-class page-turner."
—*RT Book Reviews* on *A Silken Thread*,
4 ½ stars, Top Pick

"Jackson is a master at writing."
—*Publishers Weekly* on *Sensual Confessions*

P9-DYD-113

**Brenda Jackson has written
over one hundred books featuring multicultural
romances and strong, sexy romantic heroes.
The Grangers is her newest series
for Harlequin MIRA.**

Look for Brenda Jackson's next novel
in The Grangers series,

A SON'S PROMISE,

available June 2014.

BRENDA JACKSON

A BROTHER'S
Honor

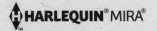

HARLEQUIN® MIRA®

Recycling programs
for this product may
not exist in your area.

ISBN-13: 978-0-7783-1433-2

A BROTHER'S HONOR

Copyright © 2013 by Brenda Streater Jackson

For questions and comments about the quality of this book, please contact us
at CustomerService@Harlequin.com.

HARLEQUIN®
www.Harlequin.com

Printed in U.S.A.

To the love of my life, my husband and best friend,
Gerald Jackson, Sr.

To everyone who will be joining me
on the 2013 Cruise to Alaska. This one is for you!

To my Heavenly Father
who gave me the gift to write.

Be devoted to one another in brotherly love.
Honor one another above yourselves.
—*Romans* 12:10

Prologue

"Foreman, has the jury reached a verdict?" the judge asked in the still, quiet courtroom, packed to capacity. The trial of the State of Virginia versus Sheppard Granger had lasted for five weeks, and the eight men and four women had deliberated for sixteen hours.

"Yes, we have, Your Honor."

"Will you hand the verdict form to the court, please?"

Within seconds, the bailiff presented the form to the judge, who took a moment to read the document before handing it in turn to the clerk who faced those in the courtroom.

Sheppard Granger showed no emotion as the clerk began reading what would be his fate. At one point, he was tempted to glance over his shoulder to look at his three young sons—Jace, sixteen; Caden, fourteen; and Dalton, who would be turning twelve in a few days. He hoped and prayed that, no matter what the jury decided, they would believe he was an innocent man. There was no way he would have killed the mother of his beloved sons.

Instead, he listened as the clerk spoke the words...
"Of the charge of first degree murder in the death of
Sylvia Granger, we, the jury, find Sheppard Granger
guilty."

Sheppard suddenly felt his knees weaken, but he refused to go down, and he refused to glance back at his
sons. His father, Richard Granger, would know what
to do now. Richard would now become responsible for
his grandsons, and he would be there for them since
Sheppard would not.

The judge was talking, addressing the court. But
whatever he was saying Sheppard couldn't hear for
the pounding in his head. As far as Sheppard was
concerned, nothing else mattered. Only one thought
repeated itself in his head with blinding clarity—his
life as he'd once known it was over.

PART I

We do not remember days; we remember moments.
—Anonymous

Chapter One

Hoping it wasn't obvious that he was watching the time, Jace Granger took a sip of his wine and looked straight ahead at the huge clock hanging on the wall, directly above the entrance of the upscale Los Angeles restaurant. He'd been there for exactly one hour and twelve minutes, and was biting at the bit to call it a night.

He appreciated his friend Alan Carter's concerns about his solitary life, but blind dates had never been Jace's thing, and he had known after the first ten minutes that he'd made a mistake by letting Alan talk him into one tonight. No doubt Angela Farlow was a looker—he would give her that, but so far it had been one hell of a night. For starters, she talked too damn much. She had a lot to say…a lot about practically nothing.

Jace took another sip of his wine and listened…or at least pretended to do so. The last couple of times he had tried interjecting his own thoughts and views, she had unabashedly cut them down, letting him know what she thought of any opinions other than her own.

Noticing a lull in the conversation, Jace shifted his gaze from the clock back to her and saw the sultry pout that touched her lips.

"Why do I get the feeling that I'm boring you?" she asked in a low tone.

Because you are, he was tempted to say. But being the gentleman that he was, instead he said, "On the contrary, I happen to find you anything but boring," plastering a smile on his face. "In fact, I find you simply fascinating." Now, that wasn't a lie. He doubted there were many women like her. Hell, he hoped not.

"Well," she said, smiling all over the place at the compliment. "I've talked enough about me. Now I want to hear about you. Alan tells me the two of you went to law school together and that, as a government attorney, you're in charge of making sure the great state of California stays on a straight and narrow path."

She rested her chin on her hands. "What made you want to work for the government instead of going into private practice? Alan said you graduated from UCLA at the top of your class."

Jace forced his body not to tense, something that usually happened whenever he was questioned about his decision to work in the public sector instead of the private, where he could have become a millionaire if he'd set his mind to it. Little did she know he had been groomed for just that kind of life and had intentionally walked away a long time ago.

His shoulders mimicked a careless shrug before giving her the same spiel he gave anyone who had the audacity to inquire. Briefly and thoroughly, with a not-so-smooth edge, he basically told her that he preferred working for the people instead of kissing asses for any amount of money. He really didn't expect people to understand and didn't really give a damn if they didn't.

He took a sip of his drink and smiled inwardly. The woman was finally at a loss for words, and he understood her dilemma, honestly he did. She thought the same way his ex-wife did. Eve's belief had been that the more money you had, the happier you were. All he had to say to that theory was *bullshit*.

It didn't surprise him when his date suggested they end the evening. That was fine with him, since the last thing he wanted was to become involved with another woman who had the same mindset as his ex-wife.

An hour later, he was entering his condo, grateful the evening with Angela had ended and that his path wouldn't cross hers anytime soon. He figured she was probably on the phone with Alan at that very moment, giving him a piece of her mind about setting her up on a blind date with a man who evidently hadn't any plans of making anything of himself.

Jace pulled off his jacket and was about to take it to the closet and hang it up when his cell phone rang. He wondered if it was Alan calling him already. He checked caller ID and saw it wasn't Alan but his grandfather. It had to be past midnight in Virginia, and he wondered why the old man was calling so late.

"Yes, Granddad?"

"Jace?"

He frowned. It was not his grandfather's deep, authoritarian voice but that of a woman. A woman whose voice he recognized immediately as the family's housekeeper's. "Hannah?"

"Yes, it's me. You need to come home immediately."

His heart nearly stopped at the thought of returning there, a place he hadn't thought of as his home for years. "Why? What's wrong?"

"It's your grandfather. He's had a heart attack, and it doesn't look good. It's serious, Jace."

Jace drew in a deep breath. His strong, robust grandfather? Heart attack? But he knew Hannah. She had been housekeeper to the Grangers for years. She wasn't one for theatrics or drama. If she said it was serious, then it was. He rubbed his hand down his face. "All right, I'm on my way."

"What about your father, Jace? Can you get word to him?"

"Yes, I'll contact Warden Smallwood right away."

"All right. I tried calling Caden, but I couldn't leave a message. His voice mail box is full, and I have no idea how to reach Dalton. He changes phone numbers probably more than he changes his underwear," she quipped.

Jace couldn't help but smile. Hannah was still Hannah. "I'll get ahold of them, don't worry." He pushed to the back of his mind the memory of the heated argument between him and his brothers when they were together last year.

"But I am worried, Jace."

He knew she was and he could hear it in her voice. The usual no-nonsense tone was diluted with distress. Something that was uncommon for his grandfather's unflappable housekeeper. "Okay, just take it easy. We don't need you in the hospital, as well. Granddad's at St. Francis Memorial, right?"

"Yes, on the Ava Granger wing."

"Okay," he said, trying not to think about the fact that his grandfather was in the part of the hospital that had been dedicated to Jace's grandmother over twenty years ago. Jace could remember that day well, especially the ceremony. They'd all been there. His grandfather, his brothers, his father...and his mother.

He immediately pushed the thought of his parents from his mind. To think about his mother meant remembering how she had died and that the law had decided his father had been the one responsible for ending her life.

"Jace, it will be good seeing you again, although I wish the circumstances of your coming home were different."

He wished the circumstances were different, too. "I'll catch the next available flight out, Hannah. Hold down the fort until I get there." He clicked off the phone and immediately called the airlines. He knew how to reach his brother Caden, but getting in touch with Dalton would be a challenge.

Moments later, after securing a flight, he went into the bedroom to pack.

Chapter Two

"Ladies and gentlemen, let's give a round of applause for the man who has become one of the greatest saxophone players of all time, Caden Granger."

Caden emerged on stage amid bright lights and faced the crowd that had packed the MGM Grand Garden Arena in Las Vegas. This was a musician's dream come true and a testimony that he had arrived. It seemed only yesterday when his first gig out of college had been at a small local watering hole in Austin. At the time, he'd been part of a band—The Depots.

The group disbanded a few years ago when most of the members decided to enter the private sector after marrying and starting families. Only Caden and two others continued to pursue their dreams, and now all three had become successful in their own right. Royce Billingslea was lead drummer with Unexpected Truth, a rock group whose last two records hit number one on the pop charts, and Robert Tyndale and his guitar were the opening act for Beyoncé.

Caden smiled for his audience before lifting the sax to his mouth to belt out the first soulful number and get them in the groove. Then he would play a string of medleys to loosen them up before ending with several numbers that would have them not only letting their hair down but getting out of their shoes, as well.

He loved this. Performing. Stimulating the crowd while he himself became energized. Being on stage was always invigorating. Never a dull moment. And the ladies who paid top dollar for front-row seats were determined to make it worthwhile. A real kick to the ego…if you were a man who needed it. Luckily, he didn't. However, that didn't mean he didn't appreciate their efforts in getting his attention. Whether it was wearing tops that showed more than an ample amount of cleavage, sitting with their legs wide-open, proudly flashing the fact they'd left their panties at home, or boldly licking their lips and swirling their tongues in a way that gave him more than an idea of what they'd like to do with their mouths if given the chance.

Unfortunately, they would be disappointed to know that when he played his sax, he tuned all of them out since his focus was on his music. Everything else became secondary. His music was and always would be his primary focus.

And it was only at this time that he allowed himself to be overcome with the one emotion he didn't want to feel until now. The people who crowded the MGM Garden Arena were only listening to the music. However, he knew the unsung lyrics spoke of a pain that wouldn't go away. It was pain that had been a part of his life for nearly fifteen years.

He would give anything…everything…to feel an ounce of his previous happiness. That was a state that eluded him at every turn, and if the way his life was going was any indication, it wouldn't be anything he found anytime soon. He knew it and accepted it, but that didn't make it right.

His life of happiness had ended the day his father had been locked up for a crime he didn't commit. No matter how many others believed differently, he knew Sheppard Granger was an innocent man, but he just couldn't prove it.

Then there had been his teen years that had been snatched away from him—he and his brothers had been ostracized by people they'd known most all their lives. People hadn't wanted their children to be friends with the sons of a criminal. And last but not least there was Shiloh, who had caused him the greatest pain of all.

So he played the music that went with his songs of lost love, lost friends and elusive happiness. The music always started out this way for him. Low-key with a melody that he felt all the way in his bones. But then it began stirring his soul, seeping through his bloodstream and becoming a cleanser, ridding his mind of so many painful thoughts. And as he continued to play his music, he found a semblance of peace from a past he couldn't forget.

"You deliberately egged her on."

"Excuse me?" Caden asked the woman who'd rounded on him. Chin up, spine straight, Rena Crews's pupils flared with the look of a woman totally pissed. Caden had seen that look before, and frankly, he was getting tired of it.

He had brought Rena on as a guitarist in his four-piece backup band last year. The ensemble would join him on stage for a couple of songs midset. She was a damn good musician, and he admired her talent. What he didn't like was her possessiveness.

They were lovers, and as far as he was concerned, that was all they were. She knew that, because he'd told her more than once that he wasn't married to anyone, nor was he involved in a serious relationship. She claimed she understood, and if that was the case, then why the drama?

She crossed her arms over her chest. "That woman who was sitting in the front row, seat ten. You know the one I'm talking about."

"Yes. What about her?"

"She had no right to sit there and all but strip in front of you. She unbuttoned her blouse nearly to the waist."

Caden lifted a brow. "Is that why you were off-key?"

He saw her flinch and knew his observation had been a direct hit. Rena was a perfectionist, good at what she did. Being off-key even for a second wasn't acceptable to her.

"Anyone would have…considering the circumstances."

"I disagree. Neither Roscoe, Salem nor I were distracted. Only you."

She was scowling when she said, "But surely you understand why."

No, he didn't, and he was a little confused as to why she thought he would. "If there had been a need, Rena, security would have handled it. The only thing I understand is what I assumed you understood, as well. We were lovers for a while and nothing more."

She lifted her chin at an angle that more than told him she was pretty pissed. "Were lovers?"

"Yes. *Were* lovers." He was letting her know that their affair was officially over, a thing of the past. "I told you in the beginning where I stood when it came to serious involvements or women who were looking for a commitment. You accepted my position." Or so she'd claimed.

He rubbed his hand down his face, not believing he was having this conversation with her. It wasn't as if he considered himself a playboy or anything; he just didn't need or want a steady woman in his life for this very reason. It would take a special woman to put up with the long hours of practice, weeks of touring and groupies that came with those things. And then there was the fact that he didn't want to share himself with anyone...other than in the bedroom.

She broke eye contact with him to snap closed her guitar case. "So now I know where you stand."

"You should have known all along, Rena. So things end here and now. We go back to the way things were in the beginning. You stay in your bed, and I stay in mine."

He paused a second and then added, "And what I do in mine and with whom is none of your business."

He saw a flash of anger in her eyes, and when she started walking away, he fought back the feeling that he was behaving like an asshole. But he immediately convinced himself there was no reason for him to feel that way, since he'd told her up front how things were between them.

As soon as the door closed shut behind her, a little

more forcibly than necessary, his cell phone went off. It was his private number. Few people had it.

Caden quickly pulled the phone from his back pocket and furrowed his brow when he saw it was Jace. It was unusual for his brother to call at this hour. Jace knew the best time to catch him was early in the mornings, before he headed out for the gym.

"Jace?" he said, after clicking on the call. "What's up?"

"Hannah just called. It's Granddad. He's had a heart attack."

Chapter Three

Dalton Granger sat by the bed, leaned back, stretched his legs out in front of him and sipped his wine while gazing at the naked woman. Lady Victoria Bowman had her curvy English ass reclining in bed, waiting for him to get a second wind.

If he didn't know better, he'd wonder just what meds she'd taken, since it had been one orgasm after another since he got here. But he did know better. Victoria cared too much for her body to ever use anything that would eventually harm it.

Dalton couldn't help but smile. He was twenty-seven to her forty-seven, and if she thought she'd gotten the best of him, she had another thought coming. Next time around, she would be the one getting her next wind and not him. He would guarantee it.

He took another sip of wine and continued to look at her. She was an extraordinary beauty with a figure that drew envious looks from much younger women. It was the norm for them to get together whenever he was in London, and it seemed over the past year that his business interests had brought him here a lot.

He glanced around the bedroom, staring at all the elegance around him. He bet that bedspread alone had cost a few thousand. The daughter of a wealthy businessman, Victoria was used to the best life had to offer and had grown up not expecting any less.

So had he.

The tragedies of life had spared her but not him...or the entire Granger family, for that matter. His brothers were doing okay. Jace was an attorney out in L.A., and Caden was a musician, performing somewhere in the States. They got together at least once a year, but the last time, around September of last year, hadn't been pretty.

Caden and his group had been in Paris performing, and it was decided that Dalton and Jace would join him there. Things had been going great until that last night when Jace had suggested they surprise their grandfather and go home for the holidays.

Home?

Now that was a damn joke. He hadn't thought of Sutton Hills, the Granger estates in Virginia, as home since the day he'd left for college. He was eighteen at the time and had no reason to return. He and his grandfather had never gotten along, and there was no need to pretend they had.

And then there was the fact that the old man had made sure Dalton hadn't been able to touch his trust fund when he'd turned twenty-five like his brothers, claiming Dalton was too much of a playboy and would lose every cent within a year. If Richard Granger expected that to keep him down, he'd been wrong. Instead, Dalton had pushed himself, determined never to have to go to the old man for anything. He'd excelled in sports and had gone to the NFL straight from college. The signing fee alone had been nice, and the two-year stint had led to lucrative endorsement contracts.

Okay, he would admit he'd almost proven his grandfather right by nearly losing it all through a few shady investments and living in the fast lane. But in the end, he'd managed to pull his shit together and become the self-made billionaire that he was.

"Are you going to sit over there for the rest of the night, Dalton?"

He chuckled and slowly rose to his feet. Like Victoria, he was as naked as the day he was born. "And just what has you in such a horny state, Victoria?" he asked, sliding his naked body back in bed beside hers.

Instead of answering, she glanced away. But not before he saw the sheen of tears in her eyes. "Victoria?" he asked softly, pulling her into his arms. They went back a long way. Sometimes he thought too long. Three years ago, almost down on his luck, he had met her father at a party while in London. Stuart Hunter, Earl of Falmouth, was nothing short of a financial genius.

For some reason, the old man took a liking to Dalton and invited him to one of his seminars. A year later, Dalton became the owner of more than twenty million in investment properties, including a number of apartment complexes in Paris and several shopping malls in Switzerland and the United States.

Victoria looked back at him and he saw even more tears. "It's Derek. Father told me today he heard Derek is remarrying," she said in a broken voice.

"I see." And he did, more than he cared to. He knew that although five years ago she had divorced the bastard for screwing around on her, Victoria was still in love with the man.

"I gave him twelve years of my life, Dalton, and I thought they were good ones. I assumed our marriage was solid. He showed me in the worst possible way that it was not. And then to make matters worse, the woman is young enough to be his daughter," she added snippily.

He decided now might not be a good time to remind her that she was old enough to be his mother. *His mother.* He pushed the painful memories of his mother and father away…and tightened his hold on Victoria. "Forget him, Victoria. He's caused you nothing but pain. You deserve better."

He'd told her that a number of times before. So had Stuart. But she refused to let go of a love that evidently controlled her heart. He couldn't imagine loving anyone that much and that deeply.

"I tried forgetting him, Dalton."

"But not hard enough," he said with irritation in his voice. He thought of everything she had going for her and figured she didn't need this drama. Hell, when it came to her, he couldn't help but feel protective. They weren't just occasional lovers; they were friends.

In a smooth move, he shifted their bodies to ease her on her back and glide between her legs. "I promise not to dwell on that million I lost last week if you promise not to think about that prick of an ex-husband of yours."

She looked up at him, eyes widened. "You lost a million dollars? Does Father know?"

"No, and I don't plan to tell him. I had it to lose,

Victoria. Besides, I don't want to hear one of his damn lectures."

She nodded. "All right. Mum's the word."

He lowered his mouth, ready to take hers, when his cell phone went off. He wanted to ignore it but recognized Jace's ring. His brother never called him at this hour just to shoot the bull. Something had to be wrong.

Victoria had seen the concerned look on his face and had reached over to grab the phone. She handed it to him. "I think you should take this."

He thought so, too. He clicked on, putting the phone on speaker. "What's up, Jace?"

"It's Granddad. He had a heart attack, and we're needed at home."

Dalton shifted off Victoria to ease back against the pillow. "And who the hell are *we?*"

"Damn it, Dalton. This isn't the time to act like an ass. Hannah called. It's serious."

"And I should care...why?"

Jace didn't say anything for a minute and then in an angry tone, he said, "Because he's your grandfather."

Dalton hadn't meant for those words to affect him, but they did. "The old man never cared about me and wouldn't care one way or the other if I were there or not. Everyone knows you were his favorite, like Caden was Dad's. I only had..." A lump formed deep in his throat when he finished by saying, "Mom."

He forced a smile through all the painful memories that suddenly emerged. Yes, he had been his mother's favorite. He'd known it, and so had his brothers. But he had been the youngest, so it stood to reason he'd found a special place in Sylvia Granger's heart.

"You won't let things die, will you? You like hold-ing on to crap," Jace accused.

Yes, he did, mainly because years ago he'd decided to never allow anything or anyone get close enough to hurt him again, and clinging to crap made sure there was distance. As far as Dalton was concerned, he'd already lost both parents, so losing the old man wouldn't destroy him.

"Look, Dalton, my plane is boarding now. I'm on my way to Virginia. I got word to Dad through the warden and I talked to Caden a few moments ago. He's meeting me at the hospital, St. Francis Memorial."

"Just keep me posted."

"Is that all you got to say?" Jace asked angrily.

"Yes. Goodbye, Jace." And then he clicked off the phone.

Victoria took it out of his hand and placed it back on the nightstand. "You should go, Dalton."

He frowned at her. "Why?"

"Because he is your grandfather."

His frown deepened. He had confided in her years ago, so she knew his family history. The good, the bad and the ugly. "And?"

"And if you think what he did to you all those years ago, denying you access to your trust fund until your thirtieth birthday, was so wrong, then go and let him see that in spite of what he did, you became a huge success."

She paused a moment and then asked softly, "He doesn't know, does he?"

Dalton shook his head. "No." In fact, he doubted even his brothers knew of the vast amount of his wealth. His family assumed he was an American gigolo in England living off women.

"Then maybe it's time he did, before it's too late."

He shook his head. "It doesn't matter."

"I think it does."

He bit back a retort, one that would have burned the hell out of her ears. "You're wrong." He lay there a moment wondering who he was shitting. It did matter, and it bothered him that it did.

Wanting to force Jace's call from his mind, he reached for Victoria, captured her mouth and hungrily began mating with it. And when he felt her passion beginning to stir, he lost himself in her incredible heat.

Chapter Four

The moment he entered the hospital room, Jace wrenched his gaze from the doctor standing by his grandfather's hospital bed. And for a minute it was hard to believe the man lying there was actually Richard Granger. The once-tall, robust man looked as if he'd shrunk into an unconscious body that was now connected to various machines.

Jace had last seen the old man during the holidays. Although he'd tried talking Caden and Dalton into spending Christmas and New Year's at Sutton Hills, both had declined. At least Caden had had an excuse with his holiday concerts being sold out. Dalton hadn't needed an excuse. He'd simply said, "When hell freezes over." Or words to that effect.

"Glad you made it, Jace."

Jace moved his gaze from his grandfather and back to the doctor, who knew him by name. Jace didn't recognize him, so he zeroed in on the name tag pinned on his medical coat. Sedrick Timmons. He remembered Sedrick and remembered when he'd always wanted to become a doctor. Over the years, his looks had changed. Gone was the tall, gangly male. This Sedrick, though still somewhat tall, was a little pudgy around the waist, wore thick-rimmed glasses and had a receding hairline.

The Timmonses had been a family of four and the Grangers' closest neighbors, although their estate was a good five miles away. In addition to the parents, Sedrick had a younger sister named Shiloh. Jace and Sedrick had played together as kids and had pretty much remained friends until their teen years.

Then Jace's mother's death and his father's trial had happened. After that, the Granger name had become a bad word to some, and the Timmonses had forbidden their children from ever associating with the Grangers again. The Timmonses had led the pack by distancing themselves, and even now, Jace could remember how being ostracized that way had felt.

Deciding there was no need for any "how have you been" dialogue, especially since their friendship had ended so long ago, Jace closed the door behind him and went right to the heart of the matter by asking, "How is he, Dr. Timmons?"

"Resting comfortably." The doctor then motioned for them to step outside the room. He and Jace moved into the corridor, closing the door behind him.

Jace saw the grim look on Sedrick's face and steeled his body for whatever news he was about to hear. "Well, how is he really?" Jace asked, needing to get it over with.

"Not good, Jace. The reason I wanted to step out into the hallway was that, although your grandfather hasn't responded since he was brought in yesterday, there's a possibility his hearing is still intact."

Jace nodded. "I understand."

Sedrick then rubbed the back of his head, a gesture Jace remembered from years past when Sedrick was about to do something that he really didn't want to do. Sedrick then dropped his hand, looked Jace straight in the eyes and said, "He's in pretty bad shape, Jace. Test results show severe damage was done to his heart. I'm surprised he's still here. It's like he's hanging on for a reason. And because I figured you'd want one, I got a second opinion from Dr. Paul Hammonds. He's the best in the field here at St. Francis."

Sedrick paused a moment and then added in a solemn tone, "I suggest you call your brothers...and get word to your father."

Because of the way Sedrick had said it, Jace could only assume Sedrick thought he hadn't done either. "Everyone has been notified."

That was all Jace intended to say on the matter. "Now, I want to spend time with my grandfather."

Sedrick nodded. "Sure, and welcome home, Jace. It's been a while."

With a bland expression that showed none of the irritation he was feeling, Jace drew in a deep breath. How would Sedrick know how long it had been? And anyway, he had assumed incorrectly. "No, it hasn't been a while, Sedrick. I was home for the holidays. In fact, I usually come home at least twice a year."

Surprise showed in Sedrick's eyes. "Sorry, I wasn't aware you ever returned to Sutton Hills."

Jace shrugged. "There's no reason you would have known."

Instead of saying anything, Sedrick shrugged and began rubbing the back of his head again. There was nothing he could say, really. Growing up, he and Jace had shared a close friendship. But that had changed, and Sedrick could tell their conversation—other than the important matter at hand—was rather awkward.

"Will you need to do any more tests?" Jace asked, thinking that getting the conversation back on his grandfather's condition would be safer ground for Sedrick. Jace didn't want him to nervously rub away the little bit of hair he still had left.

"No, not unless we detect an improvement of some sort. There's a possibility he might regain consciousness, but it won't be for long, and unfortunately, doing so might cause more damage to his heart."

Jace frowned. "Why?"

"Because if he's awake, he'll run the risk of getting excited, which could overtax the heart muscles."

At that moment, a nurse approached and offered an apology for the interruption before informing Dr. Timmons of an emergency in another patient's room.

"If you have any more questions, Jace, just have someone page me," Sedrick said, rushing off.

Jace nodded and moved to return to his grandfather's room. He hated hospitals. Always had and always would. Pulling up a chair close to the bed, he sat there and stared at his grandfather, remembering better times. He had always understood the old man when Caden and Dalton had not. That was one of the reasons everyone claimed he'd been Richard's favorite. People thought that, but Jace was fully convinced his grandfather loved all three of his grandsons the same.

Jace heard his phone tweet, letting him know he'd

gotten a text. Pulling his phone from his back pocket, he saw the message had come from Caden.

Plane just landed. Should arrive at hospital in ½ hour.

After putting his phone away, Jace drew in a deep breath, leaned back in his chair and drew his gaze back to his grandfather. At that moment, he felt an enormous pain grip his gut. His grandfather had always been there for Jace, and now Jace wanted to be here for him. But he wasn't sure how much he could take of seeing Richard lie there with tubes connected to his body and machines beeping out the only sounds in the room...except for that of his grandfather's labored breathing.

Richard Granger had celebrated his seventy-fifth birthday last year, and both Jace and Caden had come home for the occasion. Dalton hadn't, which had been no surprise to anyone.

Jace drew in a deep breath, not wanting to think about the animosity Dalton still had toward the old man. Instead, he shifted his thoughts to days past when he and his brothers were younger, happier. And their parents were together and both his father and grandfather ran the company...

His thoughts trailed off as he remembered the billion-dollar company his family owned and which his grandfather had practically run alone after his son had been incarcerated. It had been fifteen years now.

The shock of hearing about his grandfather's heart attack was so great that Jace hadn't given any thought to Granger Aeronautics. Had Hannah known to contact Titus Freeman, the executive vice president? If not Freeman, then surely Vidal Duncan. Vidal was not only the company attorney but also a longtime family friend. He would know what to do.

Any thought of Granger Aeronautics flew from Jace's mind when he noticed his grandfather's breathing had changed. It had become labored, forced. Fear gripped him as he stood to press the nurse call button. The change in breathing might not necessarily mean anything, but he wanted to be certain.

"Granddad," he said, leaning close to the bed as Dr. Timmons and a nurse rushed in. "It's Jace, and I'm here," he said in a soft voice. "You're going to get better. There's still a lot left for you to do. And you're not a person to half finish anything."

He reached out and gently gripped his grandfather's hand in his, ignoring how weak it felt as well as how frail it seemed. And he pushed to the back of his mind how unresponsive his grandfather's hand was to his touch.

Jace was glad Caden was on his way, because he didn't want to handle this alone.

"What happened?"

The sound of Caden's voice was a welcome relief, and Jace turned and looked into his brother's concerned face. Dr. Timmons and the nurse assisting him glanced up, as well.

"Jace brought it to our attention that your grandfather's breathing had changed, so we're making sure everything is okay," Sedrick spoke up and said.

"And is it?" Caden asked, walking into the hospital room and placing his sax case against a wall.

"Yes. He's resting comfortably," was the doctor's response.

Jace moved toward his brother and engulfed him in a fierce bear hug. "I'm glad to see you, Caden."

"Same here." Caden then glanced over at Dr. Timmons. "Good seeing you again, Sedrick." Moving across the room, the two shook hands.

Jace raised a brow, surprised Caden had easily recognized Sedrick when he had not.

"Same here," Sedrick said, smiling. Jace figured it was because Caden was definitely being friendlier toward him than Jace had been.

"Sorry about this situation with your grandfather," Sedrick added.

"I am, too." Caden then glanced over at Jace. "Did you reach Dalton?"

"Yes." Jace pretended to stretch his body and knew Caden intercepted the code they'd developed years ago that meant…*we'll discuss it later*.

"He's back to resting calmly now," Sedrick said. "If it happens again, let us know."

He was about to leave the room with the nurse following in his wake when Caden asked, "How's Shiloh?"

"She's fine and back in Virginia. She returned six months ago when my father became ill and stayed to help out with Mom after he died."

"I was sorry to hear about your dad's passing," Caden said.

"Thanks."

Sedrick closed the door behind him, and it was then

that Caden glanced back across the room at Jace, who said, "You handled that well."

"What?"

"News that Shiloh is back in Virginia."

Caden shrugged and his jaw tightened. "Doesn't matter to me one way or the other."

"Yet you asked about her," Jace couldn't help pointing out.

"Out of curiosity and nothing more."

Jace decided not to also point out that curiosity didn't mean a damn thing unless it mattered.

"So what's going on with Dalton? Is he coming or not?" Caden asked brusquely.

Jace stretched once again, followed by an incline of his head toward the bed after pointing at his ear.

Caden understood and nodded. "Fine."

Caden then moved toward the bed and settled down in the same chair that Jace had vacated earlier. Jace studied his brother. Although there was a two-year difference in their ages, Caden was an inch taller but somewhat thinner, especially in his facial features. He looked tired, through-to-the-bone worn, and in need of a lot of rest. Jace figured doing all those concerts and not eating properly in between, in addition to not getting enough rest, was taking its toll.

Caden reached out and took their grandfather's hand in his. "If this was your idea of getting us all back in one spot, then it worked," he said. "But just so you know, I don't like seeing you this way, so knock it off."

Jace couldn't help but smile. Years ago, Caden had found a way to bypass the old man's toughness to deal with him on a more playful level. Very few people could do that. A part of Jace wished Dalton had tried, but there had been too much anger, probably on both sides.

"His hand feels weak," Caden said, shifting his gaze from their grandfather to Jace.

"I know." Jace then glanced at his watch. "I know you just got here, but how about us going downstairs and grabbing a cup of coffee while Granddad's resting? Besides, I need to call Hannah and let her know we're here."

Caden nodded. "It's late."

Jace chuckled. "Yes, but how much you want to bet she's still up?"

Caden grinned as he stood to his feet. "You're probably right."

"You know I am," was Jace's reply as they headed for the door.

At two in the morning, the hospital's break room was empty, and as Caden settled down in a chair at one of the tables, the only thing on his mind was that Shiloh was back in Virginia.

"Still take yours black?"

He glanced over at Jace, who was standing at the coffee vending machine. "Yes, that's the only way to fly."

"Only if you pull all-nighters as you've evidently been doing," Jace tossed back.

Caden wasn't in the mood to go any rounds with his brother about his late nights. Hell, he knew he needed to do better in the rest department, but doing Vegas was any entertainer's dream come true. Luckily, it had been his last night, so he didn't have to cancel any performances. But he did have that gig coming up in New York in a few weeks. It was only two weeks, but the pay and the exposure were awesome, not to mention he was already committed.

"Here," Jace said, setting the coffee in front of Caden and interrupting his thoughts. Just as well. Caden didn't want to think about the future until he knew his grandfather was out of the woods.

"Thanks. So what are the doctors saying about Granddad?" Caden asked.

He watched his brother slide into his chair and recognized that someone who knew Jace as well as he did would be sure that whatever he was about to say wasn't going to be good. The words *bad news* were written all over Jace's face.

"Not good. In fact, Sedrick is surprised he's still here. The heart attack did a lot of damage to his heart muscles."

Although Caden had inwardly steeled himself as much as possible against what was about to come, Jace's words were still a devastating punch in the gut. "We'll get a second opinion," Caden said after taking a sip of his coffee.

"We got one, Caden. Results are the same."

Caden held his brother's gaze. "So what are you saying?"

Jace rubbed his hand down his face before saying, "We're losing him."

Caden closed his eyes and switched his gaze off Jace to some abstract picture on the wall. The thought of losing the old man was hard on him, almost as hard as it had been to lose his dad. The only difference was that his father hadn't died, and Caden could go see him whenever he wanted…in accordance with the penitentiary's visiting hours, of course. And he made it a point to visit his dad as often as he could. It had been fifteen years. Fifteen hard and lonely years without his father being free.

He looked back at Jace. "Have you told Dad?"

Jace nodded his head. "Yes, I contacted him before flying out here and spoke to Warden Smallwood. He promised to get the message to Dad. But Dad has no idea of how bad things are."

Caden didn't want to be the one to tell him and knew Jace didn't want to be the one, either. He took a sip of his coffee and studied his brother. This had to be hard on Jace, since he and their grandfather were extremely close. Caden had always chalked it up to Jace's being the firstborn grandson and all that. But later, as they got older, Caden realized just how much like Richard Granger Jace truly was. He had the ability to put everything in the proper order. He could be tough when there was a need. Uncaring, firm, rigid, inflexible…and all those adjectives that meant the same thing. But then there was a side of him that demonstrated he had to be the most caring person in the world. You just had to know how to work it to get that side exposed.

"Jace, are you okay?" Caden asked softly.

Jace, who'd been staring down into his cup of coffee, lifted a tormented gaze to him. "Not really. Remember how after Dad's trial we thought our world had ended? After losing Mom, we had to hear all that bullshit about Dad killing her, losing our friends and seeing what asses our neighbors were?"

Caden recalled those difficult days. "Yes."

"It was hard for me, but the one bright spot was Granddad. He was there, and I'm sure it wasn't easy for a sixty-year-old man to take on raising three teenage boys."

Caden agreed. It probably wasn't easy. "And he did so while keeping a firm managing hand on Granger Aeronautics. Who'll be looking over things now?"

Jace shrugged. "Probably Freeman. He's vice president."

"Only because the old man couldn't convince you to move from out West and into the spot. He always wanted you to take his place, Jace."

Jace's dark brown eyes narrowed at his brother. "It's kind of late for that, isn't it? Besides, if I remember correctly, he wanted *all* of us to take a part in the company, not just me."

"Yes, but with you being the first Granger grandchild, it would have been your place more than mine or Dalton's. It was expected."

And it had been. Richard had made sure all three of his grandsons worked for the corporation during their summer months of high school and college, whether they had wanted to or not. He had been crushed when all three told him they had no desire to work in the company their great-grandfather had formed. But that decision from Jace had disappointed him the most. He still held hope that Jace would change his mind and take his father's place once he completed law school.

When he saw Jace wouldn't change his mind, Richard had finally left the matter alone.

"And it wasn't expected of you?" Jace asked with an edge to his voice.

Caden refused to back away from the truth. "Not as much. He knew I was too much into my music to think of ever fitting in with the business suit crowd. I wouldn't last a year. I would have been fired for playing my sax during work hours."

Jace nodded. "And Dalton?"

Caden grinned. "Our baby brother wouldn't have been able to keep his hands to himself when it came to a pretty woman."

Jace threw his head back and laughed. "Now, that's the truth."

It felt good to hear Jace laugh, Caden thought. He wondered how often his brother laughed at all anymore. And what about Dalton? How many times did he laugh these days? Caden could only speak for himself, but his own laughter was a rare thing, with long stretches in between.

"And speaking of Dalton," Caden spoke up to say. "Where the hell is he? And don't tell me he doesn't plan on coming."

The amusement was immediately wiped from Jace's face. "Okay, I won't tell you."

"Why?" Caden asked, and heard the disgusted tone of his own voice. "Did you not tell him how serious things were?"

"Yes, I told him, and it's his feeling that the old man wouldn't care one way or the other if he were here or not."

"Bullshit."

"I know, but Dalton has a hard head and is stubborn to a fault. He never forgave Richard for not letting him claim his trust fund when he turned twenty-five."

Caden frowned. "Granddad had good reason for doing what he did, and you and I both know it. Dalton was chasing anything in a skirt and had already blown most of that endorsement money, which should have set him up for life."

"Yes, but evidently Dalton doesn't see it that way. Having to wait until he's thirty to get what we got at twenty-five is a thorn in his side," Jace said.

Caden didn't say anything for a moment, and then, after taking another sip of his coffee, he said, "I could have waited since I haven't touched mine, anyway. What about you?"

Jace shook his head. "I haven't touched mine, either."

Neither man said anything else for a while, and then Caden asked, "How much did you tell Hannah?" Jace had made the call before they'd stepped on the elevator. Hannah was glad they'd made it to Virginia but was disappointed Dalton hadn't come.

"Exactly what Sedrick told me," he said, standing. "She's not handling it well."

"I can imagine," Caden said, easing from his chair while thinking just how long Hannah had been with the Grangers. Close to fifty years. They didn't consider her a housekeeper but a member of the family. Their grandfather had depended on her a lot when he'd taken on the task of raising his grandsons. "So what are you going to do now?"

Jace glanced over at him as they headed for the elevator. "I'm operating on Pacific time, so I'm good. I plan to stay here so that if Granddad wakes up he'll know one of us is here. You can go on home and—"

"Home?"

"Sutton Hills," Jace clarified. "Keep Hannah company. I doubt she'll get any sleep tonight anyway."

"I'd prefer to stay, too," Caden said. "Like you insinuated earlier, I'm a late-nighter."

"All right."

The two had made it back to their grandfather's room and had pulled chairs close to the bed where they planned to park it for the night when a nurse walked in. She offered to bring in cots. After all, she'd said, their money had paid for this particular wing, so it was the least she could do.

She'd done more by bringing in fluffy pillows and blankets, as well. Since the room was pretty sizable, probably the largest one in the wing, Caden and Jace figured they could make themselves pretty comfortable.

Deciding to end all conversation so as not to disturb their grandfather, they settled in for the night. A few hours after they'd dozed off, they were awakened by the creaking sound of the door opening. They figured it was a nurse coming in to check on their grandfather. Suddenly, the fluorescent light burst to life overhead, nearly blinding them.

"Now why am I not surprised to find the two of you here, goofing off?"

Jace leaned up and his mouth dropped open in surprise. "Dalton?"

"Hell, yeah, it's me."

"I thought you weren't coming," Jace said, squinting against the bright light and inwardly downplaying just how good he felt that his brother was here.

"I changed my mind."

Caden tossed off the blanket and sat up on the cot. "Fine time for you to show up, just when we were trying to get some sleep."

"Go to hell."

Dalton then glanced past them to the man lying in the hospital bed. And as if what he was seeing was way worse than he'd expected, he leaned back against the hospital room door and said, "Holy shit."

Chapter Five

"Just what had you expected to find when you got here?" Jace asked his brother when he and Caden found themselves downstairs in the break room drinking coffee once again.

Dalton, his face still ashen from shock, shrugged. It was obvious he could have used something a lot stronger to drink than coffee. "Hell, I don't know. But the last thing I expected was for the old man not to look like himself. Flat on his back. Shit. I don't recall him ever being sick or looking this bad. He was always bigger than life. Strong as an ox. Unconquerable."

Caden rolled his eyes. "He had a heart attack, Dalton."

"Yes, and so did Victoria's grandmother. But the old girl was up and about and back to playing bridge with her friends a few weeks later," he explained, then took a sip of coffee as if it would calm his frazzled nerves.

"She probably had a light heart attack," Jace said and had a sudden flashback of this Victoria, the older Englishwoman his brother had been involved with for a while. He'd had a chance to meet her when Caden had performed in Paris. She looked good for her age, he would give her that. But a twenty-year difference? Christ. As far as he was concerned, that was too wide a gap.

He took a sip of coffee, deciding the less he thought of his brother's affairs, the better. "According to Dr. Timmons, Granddad suffered a massive one. It destroyed most of his heart muscles. I told you over the phone how serious it was," Jace said, then sipped his coffee again.

"But I didn't fully believe you. I thought you were just saying that to get me home," Dalton responded.

"I'd never pretend about something like that. And if you didn't believe me, why are you here?"

Dalton didn't say anything for a moment and then, "I figured the old man and I had a few things to discuss."

"Like you pressing him to lower the age for your trust fund?" Caden said, sitting upright and glaring over at his brother.

Dalton glared back. "And if I was, it's none of your business. Besides, I don't need the trust fund now." He quickly decided to change the subject before he was asked to elaborate. "Did you get to talk to Dad when you called to tell him about Granddad?" he asked Jace.

Jace shook his head. "No. I spoke with the warden. He'll get the word to Dad."

Dalton nodded slowly. "And how is Dad?"

"You wouldn't have to ask if you took the time to go see him for yourself," Caden said angrily.

"Fuck you, Caden. I was talking to Jace."

Caden leaned over the table, nearly in Dalton's face.

"And I was talking to you. When was the last time you saw Dad? Five years? You're one damn poor excuse for a son."

"Hell, you don't understand. I'm not like you and Jace. I can't handle seeing Dad that way. Locked up, talking to us through a damn glass partition and wearing that same blue outfit. We're not talking about some street bum, gangster or drug pusher. We're talking about Sheppard Granger, respected businessman, wealthy entrepreneur, law-abiding citizen, who never had as much as a speeding ticket."

"So your infrequent visits had nothing to do with your thinking that perhaps Dad was guilty after all?" Jace asked calmly while watching Dalton with an intense gaze.

"What the f—? No. That's not the reason," Dalton said, looking first at Jace and then at Caden, who was staring at him just as intently. "How could you guys even think something like that?"

Jace shrugged. "Because it's been fifteen years, and whether we want to discuss it or not, we of all people have reason to think Dad had the motive, especially after the argument we heard that night and what was said."

Silence ensued for a few moments, and although no one said anything, they were each remembering that last night their mother had been alive and the heated argument their parents had had. They had heard it, yet when the authorities had questioned them together and then individually, they had denied knowing anything. They had refused to say anything that would have incriminated their father even more.

Even at their young age, they'd had enough sense to talk with Hannah, who had heard the argument, as well. She had encouraged them to discuss the matter with their grandfather, and the five had decided in their hearts there was no way their father could have done such a thing, no matter what threats he'd made against their mother that night.

"You never said why you stopped visiting Dad," Jace said to break the silence. "Not to me, Caden or Granddad. And especially not to Dad. He never asked, but he wondered if that was why. That you had begun to doubt his innocence."

"Well, that's not it. Because I knew—" Dalton caught himself and stopped talking in midsentence. Not meeting his brothers' gazes, he lowered his head to sip his coffee.

Caden wasn't going to let him off that easily. "Because you knew what?"

"Nothing," was Dalton's quick response.

Jace had opened his mouth to say something when a nurse suddenly appeared seemingly out of nowhere and stood beside their table. "You have to come quickly. Mr. Granger is awake and asking for you."

The three were out of their chairs in a flash. "He's awake?" Caden asked.

"And talking?" Jace inquired, remembering what Sedrick had said about the danger of their grandfather regaining consciousness and then overexerting himself.

"Which one of us does he want to see?" Dalton asked as all three of them quickly followed the woman to the nearest elevator.

She waited until the elevator door swooshed closed

before providing any answers. She turned to Caden. "Yes, he's awake." Then to Jace she said, "He's talking, but we're keeping him calm as much as we can."

To Dalton, she simply replied, "He's asking for all three of you, and Dr. Timmons sent me to find you."

Sedrick was standing in the hallway near the door when the Granger brothers arrived on the floor. "We heard he's conscious," Jace rushed over and said.

Sedrick didn't say anything for a second and then, "Like I told you earlier, it was as if he was holding on for a reason. Evidently, it was for the three of you to arrive, because he's asked to see you."

Jace frowned. "But I thought you said the less talking he does, the better it will be for him."

Sedrick nodded. "Yes, but he's determined to say what he has to say, and I think he should." He then looked past Jace and Caden to Dalton. He stretched out his hand. "Dalton, you probably don't remember me but—"

"I know who you are," Dalton said, not bothering to accept the man's hand. "You *used* to be a good friend of Jace's."

Dalton's actions and sarcasm weren't lost on anyone, and Sedrick blushed with embarrassment. "Yes, when we were teens."

As if Sedrick's words weren't of any significance, Dalton said, "Whatever. Can we see the old man now? You're blocking the door."

"Certainly." Sedrick moved aside. "I'll remain in the area until after you've had your talk." He then walked off.

Before Jace could say anything, Caden had pushed open the door to their grandfather's hospital room.

Richard Granger's body was racked with pain, and it hurt him to breathe. The doctor had given it to him straight. Surgery wasn't an option. In other words, he had a lot to say to his grandsons but a short time to say it, so every second counted. Whether they wanted it or not, the legacy was now theirs. He had tried to do right by them and raised them as Sheppard would have.

Sheppard.

He drew in another painful breath. And that was another thing. He would have to make sure they succeeded where he had failed, in making sure their father was a free man. Fifteen years had been wasted already. It had pained his heart to know that his son, innocent of any crime, had been found guilty of murder. He had hired some of the best investigators to clear his son of the charges, but it seemed someone was out there, making sure Shep stayed put. Richard mustn't lose sight of the fact that the real murderer had gotten away and was walking around free. And probably intended to stay that way.

And all of this because of the woman he hadn't wanted his son to marry. It hadn't mattered one iota that she was born a Gadling. He had known Sylvia was bad news from the first time she had been invited to his home. But Ava had wanted the union, thought Sylvia was the perfect woman to give her those grandchildren she'd wanted. So he had gone along with it. And he had regretted it every day since.

"Granddad?"

Richard heard his name and recognized the voice.

Jace. His firstborn grandson. The one he had dreamed of one day taking over the family business for future generations of Grangers. He forced his eyes open and fought to keep them there as he stared up at the faces staring down at him. They were here. All three of them. Somehow, in his heart, he knew if he ever needed them, they would come. So sorry this time it was to say goodbye. But first...

"Jace. Caden. Dalton." His voice sounded weak and slurred, even to his own ears. "I need to tell you something. I need—"

"Granddad. Don't try to talk. You need to save your energy for—"

"No. Listen and let me talk." He saw the defiance in Jace's eyes and then he pleaded in a hoarse tone, "Please."

Jace held his gaze for a second and then nodded. The three grandsons crowded closer to the bed. Richard forced his eyes from Jace to settle on Dalton. He wasn't as close as the other two. The youngest even now wanted to be detached from the others. But no more.

"Dalton?"

He saw the surprised look on his youngest grandson's face when he called Dalton's name. It was only then that Dalton moved closer. "Yes, Granddad?"

Richard swallowed back both pain and regret. "I only wanted to make you a better man. You were Sylvia's baby. She spoiled you rotten. Things came too easily for you, and you were beginning to act entitled. But I've kept up with you over the years."

He saw the surprise that lit Dalton's eyes. "Yes," Richard said unashamedly. "I kept tabs on you even when you didn't know I was doing so. You made your own way to success, and I can look you in the eye and say that I am proud of the man you've become... without my help or that of the Granger name."

Richard paused a moment when he felt a sharp pain slice across his chest, and for a few moments he felt dizzy as the faces of his grandsons swirled around him.

"Granddad, you okay? Get the doctor, Caden."

"No," Richard said in as firm a voice as he could manage. "I need the three of you to listen carefully. First, the company. I know you all have your own lives, but Granger Aeronautics is your legacy, and I need you to claim it. Something is going on. I don't know what. Promise me that the three of you will work together to bring the company back. I delegated responsibilities to the wrong people, and only the three of you can turn the company around."

Richard coughed a few times, which caused Jace, Caden and Dalton to move closer to the bed and lean down to listen when Richard said, "I need your promise that you won't let the company fall. Promise me."

"We'll take care of the company, Granddad," Jace said. He glanced around at his brothers before adding, "We'll do it together."

"I need your individual promises," Richard implored. "Caden?"

"I promise to do what I can, Granddad."

Richard nodded. "Dalton?"

"Same here. I promise," Dalton said.

Richard nodded. "And another promise I need is for you to try to free your father. Prove he's innocent. Promise me you'll try."

Again, his three grandsons made promises.

A satisfied smile touched Richard's lips. Now he could go. "Thank you. And remember everything I taught you. Always watch each other's backs."

And then Richard closed his eyes, never to open them again.

Chapter Six

Sutton Hills.

Jace stepped out on the porch in the early morning with a cup of coffee in his hand and glanced around. Although he wished he could deny it, it felt good to be back at Sutton Hills. However, he would be the first to admit it felt strange without the presence of his grandfather. The adjustment would be hard, just as it had been when he had to make peace with the loss of his parents. One through death and the other through incarceration. It hadn't been easy during his teen years without them, and it wouldn't be easy without the old man.

Sutton Hills encompassed over two hundred acres near the foothills of the Blue Ridge Mountains. A thirty-minute ride from Charlottesville, the area consisted of the most beautiful land anywhere. The sunrises and sunsets were spectacular and could honestly take your breath away.

Located at the main entrance to Sutton Hills was the equestrian center where the horses were kept. His father's and grandfather's pride and joy. Even now,

Sutton Hills was considered a horse ranch because of the beautiful Thoroughbreds here.

The acreage was divided into four major plots. First, there was the main house where his grandparents had lived, a mile down from the equestrian center and sitting on fifty acres of land. The two-story structure was an architectural masterpiece and backed up against Mammoth Lake.

To the east of that was what had been his parents' homestead and where he had lived for the first sixteen years of his life. His grandfather had closed up the house after his father had been convicted. After the trial had ended, they had gone back just long enough to pack up their things to move to the main house with their grandfather.

Jace looked to the west to where the boathouse was located along with the entertainment center where his parents had hosted most of their parties. But his gaze stayed fixed on the boathouse because it was there, one noonday in late October, that his mother had been found dead. Shot to death. And according to the authorities, their father's fingerprints had been on the murder weapon.

"Hannah still makes the best coffee," Dalton said, opening the door to join Jace on the porch.

Jace turned, grateful for the interruption. He was about to travel too far down memory lane to suit him. "See what you were missing all those years you refused to come back here?"

"Yeah, I see." Dalton got quiet, and Jace figured he was thinking, about the past, about the present and now the future. Jace pondered the future. They had made promises, but none of them had talked about those promises since making them at their grandfather's deathbed.

Their grandfather had flatlined immediately after his last words to them, and they'd finally had to accept that Richard Granger was now gone from their lives. It had been hard going to Sutton Hills to deliver the news to Hannah and even harder to notify his father and make funeral arrangements without him.

Yesterday's memorial services had brought out people Jace hadn't seen in years, trickling in to pay their last respects to a man a few might have feared, others respected and some would have envied. What others thought of him didn't matter to Jace. To him, Richard Granger was a man to be admired. A man who didn't take crap from anyone, and he had raised his son the same way. Except that Sheppard had a softer side that he'd inherited from his mother.

One or two mourners who'd attended had asked about Jace's father, but most made solicitous statements about the old man and avoided the topic of Sheppard Granger altogether. The services were short. That's the way Richard would have wanted it. It was over, but the grief was still there for Jace. Every room in the house held memories.

"I wondered where you two had gone off to," Caden said, stepping out on the porch, as well.

"Where were you?" Dalton asked, deciding to ease down to sit on a nearby step.

"Talking to my manager. I'm supposed to be in New York for two concerts in a couple of weeks."

When his brothers just stared at him without saying anything, Caden said, "And no, I didn't forget the promise. However, I made a commitment that the band and I need to keep. I do have a life."

"You're not the only one," Dalton mumbled. "I can't believe we made that promise. Shit, I haven't done this kind of work in years."

"You mean prostituting yourself to the oldest bidder wasn't real work?" Caden sneered. "Being a boy toy has it benefits, evidently." He had met Dalton's lovers on two occasions, and both had been old enough to be his mother. Caden really shouldn't be surprised. Dalton was thought of as the extremely handsome Granger with looks that could turn heads no matter the age. And because of those looks, women had always been his baby brother's weakness.

"Hey, don't hate me. And didn't you hear what Granddad said before he died? He was proud of me because I had made something of myself."

"Evidently, he knew something that we don't," Jace said, rubbing his chin as he gazed at Dalton. He had wondered about the old man's words, but he'd been too occupied to dwell on them until now.

Dalton met his brothers' gazes, smiled and then bragged, "I'm a billionaire."

It seemed the air vibrated under Dalton's words. Jace heard Caden's chuckle of disbelief. But for some reason, Jace believed Dalton. "And how did you manage that?" he asked. "Did your duchess die and leave you a few castles, a number of pubs and a boatload of expensive jewelry?"

What Jace thought of as a devilish grin tugged at Dalton's lips before he said, "Victoria's not a duchess, she's a lady—of English nobility—and she's very much alive." He took a sip of his coffee and then asked,

Brenda Jackson

"Have you ever heard of Stuart Hunter, Earl of Fal-mouth?"

Jace raised a brow at the name and before he could respond, Caden piped in and said, "If Jace hasn't, I have. He's a well-known English investor. Filthy rich. Invests in a lot of Hollywood movies as well as space travel." Caden stared at his brother. "Why?"

"I met him while in England at a party. We hit it off. He became my mentor. He's also Victoria's father."

When neither Jace nor Caden said anything, Dalton added, "So with Stuart's help, I made a lot of nice financial moves that paid off. And for the record, Victoria and I are nothing more than friends with benefits."

"How did Granddad know? About you being successful—not about Victoria and you being friends with benefits," Caden clarified.

"Wouldn't surprise me if the old man didn't know that, as well. And I don't know how he knew. He must have kept up with what I was doing," Dalton said, staring down into his coffee as if analyzing the dark liquid. Had he been spied on when he hadn't known it? And the sad thing was that he couldn't be mad at his grandfather because that meant he cared. He then glanced up at his brothers. "How do the two of you feel about making those promises?"

Jace shrugged. "We made them, so there's nothing we can do about it. We gave him our word on his deathbed."

Dalton took another sip of coffee. "That might be true, but I don't know a damn thing about running Granger Aeronautics."

Caden rolled his eyes, knowing Dalton was about to start whining. "You worked there during the summers like the rest of us. Your mind should have been focused on the job instead of on every woman with big boobs who passed you in the hallway."

Dalton smiled. "Okay, I admit I wasn't focused."

"At least not on work," Jace said, brushing a fallen leaf off his shirt.

Dalton smiled and glanced over at Caden. "I saw Shiloh yesterday at the services. I checked her out for a good five minutes before figuring out who she was. Boy, she looked good. Who would have thought she would have filled out like that?"

Caden frowned over at his brother. "If you got something to say, then say it."

Dalton chuckled. "I just did. And since I got a rise out of your ass, I guess that means you liked what you saw, as well. She was always your—"

"Best friend and nothing more," Caden cut in, glaring at Dalton. "And that was ages ago."

"And she defected like everybody else when the going got rough," Dalton said, his voice tinged with anger and bitterness. "I want to know why half the people who came to the services yesterday were there. They acted as if the Grangers had HIV when Dad was sent to prison. You don't know how close I came to telling a few of them yesterday to kiss my ass with their condolences. And it really pissed me off when a few approached me with that lie about how good it was to see me again."

Jace didn't say anything as he leaned back on his elbows. He momentarily tuned out Dalton's angry ramblings and fixed his gaze on Caden, who'd seemed to tune Dalton out, as well. Instead, Caden was standing with his back to a post, sipping his coffee and looking as if his thoughts were a million miles away. He wondered what was on his brother's mind. Had Dalton hit a nerve by bringing up Shiloh?

"Joe Crowder is supposed to be here at eleven," Dalton said, reclaiming Jace's attention.

Joe was the family attorney. Their grandfather's will was to be read today. Vidal Duncan, the company attorney, was scheduled to meet with them, as well, after the reading. As expected, Titus Freeman had attended the funeral services. If he was aware of the promise the brothers had made to their grandfather, he hadn't let on. Just as well, since Jace had no idea how the man felt about being ousted from such a high-level position.

Dalton stood to stretch his legs and, as if pulled by a magnet, his gaze moved across the pastures in the direction of the home where he had lived as a child. "Has anyone gone back there since the day we left?" he asked.

Jace and Caden followed his gaze. It was Caden who answered first. "I haven't. Haven't wanted to."

"Neither have I," Jace said, finishing off the last of his coffee.

Dalton nodded, tucking his hands into the pockets of his jeans while he continued to scan the area. "Just wondering."

There were no surprises with the reading of the will. Everything Richard owned he bequeathed to his son, Sheppard. However, Jace, Caden and Dalton shared the handling of those properties and shared the inheritance in case of Sheppard's death. Since Jace was the oldest, he received a higher percentage than the others, which everyone thought was fair.

Hannah received the deed to her small cottage on Sutton Hills as well as papers to the car she was driving and a horse she'd grown fond of over the years. And she got a very generous monetary gift that would take care of her for life should she choose never to work again. No one said anything while Joe read through Richard's requests. On occasion, the sound of Hannah's sniffing was heard. Richard had been generous to his favorite charities, including the wing at the hospital that bore his deceased wife's name.

Joe had barely left when Vidal arrived. The two men were different in looks and stature, but both were born to be attorneys. They had that *"this is the way Richard wanted it, so this is the way it is going to be"* air about them.

"So, as you can see from the way your grandfather set things up, Freeman is to step down as vice president the moment you arrive in the office tomorrow."

Jace jerked his head around. "Tomorrow?"

"Yes, the sooner you take over the better."

Jace lifted a brow. "What's the hurry? The company isn't going anywhere, is it?"

"No, but it needs your leadership. Granger Aeronautics has been operating in the red over the past year."

Jace frowned. His grandfather hadn't mentioned anything like that to him. "Red? But why?"

"Richard didn't know why," Vidal said, shaking his head. "He wasn't getting contracts like he used to and was being outbid on a number of projects."

"That doesn't make any sense," Caden said. "I'm

no business brain, but I would think someone as astute as Granddad would have found the problem and—"

"Whoa, wait a minute," Dalton said, leaning closer to the table where they were sitting. "Are you saying that Granger Aeronautics is going under?"

"It's headed that way unless the three of you can find a way to stop it from happening."

Caden looked pissed. "And how are we supposed to do that?"

Jace heard the anger in his brother's voice. Although they hadn't said it, they were wondering the same thing. Had their grandfather made them promise to try to achieve the impossible? Try to save a company that was already failing?

"I say the three of us vote to get rid of it. Stuart may know someone who might be interested in a merger and—"

"No!" Jace said, turning on Dalton, with nostrils flaring and his gaze resembling a glacier. "Damn it, we gave our word, and we're going to keep it."

"By doing what?" Dalton stormed back. "Making things worse? What did a few summers teach us at that place? Not jack shit."

Dalton drew in a deep breath and made an attempt to cool his anger before adding, "You're talking about a corporation with close to a thousand employees, Jace. Last I heard, Granger Aeronautics was the fourth leading employer in Charlottesville. We owe it to those employees to do right by them and not screw up any pensions they have coming. If we don't make things right, they lose it all. Do you want that?"

No, that wasn't what Jace wanted, but he couldn't understand how easily Dalton could give up without trying. "Granddad was right about you, Dalton. Things did come too easy for you, and you do act entitled. Now you've made your billions, but even with that, you didn't work hard. It was through investments. I think you're afraid of a little hard work."

Dalton was out of his chair in a flash, knocking it over in the process. He got in Jace's face. "I happen to believe in working smarter, not harder."

Vidal moved forward to intervene before words were replaced with fists. However, Caden touched Vidal's arm and shook his head. As far as Caden was concerned, if it came to Jace knocking some sense into their baby brother, then so be it. It was probably about time someone did. Apparently, Dalton's billions had gone to his damn head.

"For once, will you think of someone other than yourself?" Jace asked. He was so angry he felt fury race through his bloodstream.

"And just who are you thinking about, Jace?" Dalton snapped. "Clearly not Granger's employees. Maybe you see this as your break to finally leave that pissy job you hate back in California. Well, fine, you do that and move your ass back here. But how can you expect to run a company when you couldn't even keep your marriage together?"

Now that was a low blow, Caden thought, shaking his head. Leave it to Dalton not to fight fair and bring in the personal. He was tempted to break things up, but he knew they both needed to let off steam...say what had to be said. Then he would have his say.

"My marriage has nothing to do with this." Jace moved closer to Dalton.

"Doesn't it? And by the way, I never liked your wife."

"And she never liked you!"

"Okay, I think enough has been said," Caden said, finally stepping forward. He stood next to Jace and faced Dalton. "Jace is right, Dalton. The three of us gave our word. Granted, when we did so, we weren't aware of how bad things were, but Granddad loved Granger Aeronautics. He knew the situation the company was in, and if he died believing the three of us working together could fix things, then I plan to die trying. Now, are you in or not?"

Dalton faced off with his brothers. One against two. It wasn't the first time, and he knew just as sure as there was a sun in the sky that it wouldn't be the last. And the bitch of the matter was that he loved them more than anything else in the world.

He'd loved the old man, as well, and the two of them had squared up their differences in the end. But what Jace and Caden were planning to do was crazy. Hell, he'd assumed they would be walking into a company that already had its shit together and, in a few months, they could haul ass. Dalton had figured that Jace would stay at the helm, but Dalton would return to England and Caden to his music and concerts. Dalton had accepted that on occasion they would have to make trips back for board meetings or special events. But never in his wildest dreams had he expected to inherit a company ready to fold. The thought of remaining in Virginia and at Sutton Hills for more than a week or two was beginning to make him nauseated.

"Well?" Caden said, when Dalton hadn't yet answered.

Dalton frowned, ready to tell them that, hell, no, he wasn't in and planned to leave that night to return to London. But deep down, he knew he couldn't do that...even as much as he wanted to. He, Jace and Caden had made a pact fifteen years ago, on the day their father was found guilty, that they would not let anything ever come between them, and today Dalton sure as hell wouldn't let it be Granger Aeronautics.

He lifted his chin. "Yes, I'm in."

"Good," Caden said, fighting back a smile.

Dalton's anger that had flared so quickly diffused just as rapidly. "Vidal wants us in the office tomorrow, and I refuse to wear the one suit I brought with me."

"Stop whining," Jace said. "We need to walk into the company meeting tomorrow and present a united front."

"We have a problem."

The three brothers turned to stare at Vidal. Jace and Dalton had forgotten he was in the room. "What kind of problem?" Jace asked.

"While the three of you were sorting out your little disagreement, I got a call. It seems Freeman has decided he wants to keep his position and is rallying the troops."

Caden frowned. "What troops?"

"Stockholders he thinks he can win over," Vidal said, his voice filled with irritation. "He's called a stockholders' meeting for tomorrow. He wants them to vote to keep him at the top, claiming the three of you lack experience and that he's the one who can get the company back on solid footing."

"Can he do that? Stay on as top dog?" Dalton asked, not sure just how that worked. He'd made billions by investing in companies, not trying to run any of them.

"Yes, if he has the right number of stockholders on his side. There are only a few, but those few hold enough voting shares that can be used against you."

Caden frowned. "I don't see how. Jace has inherited Dad's voting shares and the three of us have a number of our own."

Vidal loosened his tie, and Caden had a feeling he wouldn't like what the man was about to say. "Yes, but last year, Richard sold off some of his shares for quick capital to compete against another company on a certain bid. He didn't want a board of directors at Granger Aeronautics, and now there are stockholders whose shares might rival yours in numbers."

"Umm, the plot thickens," Dalton said under his breath, but loudly enough for his brothers to hear. Jace glared at him, but Caden decided not to even waste his time.

"And unfortunately, if Freeman can convince them that he can pull the company through this, they will back him and cast their votes his way," Vidal added.

"Do you know who these shareholders are?" Jace asked, starting to pace.

"Yes," Vidal said, nodding.

"How soon can you get me their names?" Jace asked, moving toward the table they'd been sitting at earlier. Caden and Dalton followed.

"In about an hour."

"Good."

Dalton felt a rush of adrenaline move through his veins. Shit, this crap wasn't so bad after all. He liked excitement, and from the looks of it, there was about to be plenty. His big brother was about to do some kind of power play. He knew that look in Jace's eyes. He was pissed, and when Jace got pissed, he got to thinking. And a Jace who thought too damn much was worse than a politician who was caught with his pants down. He would find his way out of it come hell or high water.

Jace glanced around the table at his brothers. "Okay, we're about to hold our first executive meeting, right here."

Caden nodded. "What's the game plan?"

"For crying out loud, Caden, stick to playing your sax," Dalton said while rubbing his hands together in anticipation. "Even a boy toy like me can figure that out. Jace plans to take that list of names and call those people. He's going to buy up their shares."

He then looked over at Jace and smiled, thinking that was a really smart move on his brother's part. "That's what you're going to do, right?"

"Not quite," Jace said, smiling back. "The only thing you're wrong about is the part that I'll be buying their shares."

Dalton frowned. "But if you don't buy them, who will?"

"For crying out loud, Dalton, even a saxophone player like me can figure that out," Caden said, grinning. At Dalton's blank look, he then added, "*You* will be buying them, Mr. Billionaire."

Five hours later, the brothers, along with Vidal, were still at the table going over the results of their efforts. Hannah had served them a lunch fit for a king, since it had included slices of her mouthwatering peach cobbler.

Jace had been able to speak with their father personally, to let him know what was going on. Although the call was short, it had been productive. Sheppard Granger approved of their strategy. "Okay," Jace said, leaning back in the chair. "Eight people have defected, but we won't know until tomorrow if that will be enough to pull things off."

"It better be," Dalton said, grumbling. "My bank account is minus a few million dollars."

"For Pete's sake, stop whining, boy toy," Caden said, studying one particular name on the list. Samuel Timmons. Timmons had owned over thirty shares of stock. More than likely, they all belonged to Mrs. Timmons now that Mr. Timmons was deceased. Jace had called to speak with Mrs. Timmons, but the housekeeper told him that she was out of town and wasn't expected back until late tomorrow.

One of the stockholders who defected mentioned that Freeman had called earlier to ensure that everyone showed up for the meeting and voted in his favor. So the question was, had he reached Mrs. Timmons, and if so, would she vote by proxy in Freeman's favor? Caden wouldn't be surprised if she did. Samuel and Sandra Timmons had been close friends of their parents, and their testimony had been damaging in his father's trial. And then once the trial was over, they'd forbidden their children to have anything to do with the Grangers' sons.

"Caden?"

He looked up at Jace. "Yes?"

"So what do you think?"

A slow smile touched Caden's lips. "I think we should show up for tomorrow's meeting ready to kick ass and take names."

"Now you're talking," Jace said, grinning with anticipation.

"Well, I hate to be the one to burst your oversize bubble," Dalton said. "But there are four people on that list who could either be with us or with Freeman, and their votes might be the deciding ones."

"And we can't lose our hair over it," Jace replied. "If we portray Grangers who're ready to come in, roll up our sleeves and turn the company around, I think they'll go our way. Most of them have been loyal to Granddad over the years and hopefully will want us to carry out his wishes."

"May I offer a suggestion?" Vidal said, presenting a business card to them. "Her name is Shana Bradford, and she's only twenty-eight, but she's been getting a lot of attention since her company relocated here a few years ago."

Jace glanced at the card. *Shana Bradford, Bradford Crisis Management Firm.* "Is she good?"

"Her firm has turned more than one company around, getting them out of the red very quickly. She definitely has a proven track record. I suggest you bring her on."

Jace glanced at his brothers. "What do you think?"

Caden smiled. "It's your decision to make, Mr. CEO."

Dalton shrugged broad shoulders. "I vote we hire her only if she looks good."

Jace rolled his eyes and glanced back at Vidal. "If things go in our favor tomorrow, I'll give her a call."

After hours of tossing and turning, not able to sleep, Jace got out of bed, slipped into his robe and headed downstairs to the kitchen for a glass of warm milk. He stopped when he saw Hannah sitting at the kitchen table, staring down at her folded hands.

He turned to go back to his room, not wanting to intrude on her private moments. But then he recalled something she had told him when his grandmother Ava had died and he had been filled with grief. *At times it's better to talk through the pain with someone else who cares.* At that moment he made a decision.

"You couldn't sleep either, huh?" he asked, moving to the table to sit across from her, while pretending not to see the tears glistening her eyes. Tears that she quickly swiped away before smiling over at him.

"I was just sitting here thinking about what I'm preparing for Sunday's dinner. It's so nice to have the three of you home again. I want it to be special."

Jace nodded. He couldn't speak for his brothers but deep down he was glad to be back. He hadn't realized just how much he'd missed this place. Until now his visits had been brief, but this time he was back to stay. "Well, don't get carried away, Hannah. The more we eat the harder it will be to work off later."

She chuckled as she took a sip of her tea. "There's more tea where this came from if you want a cup."

"Thanks, I think I will," he said, getting up from the table. "I came down for a glass of warm milk but I think the tea sounds better."

As he poured the hot water in the cup he glanced over his shoulder at her as she stared down into her tea. Hannah had been with the Grangers for years. His grandparents had hired her as nanny and housekeeper just weeks after his father was born. And twenty-five years later she had gone to live with Sheppard and his wife when Jace came into the world, then remained to care for Caden and Dalton, as well.

Hannah's husband, Raymond, had died years ago and she had taken the death hard. She and Ray had one child together, a daughter name Maretha, who'd made Texas her permanent home after attending college there.

He could not remember a time when Hannah had not been a part of their lives. She had been there when his grandmother had died, and had helped them deal with the loss of their mother and the incarceration of their father. And she was here for them now. But she was dealing with her own grief as much as theirs. He knew his grandfather considered her more than just a housekeeper. She was part of the family.

And Jace knew that his grandfather had loved her.

He hadn't been surprised when his grandfather had confided in him the last time he was home. Jace knew neither Caden nor Dalton had a clue, mainly because they hadn't come back to Sutton Hills as often as he had. He had been able to watch the two of them interact on a daily basis. But no one had seemed surprised with the generous bequest Richard had left for Hannah. Probably because they felt she deserved everything she got for putting up with the Grangers for as long as she had.

As certain as he was that his grandfather loved Hannah and she loved Richard in return, Jace knew the affair had only developed after he and his brothers had left for college. Loneliness had been a factor, as well as the fact that Hannah looked pretty good for her age. To Jace's way of thinking, she had begun looking younger and prettier each and every time he came home to visit. And Jace more than anyone was glad she had been there as someone Richard could trust and spend happy times with.

He moved to rejoin her at the table. "He loved you, you know."

She jerked her head up and stared at him and his heart twisted at the tears he saw swimming in her eyes. "You knew?" she asked in a shocked breath.

"Yes, he told me and I was glad," he said, reaching out and placing his hand on hers.

She swallowed. "Do you think Caden and Dalton…"

"Know?" he finished for her. Shrugging, he released her hand. "Not sure if he told them, too, but it doesn't matter. Granddad probably wasn't an easy man for a woman to love so I believe what the two of you shared was special."

"Thank you, and it was," she said, swiping away her tears. She got up from the table to grab a tissue and then returned to sit across from him once again. "You boys are doing the right thing, Jace. Your granddaddy loved that company and he would not ask the three of you to take it over if he didn't believe you could do it," she said softly.

Jace didn't say anything for a minute, then sighed deeply. "I hope you're right, Hannah. I feel like the weight of the world is on my shoulders right now. I have big shoes to fill and I don't want to let him down."

She reached out and placed her hand on his. "You won't. He believed you can do it, and I do, too."

He couldn't help but smile. It had always been that way with Hannah when it came to him, Caden and Dalton. She made them feel special in ways his own mother hadn't. Sylvia Granger hadn't been the easiest woman to get along with, and Jace had known it.

"Thanks." He took a sip of his tea and then said, "Tomorrow is a big day but I think we're going to get through it."

She nodded. "You *will* get through it. Running Granger's is in your blood. You'll see."

He didn't say anything for a minute and then asked, "Did you know the company was in such a dire state?"

She shook her head. "No, Richard never talked about work with me. That was our rule. I wanted to be his escape from all of that. I wanted him to be able to relax without worrying about Grangers. I wanted only happy times for us."

"And considering everything," Jace said softly, "you deserved those happy times. You both did. It's okay for us to grieve now, but I believe happy times will return for all of us one day."

She paused a minute and then said, "Do you know what would make me extremely happy?"

He glanced over at her. "No. What?"

"For you to settle down one day, remarry and give me another generation of Grangers to raise."

Jace chuckled. "Let's conquer one thing at a time, please. I'll be married to Granger Aeronautics for a while."

Hannah snorted. "That company won't keep you warm at night. Remember that."

He leaned back in his chair and gazed at Hannah and smiled. He had a feeling she would not let him forget it.

Chapter Seven

Brandy Booker, the receptionist who was manning the spacious lobby of Granger Aeronautics, looked up from her desk and stared into three pairs of light brown eyes. She remembered seeing the three a few days ago at the funeral services for Richard Granger. They were his grandsons, and never had she seen such sexy, handsome men before. Sunlight filtering through the huge window seemed to shine directly on them, making them appear almost bigger than life and even more handsome.

They were impeccably dressed in expensive business suits, white dress shirts and fashionable ties. Two of the men wore serious expressions, while the third was giving her a flirty grin, which she was tempted to give back to him. She cleared her throat. "Yes, may I help you?"

"We're the Grangers, and we're here for the stockholders' meeting," one of the men said. She knew he was Jace Granger, the eldest. She recalled he had delivered his grandfather's eulogy.

Rumors were going around that Mr. Granger had

left the business to his grandsons, and she had a feeling things were about to get pretty interesting around here. Especially since Mr. Freeman, the VP, had been running around like a chicken with his head cut off all morning. He liked power and was fighting like hell to retain it.

"Yes, Mr. Granger, the meeting is about to begin." She wondered if their timing was deliberate to make some sort of grand entrance, and she could certainly see them making one. "I'll be happy to escort you in."

Jace, Caden and Dalton walked into the huge conference room, and everyone seated at the table glanced their way. Seeing three empty seats, they took them. Jace saw the disappointed look that flashed in Freeman's eyes and figured the man had been hoping they would be no-shows.

Once seated, Jace glanced around the room. Everyone who he figured would be here was, and since there were a few people he hadn't expected, he could only assume they were voting by proxy. One in particular, he knew, was drawing Caden's attention. Shiloh Timmons.

Jace glanced over at Freeman. His secretary had called to advise them of the meeting late yesterday, and Jace was certain it was a deliberate move on Freeman's part. It would have been too late to form any type of strategic countermove. Freeman would be surprised to learn he didn't have the upper hand he assumed he would.

At exactly ten o'clock, Freeman called the meeting to order. Since this was an unscheduled meeting, he asked for a motion that the secretary not read the minutes from the last meeting. His motion was seconded.

Freeman then addressed the meeting, once again offering his sympathies to the Granger family for their loss. He then, pretty elegantly Jace thought, indicated the reason for the meeting. Freeman stated that the company was about to change leadership and direction at the worst possible time. And that although he respected Richard's decision in wanting a Granger to run the company, he had been vice president for two years and felt more than capable of taking the company where it needed to be. He offered to have the Grangers work under him for a while to learn the ins and outs of the company, after which time, he would gladly step down and let the brothers take things over. However, he stressed that now was not the time.

Jace glanced around the table. Everyone was listening attentively, a few were taking notes and some had nodded. He was glad they'd made the move to buy up stock yesterday. His keen sense of discernment allowed him to pinpoint the people Freeman already had in his pocket. So Freeman's claim that he would only take over for a short while was a bunch of bullshit, and they all knew it.

After Freeman stopped talking, the secretary asked if anyone had anything to say before votes were cast. Jace knew it was his time to speak, and he stood up to do so. "This company was started by my great-grandfather over seventy years ago and was later run by my grandfather, father and then, in my father's absence, my grandfather again. On his deathbed Richard Granger asked that my brothers and I take over the day-to-day operations of Granger Aeronautics. All of you know how much my grandfather loved this company, and he would not have made such a request had he not felt that we could succeed in what he was asking us to do and that it was in the best interest of this company. He had faith in us, and I'm hoping you do, as well. I am ready to take over as CEO and move this company in the right direction. I ask for your vote of confidence."

Freeman then asked for a vote, indicating for his secretary to do a roll call. From the smile on his face, it was apparent he was fairly certain he would come out on top. However, Jace saw that smile turn to concern when, during the roll call, it was obvious that a number of stockholders had gotten rid of their stock yesterday.

The roll call had been done in alphabetical order, and Jace wasn't surprised when Freeman had five times the number of votes Jace could cast due to proxy. He saw shock and then anger appear in the older man's eyes when he saw how many voting shares Jace, Caden and Dalton had obtained.

It was a close vote, and the last person on the roll call was Sandra Timmons. Shiloh was her proxy. She had enough shares to cast the deciding vote. Jace refused to look over at her, figuring that Caden had been doing it enough for the both of them.

The secretary spoke up. "Shiloh Timmons, proxy for Sandra Timmons. How do you want to cast your vote?"

Jace literally held his breath. He didn't release it until he heard Shiloh say in a clear voice, "I am voting for Sandra Timmons, thirty shares for the Grangers."

"Your girl saved the day, man," Dalton said after the meeting had adjourned. "I was sweating bullets there for a minute."

"She's not my girl," Caden said as he stood at the window in the conference room and looked out. "And I wish you'd stop insinuating that she is."

Dalton, who was leaning back lazily in one of the conference room chairs, shrugged broad shoulders. "You and Shiloh were close growing up."

Caden turned around. "Yes, and if you recall, that was before…" He paused, knowing he didn't have to go into any details. Dalton knew. Each of them had felt the pain of suddenly being ostracized by their friends.

"She was just a kid, Caden. A kid who had to do what she was told. Can you imagine her going against old man Timmons? If you remember, the man was an asshole."

Caden did remember, but there was more to his and Shiloh's history than Dalton knew. More than anyone knew. And he wasn't about to enlighten his brother about anything now.

Jace entered the conference room. "I just talked to Vidal. He'll make sure the transition is done as smoothly as possible. Everything is set."

"Set how?" Dalton wanted to know. He had several million dollars in Granger shares, and he intended to get a return on his investment. Stuart would have a cow when he heard about what he had done. The first rule when investing is to make sure you don't lose money. That meant he needed to stay on top of things so that rule was not broken.

"Freeman and I have reached an understanding," Jace said easily.

Dalton sneered. "Understanding, my ass. I don't trust him."

"Neither do I," Caden said, leaning against the wall.

"Hell, Jace, the man was trying to take the company right from under our noses."

"He didn't think we were ready to take over things," Jace said somberly.

"Can't blame him, since I thought the same thing myself," Dalton said. "But I still don't like what he tried to pull. So now that we're in, are you going to give Ms. Bradford a call?"

Jace pulled the business card Vidal had given him from his pocket. "I might as well. Vidal showed me a number of profit and loss statements, and this company is so deep in the red it's not funny."

That's not what Dalton wanted to hear. "But it can be turned around?"

Jace heard the concern in his brother's voice. "You'll get a return on your investment."

A hopeful look appeared in Dalton's eyes. "Promise?"

Jace held his brother's gaze. "You know I don't make promises, Dalton."

How could I forget? Dalton thought. The last time he had asked Jace to make a promise had been during their father's trial. He wanted Jace to promise him that their father would not have to serve time, and that he would be back home with them when the trial ended. They'd already lost their mother, and the thought of losing a father had been unbearable to Dalton. Jace had refused him that promise, and Dalton was glad he had. It would have been a promise that was broken.

"Yes, I know," Dalton said. "I forgot. I usually don't get out of bed before noon, and my brain was not functioning so well this morning."

"But I see your eyeballs are," Jace said. "When

you were checking out that receptionist this morning, I could swear you had X-ray vision."

Dalton chuckled as he loosened his tie a bit. "Wish I had. Damn, she looks good. I want her for my office assistant."

"If you do get an office assistant, I'm going to make sure she is not on the list." Jace eased down to sit on the edge of the table. "Speaking of your own offices, they'll be ready for you to move in before the end of the day."

"I only want an office if I get to pick my office assistant, and I want her on the list, Jace," Dalton said, grinning. "And I don't want my office next to Caden's unless it's soundproof. You know how he has a tendency to play his sax at odd times."

Dalton had expected Caden to come back with some ear-blistering retort, and when he didn't, Dalton turned to gaze over at his brother. Jace looked over at Caden, as well. Caden had gone back to staring out the window, dismissing their presence.

"I think what Shiloh did at the meeting got to him," Dalton whispered under his breath.

"You think so?" Jace asked. Personally, he thought so, too. And he had a feeling there was something else going on there but had no idea what. Why was Caden acting so uptight about a woman he hadn't had any contact with for close to fifteen years?

"Which office do you get?" Dalton broke into Jace's thoughts to ask, deciding to leave Caden to whatever thoughts were going through his mind.

"The one that was Granddad's. I'm keeping Dad's office the same way Granddad has kept it all these years. Intact."

Richard had always assumed his son would be freed and had kept Sheppard's office basically as he'd left it. Jace planned to do the same. That was another promise they'd made, the one regarding their father. And it was another he intended to keep.

"I want to go see Dad." Dalton broke into Jace's thoughts.

Jace looked at Dalton. He noted from the corner of his eyes that Dalton's statement had also grabbed Caden's attention.

"I suggest we all go see him," Caden said, moving closer to the table. He dropped down in one of the chairs.

"Sounds like a plan. I'm sure losing Granddad was hard on him," Jace said, glancing at his watch. "Getting out to visit him today or tomorrow might be difficult with everything that is going on. I'm trying to set up a meeting with Shana Bradford as soon as I can. According to Vidal, if anyone can get us out of the red, she can."

Shana Bradford smiled up at the man who'd made her coffee. "The coffee is great as usual, Dad."

He was the one man she most admired. Widowed, her father had raised her and her sister Jules alone, which hadn't been easy while working as a policeman defending the streets of Boston. He had retired a few years ago, wanting a quiet life, and had decided to settle in Charlottesville, the place where her parents had first met while attending college.

Jules had been the first to follow their father to Charlottesville, where she established a private investigating firm. Shana had begun liking the area more each and every time she came to visit and, three years ago, after her breakup with her steady boyfriend, she decided to move her own firm here. She was glad she had. She loved Charlottesville and liked having her family close by again. And she made certain that she carved out time during her busy schedule to drop by to visit her dad and grab a cup of coffee, bring him lunch or show up for dinner.

She took a sip as she watched her father move around the kitchen. The space wasn't all that large, but he actually looked lost. That was unusual, since her father generally exuded a strong presence. She immediately read the signs. Something heavy was on his mind.

"Dad, is there something bothering you?"

He quickly turned and looked at her, and she immediately noticed that his smile was tentative, nervous. He placed the dish towel on the counter, moved back toward her and sat down with her at the table. "No, there's nothing bothering me, but there is something that I need to talk to you about."

She lifted her brow as she set her coffee cup down. She couldn't hide the concern in her features. "Okay, what is it?"

He didn't say anything for a moment, and then he looked at her and gave her that same smile she'd grown accustomed to over the years while growing up. It was that smile that let her know everything was going to be all right and that he would be there for her, no matter what.

She waited…and then he released the bombshell by saying, "I'm thinking about remarrying."

Shana was glad she had stopped drinking her coffee, because otherwise she would have choked on it.

Remarry? Her father? She drew in a deep breath before saying, "I wasn't aware you were seeing anyone."

Had Jules known and just not mentioned it? No, there was no way. That would have been headline news in Jules's book, and her sister would have had the woman thoroughly vetted by now.

"I'm not seeing anyone, technically. Mona and I run into each other every so often in the grocery store." He chuckled. "We talk over the fresh vegetables, but haven't gone out on an official date."

Shana was trying desperately to follow him. "And already you're thinking about marriage?" she asked. Those had to be some strange-idea-inducing vegetables in that grocery store. Her father had to be the most logical man she knew, and she was beginning to worry because he was thinking illogically.

"Yes, just thinking of the possibility. She's the first woman I've had thoughts about since your mom, so that must mean something. You know the story of how your mom and I were attracted to each other at first glance when we met that day in class?"

Yes, she had heard the story and had always thought it was special that the two had begun dating in their sophomore year and married a month after graduation, two years later.

"So tell me, what is there about her that makes you think of marriage?" she asked, picking up her coffee cup and taking a sip.

"She's pretty. Dresses nice. Smells good."

He'd gotten up that close to the woman? "What do you know about her, Dad?"

Her father leaned back in the chair and the smile that appeared on his face at that moment was one she had never recalled seeing before. It was different some-how from the ones he had for her and her sister, Shana thought.

"I know she's friendly with a pleasant personality, and I like that. She's also kind and generous. Everyone at the store knows her. And she teaches."

Shana raised another brow. "She's a schoolteacher?"

"No, a college professor at the University of Virginia. Political Science. I never liked talking about politics until now."

Shana leaned back in her chair, as well. She just couldn't imagine her six-foot-three-inch, sixty-two-year-old father hanging around the vegetable stand in some grocery store talking politics with anyone, never mind a woman.

But, then, to be fair, in all the years since her mother died, Shana had never known Benjamin Bradford to be involved with a woman. Oh, she knew he'd dated once in a while—she could still recall the packs of condoms she and her sister had found in his drawer one year. But he had never brought any of those dates home for his daughters to meet. Their mother had died of pancreatic cancer thirteen years ago, right before Shana's fifteenth birthday. Jules had been thirteen. Now they were grown women with lives of their own, so it stood to reason that if he was ever going to be seriously interested in a woman, it would be now.

But still… Marriage?

"So her first name is Mona. What's her last name?" Shana decided to ask. There was no harm in Jules checking her out. This was their father they were talking about.

"Underwood. Her name is Mona Underwood."

"How old is she, Dad?"

He chuckled. "Hey, I never ask a woman her age."

"Yes, but I'm sure you have some idea. Take a guess."

He scrunched up his forehead. "I recall she said she was thinking about retiring in a couple of years when she turned fifty-five. So I guess she's in her early fifties."

That meant he was anywhere from ten to twelve years older than this Mona Underwood. That wasn't too bad. It could have been worse.

"Is she a divorcée, widow, never been married…?"

"Divorced. I do know that."

Thank God. "How long ago?"

"For what?"

Shana rolled her eyes. "Since Ms. Underwood got divorced?"

Her father squinted his dark eyes at her. "Why do I feel like I'm being interrogated?"

She couldn't help but smile. "Because you're an ex-cop. Comes with the territory."

She was about to ask a few more questions when her cell phone went off. "Excuse me a minute, Dad," she said as she pulled her phone out of her purse. It was her office calling. "Yes, Joyce?"

"Potential new client. Jace Granger of Granger Aeronautics. He would like to talk to you in person and wants to know if you can drop by the office. And by the way, he has *such* a sexy voice."

Shana smiled. "Calm down, single mother of three. Rein in those raging hormones." Joyce, her office manager, was thirty-three and had been a divorcée for a year or so. Since she'd started dating, she seemed to be going buck wild.

A few moments later, after getting the information she needed from Joyce, Shana hung up the phone. "Okay, Dad, I need to go. I have an appointment," she said, standing and heading for the door.

"Have I told you lately just how proud I am of you?"

Shana dropped her hand from the doorknob and turned around. Smiling, she walked back to her father, leaned down and placed a kiss on his cheek. "Not lately, but just knowing you are, is special."

"I'm proud of Jules, too, although I worry about her sometimes."

Shana nodded. Following in their father's footsteps, Jules had been on the police force for two years before making detective. When it came to solving cases, she was a whip. Jules had finally fulfilled her dream and opened an investigation firm. Her cases took her all over the place and at twenty-six and single, her sister was loving it.

"Jules can take care of herself. We both can. We're Ben's girls, and he taught us how to fend for ourselves."

A short while later, before starting her car, Shana punched in the phone number Joyce had given her. She leaned back, thinking of the conversation she'd had with her father. Jules was working a case in Miami, but as soon as her sister returned, they would talk. Ben Bradford remarrying? She wanted her father to be happy for the rest of his life, but she didn't want him to settle for the first woman he found interesting, pretty, well dressed and good-looking.

"Jace Granger."

The deep, masculine voice pulled her concentration to the phone call.

"Yes, Mr. Granger, this is Shana Bradford. My assistant relayed your message. I understand you would like to set up a meeting?"

"Today if possible."

She glanced at her watch. That was unexpected, but it just so happened that her calendar was clear for the rest of the day as the Williams meeting had been canceled at the last minute. "I have some time right now as a matter of fact. Shall I meet you at your office?"

"No, not here. It's almost lunchtime. Can we meet for lunch…that is if you haven't eaten already?"

"No, lunch will be fine. Do you have a place in mind?"

"What about Vannon's? Do you know where it is? If I recall, the food there is excellent."

"It is excellent. It shouldn't take me more than twenty minutes to get there."

"It will be the same amount of time for me. I appreciate your flexibility, Ms. Bradford."

"No problem. I'll see you in about twenty minutes."

She clicked off the phone. It wasn't unusual for clients to want to meet somewhere other than at their offices. Ninety percent of the time she was called in when there was trouble. If there was a problem within the firm, it was best for the employees not to find out about it until management had it under control. Understandably, people became antsy over the possibility of losing their jobs when a company wasn't performing the way it should be. That was her job, going into failing corporations and doing what could be done to turn their businesses around. And she was justifiably proud of her track record.

Shana wondered what the problems at Granger Aeronautics were. She remembered hearing that the CEO had passed away. That in itself could cause turmoil within a corporation. The prospect of change in any form had a way of getting to people.

As she turned the ignition in her car to pull out of her father's driveway, she couldn't help but agree with what Joyce had said earlier. Jace Granger had a sexy voice.

Shana then punched a knob on her console for Greta, her automated search engine. Bruce Townsend, a computer whiz who worked for both her and Jules, had invented the device, which was great for those doing investigative work. Shana had one installed in her car that shared her office network. All you had to do was tell Greta what info you wanted, and within minutes, she would recite all you needed to know.

"Greta, search your engines for information on Granger Aeronautics."

"Affirmative," was Greta's quick, automated reply.

By the time Shana had turned the corner, Greta was reciting the history of Granger Aeronautics.

Chapter Eight

Jace arrived a few minutes early, so he sat near the restaurant's window to enjoy the outside view. It was a beautiful summer day with a little breeze to offset the hot temperature. Traffic hadn't been so bad coming from the office, and he had the opportunity to familiarize himself with the roads that hadn't been there the last time he'd been in Charlottesville. It was progress that he appreciated, since they helped eliminate traffic buildup on the expressway, which was something he was used to in Los Angeles.

His thoughts shifted to the office he'd left. It surprised him that Freeman had suddenly decided that Jace, Caden and Dalton were the best thing for Granger Aeronautics and that he would be happy to work with the three any way he could. Jace shook his head. Did the man really have a choice?

On another note, someone had spread the rumor that the company was in financial straits, and employees were beginning to worry. Several who had worked for Granger for years, some before the day Jace was born, had cornered him in the hall and requested a private meeting. They had assured him he would have their loyalty the same way his grandfather had had through the years. He appreciated that. One even went so far as to warn him to keep an eye on Freeman.

Jace's main concern was dealing with rumor control, since it was sending a panic wave through the company that the doors could be closing within a few months. Their biggest client was the federal government, and the last thing Granger Aeronautics needed was for the government to have a reason not to renew their contracts.

He took time to glance at the reports he'd reviewed right before leaving the office and noted they had not gotten as many jobs from the government as they had in the past, which was probably one of the main reasons for the decline in revenue. Over the coming weeks, he would have to roll up his sleeves and dive into every aspect of Granger Aeronautics to figure out why.

Jace rubbed the back of his neck, hoping he hadn't bitten off more than he could chew. Over the years, his grandfather had kept him abreast of things going on in the company…although the old man had never told him about the recent turn of events in the company's financial situation. But Jace was aware of their clients, the people depending on their products, and he wanted to make sure they were kept happy.

Granger Aeronautics had been one of the leading employers in Charlottesville for years. His great-grandfather, Sutton Granger, had been a Tuskegee Airman during the Second World War. At the end of the war, he and a fellow airman mechanic, Aaron Mann, had basically risked everything they had to form Granger-Mann Aerospace, located in Birmingham, Alabama.

Aaron Mann died unexpectedly in a boating accident, and since his family wanted no part of the company, Sutton bought them out and changed the name to Granger Aeronautics. A year later, the company moved to Charlottesville.

Jace knew the history; they all did. Their grandfather had drilled it into them and so had their father... although not quite as hard. He'd known it had been a disappointment to Richard when none of his grandsons had shown interest in continuing the legacy, but Jace figured their grandfather had known why, although he might not have agreed with it. It hadn't come as any surprise to the old man that Jace, Caden and Dalton had wanted to move as far away from Charlottesville as possible. Their teen years after their father's death hadn't been easy, and the town had made it downright difficult at times. They had become known as the sons of a convicted killer.

Richard had planned to retire and leave things in his son's capable hands before the murder happened. When Sheppard had been convicted, retirement had no longer been an option for Richard. He had worked tirelessly for the next fifteen years to keep the company afloat—for his grandsons, and for the return of his only son.

Jace, of all people, knew that his grandfather never gave up hope that one day the verdict would be overturned and Sheppard would walk out of prison a free man. When Sheppard had entered prison fifteen years ago, he had started positive programs for the inmates such as Toastmasters, Future Leaders of Tomorrow

and the GED program. His efforts had been successful and were recognized by the media and even the
governor.

Five years ago, upon the recommendation of the
warden, the governor had approved Sheppard's transfer
to Delvers, a prison that housed less-serious offenders.
For the past five years, Sheppard had worked closely
with the warden as a trustee, initiating various projects to ensure that the less-serious offenders didn't
become serious offenders in the future.

Jace was not surprised. His father was a born leader
who cared for others, which is why he knew that his
father was not responsible for his mother's death, not
even as the crime of passion the prosecution had made
it out to be.

"Jace Granger?"

He looked up into a very attractive face. The first
thing he noticed was her eyes. They were oval-shaped
and a deep, dark chocolate. Beautiful. And so were
her other features. "Yes, I'm Jace Granger," he said,
standing.

She extended her hand to him. "I'm Shana Bradford.

Shana sipped her wine and recalled the stats Greta
had provided on the man sitting across from her, Jace
Granger. He was a thirty-one-year-old divorcé and attorney with a government agency in Los Angeles. He
was highly respected and considered a hard worker.
However, some thought he was limiting his abilities
and questioned his lack of motivation. And something
she found odd was that there was a million-dollar trust
fund established by his great-grandfather that he'd be-

come eligible to receive at twenty-five. Yet he hadn't touched any of it. He lived a modest life, was a liberal and donated thousands each year to charity.

She also knew about his father, Sheppard Granger, as well as his brothers, Caden and Dalton. Greta had been very thorough during the twenty minutes it had taken Shana to arrive at Vannon's.

Now that her brain had rehashed Greta's info, Shana streamed through her mind what she was seeing for herself. First of all, Jace Granger was a very handsome man. She would even throw in sexy to match the voice. He had a beautiful pair of light brown eyes and creamy, caramel-colored skin, black, close-cut hair that was nicely trimmed and a pair of full lips. She figured to get teeth that white and perfect, a lot of money had to have gone into his mouth as a child. And he had a dimple in his chin and a strong jawline. His eyebrows appeared perfectly arched with long lashes, the kind most women would kill for. He had big hands and the long fingers of a piano player. When he stood, she couldn't help but admire the way he filled out his suit. He was tall, with broad shoulders and a pleasing smile. Altogether, she thought he was definitely a nice-looking, well-built package.

"So you think you can help Granger Aeronautics?" he asked, taking a sip of his wine, as well. She was intelligent enough to know that while she'd been sizing him up, he'd been doing the same with her. She had no problem with that. Thanks to her parents' strong genes and facial bone structure, she knew she wasn't bad to look at. She had honey-brown skin, dark brown eyes and a head of healthy hair that she liked wearing straight in long graceful curves to her shoulders.

Her lips were full, and she was blessed with a dimple in one cheek.

Although she and Jace were doing a good job of downplaying the attraction, it was there. But she was well aware that attractions came and attractions went. It was no big deal to her unless it got in the way of business, and she didn't intend to let that happen. She was too focused for that. Too much of a professional.

There was never a time when she couldn't control her hormones when it came to a man—even Jonathan Hickman. He was the last man she'd been seriously involved with and that was a few years ago. Shana had thought she was in love with him…yet he claimed she was too in control, a damn robot without emotions and feelings. He'd been wrong. She had emotions and feelings. Maybe had he known that, he would not have hurt her the way he had.

Both she and her sister were blessed with high IQs, and Shana had been told by a lot of her college professors that hers was too high for her own good. She was a curious soul by nature, and when things were wrong, she always liked making them right. The story of her life.

"I know I can help," she said, setting down her wineglass. "I've familiarized myself somewhat with your company."

He raised one of those arched brows. "You have?"

"Yes." He was probably wondering when she had had time to do that. "I have Greta, a very high-tech search engine in my car. I was able to listen to the stats on the drive over here."

"Oh, I see."

She wondered if he really did. She had not only researched his company, but had obtained information on him, too. She liked knowing who she was dealing with.

Jace thought Shana Bradford was hot. The dark brown business suit looked great on her, although he was sure it was meant to look conservative. Instead, it deepened the color of her eyes and made her complexion that much smoother looking. And the conservative look did nothing to hide what a gorgeous pair of legs she had. And she was wearing panty hose, something few women still did these days. In L.A., he was used to seeing bare-legged women all the time, even in business suits, and he appreciated the lack of hosiery on any nice pair of legs. But seeing Shana in panty hose had him rethinking that position. The ones on her legs were flesh tone, barely noticeable, silky. For some reason, they managed to extend her legs' beauty to a level of sensuality that he found breathtaking.

The woman was also candid. Some might think a bit cocky, conceited and way too sure of herself, but he wasn't one of them. She believed in her abilities and knew what she could do, and Jace couldn't help admiring that trait in a woman. He'd done a Google search on her company. She had an MBA from Harvard, graduating at the top of her class, two years earlier than the norm. Since opening her business a few years ago, she had reinvented several corporations, and her success ratio was astounding.

And Shana Bradford was a very striking woman. Any man would take a second look at her any day of the week. The total package, a combination of professionalism and sexiness, was doing everything to rev up his libido. He drew in a deep breath, knowing that he shouldn't be thinking of her in those terms. What he should be thinking about was that she was someone who could help him. Unfortunately, she was making that task pretty damn impossible while sitting across from him looking as scrumptious as the wine he was drinking and just as appetizing. He was certain he would get his mind back strictly on business, but right now, he wanted to analyze her as the desirable woman that she was. He liked her looks, and she smelled good. Whatever perfume she was wearing she could claim as hers. And he liked her voice. She was articulate and looked you right in the eyes when she spoke.

"Before the waiter delivers our food, I would like you to tell me why you want to hire me," she said, interrupting his thoughts.

His lips quirked into a smile. "I thought you knew what was going on at Granger."

She quirked her lips right back at him. "I know enough, but I want to hear your version."

"All right." He began talking, and she took it all in, every detail, specific or otherwise. He spoke smoothly, elegantly and with confidence, even when she doubted he was truly feeling it. He told her she was recommended by their company's attorney, who was also a longtime family friend. He went into details about the buying up of additional shares and the stockholders' meeting that was held that morning. He went over his agreement with Freeman—the two of them would work together to ensure the success of the company.

He ended by saying, "Well, that about covers it."

She studied his gaze for a moment, thinking he wasn't a man someone could read easily and, for a woman, not at all. She sipped her wine and then said, "Mr. Granger, you called me to help bring your company around. I'm capable of doing that. However, you will have to be straight with me on all levels. You did not tell me everything."

She saw his eyes darken, shadowed with irritation at her accusation. "And just what is it that I haven't told you, Ms. Bradford?"

"Why three men who once swore never to work for Granger Aeronautics are suddenly doing so. I understand about your grandfather's death and all that, but the three of you could have easily let Titus Freeman run things…after all, he was vice president. You were satisfied with your job at that government agency in Los Angeles, your brother Caden is a professional musician with quite a following and your younger brother Dalton is pretty much known on the European circuit as quite the ladies' man. A number of women have nicknamed him 'Cocoa Puff.' And probably what most people don't know is that he's a billionaire, not from taking advantage of any of his older lovers, but from investments. So my question to you is, why are the three of you here?

Jace didn't say anything for a moment, wondering how much to tell her. Then after looking in her eyes, observing that *you-better-not-bullshit-me look,* he decided to come clean. "It was a deathbed promise. My grandfather asked the three of us to take over the running of Granger Aeronautics. And it's a promise I intend to keep."

She could admire that, but still…why would his grandfather ask the three of them to do that? Richard Granger knew they had lives they were more or less content with. Why would he ask them to give up their livelihood for a company they'd walked away from years ago?

Evidently, she had a confused look in her eyes, because he said, "I don't know why he asked that of us, considering everything. But we knew our grandfather. We don't think it was last-minute manipulation. I honestly believe he thought we could do a better job than Freeman. Why he felt that way, I'm not sure. Granddad loved Granger Aeronautics. He wouldn't turn the running of it over to us unless he felt we could do it."

She took a sip of her wine and then asked, "For how long?"

"Excuse me?"

"How long will you stay at Granger? Just until I get it out of the red? I understand you didn't resign from your company in California, but took a leave of absence."

Jace frowned, wondering how in the hell she knew that. She wouldn't have been able to find that out in twenty minutes. But from the self-confident look in her eyes, he had a feeling she had. She must have some damn good contacts.

He took a sip of his drink, because at the moment he couldn't answer her. All he knew was that he was staying put, but he had a feeling his saying that would not be good enough for her. "Just what do you expect of me, Ms. Bradford?"

"Maybe you ought to be asking yourself what those employees of Granger Aeronautics expect of you, Mr. Granger. I would think they'd want someone who plans to do right by them and not leave them out in the cold.

They worked hard for your grandfather, and most were loyal. They expect a leader who would remember that."

And he had remembered that. He knew then what his answer to her question would be. "I can only speak for myself, but I'm staying."

At that moment, the waiter interrupted by bringing out their food.

Over lunch, Shana asked Jace several questions that she felt he answered truthfully. He even told her about the other promise they'd made regarding her father. She definitely felt he had a lot on his plate but was confident he knew how to handle his business.

He asked her more questions, specifically how she would go about evaluating the company if she accepted the job. She made sure he knew she hadn't decided whether she would work for him or not before she went into explaining her company's in-depth evaluation process. Although, in the end, he didn't have to implement all her recommendations, but the success ratio would increase if he did so. She could almost guarantee it.

She appreciated that he was honest enough to admit that in some areas he felt like a fish out of water, but over the years his grandfather had kept him abreast of some things, so he was familiar with the day-to-day operations.

"If you take the job, I think having you work on the premises would be a plus," he said, pushing his plate away.

She glanced over at him. "I'm surprised you would want your employees to know the company is in a dire enough situation that I had to be called in."

He shrugged. "They know anyway, and I have an idea how they found out."

Shana considered his words and said, "I know Freeman would be the logical culprit, but I've discovered the logical one is not always the guilty party. You would be surprised what's tucked away in closets that I usually expose. People you thought you could trust can prove otherwise. I would suggest you watch your back, not just with Freeman but with others. Some might think you don't know what the hell you're doing and try to take advantage."

"Thanks for the advice."

The waiter came to remove their plates. Wineglasses were replaced with coffee cups, and they continued talking. She was being evasive about whether she would take on Granger Aeronautics, and with good reason. She had just come off a big, lengthy assignment and had looked forward to taking a month off to do practically nothing. She had considered accompanying Jules on one of her easier assignments, just to have girl time with her sister, since both of them were usually busy. If Shana took on this job, she would be back to working from sunup to sundown. Her weekends would be filled with endless time spent at her computer. Besides Joyce, she had two other assistants, but like her, they were looking for a break between cases. They would still get theirs, she would see to it. They needed it. That meant she would have to work even harder.

And then there was the issue with her father. She might need to spend time with him as well if he was thinking about remarrying and the likely candidate was a woman he'd only gotten to know in the grocery store. She could understand any man wanting female companionship at any age, but getting married was a whole different topic. She couldn't wait to discuss it with Jules.

She noticed there was a lull in the conversation and she glanced across the table to see Jace staring at her. She didn't have to ask him why. He was still checking her out. She understood it was a man thing, but he was working overtime. Too bad it was an interest that wouldn't go anywhere.

She sipped her coffee and for the moment appreciated the quiet time that allowed her to think. And the one thing she couldn't help but admit was that she liked him. She liked that he had loved his grandfather so much that he was willing to make sacrifices. Finding his way around Granger Aeronautics wouldn't be easy, and like she'd told him, he would be a target. It took no time at all to tell that he was highly intelligent and had those same leadership qualities he'd praised his father and grandfather for having. For some reason, she wanted him to succeed, and she knew there was a possibility he would do the latter without her company's help.

"I've decided to handle your case, Mr. Granger."

He held her gaze for a moment and then said, "I appreciate that. For a moment there, I was thinking that you wouldn't."

She'd figured as much from the surprised look in his eyes. "I considered walking away but only because you hadn't completely leveled with me at first. Now you have. You made a promise, and what I admire and respect is that it's a promise you intend to keep. Your job as an attorney didn't motivate you. You did it, and you did it well, but there was no challenge. You need a challenge, Mr. Granger. One that you know will pay off not only for your employees but for your grandfather and father, as well. You will be dedicated. Turning your company around won't be easy, but you intend to make it work. And you'll succeed because you're willing to make changes, even sacrifices, to reach your goal. And most important, you have waylaid my fears that you're not in it for the short-term. I believe you're in it for the long haul."

She paused a moment and then added, "However, I'm not sure about your brothers. I intend to speak with them soon, because even though you're your own man, you're also their brother, and the oldest. And you want them to want this as much as you do. Call it a brother's honor, but you want their support. You want it, even though you don't necessarily need it. You're going to do whatever you feel needs to be done anyway. But I admire that you care for their feelings, and I can understand that. I have a younger sister, and I can see putting her well-being and interest before my own."

Jace didn't say anything for a moment as he sipped his coffee. She was right. He was in it for the long haul. He hadn't accepted that until now. He wasn't sure about his brothers, but he could safely say he was in. And he wanted his brothers in with him, but would understand if down the line they wanted out. They had their own interests and careers. It was an individual thing. Working in a corporation wasn't for everybody.

"You want to know what I think?" she asked.

He glanced over at her, met the darkness of her eyes, felt the stirring in the pit of his gut and willed it away. "Yes, I want to know what you think."

"Granger Aeronautics has always been your legacy. But I think that today you've realized it's your destiny."

He didn't say anything because he was thinking about how long he hadn't wanted to claim his legacy and how adamantly he'd been against it. Yet here he was, ready to jump in with both feet and not look back.

"Now that we've gotten all of that taken care of, I do have a request, although my common sense dictates otherwise, Mr. Granger."

"Before you say anything, I think since we'll be working together it would be appropriate for you to call me Jace if you don't mind my calling you Shana." At her nod, he then asked, "So what request do you have?"

She smiled over at him. "That I order dessert. I have a weakness for chocolate."

Chapter Nine

"So, how did it go?"

"How does she look?"

Jace wasn't surprised his brothers were in his office waiting on him when he returned from his meeting with Shana. Tugging off his jacket, he glanced over at Caden to address his question. "The meeting went well, and she's agreed to help. She'll have a place here in the office just to be visible. Hopefully, that will put employees at ease."

Then, answering Dalton's question, he said, "She's a beautiful woman who has a pleasant personality, but at the same time pulls no punches. She's sharp and highly intelligent."

Dalton grinned. "Boy, aren't we full of compliments?"

"And she deserves every one. I think she's going to get us through this."

"Hell, I hope so. I'm missing Europe already," Dalton said, smiling all over himself.

Jace sat on the edge of the desk and studied his younger brother for a second before saying, "I'm sure you are, Cocoa Puff."

Surprise lit Dalton's eyes. He then grinned sheepishly and said, "Hey, what can I say? When you got it, you got it. I guess your girl-wonder checked me out."

Jace smiled. "Yes, she did."

Caden laughed. "Cocoa Puff?"

Dalton frowned. "Well, I bet she can't tell you where my tattoo is."

"I wouldn't be too sure of that. Like I said, she's good."

"And I bet you checked her out real good," Dalton said.

The smile left Jace's face as he moved around to sit behind his desk. "This is business, Dalton. I don't see every female with a nice pair of legs as a sex object."

Dalton rubbed his chin as his smile widened in approval. "So she has a nice pair of legs?"

Jace refused to be baited, so he changed the subject, asking, "Anything interesting happen while I was gone?"

Caden shook his head. "It's been quiet. Almost too quiet. I think everyone thinks Caden and I are spying on them. When will your wonder-woman start working?"

"Tomorrow. So we need to make sure she has an office ready."

"I'll be happy to help her move in," Dalton volunteered.

Jace gave that some thought. His brother was such a bullshitter, and Shana Bradford was just the woman to give Dalton a firm kick in the ass. But he didn't want Shana to have to deal with drama on her first day. "There's no need, Dalton. I'm sure she can manage just fine on her own."

He didn't say anything for a minute then added, "Warning, Dalton. We need Shana Bradford, so don't make a pest of yourself."

"Okay, Shana, you've been blowing up my phone. What's going on?" Jules Bradford asked her sister as she tossed her backpack on the hotel bed. Today had been extra long. She was investigating a kidnapping that happened over two years ago. During a custody battle, the father had kidnapped his son and faked their deaths. The mother never believed her husband and son were dead and had hired Jules to prove otherwise. Her search had led her here to a small town in Mexico. She had spent an entire day trying to get information from some of the locals, and no one was talking.

"It's about Dad."

Jules stopped in her tracks and held the phone tight in her hand. "What about Dad?"

"He's thinking about remarrying."

I must have heard wrong, Jules thought, dropping down on the bed near her backpack. "What are you talking about, Shana? Dad isn't even seeing anyone."

"I know." Then Shana gave her sister the details. The same ones her father had given her.

Moments later, Jules said, "Umm, probably a phase he's going through. I'm sure most men his age have gone through it. Dad's been a widower for over thirteen years with no serious involvements that we know of. He probably saw this woman a few times, thought she was hot, talked to her, decided he liked her and that was it."

Shana, who was sitting in her office, having taken a break from doing more research on Granger Aeronautics, rolled her eyes. "That's not it. You were not there when he was telling me about this Mona. I saw that sparkle in his eyes. It might be more than a phase, Jules."

"Then we'll stop it. Work up a plan, and we'll implement it when I get back."

"Just listen to what you said. Our father is happy, and you want to jeopardize it? Would it be so bad if he truly likes this woman and wants to marry her?"

"For crying out loud, Shana, just listen to yourself! What cloud are you floating on? Dad barely knows the woman, and he's thinking marriage? And there is a big difference between happy and hot. I'm still going with the idea of him being in the hot prime of his life."

It was times like this when Shana knew she needed to end the conversation with her sister. "You must have had a bad day," she said.

Jules stood and began stripping. "Why do you say that?"

"Because you sound like you could chew a couple of people up and spit them out."

Jules smiled. Her sister knew her well. "And I would begin with a number of the people I interviewed today. They were lying through their teeth about not recognizing a picture of Marcos Rodrigo. The man is hiding out here someplace with his son. I can feel it."

"Then I'm sure you'll find them," Shana said, closing one document on her computer and opening another. "Look I'm in the middle of research and I—"

"Whoa! Wait! Research? I thought you were taking a month-long break!"

Shana wished she hadn't been reminded. "I was, but I got a client who needs me."

"Don't they all, Ms. Fixer-Upper? What makes this one so special you're giving up a month of fun and sun?"

Shana's hands stopped stroking the keys, and she paused before entering a name in Google. "I didn't say he was special."

"*He?* Sounds interesting. I hadn't said anything about a 'he.' I think you just told on yourself."

Shana frowned. Leave it to her sister to grasp any little thing and run with it. "Mistake on my part that wasn't intentional, but understandable since Jace Granger is now the CEO of Granger Aeronautics. I met with him earlier today and agreed to help bring his company around."

"So, again, I ask, what's so special about him that made you give up your time off?"

Shana thought long and hard about her sister's question before saying, "A number of things, but most of all his integrity. It was a deathbed promise he intends to keep. You know how I am about those sorts of things."

If anyone would know, it would be Jules. They had both promised their mother while she lay dying of cancer that they would be good girls and not cause their father any problems after she was gone. It was a promise they had both kept. Graduating from high school with honors, they had both finished college in three years instead of four, going practically year-round.

"Yes, I know. Is he good-looking?" Jules asked, picking her clothes up off the floor. Whether her sister knew it or not, her defensive tone was telling on her.

"Yes, he is good-looking. I'll give him that."

Jules laughed out loud. "And that's about all you'll give him. Jonathan ruined you for any other man."

Shana frowned at the mention of her ex-boyfriend. "He did not ruin me."

"Then why haven't you dated anyone seriously since then? Makes me think you're pining away for him."

"You're wrong. I want to focus on my business. Men aren't a necessity for me like they are for some women. And I don't recall the last time you went out on a date."

"I went out with James last month, remember?"

"I mean a serious date and not one of your stake-outs, Jules. You were trying to bust a cheating husband." Shana glanced up and waved as Joyce headed for the door. At least she made sure her workers went home at a decent time.

"And it was successful, I might add," Jules said, grinning, sounding proud of herself. "And that's probably one reason I don't take men seriously. Most of my cases are about cheating husbands, which in my book makes a statement. Unless his name is Ben Bradford, no man is to be trusted."

Jules headed for the bathroom with discarded clothes tucked under her arm. "I need to shower now. Don't expect me back in Virginia for another two weeks. In the meantime, keep an eye on Dad and the veggie lady."

Jace glanced at his watch, noticing it was nine o'clock already. He pushed the documents he'd been reading aside and stood to stretch his body. The office had closed hours ago, yet he was still here, reading as much information as he could. This was sort of like cramming for one of his law exams.

Caden and Dalton had moved into their offices down the hall and at six had quickly headed out for the bar and grill down the street. They had invited Jace to join them, but he had declined. He had received an email from Shana, asking that specific documents be available for her to review tomorrow, and he figured he needed to go over those documents, as well.

He glanced around the office that had once belonged to his grandfather. He'd decided not to change a thing for now, although the green drapes with the matching carpeting didn't do anything for him. Jace smiled, recalling that grccn had always been Richard Granger's favorite color, in all shades.

They would be visiting their father next weekend, and Jace was looking forward to it. Caden would leave to wrap up a few events he'd scheduled and would return in two weeks. Jace was grateful Dalton hadn't made some excuse to fly to London and wondered if that receptionist downstairs had anything to do with it.

Jace was about to head back over to his desk and read the last of the documents when his phone rang. It was a number he didn't recognize. "Hello?"

"You could have at least called to let me know your grandfather had passed."

Jace drew in a deep breath. It was his ex-wife, Eve. "Why would I have bothered? It's not like the two of you were close. And if you're calling to see whether you were left in his will, you weren't."

"That's cold, Jace."

"Goes with the territory, since I recall your calling me a cold bastard the day you were served with divorce papers."

As if she hadn't heard his words, she said, "I hear you're in charge of the place now that he's gone. I'm happy, since that's all I wanted for you."

"That's what you wanted for yourself, Eve. Let's get that straight. You were never satisfied with the money I was making as an attorney when you figured I could be making millions working alongside my grandfather. That's the truth, and you know it." He dropped down in his chair and added, "And then there was the issue of your not getting your hands on my trust fund. That really teed you off."

He couldn't help but smile. She figured she had it all worked out just how much of his trust she would milk out of him. But thanks to his grandfather, things hadn't worked out that way for her, which is why she couldn't stand the old man.

"Why do you keep trying to paint me as a gold digger, Jace? When we married, I had just as much money as you."

"The underlying word is *had*. By the time we divorced, you didn't have a penny. You had spent all of yours and were trying to run through mine, as well."

"I like nice things."

"No, you like expensive things and then choose not to work to pay for them."

"I was the wife of a Granger. There was no reason for me to work. Had I given in and stayed pregnant like you wanted, then everything would have been fine. Why can't you understand that although you wanted a baby, I didn't? I wasn't ready, Jace. I was still—"

"Having too good a time to settle down and become a mother, I know," he interrupted. "But was that any reason to have an abortion behind my back?" he asked in anger. It pained him every time he thought about it. And the sad thing about it was that she never planned to tell him. All the arrangements had been made while he was out of town. When he had returned unexpectedly, he had found out the truth.

"Eve, let's end this call while we can remain civil. Goodbye, and do me a favor and delete my number."

She clicked off the phone. It wouldn't be the first time she'd hung up on him, but if she did what he'd said and deleted his number, then it would definitely be the last.

He had picked up another report when his cell phone rang again. He thought it was Eve calling his bluff by calling him back when he noted the call was from Shana Bradford. "Yes, Shana?"

Shana took a deep breath, thinking there was that sexy voice again. She hated admitting it, but she liked the sound of her name on his lips. "I figured you would still be at the office. Chocolate is known to boost your energy level, and I noticed that your slice of cake at lunch was a lot bigger than mine."

She heard his rich, masculine laugh and thought it was sexy, too.

"You noticed, huh?"

"Yes." She smiled, recalling how he'd devoured the entire slice. "I won't keep you, but I was wondering if I need to bring my own computer or if you've got one there for me?"

Jace lifted a brow. "Some companies actually make you bring your own computer?"

"Yes, and it's no big deal if that's the case. I just like knowing beforehand."

Jace leaned back in his chair, suddenly feeling calm and relaxed. Both feelings were much appreciated after his phone call with Eve. "Well, that's not the case. In fact, I took charge of things myself."

And he had. He had decided to give her the office next to his, the one that had a connecting door to his grandfather's and his father's offices. Since it was in the middle of both offices, it had served as a private meeting room for the two men. It was roomy and large enough for Shana's temporary office and had a beautiful view of the Blue Ridge Mountains outside the window.

The maintenance department had already removed the huge conference table and replaced it with a desk, a couple of file cabinets, a bookcase and other accessories. His grandfather's secretary, who was officially now Jace's secretary, had gotten the office organized with supplies, including the latest computer. The receptionist from downstairs had assisted his secretary, which had probably made Dalton's day. Fortunately, it was a task that hadn't taken long to complete.

"I appreciate it and intend to be there first thing in the morning—around eight."

"All right, and you have a spot reserved in the executive parking lot."

"My-oh-my, don't I feel special?"

She had a nice phone voice. Silky-sounding. He had thought that yesterday and was thinking it again today. "If a parking space does that, then wait until dress-down Friday. I understand that's a big event here. They like to get out of their dresses and suits and go straight to the jeans."

"Doesn't take much to satisfy some people," she said.

He wondered what it would take to satisfy her... or whether she was one of those women like Eve who couldn't be satisfied. Nothing for her was ever enough.

"I almost forgot to mention something, Jace."

"What?"

"I have my own computer expert, and I prefer using one of my own networks. So if it's okay, he'll be there tomorrow to put me on a different computer system than you have at Granger. It will be best for security for the work I intend to do there."

"Okay, I don't have a problem with that. I'll let my technicians know."

"No, I prefer no one knows but you and I. Bruce will make it seem like I'm still using the company's server, but I won't be."

"Oh, okay."

"I'll be seeing you in the morning, Jace."

"Sleep well."

"I will."

Jace hung up the phone. He'd heard her fighting back a yawn a few times during their conversation and wondered if, like him, she was still at the office. As he picked up the file he'd been about to read earlier, he couldn't help but smile at the thought of seeing her again tomorrow.

A few hours later, Shana slid into her jacket ready to leave her office, confident that she was prepared for her first day at Granger Aeronautics. She found everything about it fascinating, even the fact that it was losing its place as one of the top leaders in aerospace engineering. Why? What she'd read was only out there for public consumption, and she couldn't wait to delve into the real stuff.… Present clients. Past clients. Business models. PR focus. Product designs. Returns on workforce investments…

All those things made up the success or failure of any company, and she intended to see if any ratio of them might be hurting Granger. She appreciated the fact that, although she might have kept long hours tonight, Jace Granger had done so, as well. Not tit for tat, but because he was demonstrating a strong desire to move his company forward and was committed to doing so.

She turned at the familiar knock on the door. "Come in."

Kent, who worked for her company as a troubleshooter, rolled in. A veteran of the Iraq war, Kent had been left paralyzed in both legs by the shrapnel from a missile blast. He didn't let being wheelchair-bound stop him, and she found his tenacity and determination to succeed in spite of his injury truly admirable. Accepting his disability as a bump you could get in your life and not a death sentence, he was good at what he did. She considered him a key player in her organization. He worked hard, sometimes too hard, and Shana often had to conspire with Kent's wife, Marsha, to slow him down at times.

"Figured you'd still be here," he said, his ocean-blue eyes flickering in a smiling glance.

She frowned, or at least she tried to. "I know why I'm here, but why are you here? I gave you and Todd a month off, with pay. You deserved it, so why are you here working at this hour?"

He chuckled and pushed a lock of blond hair out of his eyes. "You took on another client. So that means we all took on another client. We're a team, Shana. Besides, I figured I could at least give you the rundown on Granger Aeronautics' top executives. I loaded the new info into Greta so you can listen to it on the drive home. A hard copy will be ready for download anytime you want."

She nodded. That was one of the reasons she appreciated her team so much. "Anything interesting?"

"I'll let you decide."

She tilted her brow. That meant there *was* something interesting. "All right."

Half an hour later, after listening to Kent's report on the four men who were the top executives under Richard Granger—Titus Freeman, Cal Arrington, Shelton Fields and John Fulmer—Shana realized that Kent was right; there was definitely something interesting. Already, questions were taking root in her head, and whenever that happened, she was pushed to dig deeper. And she would.

Chapter Ten

Jace walked in at seven-thirty the next morning to find Shana sitting at the desk in the office she'd been given, already buried knee-deep in paperwork. He paused in the doorway a second and watched her read various documents. Even the pair of cute glasses perched on her nose did nothing to detract from her attractiveness.

And he couldn't help noticing a few other things, like how smooth and creamy-looking her skin appeared to be and that instead of being tinted with lipstick, her lips appeared shiny with gloss. The strands of her hair were a lustrous black, and the few loose tendrils would have softened her features had it not been for the way her lips were pursed together. But even with that, she looked good enough to eat—at least as good as the hot bagels in the bag he was carrying.

He felt his gut contract and immediately thought it was way too early to be thinking such things, but then he reconsidered. A beautiful woman could be appreciated at any time and any place. He decided now was the time to let his presence be known. "Good morning."

She glanced up and smiled. "Good morning, Jace."

"We said eight o'clock, but I had a feeling you'd be early. I hadn't counted on this early," he said, walking in and setting down the bag on her desk. "Fresh, hot bagels from Jennie's."

A smile tipping the corners of her lips widened. "Ahh, one of my favorite places. Thanks."

He had ordered a coffee machine be provided for her, and from the look of things, she'd already had a cup. "I hope this office meets with your approval."

"It does," she said, glancing around. "Almost too much. I had to fight to buckle down and get started instead of staring out the window." Still smiling, she stood up and sighed in satisfaction. "This is such a beautiful view."

"I think so, too," he agreed, scanning his gaze over her and knowing they were talking about two different things. She was wearing another conservative business suit. This one navy. And, like the brown one, it was meant to make a conservative statement, definitely professional. It did, but he was capable of seeing beyond all that. He could imagine her in a halter top with her firm breasts barely contained and a pair of khaki shorts that showed off her gorgeous legs. He wasn't sure why that image was stamped in his mind, but it was.

"What time is the meeting this morning?" she asked, cutting into his thoughts.

Since he'd agreed it was best that she work on the premises, she suggested that a meeting with his executive team and department heads was the best way to let them know why she was here. It was best to get it out in the open instead of having them speculate. He had agreed. "Around ten. My administrative assistant sent an email out yesterday afternoon."

"She seems like a nice lady."

"Who?"

"Your administrative assistant, Melissa Swanson."

"Yes, and she appears rather efficient. The woman who worked for my grandfather and then for my father for thirty-plus years retired a couple of years ago. That's when he hired Melissa. I understand she was promoted from a clerical position downstairs."

He glanced down at her desk. "I see you're busy already."

"Yes. I hope to have my first report to you in a week. It will be a preliminary one, but one I feel would be the first step to get Granger back on track." She paused a minute and then said, "But first, I believe I need to address something," she said, walking from behind her desk. She strode to the door.

He could tell from her expression that whatever she had to say was serious. But that did nothing to deter him from catching her scent as it floated through the air, or the male appreciation he couldn't fight as he watched her movements, a natural sway of her hips with every step she took. Inhaling a deep breath, he couldn't recall when he appreciated a pair of feminine legs more.

After closing the door, she turned on her three-inch heels and walked back to him. She had removed the glasses, and he quickly concluded her eyes were even prettier today. In fact, he thought all of her features were more beautiful. That magnetic pull he'd felt yesterday was back and in full force.

"I believe we need to have a little talk, Jace," she said, coming to a stop in front of him.

His arched brow rose inquiringly. "What about?"

"Your libido and my hormones."

At his surprised look, she shook her head. "Don't look so shocked that I would bring such a thing up, Jace. Normally I wouldn't, but those two things seem to be working overtime with us and have no place here in the office. And since I have a policy never to get personally involved with my clients, they don't have a place anywhere."

Jace figured she couldn't state things any clearer than that. There was no need to play dumb, since he was well aware of the attraction between them. But Jace hadn't realized that Shana had been as aware of the pull between them as he was. And he definitely hadn't expected her to address it. At least now he knew the attraction was mutual. He also knew it was something they needed to work on curtailing since it wouldn't be going anywhere.

"Do I make myself clear, Jace?" she asked with that serious look back on her face.

He nodded slowly. "Very clear. And I promise to try keeping my libido in line."

Lord, she hoped so, Shana thought, feeling more relaxed and letting out a relieved breath. And she would try to do her part, as well. In fact, she needed to do more than try, because anything otherwise wasn't an option. But it wouldn't be easy. No man had a right to look so doggone handsome that early in the morning.

In the business suit he was wearing, he exuded power and displayed a male physique that actually made her mouth water.

First, she had glanced up to see him standing there, his tall, well-built, nicely proportioned body leaning against the doorjamb. And then he had moved closer to her desk, and she couldn't help but appreciate such an impressive pair of broad shoulders and a well-muscled chest. And he walked with an easy grace and style lined with an air of confidence that she found commanding.

She'd known she'd be in trouble if she didn't address what could become an issue. They were adults, but more importantly, they were professionals. And now that her concerns were out there, together they would deal with them in a way that was satisfactory to both. No need for pretending.

"Now that we've gotten that matter taken care of," she said, moving back around to her desk, "I wonder if I can have a short meeting with you thirty minutes before we meet with everyone else. I'd like to go over the items I'll be requesting from them."

"That will be fine. Let me get settled in for today, and we can meet in my office." He checked his watch and then glanced back at her. "Let's say, in around a half hour?"

"That will be perfect. And your brothers. I'd like to meet with them afterward."

"That can be arranged, as well. I'll let you get back to your work." He turned to leave, and she watched the well-muscled body move toward the door. He opened it, and without looking back at her, he walked out and closed it behind him.

* * *

Jace stood at the window in his office. Although he had agreed to Shana's request, he knew mere words couldn't block out the attraction he felt toward her. But it would be a start, because he did agree with her that it was an attraction that would not go anywhere. They had bigger, more important things to deal with than physical attraction.

He turned when he heard the buzzer on his desk and walked over to press it. "Yes, Melissa?"

"Your brothers are here to see you."

He smiled to himself as he spoke. "Send them in." Before leaving that morning, he had told them to be at the office at eight. It was close to nine, but at least that was a start. Neither of his brothers was used to keeping banker's hours. And Dalton wasn't used to keeping any hours at all.

The door swung open and Caden walked in smiling, but Dalton had a fierce frown on his face. "How are things going?" Jace ventured to ask.

"Fine."

"Lousy."

Both answers came simultaneously. Jace sat down after seeing his brothers head toward separate corners of the room. Caden stood to glance out the window to enjoy the view, and Dalton dropped down in a chair. Jace resigned himself that it would be one of those days and figured it best to start with Caden since he was smiling. "So, what's going on with you?"

Caden's smile widened. "I got a call from my manager. Cameron will use a few of the pieces off my last album as part of the music score for the movie he's filming now."

Jace's lips curved into a smile. "That's great news. Congratulations." He had seen James Cameron and Caden speaking briefly at his grandfather's memorial service. Afterward, Caden had mentioned that Cameron might be interested in using some of his music for a film soundtrack. Cameron and Richard had become friends over twenty years ago when Richard had been one of the investors for Cameron's earlier films.

He then turned to Dalton and shot him a curious look. His brother's frown had worsened. "And what's up with you?"

"Not a damn thing."

Jace glanced over at Caden, who merely shrugged with that *I don't know and really don't care* look. He decided to follow Caden's lead and take that same approach. Dalton would unload when he was good and ready.

"I'm glad the two of you made it in at a reasonable hour. There's an important meeting I'd like you to attend in ten minutes. Shana wants to meet with everyone."

Dalton raised a brow. "Shana?"

"Yes, Shana Bradford of Bradford Crisis Management."

Dalton rolled his eyes. "I know who she is, Jace, I just wasn't aware the two of you were on a first-name basis."

Jace leaned back in his chair and gazed at his brother intently. "She'll be working closely with us for the next month or so. Any reason I shouldn't?"

"No, I guess not."

Dalton's disdainful expression was unnerving, but Jace was determined not to let his brother's foul disposition bother him this morning. Jace was about to brief them on his meeting with Freeman yesterday when his administrative assistant buzzed. "Yes, Melissa?"

"Ms. Bradford is here for your meeting."

Jace stood. "Send her in."

Dalton murmured as he and Caden stood, as well, "Can't wait to meet the wonder-woman."

Jace shot his brother a warning glance before the door opened. Afterward, his gaze became fixated on Shana, but he heard Dalton's low whistle before he said, "Be still my heart."

A nervous little shiver ran down Shana's spine, and she forced it away. It was bad enough to have to confront one incredibly handsome man, but now she had to somehow deal with two more. It was easy to see that Caden and Dalton were Jace's brothers. With the three of them in a room together, the similarities were striking. Although she was sure there were aspects of their personalities that set them apart, all three were ruggedly handsome and powerfully built.

Caden, she thought, appeared smooth and laid-back. Although it wasn't obvious, she could tell he was sizing her up both physically, because he was a man, and then mentally, because he was curious about her. His preoccupation appeared more with the latter than the former.

Dalton, however, was another story. The flirty look in his eyes and the buttery smile told her everything. All three men were impeccably dressed, but this one's suit had a designer touch. There was no doubt in her mind that he was a man used to getting whatever he wanted easily and he would try his moves on her. He jauntily tilted his head to the side and openly checked her out as his gaze roamed up and down her. His lips were full and sensual when he said, "I wish I had met you first."

She smiled back. "It would not have mattered if you had. I'm here for business reasons and not entertainment purposes. It will behoove you to remember that."

Jace stood on the sidelines, bracing himself for his brother's response. Shana had put Dalton in his place and rightfully so, but he knew his baby brother. Dalton assumed that coming on to every woman was his birthright.

The beginning of a smile touched Dalton's lips even after being put in his place, albeit in a diplomatic way. He wasn't mad at her, just even more intrigued. And Dalton wasn't stupid. Jace could claim indifference all he wanted, but there was an interest there, and Dalton would willingly bet it was on both sides. He had picked up on something he recognized as strong sexual tension between them. And it amused Dalton that Jace and Shana were evidently fighting it. He inwardly chuckled, thinking it was their fight and not his. But he didn't have a problem shaking things up a bit. If he had to be stuck here in this city for a while, he didn't have anything better to do.

"Are you sure that's what you want?" he asked, taking a closer step.

She took one also and looked dead into his eyes. "Positive."

Dalton's smile deepened. She was as tough as she was hot, and he hoped like hell that Jace could handle her. He took a step back. "Then I concede."

"You, Dalton Granger, have no choice."

Dalton threw back his head and laughed, and it felt good to do so. He had awakened that morning pissed at the world in general, mainly because he preferred being anywhere other than Sutton Hills. Shana was a bright spot in his morning.

Vidal arrived, and Jace introduced him to Shana. She thanked Vidal for the recommendation that had brought her to Granger Aeronautics. "No problem," Vidal said, smiling. "On occasion, Jerome Haler and I play golf, and he couldn't stop singing your praises about how you were able to pull his company out of that slump. He said it would take a miracle, and in the end, you were it."

"Thank you," Shana said, smiling.

"Now that introductions are out of the way," Jace said, "Shana and I will be going over a few things before our meeting this morning, and you're invited to stay," he said to his brothers and Vidal.

Jace thought that would be Caden's and Dalton's cue to quickly skip out, but to his surprise, both chose to remain. Caden wore a serious expression, but Dalton's lips twitched as if he were amused by something. Shana took the chair in front of Jace's desk. Over the next twenty minutes, she went over the items she would be requesting from each executive and department head and why. "Your company is paying each of these individuals a good salary to do their jobs, and I want to make sure they are doing so as efficiently as possible."

"I have no problem with that, and they shouldn't, either," Jace said, checking his watch and then standing. He tightened his tie before reaching over to get his jacket to slide it on. "It's about time for our meeting," he said, gathering up the papers on his desk.

As much as she didn't want to, Shana felt a stirring in her stomach when Jace had eased his jacket over massive shoulders rippling with virility. Then, of all things, her heart began pounding furiously in her chest. She knew what was bothering her, and it irritated her immensely that she wasn't practicing what she had preached a couple of hours ago.

She drew in a deep breath while thinking that, okay, she had weakened and broken down her defenses this once, but it wouldn't happen again. The thought that she was back in control sent her spirits soaring until she glanced over at Dalton Granger. He gave her a smile that sparked, revealing his amusement, before he flashed a huge grin. She had a feeling he was up to something but had no idea what.

Her gaze left Dalton and returned to Jace to find him watching her. "Ready?" he asked, and to her way of thinking, a huskiness seemed embedded in his tone.

"Yes, I'm ready."

"I'll go on ahead," Vidal said, smiling. He moved close to Jace and whispered privately, "I told you she was good." He then quickly left the room.

Coming around to the front of his desk, Jace escorted Shana out of his office with Dalton and Caden bringing up the rear.

Chapter Eleven

When they arrived for the meeting, it appeared that all of the key players were in the conference room waiting with a mixture of curiosity and expectancy on their faces.

Jace glanced around the room while escorting Shana toward the front with him. He would be sitting at the head of the table, and he had asked his administrative assistant to reserve a chair for Shana at his right and two chairs for his brothers on his left. This would be the first official meeting he would hold as CEO. He had made his rounds yesterday morning and met briefly with every man and woman in the room at the time. All had kind words to say about his grandfather, and Jace recalled having seen many of them at the memorial service. However, he knew they were all wondering what was on his mind. The rumor mill was hard at work, and Jace needed to get control quickly and decisively.

"Good morning. I appreciate your flexibility in changing your schedules to accommodate this meeting. However, we have an important matter that needs to be discussed," he began, glancing around the table.

"To put it bluntly, Granger Aeronautics has lost a number of major clients over the past twelve months, and I intend to find out why so that we can reclaim our position as the number one provider of aerospace products and services. To do so, Shana Bradford of Bradford Crisis Management will be working with us in the coming weeks. Her firm has a stellar reputation for reinventing companies."

A hand rose, and Jace recognized the tall man with the bald head as Cal Arrington, third VP and currently in charge of the products and designs division. He had held that position for close to fifteen years. "Yes, Cal?"

"Honestly, Jace, do you think such a move is necessary? I agree we need to consider better ways to market our products, but the clients we do have are firm. I don't believe your grandfather would have considered such a move."

He saw several department heads nod, agreeing with Cal. Jace had known he wouldn't get everyone to buy into what he was doing. "Yes, I think the move is necessary and is one my grandfather would have considered. In fact, he had planned to do so before his untimely death."

He hadn't mentioned it to Shana or his brothers, but when he worked late that night, he had remembered the code his grandfather had given him years ago to access a special folder in Richard's computer—it was Jace's name spelled backward along with Sheppard's date of birth. The folder contained Richard's thoughts and concerns that he would jot down for future use. Jace had seen Richard's notes that outlined the idea of

bringing on Shana's firm because he suspected someone had shared trade secrets with a rival company.

He looked over at Freeman, who was sitting at the
table with tight lips. Jace figured the man was probably
annoyed that Jace hadn't run the idea by him first. "I'm
giving the floor to Ms. Bradford, who will advise you
about what information she needs from each of your
departments. She will be working in the office next to
mine, and I'm hoping her presence will assure every
employee that I am taking steps to regain Granger's
position as number one in the aerospace industry."

He glanced around the room. There were those who,
like Cal, hadn't bought into the idea, and the expressions on their faces made it obvious. But then there
were others who, by their nods and smiles, clearly
agreed with his bold move.

Shana stood. "Good morning."

Jace leaned back in his chair, confident that Shana
was capable of handling things from there. He knew
she would win some over, and others she would not.
But in the end, she had a job to do, and there was no
doubt in his mind that she would do it and do it well.

After her presentation, the questions began in ear-
nest, and she fired back the answers. He glanced
around the room, and he saw a level of respect in some
eyes and wariness in others. One or two tried being
forceful with their thoughts and ideas, and she stood
her ground, the authority and confidence in her tone
putting several on notice that she was not a pushover.
His admiration of her went up another notch.

He felt Dalton's eyes on him and glanced over at his
brother, who appeared to have an intense yet secretive
expression on his face. Jace stared back at his brother

before switching his gaze to Shana once more, wondering what game Dalton was playing.

Twenty minutes later, the meeting ended with the executives and managers heading out the door with muttered remarks, both approving and disapproving. Shana glanced over at Jace. "I didn't expect to win them all over."

He nodded. "Neither did I, but you're here now, and one day the naysayers will appreciate your presence when the company moves forward."

Caden patted Jace on the back. "Both Granddad and Dad would have been proud of how you handled the old guard today, Jace. When it comes to this kind of stuff, you're a true leader. I bet Cal is concerned because he hasn't brought on a new project in years."

Jace lifted a brow. "And how would you know that?"

Caden chuckled. "You aren't the only one spending his time reading. Thought I would do as much as I could before I left next week." Caden would be leaving for a couple of weeks to perform at two previously scheduled concerts in New York that were too costly to get out of.

Jace glanced over at Dalton, who was still sitting at the table and not saying a word. "So how do you think the meeting went, Dalton?"

Dalton didn't say anything for a while and then stood. "Caden's right, you're the right one to come in here and kick asses into shape or out the door. Freeman's pissed, although he's trying not to show it. I could hear the sound of his teeth grinding when you introduced Shana. He doesn't want her here. I think he feels threatened again. And I agree with Caden.

Dad and Granddad would have been proud of how you handled things. Caden's right. You're a true leader."

"Thanks."

Dalton then turned his attention to Shana and smiled. "For some reason, they see you as a threat, Ms. Bradford, and I'm curious as to why. I understand that no one likes change, but I felt it was more than that."

Jace lifted a brow, intrigued by his brother's observation. He hadn't truly expected it. "Why?"

Dalton shrugged, and then his smile widened. "Not sure, but I'm sure Ms. Bradford will make it her business to find out. Won't you?"

Shana returned his gaze. "Yes, I will definitely find out."

It didn't take long for word to spread through Granger Aeronautics that Bradford Crisis Management was not only on board but intended to bring the firm back up to snuff. Jace had encouraged all his department heads to meet with their teams to squash any rumors that needed addressing. Freeman had sought him out after the meeting, claiming the stockholders' meeting hadn't been his idea but had been initiated by a concerned stockholder. Jace knew that wasn't the case but hadn't called the man out on it. All he cared about was getting Grangers back on top, and he felt he had a chance with Shana's help.

During the following week, Jace noticed an improvement in morale among the employees. Smiles were in place, and he was met with friendly greetings when he passed through the halls to visit various departments for cross-training. Not surprisingly, Freeman had resigned, and as far as Jace was concerned, he had done the right thing since he could no longer be trusted.

Jace worked late every night, and so did Shana. He was well aware that she was still in the office, hard at work, when he left each day. He made a habit of sticking his head in the door to bid her good-night, and usually she was so buried in the various reports she was reading that she didn't bother to glance up. She would merely throw her hand up to acknowledge she'd heard him.

At the end of the day, Dalton walked into his office and dropped down in the chair across from his desk. "We need to talk, Jace."

Jace pushed aside the papers he'd been reading, giving Dalton his undivided attention. "All right. What's going on?"

"I can't handle being at Sutton Hills and will look for a place in town."

Jace didn't say anything for a few moments as he nodded slowly. Then he said ruefully, "To be honest, you lasted longer than I thought you would."

Dalton met his gaze and then released a deep sigh. "I was worried you would think I wasn't going to uphold my end of the promise."

"No, I don't think that. Besides, thanks to you, we were able to buy back all those shares, which put us in a good position. Even Dad said it was a good move on our part when I talked to him on the phone."

Jace, Caden and Dalton were preparing for the trip to visit their father this weekend, and it was a visit that Jace was looking forward to making. He was sure the same held true for Caden. However, he couldn't help but be concerned for Dalton. Although his brother had expressed a desire to see their father, Jace knew how hard it would be for him. Of his own choice, Dalton hadn't seen their father in over five years. It would be hard for Dalton, but it would be hard for Sheppard, as well.

"I'm glad he thought so," Dalton said.

The room got quiet for a moment, and then Jace spoke up and said, "Losing Mom was hard on all of us, Dalton, but I know it was especially hard on you, and I realize that. The two of you were extremely close, and to be honest, I worried about you. Especially when you didn't want to go see Dad as often as the rest of us. I thought you believed all the trash the media was spreading."

Their grandfather had shielded them from the courtroom drama by not allowing them to go to their father's trial. But they had gone on the day the verdict was read. They had been so sure the trial would end differently.

Dalton glanced down and studied the floor awhile and then glanced back at his brother. "I had my reasons back then, Jace."

"Did those reasons have anything to do with the question of Dad's innocence or guilt?"

Dalton's expression stilled for a minute, and then he looked over at Jace. "I would be lying if I said it never crossed my mind. Like you said, Mom and I were close. But Dad was such an easygoing person. I know anyone can get mad enough to snap, but Dad would still have thought of us and not hurt Mom. I believe that."

Jace believed that, too, although initially, like Dalton, he hadn't been sure, especially since the three of them had heard their parents' argument the night before. "Do you have any idea where you plan to move?"

Dalton shook his head. "No. I'm hiring a Realtor. I'm thinking a one-bedroom condo in a gated community would serve my purpose. If I like it well enough, I plan to buy it."

Jace knew that for his brother to be thinking of buying a place meant he would hang around awhile and wouldn't jump a plane to return to England the first chance he got. "That sounds like a good plan."

Dalton stood. "And just so you know, I like your Shana Bradford."

Jace lifted an arched brow. "*My* Shana Bradford?"

"Yes, I'm very impressed with her and have been since that meeting a week ago. She's sharp as hell, and I particularly liked how she handled Arrington and Fields. A couple of times, I thought they were out of line with how they grilled her, but she held her own with them."

Jace smiled, remembering. "I knew she would. The last thing we needed was for the company to begin panicking. But already I've noticed improvement in morale."

Dalton checked his watch. "I'm meeting Caden downstairs and we're headed to McQueen's, that bar and grill down the street. Do you want to join us?"

Jace shook his head. "Thanks, but no. I still need to finish reading all these documents. My goal is to learn as much about the company as I can."

He then tilted his head back and stared at his brother. "And how's your reading coming?" He had given Caden and Dalton the same documents, and he knew they hadn't yet put any dents in them.

A sly smile curved Dalton's lips. "Let's just say it's coming. Besides, you're the big chief. Caden and I don't need to know everything. We're merely here to have your back."

"I don't see things that way," Jace said blandly. "Your positions are just as important as mine."

"Whatever," Dalton said, smiling and heading for the door. "We'll see you at home later."

Jace pushed away from his chair, knowing he would work late tonight to read the documents regarding the last government contract they'd been awarded and the most recent two they did not get. It appeared their biggest rival in the industry, Barnes Aerospace, had outbid them twice. Was that the reason his grandfather suspected someone was passing trade secrets? Jace didn't mention his grandfather's suspicions to Shana since he was curious to see if her report would verify his grandfather's hunch.

Standing, Jace stretched his body and tried to ignore the growl of his stomach. He hadn't eaten since lunch, and even that meal had been pretty skimpy. Now his stomach was protesting and rallying for its next meal.

Deciding to grab a bag of chips from one of the vending machines, he opened his office door and stepped out into the lobby and collided with a soft, feminine body.

"Oops."

Jace reached out and caught hold of Shana's arms before she could lose her balance. She glanced up at him. "Thanks, Jace. Sorry, I wasn't looking where I was going. I got a little hungry and figured I'd grab something out of the vending machine. I should not have skipped lunch."

"No, you shouldn't have," he said, trying not to notice that, even at this late hour, her makeup was flawless. What got to him most, right below the gut, were her full and sensual lips. She had removed her jacket, and her blouse still looked crisp while pressed against a pair of firm breasts.

"I did eat lunch but got munchy, too, and was on my way to the vending machine," he added.

Shana noticed that Jace had removed his jacket and tie, and the top two buttons of his shirt were undone, revealing a portion of a hairy chest. Another thing she noticed was his scent. It was a masculine aroma she'd noticed that first day when they'd met at the restaurant.

She had seen him when she'd first arrived for work but hadn't seen him for the rest of the day. But seeing him that morning had been enough to overload her senses. And she'd had the unfortunate duty of riding the elevator up to their floor with him. She was grateful others were on board; otherwise, she would have been forced to engage in small talk with him and was glad she had been spared that.

"And another thing you should not be doing is working too late," Jace said, reclaiming Shana's attention. "It's been almost two weeks now, and you're still at it."

She waved off his words. "I'm fine. I prefer doing it here than at home."

He glanced down at her hand and then chuckled. "What's so funny?" she asked.

"These," he said, touching the items she'd purchased from the vending machine. "Do you need that many Hershey bars to tide you over?"

Her face split into a huge grin. "Like I said, I didn't eat lunch, and I have a thing for chocolate."

"Then why not order lunch in?"

"Don't want the hassle of clearing things through security. Besides, I'm okay. My dad called a while ago to say he'd made a pot of spaghetti and was sharing. He has a key to my place, so it will be there when I get home."

"You and your father are close?" He recalled that she had mentioned a sister but not a parent.

"Yes, very." Knowing it was time for her to retreat to her office, she took a step back. "Well, it's time for me to get back to work. I'll see you later."

"Wait, let me get this," Jace said, reaching up and pulling a piece of lint out of her hair. He liked how the silky strands felt against his fingers.

"Thanks."

"Don't mention it."

Shana tried breaking eye contact with Jace and found it hard to do so, mainly because of the intensity with which he was staring at her. She felt helpless to do anything but stare back. And then she felt it—that gentle yet heated stirring in the pit of her stomach. It was the same sensation she fought to ignore each and every time she saw him.

The air surrounding them seemed to vibrate, and she felt the tremble through every part of her body. Suddenly a rush of desire swept right between her legs. An incredible hunger began spreading from one part of her body to the other. She couldn't remember the last time she had been this attracted to a man. Her mind nearly froze at the thought.

Before she could draw in her next breath, Jace closed the distance between them, and instead of re-treating, she stood her ground while watching the fierce hunger flare to life in the depths of his eyes. Heat was blazing between them, and she felt its intensity. Potent. Stimulating. Arousing.

And when his gaze shifted from her eyes to her mouth, her lips felt a magnetic pull toward his as he began lowering his head. His lips were so close, she could almost taste them and...

The sound of one of her candy bars hitting the floor made Shana jump back. She was appalled at what she and Jace were about to do. Out in the open. In the middle of a corridor. "I need to get back to work," she said after picking up her candy bar.

He took a step back, as well. "Yeah, and I need to grab a bag of chips out of the machine." After she'd taken a few steps, he called after her. "Shana?"

She stopped and turned around. "Yes?"

"I am trying," he said. She knew exactly what he meant.

She nodded. "And I'm trying, too. I guess we need to try a little harder."

She then opened the door to her office and slipped inside.

"Drop, damn it!" Jace muttered while pounding on the front of the vending machine with his fist. He knew his anger was not at the bag of chips stuck in the machine but was directed at himself for what he'd almost done with Shana. He'd come close to kissing her, claiming the most sensuous lips he'd ever seen.

In one single instant, he'd come close to destroying all the resistance he'd fought so hard to build up with her. There was no excuse for not being able to handle his sexually deprived testosterone.

"Damn it, drop!" he said in frustration, pounding on the vending machine again.

"What the hell is going on out here?"

Jace swiveled around and stared Caden in the face. "What are you doing here? I thought you and Dalton left hours ago for dinner and drinks at McQueen's."

"We did," Caden said, coming up, pulling coins out of his pocket and inserting them into the machine. He chose the same chips Jace had, which made both his and Jace's bags drop down together. Caden gave Jace his bag of chips. "That's how you do it, Jace, not by giving the machine a beat-down."

"Whatever," Jace said, opening the bag of chips. "So if you left with Dalton, then what are you doing back here?"

Caden opened his own bag of chips, and the brothers began munching as they walked back toward Caden's office. "I believe in the theory that three's a crowd. Dalton met someone, a real hot number with a gorgeous pair of legs. I didn't want to be the one standing in the way of heated desire and unquenchable lust."

"I see your point," Jace said, dropping in the chair in front of Caden's desk.

After sitting down behind his desk, Caden glanced over at Jace. "I understand Dalton talked to you about moving out. I'm glad you didn't give him any grief about it."

"I wouldn't have done that, because I understand.

I've always understood, Caden. Just like I understood the pain you endured losing your best friend."

Caden didn't say anything, but he knew his brother was referring to his childhood relationship with Shiloh. Jace was observant, and Caden wondered when his brother would get around to asking questions. And they were questions Caden wasn't ready to answer just yet. So he decided to change the subject. "You'd be happy to know I've finished reading this stuff," he said, motioning to the stack of papers on his desk.

"Interesting reading once you get into it. I don't know how Dad and Granddad handled it all. It's too much to know," Caden added.

Jace shrugged. "It's not so bad."

Caden released a deep chuckle. "You can say that since Granger Aeronautics is in your blood. I see how easily you handle board meetings and those arrogant executives and managers who think you're a wet-behind-the-ears, don't-know-shit CEO. You're proving them wrong every day. You're a natural. A perfect fit."

Jace appreciated the compliment. "What about you, Caden? You have a business degree."

Caden's eyes became openly amused. They always did when he was reminded of that. "I love my music and only got that degree because Granddad all but threatened to disown me if I didn't."

Jace nodded. Dalton had a business degree, as well, but no one had ever expected him to use it, since they'd all known his position on the matter. He wanted to play football and impress the women, and he figured the sport endorsements and trust fund would be more than enough to tide him over and keep him rolling for the rest of his life.

"How long do you think Dalton will hang around before the lure of Europe gets too much for him?" Jace asked, curious to hear Caden's answer.

"I honestly don't know. It's been almost two weeks, and he still whines from time to time. Says he has things to do, places to go, women to fu—"

"Okay, I get it," Jace broke in, not allowing Caden to finish. Didn't take much to figure out what he'd intended to say.

"Well," Caden said. "I take Dalton out, feed him, order a couple of drinks and buckle down for his gripe session so that you won't have to. You have enough on your plate with Granger Aeronautics…and with Ms. Bradford."

A frown touched down in Jace's features. Caden couldn't help but be amused at his brother's reaction to what he'd said. "Come on, Jace. Are we not supposed to know you have a thing for her?"

"I don't have a thing for her."

"Okay."

Jace decided to leave it alone since he'd never been able to lie worth a damn with Caden. He stood. "Time to get back to work if I want to make it home before ten."

"And it's time for me to leave, too," Caden said, getting to his feet. "I'd completed the last of reading that report when I heard you pounding out your sexual frustration on the vending machine."

"You're imagining things."

Caden chuckled as they walked out of his office. "Am I? Fine, if that's what you want me to think. But that kind of frustration needs to be taken care of, or it'll come to a head in the worst possible way."

Chapter Twelve

"Hold the elevator, please!" Shana called, her movements purposeful and swift as she quickly strolled toward the bank of elevators and stepped on. "Thanks."

"No problem."

She froze at the sound of *that* voice. And then she glanced over her shoulder at the only other person in the elevator and her breath caught. Impeccably dressed, he looked good as always. "Good morning, Jace."

"Shana. You're eager to get started this morning."

"Yes, I am."

What she was really eager about was the weekend and couldn't wait for it to begin…although she had nothing planned. Jules wanted her to go grocery shopping with their father to meet the mysterious Mona. If she did, then that would be the only thing on her "to do" list. All she wanted to do was rest and relax. It had been one vigorous week, and there was still work to be done. She could handle that. But what she couldn't handle was the way her thoughts would shift throughout the day to begin focusing on the CEO instead of the company. She'd been doing that a lot lately. Too much for her peace of mind.

"Ready for the weekend?" he asked her, and she thought she heard him shift positions behind her but refused to look back to see.

"Yes, what about you?" she countered, frowning. Did she hear him move again? She was tempted to glance over her shoulder to verify that he hadn't.

"Looking forward to it," Jace said.

She could imagine. Men who looked like him had dates lined up aplenty. The fact that he'd returned to town less than a month ago meant nothing. Men were known to act fast, and he was a divorcé. No reason for him not to date. "Big plans?" she asked, telling herself it was merely for conversational purposes and not because she really wanted to know.

"Yes. My brothers and I are going to visit my father."

"Oh." Not what she'd expected, and for some reason something within her swelled. "That's nice," she said, glancing over her shoulder, and for the second time that morning she froze. Jace was no longer standing back against the panel wall but was there, close to her back. Too close. All at once, she was aware of every aspect of him—the strength of his shoulders beneath his jacket, and especially the rippling muscles in a chest that was too close to her back for comfort. All she would have to do was lean back a tad and she could be pressed against him, like she had been in her dreams so many times.

Smothering a groan, she turned toward him, lifted her chin and met his gaze. Like last night, it was intense, filled with a flickering fire that was heating her in places it shouldn't. Annoyed with herself and irritated with him, she said, "Why are you standing so close to me?"

Instead of answering, he said, "You look good. You always look good. Even in your business suits, panty hose and pumps. You have the ability to turn dressing conservatively into a sensuous thing, a damn sexy thing."

Shana tightened her hands on her purse and tried to stop them from trembling. She didn't want his compliment to get to her, nor did she want the male rawness of him in a business suit to wear down on her senses.

The elevator door swooshed open, and he quickly reached out and pressed a button to close it back. Then he pressed another button to keep it from moving to another floor. "What do you think you're doing?" she asked, going from irritated to incensed.

He stepped closer. "Melissa is taking the day off, and my brothers won't be coming in until noon, which means it's just the two of us up here. To answer your question, what I think I'm doing is what I should have done yesterday when I had the chance."

She had an idea of what he intended to do, especially when he reached out and placed his arms at her waist. It would be so easy to use one of her martial arts moves on him, but she didn't. It wasn't that she was easy, either, because she wasn't. But she was curious. She needed to know why thoughts of him found their way into her mind during the day and in her dreams at night. And why did the scent of him arouse her to the point that the area between her legs throbbed mercilessly?

And why now, when she should demand that he back off, was she standing there, willing him to bring it on?

Jace's gaze was trained on Shana's face, and he liked what he saw while wondering what she was thinking. He knew the thoughts going through his own mind and figured if she had a clue, she wouldn't appreciate them.

"Is there a reason for this?" she asked in an irritated tone.

Yes there was. "I think we acknowledged my testosterone and your hormones have a tendency to get a little crazy around each other," he said. "We agreed to try to keep the craziness at bay. That would have worked for me if you didn't turn me on each and every time I see you. And I think there's something about me that heats you up, as well. Am I on the right road?"

Yes, not only was he on the right road, he was driving on that road masterfully. "And what of it?"

His smile sent her pulse racing. "Yesterday, you said we were trying, and I agreed," he said. "You said we had to try harder, and I agree with that, too. I also know this craziness is not only unwise but it would be a bad move on our parts to do anything about it. Get crazier. Follow me?"

Unfortunately, she did. "Get to the point, Jace. I have work to do."

So did he, he thought, mesmerized by that mouth of hers. And her scent was getting to him like it always did. "My point is that I want you."

At the glare that flared in her eyes, he quickly added, "And I know it's wasted longing on my part since you've made it clear there can't be an involvement between us. But there is something, this one thing that I have to do, and I hope doing so will get you out of my system. I believe it will, and when I'm done, I'll be okay."

Shana drew in a slow breath, wondering if he'd considered his words. Just in case he hadn't, she decided to reemphasize. "When you're done, *you'll* be okay?"

"Yes."

And as if he belatedly knew her thoughts, he smiled and said, "I'm convinced that you'll be okay, as well."

And then he lowered his mouth to hers.

It was as if a sharp bolt of lightning hit the confines of the elevator and sent shock waves all through Shana. She closed her eyes, knowing she would remember every movement of his tongue inside her mouth and how diligently it was mating with her and causing her to sink against the solidness of his chest. Primitive urges she hadn't encountered for years seemed to seep into her bones, building a fire that was spreading all through her.

His kiss was way too intimate, and she reveled in the feel of his hands that had moved from her waist to boldly cup her buttocks. No man had ever claimed her mouth like this, with a tongue probing in places that made her shiver inside.

And then suddenly, he began eating away at her mouth with a hunger that elicited passion so aggressive she heard herself moan as her hands began traveling up his chest. Sensuous currents were taking her over, ripping away at her common sense with an intensity that was astounding.

Sensuous flutters were going up and down her spine, and automatically, her body pressed closer to him as his mouth continued to devour hers and send blood rushing through her as the craziness she'd tried to avoid was taking over.

Shana felt the thick muscles of his thighs, and the strength in them had her trembling with desire. This kiss was going way beyond her expectations, and her body was reacting in kind, as if it had been years since it had been satisfied with this kind of need. She then recalled that it *had* been years, which was probably why her insides were a curling mass of desire. She felt her feet move, and then her back was pressed up against the wall. His mouth was hot and had her sizzling at degrees that had her melting.

Suddenly, the buzzer sounded. Jace pulled his mouth away, and she automatically slumped against him, and his arms tightened around her. She could feel his fingers in her hair, caressing her scalp, while her breath was released in short, ragged pants.

His breathing was choppy, and the warmth of his breath was on her neck. It would be easy to ask him to take her in his office or hers and finish what they started, she thought as she sank deeper into his chest. But it would also be foolish.

"Come on, let's get out of here before a mechanic shows up," he whispered in a deep, husky voice close to her ear.

She heard the elevator opening and drew in a deep breath as she glanced up at him. Smoldering fire was still there in his eyes, and she could just imagine what he was seeing in hers. Pushing herself out of his arms, she knew she needed a reality check and would get one in the privacy of her office.

"Time to get to work," she said, already moving toward the door to her office. Craziness had begun ruling her mind and body, and the sooner she could escape from him, the better.

She should have known he would not make it easy for her, and when he said her name, she slowed and then turned around. "Yes?"

"Should I apologize?"

She wished she could tell him yes, that he should, but to do so wouldn't be fair or honest. Especially when she was certain she had enjoyed the kiss just as much as he had. Probably had even wanted it as much. "No," she said in a somewhat shaky breath. "But that doesn't make things right, Jace. Timing's lousy, and considering everything, it's not the best situation for us to be in. You hired me, so technically, I work for you, and I told you my feelings on the matter."

"Yet you wanted the kiss."

He was going to make her say it. Admit to it. "Yes, I wanted the kiss, but I want my peace of mind even more. I hope I'm out of your system, because it won't… it can't happen again."

Shana then turned and quickly moved toward her office without looking back.

"So," Dalton said, glancing over at Jace. "You think throwing a party where everyone comes naked is a good idea, Jace?"

"Yes, that sounds good."

When both Dalton and Caden threw their heads back and burst out laughing, Jace frowned. "What's so funny?"

"You are," Caden said, trying to suppress another laugh. "I don't know where your mind's at today, but it's not on anything Dalton and I have been saying. Your baby brother just asked what you thought about him throwing a nude party, and your response was that it sounded like a good idea."

Jace's frown deepened. Had he really said that? He met his brothers' gazes, and from their amused looks, apparently he had. "My mind was elsewhere."

"We figured as much," Dalton said, grinning. "So where was it?"

"Where was what?" Jace asked.

"Your mind. I hope you're not getting so wrapped up in this company that you can't think straight. If you are, Caden and I will force you to come with us to McQueen's and unwind with a few beers and good food. You'd like it."

Jace straightened up in his chair. "I'm sure I will."

When a text message on Dalton's mobile phone came through, he pulled the phone out of his jacket pocket, checked the text and smiled. He glanced over at his brothers. "Sorry, I won't be able to hang with you guys after work. I got a hot date," he said, standing. "And I probably won't be home until late—probably not at all—so don't wait up."

"You do remember we're going to see Dad tomorrow, right?" Caden spoke up to ask as Dalton quickly headed for the door.

"Yes, I remember." And then he was gone.

When the room got quiet and it was evident that Jace had reverted back to la-la land, concern shadowed Caden's features. "You sure you're okay?"

Jace blinked as if he'd forgotten Caden was there. "Yes, I'm fine."

"I wonder."

When Jace didn't say anything, Caden forged ahead. "You're working long hours, not eating properly, and Hannah's worried about you. Dalton and I have to hear it when you're not there, which is most of the time. She wants you to make the company a success but doesn't want you killing yourself doing so. Of course, Dalton came to your defense yesterday."

Jace leaned back in his chair and grasped the back of his neck with the palms of his hands. "Did he?"

A corner of Caden's mouth slipped into a smile when he said, "Yes. He told her there's a woman involved and that you were hanging around hoping you'd eventually score."

A muscle quivered in Jace's jaw. "He said that, did he?"

"Yes. He said a little bit more, but I won't bore you with the details."

"I'd appreciate it if you didn't."

Jace closed his eyes for a minute and, at the moment, refused to admit that what Dalton said wasn't far from the truth. Granted, he did have a lot of documents and reports to read, but he could easily do it at home. But there had been something satisfying in knowing he was here and Shana was there. Close by. In the office right next door.

"Jace?"

He opened his eyes and looked over at Caden. "Yes?"

"I asked you something twice, but evidently your mind was rather occupied."

"And what exactly did you ask?" Jace asked through stiff lips.

"I want to know if you'll have dinner with me at McQueen's. Share a few beers. You'd love their fries." A smile then eased onto Caden's lips. "And just in case there's even an ounce of truth in what Dalton told Hannah, I suggest we invite Ms. Bradford to join us."

Jace's eyes narrowed. "Are you trying to be funny?"

Caden tried keeping a straight face. "Absolutely not. I would enjoy her company, so ask her. The worst she can do is tell you no."

And Shana *would* tell him no, Jace was convinced of that. So why was he about to knock on her office door at five o'clock on a Friday afternoon? The office was closed, yet she was still here. But then so was he. They were both single, so why didn't they have dates this weekend or something?

Speak for yourself, pal, he muttered to himself. *For all you know, she might have a date for the weekend. She's a looker, so don't assume anything. And then there's the way she tastes…*

He rubbed a hand down his face, frustrated that he couldn't get the elevator kiss out of his mind. Christ! Never had a woman's mouth tasted so damn delectable. He felt a deep stirring in his groin just remembering it. He had drunk the sweetness of her mouth like a starving man, a man whose mouth had felt a surge of electricity the moment their lips had touched.

And he wasn't sure just how she felt about it.

She didn't appear mad, just resigned…like him. Mainly because, kiss or no kiss, she was not out of his system. If anything, she was deeper into it. And he didn't know a way to get her out. For him, it was a no-win situation.

Deciding to knock and get it over with, he did just that. "Come in."

Taking a deep breath, he opened the door and found her just as he did most other evenings—buried in stacks of papers that were spread across her desk, with a pair of glasses perched on her nose and her hair spread around her shoulders. Her scent had reached out to him the moment he stepped into the room. The scent was as luscious as how her lips had tasted.

There was a wary look in her eyes as she gazed up at him. "Yes?"

"Caden and I are going to McQueen's. I heard the food is good and the drinks are even better. Nice way to kick-start the weekend. Do you want to join us?" Damn, he'd said a mouthful.

Shana sat up straight in her chair. This was the first time she'd seen Jace since this morning after that little elevator scene. Mainly because she'd been hiding out here in her office, hoping their paths didn't cross. Lucky for her, they hadn't. But was it really lucky for her?

Ben Bradford was too proud a man to raise a coward, yet that's just how Shana had been acting today.

When did she ever let her interest in a man have her hiding out like an escaped convict?

Her attraction to Jace was an issue. And it was one she was working on resolving. But the more she thought about it, the more it sort of became a "dog in the gate" syndrome. As a child, Shana walked to school, and every day, she passed by a house with a fence and a dog protecting the yard. She was afraid the dog would somehow get out and attack her the same way a boy in her class had been attacked once. When her fear of the dog grew too great, she intentionally walked an extra block to avoid that house with the dog…until her father found out what she'd been doing.

He told her that sometimes you had to stand up to your fears, and she needed to prove to the dog that she was in control. The next day, with knees shaking, she had walked past the house. The dog had barked and acted like he was going to jump over the fence, but he hadn't. She had made it through that day and the days that followed because she believed she was in control. She still had her fears, but she had managed to take charge of them. In the end, once the dog saw she would not weaken, he eventually stopped barking at her.

She would apply that same analogy to the situation with Jace. She had work to do here for at least another three to four weeks, and she couldn't spend all that time trying to avoid Jace—being afraid of him and the way he made her feel. There would be days when they would have to meet for long periods of time, so she could not let him be her dog in the yard. He knew her position and knew she would not waver on it. The kiss was…just a kiss. Curiosity. Need. Greed. Those things had fueled it. What she needed to do was go out and have some fun this weekend. Kick back. Indulge in sex…something she hadn't done in almost a year. Charles Kincaid, a doctor she'd met a few months ago, often called her on the weekends for a date, and she was always quick to turn him down. This weekend when he called, she would handle things differently.

"Shana?"

She held his gaze. "Thanks for the invite, and yes, I'd love to join you and Caden at McQueen's."

Chapter Thirteen

Shana's exuberant laughter filled their section of the restaurant, and Jace suddenly realized it was the first time he'd heard it, and she was laughing at something Caden had said. His jaw muscles tensed as he thought that the two of them were apparently getting along great.

He hadn't expected her to come, and she had surprised the hell out of him when she said she would. And she certainly seemed to be enjoying herself. Tonight, Caden was quite the character, and Jace realized at that moment that he hadn't heard his brother laugh in a while. So maybe Shana's joining them tonight was a good thing. Jace wasn't sure what was going on with Caden but hoped if he ever needed an ear that he knew Jace was available.

Jace had a hunch that whatever was going on with Caden somehow involved Shiloh Timmons. He wasn't sure how; he was just certain that it did. That was one of the reasons he had no problem with Caden going away to do those two concerts. His brother needed to get back into his music, and Jace knew how much music relaxed Caden and soothed his ruffled feathers.

He was not worried about Caden not returning, because he would. And when he got back, Caden would roll up his sleeves to do whatever he needed to do to fulfill their grandfather's promise. If it were Dalton, Jace would probably worry. If Dalton ever got a chance to defect back to Europe, he would find any and every excuse to stay there, discovering a way to fulfill their grandfather's wishes from another continent if he could. Even if he had to do so by hologram. Jace couldn't help chuckling at the thought of that.

"What's so funny, Jace? Share it so we can all laugh."

Jace glanced over at Caden. He then looked past Caden to Shana. Before leaving the office, she had pulled her hair back in one of those fancy clips, and for some reason, the style brought more emphasis to her eyes and face. He thought this evening that she looked even more beautiful than usual.

"I'd rather not," he heard himself say. "Besides, it wasn't important."

Caden nodded. "If you say so." He then turned his attention to Shana. "What are your plans for the weekend? I bet you have a date."

Shana wished Caden hadn't put her on the spot. It wouldn't be so bad if Jace wasn't sitting across from her, leaning lazily back in his chair while nursing a glass of beer with those deep, brooding and intense eyes leveled on her. Even when the conversation had been between just her and Caden, she had been aware of Jace's focused gaze.

"Yes, I do have a date. And it's one I'm looking forward to." So she decided to tell a little white lie for now. When Charles called, which she would bet he would, then it wouldn't be a lie any longer. "My first two weeks at any corporation are usually the toughest and busiest," she continued by saying, "Granger Aeronautics is no exception. I had a lot of things I had to familiarize myself with. Hundreds of reports I had to read."

"And how are things going with that?" Jace decided to ask. He needed to wrap his mind around something other than the fact that she had a date this weekend. Was she seeing someone on a steady basis? Involved in a serious relationship? She didn't have a ring on her finger—wedding or otherwise.

A muscle in his jaw twitched. Why did he give a damn about her date when it really wasn't any of his business what she did this weekend or with whom? He was convinced that regardless of the man she might be spending time with this weekend, that strong attraction between them—the one he'd thought he could kiss out of their systems—was still there, well, alive and kicking…even if it wasn't anything but a hefty amount of lust.

"It's going great, and I think I covered a lot of ground. I should have my first report to you sometime next week," she said, intruding on his thoughts.

"So you feel good about Granger making a turnaround?" Caden asked.

"Yes, I do, as long as the recommended changes are made."

Jace noticed that an easy smile always played at the corners of her mouth while talking to Caden, but it was the opposite with him. Case in point, she glanced over at him, and he couldn't help noticing how her smile faded somewhat. A part of him wanted to think that he was imagining things, but he knew he was not.

"I don't see why the changes wouldn't be made. In fact, I'm convinced they will be, right, Jace?" Caden asked.

When Jace didn't say anything, Caden glanced over at his brother and repeated the latter part of his comment again. "Right, Jace?"

Jace shifted his gaze from Shana to Caden. "I don't agree to anything blindly, so it depends what they are." His gaze went back to Shana in time to see her flinch. She then stiffened her spine.

"I don't expect you to jump at my every recommendation, Jace. But I'm hoping you keep an open mind to know whatever I propose is designed to propel your corporation's long-term success. I don't put a Band-Aid on the problem. I fix it."

"I understand that."

"Do you?"

"Yes." Their gazes locked, held, as if testing for strength of will. Then Jace added, "You will sacrifice anything to look good."

Her mouth spread into a thin-lipped smile. "I *am* good."

One corner of his mouth twisted upward. "Yes, you definitely are."

When there was a moment of silence that had extended way too long, Caden cleared his throat. He had a feeling the conversation had somehow shifted from Granger Aeronautics to something he'd rather not know about. It was obvious they'd forgotten he was sitting there, and it wouldn't be long before one of them said something they'd rather not expose.

When they looked over at him, Caden smiled and said, "Speaking of good, I noticed the dessert for today is lemon cake with ice cream. The slices are huge. Would anyone want to share one with me?"

Shana entered her condo, turned off the alarm and then set her briefcase and purse on the first table she came to. Why was she so upset with what Jace had said? She wouldn't expect any CEO to go along with everything she recommended, but she expected him to have an open mind.

Who said he won't? her inner mind countered. *Why are you making it so freakin' personal?* Was she? Okay, maybe she was. And when he'd made that "good" statement, she had read between the lines and knew exactly what he'd been referring to. They'd ended up sharing ice cream and lemon cake with Caden while keeping up the pretense that all was well between them when she knew it wasn't. And she blamed it on that damn kiss.

Knowing she needed to chill a minute before taking a shower and getting in bed, she moved toward the French doors that led to her patio. She loved it here and knew the moment she'd been given a tour of the condo that it was hers. The screened-in patio that overlooked rolling hills and a huge, man-made lake had been a plus.

Her community consisted of a lot of both married and single individuals. Some were parents, and most were pet owners. Gloria, a flight attendant and one of her best friends, lived on one side of her, and Lonnie, a veterinarian, lived on the other. A married couple, Connie and Bill, lived across the street and were excited about expecting their first child in five months. The other neighbors kept to themselves, and she didn't know them by name, but she would throw up her hand in a wave whenever she saw them or vice versa.

Both she and Jules lived within ten miles of their father, although Jules traveled around from state to state most of the time. Still, it was convenient, and usually either of them would drop in and spend time with him. The three of them had always been close, and it seemed so strange that after all this time, he was hinting that he was interested in a woman. She, of all people, knew he deserved to be happy, but she and Jules couldn't help but be concerned, even if they were a little bit possessive.

With the darkness settling over the street, there was enough light from the moon as well as various illuminations from the two wooden decks to see a number of couples who owned boats enjoying a night on the water. According to her father, there were fish aplenty in the lake, and he liked coming over with his rod and reel whenever he got bored. She especially liked it when he did, because that meant he would end up cooking what he caught. No one fried fish and cooked hush puppies like her father.

Thinking she had chilled long enough, she went back inside and was headed for her bedroom when her cell phone rang, and she quickly sifted through her purse hoping it was Charles. She let out a disappointed sigh when it wasn't Charles but Jules. "And what do you want?"

There was a pause on the other end before Jules said, "Evidently, you're in a bad mood for some reason tonight."

Shana tapped her foot on the floor. "Yes, I am. I was hoping you were Charles."

"Charles Kincaid?"

"Yes."

She heard Jules snort. "Why him? I told you that you can do better."

Yes, she could, but at the moment it didn't matter. "The reason I was hoping it was Charles is because, although he might have his faults, he is a lot of fun, and I need fun this weekend."

"Rough week?"

"Yes. This was my third week working with Granger Aeronautics."

"That's right, it was. And how is the hunky CEO?"

A frown settled between Shana's brows. "Who said he was a hunk?"

"You did...in so many words. You said he was good-looking, which equates to a nice face and a fine-as-a-dime body. Did I assume wrong?"

All Shana had to do was remember how he had looked when she stepped on the elevator that morning. Like her, he had forgone "dress-down Friday" and had worn a business suit. He had looked damn good in it as usual. Her sister was right. Jace was definitely a hunk, eye candy of the sweetest kind.

"No, you didn't assume wrong," Shana admitted.

"You didn't say if he was married."

"He's divorced."

"Kids?"

"No. At least he never mentioned any."

"Umm. Sounds like a nice guy."

Shana wouldn't say whether he was or not. Doing so might get her into more trouble with Jules. She knew how her sister's mind worked. "So now that I've been interrogated, what's going on with you and your case? Any new leads?"

"Yes, one came in this morning. Someone wanted me to meet him in an undisclosed location. I did. He was a cabdriver and was able to not only positively identify Marcos Rodrigo but confirm that he was traveling with a child. He gave me the address where Rodrigo was dropped off. I guess he figured he had covered his tracks well because he was still there, at one distant cousin's house and living in the basement."

"You got him?"

Shana heard the smile in her sister's voice when she affirmed, "Yes, I got him and Little Marco. The first thing the kid did was ask for his mommy."

"Has she been told yet?"

"Yeah, and it took her almost a full hour to stop crying."

Shana could imagine. For a mother to be told that her child had died, burned to a crisp in an auto accident, only to find out that he was alive and had been kidnapped by his own father had to have been an ordeal from hell. And what was so sad was that the authorities had closed the case, convinced the ex-husband and child had indeed died in the fire. But Carla Rodrigo had come to Jules and had convinced her to take the case. Jules had done so because of gut feelings that had paid off.

"Congratulations, Jules. That's another mystery solved. You're getting a track record."

"So are you, with the ability to save those companies. I'm sure Dad is proud of his girls."

Shana smiled. "I'm sure of that, as well."

"And speaking of Dad, are you ready to go grocery shopping with him tomorrow?" Jules asked.

"Yes, and when are you coming home?"

"Not for another couple of weeks. Ms. Rodrigo is on her way here, but there's a lot of paperwork to get in. This is another country, so we had to get both the State Department and FBI involved since it was a kidnapping."

"Well, you be safe."

"I will."

After Shana hung up the phone and placed it back in her purse, she tried not to think about Jace Granger and the effect he had on her, and especially not about the kiss they'd shared that morning. What she needed to think about was Mona Underwood, the woman her father was interested in, and find out everything she could about her.

The last thing Shana needed was for Jules to come back to town and start digging, whether it was warranted or not. When it came to Ben Bradford, Jules could go over the top and would be a force to reckon with.

Continuing her trek toward the bedroom, Shana figured that when Charles asked where she wanted to go, she would suggest dinner and a movie. And she would reiterate that he needed to keep his hands to himself. Charles liked to take liberties he shouldn't at times, which is why she had to put the brakes on their relationship. He figured she was bedroom-ready after the first date, and she had to inform him she didn't do casual affairs. So for the past three months, he had been trying to wear down her defenses and refused to let her be the one who got away.

But she would have to admit when he wasn't focused on trying to get her into bed, he was a great conversationalist and an all-around nice guy. She needed to unwind this weekend, have a little fun. But more than anything, she needed to get Jace Granger off her mind.

Chapter Fourteen

"Good morning, everyone."

Jace glanced up as Dalton walked into the dining room, smiling all over the place and pulling Hannah in his arms for a huge kiss on the cheek that had her blushing and chuckling. Hannah's smiles had become almost nonexistent since his grandfather's death, and it felt good to see her smile again.

"Go on and sit, Dalton, before I take a broom to you," Hannah warned. "And I baked those biscuits just the way you boys like."

"Thanks, Hannah, and you are so appreciated," Dalton said, smiling and rubbing his hands together as he quickly moved toward the table.

"I thought you stayed out all night," Jace told Dalton when his brother had filled his plate and plopped down in a chair across from him and Caden.

Dalton spread his lips in a silly-looking grin. "I did. I got in less than an hour before you got up. I started to wake you, but Hannah wouldn't let me. Claimed you needed your sleep."

He leaned closer and whispered so as not to be overheard by Hannah, who was dusting the furniture in the next room. "I almost told her you had no reason to need more sleep. I'm the one who had been flexing my muscles most of the night while you were probably just curled up dreaming about doing so."

Jace took a sip of his coffee, deciding not to respond but let Dalton have his glory. Caden wasn't going to let their brother off that easy. "Still the braggart, I see. One day, you're going to meet your match."

Dalton, with a piece of bacon hanging between his lips, grabbed his heart as if Caden's words had pained him. Jace couldn't help but smile at the antics. It had always been that way growing up as teens while living here with their grandfather. He was the realist, Caden the idealist and Dalton the airhead who was getting more sex than either of them...or so he claimed.

Richard would sit at the head of the table with a newspaper held up to his face as he scanned the financial section, while Dalton whispered across the table about his sexual escapades and Jace and Caden hung on his every word. Jace always wondered whether the old man's attention had been glued to the paper or if he had been getting an earful like the rest of them.

Jace checked his watch. "Eat up. We need to be on the road in an hour."

He didn't want to admit it, but he felt like a kid about to go see Santa. He made it a point to visit with his father two to three times a year and knew Caden kept in contact even more often than that. Dalton hadn't seen their father in five years, not since Sheppard had been transferred to Delvers. This would be the first time the three of them would be visiting their father together in over ten years.

"Dad knows we're coming, right?" Dalton asked before taking a sip of his coffee.

"Yes, I talked to him a few days ago. He can't wait to see us, especially you," Jace replied.

Dalton didn't say anything at first and then he said, "And I'm looking forward to seeing him, as well."

A short while later, Jace was back in his bedroom, getting a few items he planned to take with him. He knew his grandfather and father stayed in contact and that Richard went to see Sheppard at least twice a month. He wondered if his father had been aware of the condition the company was in. And if he was, what exactly had Richard told him about it? Jace intended to find out.

As he clipped his cell phone onto his belt, he couldn't help but think about Shana. The thought of her going out on a date shouldn't be getting to him. All they shared was an attraction, and all he'd gotten out of it was a kiss. But it hadn't been just a kiss, it had been *the* kiss.

He traced his tongue across his lips, convinced three meals later that he could still taste her on his mouth. She was supposed to be out of his system about now, but things hadn't worked out that way. He would admit within himself that he wanted her more than ever. And it wasn't supposed to be this way. His divorce from Eve was like a rebirth for him, and he'd made the promise that the next relationship he got into wouldn't boggle his mind and he would be able to handle it. But there was nothing about Shana Bradford he felt he could handle. Even when she was wearing those prim, proper and traditionalist suits, she might as well be wearing nothing at all, because he could see beyond all that to expose the sexy woman he knew she was. The woman who was ruthlessly dissecting his libido bit by bit.

There was a gentle knock on his bedroom door. "Come in."

Caden opened the door and walked in with Dalton following behind. "Ready to ride?"

Jace nodded as he glanced at the two men. His blood. His brothers. "Yes. Come on. Let's go see Dad."

Sheppard stood at the window and glanced out. Delvers wasn't a bad place if you had to be locked up. In fact, as a trustee, he had more freedom here than most of the guys. Only difference was their sentences were a hell of a lot shorter than his—five years at the max. He had served fifteen years of a thirty-year sentence, making it through the halfway mark.

It was hard being locked up, denied your freedom for a crime you didn't commit, and then knowing the person who had been responsible was out there somewhere walking around scot-free. His father had asked Sheppard more than once if he had any clue as to who might have wanted to end Sylvia's life, but he'd admitted honestly that he had been and still was clueless.

Shep had known Sylvia's secrets even when she thought he hadn't. His wife had been unfaithful to him, and not the other way around like the prosecution had claimed. Her lover hadn't attended the trial and, to this day, as far as he knew, Shep was the only one who knew of the affair, other than the man's wife. She had been the one to expose it to Shep. But he couldn't even say either of them had anything to do with Sylvia's death, because at the time they were both out of the country together, trying to rebuild their marriage. He hadn't felt the need to say anything about either of them to his attorney. The last thing he wanted was to smear the name of his sons' mother.

"Mr. Shep, I just wanted to come say goodbye."

Shep turned and looked into Matthew Fontane's face, a face that looked somewhat different than the one who'd come to Delvers to serve time five years ago. Shep had been at Delvers only two weeks when Fontane had arrived, furious, full of anger and mad at the world. At eighteen, Fontane had been caught in a carjacking ring. The driver had suddenly had a heart attack and would have died if Fontane hadn't stayed behind to give the man CPR. For that, he'd received a lighter sentence than the others. However, Fontane felt he should have been able to walk free.

The warden had assigned him to Shep's team, and they had butted heads from day one. But it didn't take long for Shep—through hard work and determination—to make the young man see the error of his ways. He found Fontane, who had dropped out of school at sixteen, to be a highly intelligent and bright kid who just happened to have a smart mouth and a troubled childhood. Now five years later, while imprisoned, Fontane had gotten his GED and was only a few credits short of having a college degree in criminology. He had already been accepted at Hampton University to finish up his education. No longer was he angry and mad at the world. Today he would be set free, and Shep knew that Fontane would do just fine.

"I'm going to miss seeing you around here, Fontane," Shep said, smiling at the young man of twenty-three, almost feeling like a proud parent. "But I know you'll be able to handle anything that comes your way. You're a born leader for the right side, the side that knows crime doesn't pay."

Fontane nodded, and then his smile faded to be replaced by a deep frown. "I hate that you're being left here for a crime you didn't commit. That's the one thing I can't accept as fair."

"Don't worry about me. I'll be fine."

"Yeah, but you have fifteen more years to do. I think if I had to be in here one more day I would have—"

"Found the strength to endure it," Shep cut in to finish for him. "There was a time when I wondered how I was going to make it, knowing I had left three teenage sons behind, but somehow I found the strength."

"But it's wrong. Someone should have found your old lady's killer by now. He's free, and you're in here."

"I'm willing to do the time," Shep said somberly.

"Although you didn't do the crime? Maybe your sons will—"

"No," Shep cut him off by saying. "They have their own lives now." What he didn't add was that he wasn't sure just what Sylvia was involved in that would make someone want her dead. And he didn't want his sons' lives placed in danger because of it. The less they knew, the better. Jace, Caden and Dalton had been and always would be his primary concern.

"There you go, Mr. Shep, always looking out for people. I just wish I could do something."

Shep's face creased into a smile. "You can. Do me proud by making something of yourself. Then go out into your community and reach out to another hellion who needs a guiding hand. Give him what I hope I gave to you. A sense of purpose and pride, as well as a belief that you can be better than what those street gangs were offering you."

Fontane nodded. "Yes, sir."

Twenty minutes later, Shep was standing at the window on the fourth floor in the library and watched as Matthew Fontane walked out of Delvers a free man. A car that Shep knew was driven by Pastor Luther Thomas was there to pick him up. Luther would see to it that Fontane was acclimated back into society as easily as possible and with strong, positive influences. And Luther would make sure Fontane got the last credits he needed to finish college. Luther had promised, and Shep knew he would keep his word. Luther himself had once been a convict but had been released after being locked up for six years after his attorney fought for and won a new trial. New evidence was submitted that proved it wasn't Luther's DNA on the rape victim. The real rapist was already in jail for a series of other rapes.

Luther, even while serving time, had been instrumental in helping Shep retain his sanity during his first year being incarcerated. He had told Shep that when the world gives you lemons, you make lemonade. Being in prison didn't make you guilty; it just meant the odds had been against you, and when you knew in your heart that you were innocent, you had nothing to be ashamed about. It had not come as a surprise to Shep that, after leaving prison, Luther had gone into the ministry. The man had a way of inspiring people and would be just what Fontane needed.

As Luther's car departed, another vehicle pulled up. Suddenly, Shep felt a deep pull in his gut as a sense of pride washed over him. He knew just as sure as his name was Sheppard Maceo Granger that his sons had arrived. All three of them.

Shep managed to grip his sons—all three of them—in a tight bear hug. He needed this. To hold them close and let them feel the love from him…just as he needed to feel it from them. They were the most important people in his life. Period. Always had been and always would be. He thought about them upon waking up each morning and said a prayer for them before going to bed each night. He could deal with the loss of his freedom but could never deal with the loss of them.

He slowly drew back and studied each of their features as love continued to stir his insides. They were men who had grown up without him. Men he was proud of. The old man had done a great job of taking over where Shep had left off. He knew times hadn't been easy. Richard Granger was from the old school and believed in authority, almost dictatorship. But it was only after Shep had been locked up and had to mingle with men whose childhoods had been so different from his that he could appreciate his father's tough love. And he figured that one day his sons would grow to appreciate it, as well.

All three had that arrogant-looking Granger chin with the dimple in the center. The Granger cleft, his grandmother would call it. All male Grangers were born with it. Dalton, although the youngest, was still the tallest, and all three looked well and physically fit.

He shifted his gaze from Jace and Caden to Dalton. "I'm so glad to see you, Dalton."

"Same here, Dad," his son said in an almost-broken

voice. "I wanted to come before now but I couldn't. There were—"

"Shh," Sheppard said softly, reaching up to grasp his shoulder tenderly. "I understand. I've always understood, Dalton. You don't have to explain. Come on and sit down."

The warden had given permission for Shep to be alone in a secluded section of the courtyard with his sons. Normally, touching would not have been allowed, but Shep knew that Ambrose, the prison guard, had basically looked away.

"This place isn't so bad," Dalton said, glancing around. "I like it better than that other place."

Shep did, too. "I appreciate the governor sending me here," he said. "He figured I could make a difference, and I believe that I have," he said, thinking about Fontane.

"They trust you here," Jace observed. "That guard over there might as well not be here."

Shep followed his gaze. "Ambrose is a good man, a father himself. He has three sons." He didn't want to be reminded that Ambrose's three sons were the same ages Shep's had been when he'd been sent away.

"Here, Dad. I thought you might want to see these," Caden said, handing his father a group of pictures taken at the repast following their grandfather's memorial service. Shep felt tightness around his heart. His father had died, and he hadn't been there to pay his last respects.

He slowly flipped through the pictures. Some of the people he recognized immediately; others he did not. But then, it had been fifteen years. He lifted a brow at one particular picture and smiled. "Hey, is that little Shiloh?"

Caden's lips tightened. "Yes, that's her. I was trying to take a picture of Cameron, and she got in the way."

Dalton chuckled as he looked down at the photo. "Yeah, I just bet she did. It looks to me as if you had the camera aimed right at her."

"Well, you're wrong," Caden said, narrowing his gaze at Dalton. He reached out for the picture. "I can toss it away and—"

"Toss it away? Why?" his father said, eyeing him curiously. "It was nice of her to attend the services considering how her parents ended up feeling about the family once I was convicted."

"Yes, real nice," Caden said as a muscle ticked in his jaw.

Shep didn't say anything. He glanced over at Jace, who merely shrugged. Shep glanced back down at the picture. "She's grown into a beautiful woman, don't you think?" He decided to probe.

"I wouldn't know." Then just as quickly, Caden took the pictures from his father and put them back in the envelope. "These copies are yours, and you can look at them anytime. I think Jace wants to talk to you about the company."

"All right," Shep said, turning his attention to Jace. "How have things been going at Granger Aeronautics?"

Jace spent the next twenty minutes filling his dad in on everything, including the emergency stockholders' meeting Freeman had called. Shep smiled. "That was a smart move to buy up that stock, and it's a good thing you had the money to loan your brothers, Dalton."

Dalton, who had grown bored with the conversation, suddenly lifted an arched brow. "Loan? You mean I'll get my money back?"

Shep chuckled. "Yes, one day you will—when the company's out of the red. You didn't think you would get it back right away, did you?"

"I figured it was for a good cause." Dalton smiled. "Besides, Jace and Caden threatened me."

Jace rolled his eyes. "He's a billionaire and has millions to spare."

"Yes," Shep said. "I think you surprised a number of people, Dalton. I'm proud of you. I always knew when the going got tough you would see your way out. Dad was worried about you for a while, but I wasn't." Shep chuckled again. "I always knew you had a good head on your shoulders once you found your way out from under some woman's skirt."

Caden laughed. "Sorry, Dad, he's still lost. He hasn't found his way out from under a skirt yet."

Dalton glanced over at Caden. "Go to—"

He then remembered his father was sitting right there and quickly said, "Go to the bathroom and relieve yourself."

Shep couldn't help but smile. It was good to see that the camaraderie between his sons was good. He was certain they got on each other's nerves from time to time, but he knew in the end they would have each other's backs.

"How much do you know about Cal Arrington, Dad?" Jace asked.

"Not much. He and Freeman were hired after I left. Dad was impressed with them, and they moved up the ranks quickly. I know Vidal had some apprehensions about him doing that, but Dad's mind was made up. If you're asking if I think Arrington can be trusted, the answer is no. Right now, the only persons you can trust are your brothers." He paused a moment and then said, "So tell me about the company you're using to reinvent Granger."

Dalton snickered. "Shana Bradford, Jace's wonder-woman. She has brains and intelligence, is sharp as a tack and has a great pair of legs."

Shep's lips eased into a smile. "And of course you would notice the latter."

"Of course."

Shep shook his head. It was clear to see that his baby boy loved life and especially the opposite sex. "Why don't you tell me about her, Jace? Dalton can't get past her physical attributes. I want to know about this crisis management company. Do the three of you think you can pull things off with her help? Your grandfather believed that you could."

Jace glanced at his brothers before looking at his father and saying, "I think we can pull it off, as well."

Chapter Fifteen

Ben Bradford came down the stairs, taking them two at a time while whistling "Sweet Georgia Brown," and froze when his feet touched the bottom floor. "Shana? I wasn't expecting you to drop by today."

Shana studied her father. He'd gotten a haircut, which wasn't unusual since he always kept his hair cut low, neat and trimmed. She figured the chambray shirt was new because she didn't recall seeing it before, and he was wearing jeans. Her father never wore jeans. He wore khakis all the time but never jeans.

"Thought I would surprise you," she said, coming to her feet. "When I got here, I heard the shower going and then later all I could hear was you whistling. I started to search the house, certain I would find a few Harlem Globetrotters around here."

He chuckled. "I'm in a good mood, no big deal."

To her, it was a big deal. Her father usually had a good disposition, even-tempered and fun to be around, but she could recall very few times he went around whistling.

"I hope you didn't come for lunch, because I haven't

fixed anything. Saturday is my day to go to the grocery store, and I'm on my way out."

"No, I wasn't expecting lunch. I thought I'd ride to the grocery store with you. I need to pick up a few things and figured we could shop together."

"Oh."

Was that disappointment she heard in his voice? She pulled her list out of her purse and held it up. "See, I just need a few things. I skipped lunch a few times last week and figured I'd make myself a sandwich to take every day."

"Good idea."

"I thought so."

Her father studied her for a second, and then he leaned back against the staircase. "Okay, what's really going on, Shana Nicole Bradford?"

Shana tried keeping a straight face. "What makes you think something is going on?"

"Because one, this is Saturday, and you usually don't get out of bed before two," he said, counting off his fingers. "Two, you never go grocery shopping. Your refrigerator would break down if you ever decided to use it for what it was purchased for. And three, you know I drive the golf cart to the grocery store, and you hate riding in those things."

She hated to admit that her father was right on all three points, especially the latter. He lived in a beautiful community that was established for the seasoned crowd. It was as if they had their own little city. Homes were strategically built in the center with all the convenient places circled around them. They had their own hospital, grocery stores, movie theater, mini malls and more restaurants than any group could need. The only catch was that, to eliminate gasoline fumes, everyone had agreed to purchase a golf cart to get around for shopping, socializing and recreational purposes. The little buggers were all over the place, and she wasn't a fan of them.

She smiled tentatively. "What if I told you I'm making today an exception?"

"Then I would be forced to ask you why."

Now, that was a good question. She could tell him she hadn't gotten much sleep last night since her lips were still tingling from a kiss she'd gotten in an elevator yesterday. Or that the guy she figured would call her for a date this weekend hadn't done so yet. "Umm, what if I—"

"Before you continue, need I remind you that neither you nor Jules can lie worth a damn, and I can catch you each and every time?"

No, he didn't have to remind her of that, but since he had, she might as well come clean. "I want to meet Mona."

He cocked a brow. "You want to meet her or check her out and then report back to Jules?"

Shana's features broke into a wide smile. *Busted.* "I guess you know your daughters."

Ben shook his head. "Yes, I guess I do." He pushed away from the staircase. "Well come on, and don't complain about my driving."

The ride wasn't so bad, Shana decided while browsing through the aisle of the grocery store. Instead of going to one of the major chain stores, her father had driven here to this quaint little market nestled near a pizza shop, hair salon, drugstore and phone store.

She liked the architecture, finding the Victorian-style buildings that lined the cobblestone street lovely.

The place reminded her of the general store right off the set of *The Waltons,* and she expected to run into Corabeth at any moment. When they arrived, she read her dad's expression and saw he was disappointed. Had he expected to run into Mona here as soon as he arrived? Had the two talked and planned to meet up? She knew not to ask him, but she couldn't help but be curious.

So he wouldn't think she was trailing him, she decided to leave him for a while and go pick up a few things she needed or pretended to need. Although she didn't plan to skip lunch next week as she had for the prior two weeks, she wouldn't take a sandwich to work. She would take Jace's administrative assistant up on her offer to arrange for lunch to be delivered to her.

Shana was about to head over to the section of the store that sold homemade ice cream cones when she glanced over to where she'd left her father earlier. Her gaze latched onto him the moment a huge smile lit his face. She then shifted her gaze to the woman walking toward him.

She would put the woman's age in the fifties, just as her father had said, although she could probably pass for somewhere in her forties easily. She was no taller than five-three, if that. Like Ben, she was wearing a pair of jeans and a shirt and a pair of comfortable-looking sneakers on her feet. The shirt was tucked inside her jeans and showed off a slim waist that flared into a pair of curvy hips.

Shana thought that Mona had a very pretty face. Creamy brown skin. Dark brown eyes. Full, glossy lips and a perky nose. Her hair was cut short, with curls cascading around her face. Shana could see why her father had taken another look at Mona when he'd met her here in this store.

Standing unnoticed in a corner, Shana watched the couple's interactions when they came face-to-face, right in front of the veggie bin. Shana stood there and watched, and a few seconds later, her heart caught at what was becoming obvious.

Mona was blind.

"Your daughter is here?" Mona asked, smiling brightly. "I'd love to meet her."

"And I'm sure she would love meeting you, as well," Ben said, smiling. He tried not to stare, but he thought Mona was simply beautiful. The grace, charm and strength in her features were enhanced every time she turned her mouth up into a smile. Long lashes swept across exotic-looking cheekbones. She told him that her grandparents had come to this country from Jamaica, and he saw a trace of the island beauty in her smooth, caramel-colored skin, full lips that rounded perfectly over even, white teeth and a slanted nose. He wished he knew how to paint, because he would love capturing her exquisiteness on canvas.

Shifting his gaze, Ben glanced around for Shana and saw her standing near the refrigerated items, staring at them. He called out to her to join them. "Shana, come over here. I want you to meet someone."

Shana felt her feet moving, and the closer she got to Mona, the prettier the woman seemed to get. "Dad," she said when she reached them.

Ben smiled down at his daughter. "Shana, I want

you to meet Mona Underwood. Mona, this is my daughter Shana."

Mona turned toward Shana and reached out and grasped her hand. "Shana, I've heard so many nice things about you and your sister from your father. I had hoped to meet you someday."

"Thanks, and I've heard a lot of nice things about you, as well." *But Dad hadn't mentioned anything about your being blind,* Shana thought.

Ben then said, "I asked Mona if she wanted to join us for pizza, but she can't do it today."

Mona turned from Shana and smiled at Ben. "I told my driver to pick me back up in an hour, so I can't today, but I'd love to take a rain check for another time."

Shana watched her father beam all over himself when he asked, "Then we have a date?"

Mona chuckled, and Shana thought the sound was as charming as the woman was. "Yes, Ben, we have a date. We can talk more about it the next time you call."

Her dad had been calling?

"Sure thing," she heard her father say. And then he asked, "Need help selecting any fruit and veggies today? They look mighty good and real fresh."

Shana knew that this was probably their private time together, and she didn't want to intrude, so she spoke up and said, "I need to check out some meats in the deli, Dad." She then said, "Mona, it was truly a pleasure meeting you, and I hope to see you again."

"You will," Ben piped up.

Shana had no doubt in her mind that she would.

Shana waited until they had gotten back to her father's home and she was helping him put away the items he'd purchased at the store when she finally asked, "Why didn't you mention the fact that Mona is blind?"

Ben shrugged as he kept on what he was doing. "I don't pay much attention to the blindness since she is so independent and all. She's not completely blind but has been ruled legally blind."

Shana leaned back against the counter. "There's a difference?"

"In a way. Mona can see some things, just not clearly. She said her sight has worsened to where everything is becoming a shadow."

Shana nodded. "Do you know what happened?"

"Yes. An auto accident about five years ago. She had worked late at the university, and some student was leaving a frat party while drunk. He broadsided her when he ran a traffic light. She was lucky to survive and credits her seat belt with saving her life. The student wasn't that lucky. He wasn't wearing a seat belt and was thrown from the car and killed instantly."

"My goodness, how sad," Shana said, shaking her head at the stupidity of anyone driving while under the influence.

"Her husband told her he couldn't handle a wife who would become dependent on him, so he bailed out. A year later, he married his secretary. It seemed the two of them had been having an affair anyway."

Ben didn't say anything for a minute and then added, "Lucky for Mona, her optic nerve wasn't damaged, just her peripheral nerves. There's a possibility they can recover, but there's no guarantee that they will. At one point, she had begun to see more light and color, but now she said that is fading. However, the doctor advised her there is a fifty-fifty chance her eyesight might return or that she could lose it permanently."

Shana breathed in deeply, thinking of the sad situation Mona was in. It took hearing something like this to make you realize that your problems—the ones you thought were so big—really weren't monumental at all. "She seems nice."

"She *is* nice," Ben reiterated. "She reminds me a lot of your mother."

Shana lifted a brow. "How so?"

"They are both fighters. I remember when the doctor first broke the news to us that your mom had cancer. She was determined not to let it get her down, and every day, I watched her put her best foot forward even when I knew what it was costing her to do so. Her strength gave me strength. I can imagine how Mona must have felt when her husband walked off and left her at the time she needed him the most. But she didn't curl up and die. She adjusted her life and did what she had to do. She's still teaching at the university and fends for herself living alone."

"Any kids?"

"No, her husband claimed he never wanted any. Now he and his new wife have two. That was a low blow to Mona."

Shana tilted her head back and gazed up at her father. "You certainly know a lot about a woman you've only chatted with a few times over squash, tomatoes and zucchini."

Ben threw his head back and laughed. "They were long conversations, but now I get to take her out on a date to get to know her even better."

Shana heard the excitement in her father's voice. "And that is what you really want? To get to know Mona better?"

The radiant glow of her father's smile touched Shana from across the span of the kitchen when he answered and said, "Yes, getting to know Mona better is what I really want."

Shana wasn't surprised to receive a call from Jules the minute she walked back into her condo two hours later. It took Shana a full twenty minutes to tell her sister everything. It would have taken less time had Jules not interrupted her every two minutes to ask a question.

"So there you have it, Jules. Dad likes her and says she reminds him of Mom."

Jules didn't say anything for a minute and then said, "But she's *not* Mom."

Shana rolled her eyes, hearing the defiance in Jules's voice. "Please don't go there, Jules. It's Dad's life, and he decides how he wants to live it and with whom. I hope you don't plan to make things difficult for him. I think we can both agree that it's his time to be happy. He loved Mom, and we both know that. And he was there with her through the good times and the bad. I don't know too many men dedicated to their wives like Dad was to his."

"Yes, I guess he could have been like your *hunk's* father, who bumped his wife off."

"He's not my hunk. And how do you know about Jace's parents?"

"By asking me that, are you saying you don't know about them?"

"Of course I know."

"Well, I came by the information from research. I couldn't sleep the other night, so I decided to let Greta entertain me. I couldn't remember Mona's last name to check her out, so I checked out the man you have the hots for. Has he ever told you whether he thought his father was guilty or innocent?"

"I believe he thinks he's innocent, since he and his brothers still have a close relationship with him. In fact, they went to visit him this weekend."

"Is that why you wanted a date with good ole Charles? He was going to be a substitute?"

"No."

"So you say. And what time is Charles picking you up tonight?"

"He's not. He didn't call."

"Say what?" Jules exclaimed, surprised. "Charles finally smartened up and is no longer lapping after you?"

"I guess. Sad thing is that this time I really would have liked to go out."

"So what do you plan to do tonight?"

"I thought about calling Gloria to see if she's back from her international flight and, if so, whether she wants to take in a movie."

"Well, you can always call Charles to see why he didn't call and then ask him out. But a few weeks ago, you claimed men aren't a necessity, so do what I do sometimes and go solo."

"I just might do that," Shana said, ignoring how her sister was throwing her words back out there at her.

"Be safe if you do go out alone. Now I need to make a few calls and will talk to you later."

"Wait! When are you coming home?"

"Not sure yet. Probably not for another two weeks. Talk to you later."

Shana hung up the phone. She should be used to her sister being away a lot, but she wasn't. Not only was Jules her sister, but Shana considered Jules her very best friend.

She headed for her bedroom and sneezed for the third time that day, noticing that her throat felt a little sore. She hoped that didn't mean she had a cold coming on. Nothing like stopping it before it got started. She would call her doctor tomorrow for an appointment. Hopefully, he would prescribe some antibiotics or something. The last thing she needed was for anything to keep her from doing her job.

A few moments later, she found out that Gloria's flight from China had been delayed, so she decided to do her exercise routine, then pull out her latest J. D. Robb novel, and read in bed.

Later that night as she slid between the covers with her book, Shana felt her lips beginning to tingle again, and as much as she wished otherwise, she couldn't help but think about Jace and her attraction to him. Though her parents had experienced such a beautiful and loving marriage, so far all she and Jules had been involved in were prickly relationships. She had figured Jonathan would be her perfect mate until she discovered he'd only strung her along to find out what he could about one of her clients. From then on, she knew never to let her guard down.

She had dated since then, but the relationships were on her terms, and she didn't like being rushed into doing anything—like sharing a bed with a man. That had been one of Charles's faults, which was why she continued to hold out with him. Even with his persistence, he had yet to give her reason to think she would be anything more to him than a conquest. Sometimes she felt she was putting too much thought into it. Why not go ahead and sleep with him since a serious relationship was the last thing she was ready to get involved with anyway? But for her, it was the principle of the thing. She didn't like being pressured.

Jace wanted her—she was well aware of that, but he was not placing any pressure on her, especially since she had told him there would not be an affair between them. She would admit that, if there was any pressure, she was placing it on herself.

Why was she so attracted to him, and why had his image apparently been scorched into her brain? And why had the taste of him seemingly been embedded in her tongue? And why even now, when she thought about him, could she envision naked bodies entangled in silken sheets?

Sheets that were hers.

Refusing to think about Jace any longer, she cuddled in bed to what had become her reading position and opened her book to where she'd left off. She was determined to get absorbed in somebody else's love life. Even if the characters were fictional.

PART II

You can give without loving, but you cannot love without giving.

—Anonymous

Chapter Sixteen

Jace swiveled around in his chair and glanced at the wooden door that connected his office to the one Shana was using, wishing he had the ability to stare straight through it. Then he wouldn't have to wonder what she was doing. He figured she was probably working, which is what he should be doing. But he couldn't concentrate. His thoughts were filled with her.

It was the last day of another workweek, and he hadn't seen Shana but three times. She had made herself even scarcer than she had last week, and he couldn't help wondering if that kiss a week ago had anything to do with it. He picked up a rubber band in what was becoming a habit and began stretching it in all kinds of directions as his mind relived that moment in the elevator for the two-hundredth time. The woman had the sweetest lips, their taste as succulent as any delicious fruit he'd ever eaten. He had thought about her all weekend, even during moments when he had visited with his father. And his dreams of her had become even more turbulent, racy and stunningly raw. How was Shana able to cause so much lust to run rampant inside of him? Lust he hadn't been able to quench. And, from the looks of things, never would.

Drawing in a deep breath, he tossed the rubber band aside and went back to reading the notes he'd compiled from his conversation with his father this past weekend. It had been an enjoyable visit that had lasted six hours, and the four of them had tried to make every minute count.

Jace had gone over all the reports he'd read on the company and had brought up a couple of issues that had concerned him to get his father's advice. Granted, Shep Granger had been away from Granger Aeronautics for fifteen years, but his mind was still sharp when it came to business matters.

His father knew Granger Aeronautics inside and out, and even though technology had changed over the years, Sheppard had managed to stay on top of advanced technology through books he'd gotten from the prison library as well as on their computer systems. And he had taken classes whenever they had been offered.

Jace glanced up when he heard the knock on the door. "Come in."

He felt a knot in his throat when Shana walked in. Today, like always, she was wearing one of those conservative yet sexy business suits. This one was turquoise in color, and she had matching shoes to complement it. And today, like always, it looked good on her. "Hi, Shana."

"I don't mean to disturb you, but I have my initial report finalized and wondered if we could meet sometime today to go over it."

Jace shifted his gaze from her to glance at the calendar on his desk. "I'm free any time after two."

"If possible, I'd prefer that we meet after the office closes. I want this to be a very private meeting between you, your brothers and me."

He noted that she hadn't included anyone from his executive team. "Caden flew out today for New York. He has a couple of concerts that had been scheduled and were too costly to get out of. However, Dalton should be free."

"Great!"

"When Melissa returns from lunch, I'll have her check with him to make sure that he—"

"I'd rather you didn't. In fact, I prefer you not mention this meeting to anyone."

He lifted a brow. "Okay, let's say around six? That way we can be sure everyone will have left by then."

She nodded. "I'll see you at six. And if you don't mind, we'll meet in my office."

"All right." She then left.

He wondered just what was in her report.

Shana sat at her desk and felt her heart beating hard in her chest as both Jace and Dalton read the reports she had presented to them. This was her initial report, and once they discussed everything, she would know how to proceed from here.

She wasn't surprised that it was Jace who finished reading first. After all, he was an attorney and was used to the legalese when it came to reviewing case studies. He glanced up from the papers and his gaze snagged hers. Immediately, she felt every hormone in her body sizzle from the intensity of his stare.

Forcing her gaze back down to the papers on her desk, she drew in a slow breath while thinking that she didn't need this. Especially not now. They had a lot of work to do, and going over this report was just the start of it. But Jace's presence wasn't making it easy. His presence was taking over everything and dominating the office space, and making her very much aware of him...even with his brother in the room.

"Shit, you mean to tell us that there's a traitor in the company?"

She lifted her gaze and glanced over at Dalton. From his outburst, one would think he was more upset with what he'd read than Jace was. That could only mean one thing. Jace already had his suspicions.

"Looks that way, doesn't it?" Jace said easily and calmly, without displaying any strong emotions.

Dalton picked up on it, stared over at his brother and quickly reached the same conclusion that Shana had. "Damn it, Jace, you knew!"

"Not for certain," Jace said smoothly, switching his gaze from Shana to Dalton. "But I had a hunch."

"And you didn't tell us?" Dalton roared, offended.

"Only because, like I said, all I had was a hunch. Besides, I figured if my suspicions were right, it would come out in Shana's report."

"When did you pick up on something?" Shana asked.

Jace then shifted his gaze back to her. "My grandfather has a private file stored on his computer. He shared the password with me several years ago...in case I ever needed to get into it. It was a file where he mainly documented his thoughts or ideas. One of his most recent notations, one made a week or so before his death, indicated he suspected someone within the company of divulging trade secrets and felt that was the reason we weren't topping certain bids."

He paused a moment and then said, "And then after reading how one of our major competitors always seemed to underbid us, I began to think Granddad's suspicions had some merit."

Shana nodded. "I agree. That was the first red flag that made me take notice and start digging more," Shana said. "I have my team investigating this and we must alert the FBI."

"The FBI?" Dalton asked, surprised. "Why would you bring them in?"

Shana glanced over at Dalton. "Mainly because the theft or misappropriation of trade secrets is a federal offense. Not to mention the kind of contract this company pulls in, primarily from the government. For a few years, Granger Aeronautics was the number one producer of aircraft parts and motors, and now they've lost their edge to a competitor who's only been around a few years. If the reason they lost that edge is because someone was giving the other company…let's say bid information, then that's a problem."

Dalton leaned forward in his chair. "Do you have any idea who could be behind it?" he asked, and his voice was edged with anger.

"No, and we could be looking at more than one person," Shana replied.

Dalton didn't say anything but thought about what she'd said. "We're going to need proof."

"And we'll have it. My team is thorough and won't stop digging until they have something. Once the FBI is involved, they'll probably do their own thorough investigation and even a sting operation. I know the guy in charge, Marcel Eaton. He worked with my father in Boston when he and Dad were police officers."

"Your dad was a cop?" Jace asked, surprised, being reminded of how little he knew of her personal life.

"Yes. He retired from the force after twenty years and moved here a few years ago. Marcel is very thorough, and because of my friendship with him, he will keep me in the loop. I'm glad your grandfather suspected something."

"I'm glad, too," Jace said. "Now I understand why he wanted us to take things over. He felt no one would look after Granger Aeronautics like we would."

"Until Dad comes back," Dalton added.

Shana lifted a brow. "Your dad?"

"Yes," Jace said, drawing in a slow, deep breath, knowing his grandfather's thought processes. "Our grandfather believed that our mother's killer would eventually be caught and that our father would be set free. He believed it so much that basically nothing in Dad's office has changed. Granddad made it his business to keep everything intact, just the way Dad left it."

"For fifteen years?" Shana said, not believing what she was hearing.

Jace nodded again. "I'm sure he didn't think it would take this long. Granddad hired a private investigator who was supposedly the best in the business at the time."

"What happened?" Shana asked.

"All I know is that the man died a few years ago in a car accident. I understand he'd been drinking at the time and was on his way home from a party," Jace supplied. "Granddad thought the man was onto something big—at least that's what the investigator claimed—but no one was able to find his report."

Shana didn't say anything for a minute and then spoke. "I also made several other recommendations in the report that I'm sure you saw but that you've yet to comment on," she said to Jace.

Yes, he'd seen them, and a number of them involved massive department cuts. "People need their jobs now more than ever, Shana."

"I am aware of that, Jace, but no company can afford to bear the expense of employees not doing what they are paid to do. And, if you notice, there are several departments not meeting monthly quotas. Your grandfather passed a couple of managers over for raises last year."

Jace had noticed that, as well. "I will meet with them and put down the law. Jace's Law. They'll be given six months to turn their departments around or I'll go in and make personnel changes."

"Some of them have worked here for years, Jace," Dalton reminded him. "A few even feel entitled," he added, thinking of Cal Arrington.

"They can feel entitled all they want, but I'll be holding them responsible for the success of their departments. But more than anything, I want to know who's responsible for passing off Granger trade secrets."

An hour or so later, Shana leaned back in her chair and gently rubbed the back of her neck, trying to work the stiff kinks out of it. She released a deep breath as she thought about what Jace had said. "Jace's Law." She had a feeling he would be fair with his employees, but at the same time, his expectations would be stern. She agreed with that approach.

There were three departments that Jace would need to concentrate on, and all three of them were currently overstaffed. Granger had to redefine itself, and there was no choice in the matter if they wanted to regain their position as a market leader in aerospace. Five years was a long time not to have been awarded a huge contract instead of the crumbs that had been left over.

There was a knock on the door, and she glanced up. "Come in."

Jace walked in. "You're still here."

Shana nodded, trying to ignore the stir in her stomach and the way her heartbeat had begun throbbing in her chest. "I see you haven't left, either."

"No," he said, coming to stand in the middle of the room. "I had planned to join Dalton at McQueen's. It's becoming his favorite hangout, but some female called and he dumped me to hook up with her."

Shana couldn't help but smile. "I understand he's moving away from the family estates."

Jace chuckled. "Yes, but for him it's a good thing. Sutton Hills was never the same for him once our mother died and my father left. He was close to Mom."

"Did you continue to live in your parents' home?"

"No, we moved in with Granddad. My parents' home, although located on the grounds of Sutton Hills, was on a different part of the estate. On a good, clear day you can see the rooftop of my parents' home from Granddad's kitchen table."

Shana wondered how Dalton felt about his father being convicted of his mother's murder. "How did things go this weekend when you visited your dad?"

She watched a smile touch Jace's lips...lips that had shown her what a fantastic and passionate kisser he was. "Dad's doing okay for a man who's locked behind bars for a crime he didn't commit."

She was tempted to ask how he knew that for certain, when the evidence against his father had been so overwhelming. From what she had read, his father's fingerprints had been on the murder weapon, a gun that Sheppard owned.

"It must have been hard on you and your brothers while growing up," she said softly.

"It was, for a number of reasons. The hardest was when the parents of some of our friends—people we'd known for years—felt we were no longer good enough for their offspring to hang around with. That was hard for three teens to digest."

And then, as if he didn't want to discuss his father with her any longer, he said, "I want to run something by you that I noticed in your report. It was something you recommended."

"Okay," she said, giving him her full attention and in ways she wished she could control better. She was convinced that cleft in his chin was her weakness.

"Revamping of engineering technology."

She eased back in her chair. "I noticed it's been years since Granger has built an aircraft."

"The last time was the year before Dad went to prison. She was a beauty," he said, sliding into the chair across from her desk. "Last year, Granddad mentioned plans in the works to build another one. This one would have this special supersonic hydraulic pump. He wanted to move forward, but the Defense Department wouldn't approve the plan. They kept finding things wrong with the design. Norm Ellison is my man in charge of the designing of the aircraft, and I've asked for a detailed report. I want to know why this hasn't gotten off the ground."

Shana didn't say anything for a minute as she recalled the bio she'd gotten on Ellison. A graduate of MIT, he'd been top of his class. His name had also been on Kent's list as someone of interest.

The whole purpose of today's meeting was to provide Jace and his brothers with a list of what was wrong with Granger. A company that built air performance planes and airplane parts should be doing very well. But Granger wasn't.

"Here," she said, handing him another report. "I'm one step ahead of you. What's in that report should be included in Ellison's when he gives one to you. I wondered why Granger Aeronautics, which had been at the top of developing innovative ideas a few years ago, hadn't come up with anything lately."

The room was silent while Jace slowly flipped through pages and pages of data. She couldn't help looking at him, liked looking at him. He had perfectly angled cheekbones, and she thought the line of his jaw was set in a way that didn't leave room for guessing when he was displeased about something.

Knowing it was rude to stare, she forced her gaze down at the papers spread out on her desk. When he had walked into her office, she could tell he was tightly wound, tense, and everything inside of her had responded even when she hadn't wanted it to.

Earlier, when he had been in here, she had felt need and want sparring to unleash within him, even when Dalton had been sitting beside him. His tense state had stirred her womanly core because she knew the reason for it.

What she needed was to call it a night and go home and jump-start her weekend. Last weekend, she'd been on a mission of checking out her father's love interest. This weekend, he and Mona would go out for pizza. Her sixty-two-year-old father was acting like a teen who'd finally gotten the most beautiful and popular girl in school to go out with him.

"Interesting."

She lifted her head and looked over at Jace. He was staring at her. "I thought so, too, but didn't want to say anything until I researched it some more. But since you came in here and asked about engineering technology, I figured I'd share what I had gathered up so far. It seems Arrington gave Ellison the order not to work on the design any longer."

"You are thorough."

"Thanks, but there are still unanswered questions… like who gave Arrington the right to make such a call."

"But you will figure things out," he said smoothly.

"Thanks for the vote of confidence." She checked her watch and pushed back her chair to stand. "Time for me to leave. I promised myself that I would be out of here by eight." She crossed the room to the coatrack, got her jacket and slid it on.

He stood as well, his body tall and trim. "I see you're not skipping lunch every day like you used to, and that's good."

"Melissa is kind enough to make sure I order in something every day."

He smiled. "Then I'm grateful for Melissa."

She walked back over to the desk to get her purse

and couldn't stop the feeling of her body simmering, getting hyped, tortured by the sight of him standing there, tall, handsome, legs braced apart with hands in his pockets. "You're about to leave, as well?" She hoped not. The thought of them sharing another elevator ride was too much.

"In another hour or so. There are a few things I still need to wrap up before I leave. Have big plans for the weekend?"

She thought of Charles. After she had time to think about it, she'd figured it had been for the best that they hadn't hooked up last weekend. She had been prepared to use him to forget about the man standing in front of her. "No plans so far. I'm planning to have a quiet and restful weekend," she said, thinking that she planned to relax, lie around and finish the novel she'd been reading. "What about you?"

He eased his hands out of his pockets. The casual motion seemed seamlessly controlled. "I'll be going through my grandfather's belongings…giving most of the items to Goodwill."

She nodded, thinking it would probably be a tough task for him to do. On more than one occasion, she had heard him speak of his grandfather, and it was easy to see the two had a close relationship. "Will Dalton help you?"

"No, I doubt it's something he could handle," Jace said with a pensive expression on his face. "Although he and the old man butted heads more times than I care to remember, they were both good at hiding their true feelings."

She tilted her head to the side, considering what he said. Her father had once accused her of doing the same thing. Not with him, since with her father she was known to demonstrate an overabundance of affection, but with the men she dated. He claimed she tended to be on her guard. But the way she looked at it, no woman wanted to get burned twice.

"Shana?"

When Jace said her name, he forced those thoughts to the back of her mind. "Yes?"

"Can you give me an estimate of how much longer you think Granger Aeronautics will be your client?"

She weighed what he'd asked. "Why?"

"Because I need to know."

As far as she was concerned, his response wasn't good enough. Had he gotten it into his head that once her work with his company was finished that would mean a green light for some sort of tryst with her? She had never slept with any of her clients, while she worked for them or after her work with them was done. They had maintained a business relationship. And things with him would be no different.

Shana placed her purse on her desk while thinking exactly what he suspected she was thinking—that his question had irked her. "I think I need to get a few things straight, Jace. That kiss was just a kiss. It was not a prelude to anything more, not during or after my work here is finished, and I don't appreciate your assuming it was," she said in a tone that didn't disguise her annoyance.

"And was it *just* a kiss?"

"Yes. Let's move on. Like I said, it was just a kiss. I've had plenty of them in my day, and I'm sure you have, as well."

He took a step closer to her. "Can you look me in the face and tell me you felt nothing?"

Anger surged within her. What was he trying to get her to say, and why? If he needed to hear it, then she would say it loud and clear...although she would be lying through her teeth. Placing her hands on her hips, she stared him in the face and said slowly, articulating each and every word so he could hear and understand precisely. "I am staring you in the face, Jace, and now please read my lips. I...felt...nothing."

Judging by the snap of anger that suddenly flared in his eyes, she knew her statement hadn't gone over well. He proved her right when he said, "I guarantee that this time you will."

The next thing Shana knew, two powerful arms swept out and pulled her into them.

Chapter Seventeen

Jace had desired women before, but it had never felt like this, an edgy need that had him almost losing control. He wanted her, and she wanted him, regardless of her stating otherwise. And if she needed proof, he would give it to her. He proceeded to angle his mouth unerringly down to hers.

He felt her resistance, which only lasted for a mere second, then he felt a stunning burst of need when she began kissing him back, confirming he had gotten under her skin as much as she'd gotten under his.

Blood was bursting through his veins, and a double dose was roaring in his loins as he continued to take her mouth, devour it. Never had he kissed a woman with such wanting, longing, greed and need. He positioned her lower lip between his in a way that allowed him to deepen the kiss. Pumping his tongue all through her mouth, he used it to tease and demand. Tightening his arms around her, he continued to plunder her mouth as if he were a dying man and she was his only hope for survival. Every nerve ending in his body felt electrified, and he was filled with a passion so raw that gut-wrenching emotions began crashing through him, making his insides tremble. It drove him on to take what she was not holding back.

Shana felt her control slipping, replaced by a wild and tempestuous need that sent everything within her soaring to heights she'd never reached before. She wasn't supposed to feel this way. Lose her head. The area between her legs shouldn't be throbbing, begging, craving. But a turbulent desire was revving her body to a state of sexual upheaval that was dazing her mind. His tongue was everywhere inside her mouth, taking and demanding, destroying any resistance she cared to make and forcing her to acknowledge that her will-power was no match against mind-boggling passion.

Sensation after undiluted sensation whipped into her, and she didn't stand a chance when her body began to shudder with a level of yearning she'd never felt before. She groaned low in her throat, astounded that any man could bring her to such a state. Almost making her beg. Moaning like a hussy gone delirious and filled with an ache that longed to be satisfied. There was no doubt in her mind her panties were drenched already.

Breathless and incoherent with desire, she broke away from the kiss, looked up and locked her eyes with his while drinking in the effect he was having on her. "Take me now, and take me hard."

And to show she meant business, she reached up and shoved the jacket from his shoulders.

The depth of Shana's need tore through Jace as he heard it in her words, making his erection throb. And when she all but began popping the buttons off his shirt in her haste to get it off him, he was inflamed with desire and reached out and began tearing the clothes off her body, as well. Her jacket was followed by her skirt, and then he dragged off the shirt and bra and practically demolished her panty hose and panties. Kicking off his shoes, he jerked his belt through the loops before dropping his pants and briefs.

Jace's hands then reached out for her, desperate to touch her skin. Papers went flying off Shana's desk when he pushed her back on it, lifting her hips and spreading her thighs. And then he thrust inside of her, consuming her entire body with him. Her inner muscles clenched him tight and clung to him. And the pleasurable feeling had him moaning deep in his throat. The desire to mate was fierce, overpowering, and he gave in to his body's demand.

Shana moaned as well when Jace began moving, taking her hard, pounding into her as if his life depended on it, making her gasp in shock and moan in pleasure at the same time. His deep strokes were powerful and dominant, and they continued while she groaned out his name over and over. He kept going and going, like a wild animal mating for the last time, filling her completely and taking her in a way she'd never been taken. On and on he pounded until she felt pleasure soaking into her bones, making half sobs flow from her lips.

The sound of flesh slapping flesh filled the room, and topped with their heavy breathing and moans, she was shoved even further into an abyss of pleasure and yearning. His penis was pumping into her like a jackhammer, pushing her further and further over the edge and into a free fall of turbulent pleasure.

Suddenly, Shana could no longer bear it and cried out his name. "Jace!"

Her body shattered into a million pieces. She saw stars, colors, bright lights, all at the same time that an explosion blasted her body, from one hemisphere to the other. She felt him shudder and she tightened her legs around him as he continued to plow into her like a madman with relentless thrusts. Need was devouring the both of them, and she felt the exact moment his hot semen shot inside of her, triggering even more spasms. And at that moment, she knew two things… how it felt to get what you asked for and…how it felt to be totally and completely sexually satisfied.

For a second, their bodies went still, too dazed to do anything else. They were still stretched out on her desk, he was fully embedded inside of her, and his face was buried in her chest, between her two breasts.

But then reality began seeping in, making them aware of where they were and what they'd just done. The mere thought that he was still embedded deep inside her sent a sensuous shiver through Shana, especially since he seemed in no hurry to get out. She felt him pulsating, still throbbing, and she couldn't help but recall the ecstasy that had just moments ago roared through her world. The memory brought a pleased smile to her lips.

He pulled out of her slowly, as if trying to savor just where he'd been. And the feel of him leaving was nearly unbearable for her as he left a burning imprint inside of her. But she knew she had to pull herself together to deal with the aftermath. Before leaving her body completely, he paused to stare down at her, and at the same time they realized they hadn't used any protection.

"I'm on the pill," she quickly said in a ragged voice. "And I'm safe."

He drew in a deep breath and said in a hoarse voice. "I'm safe, as well." And then he eased completely out of her.

"Jace."

"Shana."

They had begun speaking at the same time, and each had a feeling about what the other was going to say…or thought they did. And when he said, "You can go first," she decided to do so. With as much dignity as she could, she accepted his help off her desk and quickly began putting her clothes back on.

"I'm well aware of what we did tonight," she said, easing into her skirt without bothering with her panties. "I asked for what I got, and I don't regret it. The only thing I regret is that our business relationship has been compromised."

"No, it hasn't."

"Yes, it has. I've broken a rule, and at this point, the only way I will continue to work with you is if you give me your word it won't happen again."

He was putting his clothes back on, as well. She winced when she saw she'd popped off a couple of buttons from his shirt. "I can't give you my word, Shana."

She stopped buttoning her blouse. "Why not?"

"Because I don't intend to keep it." With his pants on and his shirt open to what she thought was one hell of a gorgeous chest, he turned to her. She thought he looked sexier in a disheveled state. "I tried pretending before that I didn't want you, tried like hell to fight it, ignore it, wish it away, and you see what happened. I took you on that damn desk for heaven's sake," he said in an angered tone. "Without any thought of birth control and not giving a damn if the door was even locked."

She swallowed deeply. "Then it's best that I leave and you find another company to—"

"No, that's not the best. I think it's time we act like two adults and deal with it."

She lifted her chin. "Deal with it?"

"Yes, deal with it."

"And just how are we supposed to do that?"

Jace rubbed his hand down his face. He didn't have a clue. All he knew at that moment was that he wanted her again. It wouldn't bother him if they left here and went to her place. He'd had her, gotten a taste of what it was like and there was no way in hell he wouldn't want more. He never considered himself a greedy ass, but he did so now.

"We have this weekend to think about it," he said, reaching down to pick up his jacket off the floor.

"There's nothing to think about," she said. "I'm ending my contract with your company."

He eased his jacket over his shoulders. "You can't do that," he said, trying to keep the frustration out of his voice.

"And why can't I?"

"Because I need you."

Shana inhaled a deep breath. She would have had a defense had he said anything but that. Especially when it was spoken with such sincerity that it jabbed at her heart. She'd covered practically all of his company reports, and he was right. He did need her. At least he needed her services. She was convinced that someone was maliciously trying to destroy his company. She wasn't sure who and didn't have a clue as to why. And whoever it was seemed determined to do it at a slow pace so as not to be detected.

Balling up her ripped panty hose and shoving them into her purse, she looked up at him. "I need to think about things over the weekend. I'll let you know my answer by Monday."

Thankful that everyone had left for the day so no one could be a witness to her tousled state, she slid into her jacket. Without saying anything else, she quickly left.

Hours later, just moments after taking a shower and with the towel still wrapped around his waist, Jace stood at his bedroom window and looked broodingly out at the lake. His blood soared through his veins with the memories of what had happened between him and Shana earlier.

Even now, he had to fight his own battle of restraint and control the temptation to call her. Not to apologize for what had taken place, since he could never regret that, but for the lack of finesse with which it was done. But then he thought, with full acceptance, their intimate encounter was meant to be that way. Hot. Fiery. Spontaneous. And filled with the passionate greed of two people who'd reached their limits.

Four weeks of pent-up sexual frustration, an attraction they'd tried to ignore and sexual chemistry that was stirred every time they were within a few feet of each other had driven them to what had happened tonight. It had been inevitable, sooner or later. There was only so much control a person could have, and tonight they'd proven strong, heated desire couldn't be capped.

And the passionate fire that had raged through their bodies may have cost them.

He drew in a deep breath as he slowly nursed the beer he held in his hand. Contrary to what Shana believed, they could not go back to how things used to be. That's why things had gotten out of hand tonight in the first place. He could understand her policy of never getting involved with a client, and in some ways respected her for it. But this was one time she needed to rethink changing that rule. Now that it had been broken, they needed to act like adults and deal with it. And they could. All they needed was a plan of action, but she wasn't willing to do that. Her strategy was to pretend nothing ever happened and go back to the status quo.

What she failed to realize, or maybe she just didn't understand, was that making love to her tonight the way he had was an act of raw possession, a claiming of the most intimate kind. In other words, primal sexuality within him that had lain dormant since his divorce three years ago had awakened and now had a life of its own. It's not that he hadn't made love to a woman since then, because he had. But he could honestly say that making love with any other woman hadn't had the same effect. Never had a deep, intense desire for a female overridden anything else—self-control, common sense or his ability to put things in perspective and think logically.

Right now, the only thought that consumed his mind was that his body still craved hers.

Rubbing a frustrated hand down his face, he moved from the window. The house was quiet, and he would be the first to admit he missed the sound of Caden and his saxophone, which his brother would play at all hours of the night. It had never been a disturbing sound to him, even while they were growing up. He'd always felt and known that Caden's music was a way of calming his soul. His brother needed the music.

Just like he felt a need for Shana.

While inside of her, he had felt the passion radiating from her soft core. A core he wanted to explore again and again. He knew this weekend and whatever decision she made would be the turning point in how they would handle things. But like he'd told her, he couldn't make a promise he knew he wouldn't be capable of keeping.

Although he knew he should give her space to decide the outcome of their fate, he was fearful of doing that, knowing she would probably make the wrong decision. He needed to talk to her, find out why she was determined not to let anything develop between them. To hell with her policy.

And as he headed back toward the bathroom, he knew he had his own decisions to make.

The moment Caden walked out on stage in front of a packed house at Columbia University's huge auditorium, he felt her. She was there, somewhere in the audience. For a moment, he almost stumbled as he fought the anger and irritation that began escalating through his body.

Why was she here? He had been home in Virginia for over three weeks, and their paths had crossed more than once. They hadn't had much to say to each other then, so why was she here? Refusing to let the unanswered question get to him, he stepped into place and within minutes had begun playing his sax.

The music flowed from within him, and he closed his eyes as he felt the melody pour through his body and ease some of his tension. He exulted in his music's ability to calm him, to place him at that moment on a higher plane and for a moment to suppress his irritation under a haze of indifference. That's what he needed to get through tonight.

He flowed into the evening, belting out one number after the next, and it was only when he was about to do his last number that he saw her. How he managed to do that in a packed house of several thousand people he wasn't sure. All he knew was their gazes connected the moment he lifted the sax to his lips. He couldn't close his eyes again the way he normally did while performing. Instead he kept his gaze locked on hers as he played. He put everything he had into it, and the band behind him followed his lead.

At the end, he got a standing ovation, and he wondered if she would be coming to the private party later given for the performers. Typically, it was invitation-only, but that hadn't stopped her before, he thought, remembering that last time a few years ago.

He finally broke eye contact with her when everyone bowed for their last time. When he glanced back up at the spot where Shiloh had been sitting just moments ago, he saw she was gone.

Chapter Eighteen

One twenty-three North Pinewood Drive.

There was no doubt in Ben Bradford's mind that he was at the right house. Mona had said it was a white stucco single-story patio home that sat at the end of a brick road on a spacious lot. It was a nice house with gardens of flowering marigolds and zinnias adorning the windows. She had a perfectly manicured lawn with lush green grass that sloped into a small pond.

She'd mentioned that most of her neighbors were other professors who worked at the university. He couldn't imagine having your coworkers as your neighbors. He liked the guys who'd been on the force with him while living in Boston, but he hadn't wanted to look at their faces from sunup to sundown. When he left the precinct and went home, his main focus had been on his daughters. Ben's girls.

Like he'd told Shana the other day, he was proud of them. They were strong, college-educated, hardworking women who'd made some good decisions in their lives. Granted, neither was close to settling down and giving him the grandkids he looked forward to spoiling one day, but he was satisfied that in due time they would both meet a couple of nice guys.

Every once in a while, he wondered whether they were too strong-willed and independent. But then he knew he wouldn't change them even if he could and was convinced there were men out there just as strong who would complement his daughters perfectly.

Bringing the car to a stop in the circular driveway, he opened the door and got out. Glancing around, he could see in the distance a part of the university, the Rotunda. He drew in a deep breath, remembering how he had spent four years of his life there. He had fallen in love with a beautiful young woman named Sharon Sweet there.

He'd also played football, had been a valiant Cavalier with dreams of going pro. But a knee injury had ended those dreams. Still, his college days had been good ones, and he'd had fun. Those times had been good and he cherished the memories.

Now here he was, forty-some years later and falling in love all over again. And he was convinced he was falling in love. When it came to choosing the women to share his life with, he didn't make things complicated. He was blessed with an inner sense of knowing just who was meant for him. He had known when he'd met Sharon, and he'd known when he met Mona. Now he had to convince Mona that their futures were entwined. This pizza date was a start.

He was well aware that she was leery of a serious involvement after what her husband had done to her, and then there was the issue of her blindness. To him, it wasn't an issue. Since knowing her, he had a new-found respect for someone with a disability who was making the best of it. And she was. He'd watched how she got around the grocery store without help. Mona was a beautiful woman, a confident woman, a woman who had captured the eye and the heart of Ben Bradford. Unknowingly and without intent, she had done her job, and now it was time to do his. Operation Mona Underwood was now underway.

His heart didn't miss a beat as he headed for her front door.

Gloria McCabe stared across the table at Shana as they both sipped on their glasses of wine. They had taken in a movie and had returned to Shana's home. She studied her friend and wondered at her mood. "Is there a reason you're down in the dumps tonight, Shana? I was telling you about the couple I caught on the plane locked in the bathroom, determined to join the *Mile High Club*. I didn't get a reaction from you about it," she said.

Shana glanced up and met Gloria's inquiring gaze. She hadn't been able to comment about a couple who hadn't been able to control their urges over thirty thousand feet in the air, because she had been caught in a similar situation herself recently right here on terra firma. She wondered what her friend would say if she knew that Shana had been taken on her desk last night, and had loved every moment.

"Shana?"

Shana sighed. "Sorry, I guess I'm not very talkative tonight."

Gloria laughed as she fluffed out her blond hair

around her shoulders. "What's wrong with you? You've been quiet all evening. What gives?"

Shana broke eye contact with Gloria and stared into her glass of wine. She and Gloria had shared a lot, and Shana considered her a BFF. They had become friends before becoming neighbors. When Shana's father had moved here, Gloria had been the attendant on the flights Shana would take twice a month from Boston to visit her father and sister.

It was Gloria who'd jokingly suggested that maybe Shana should save her money and just move to Virginia. Less than a year later, Shana had done just that. And it had been Gloria who'd told her about the condo that was for sale right next door to hers.

A friendship had been born, and since then, it had been nourished into the trusting relationship it was now. She knew all about Gloria's abusive ex-husband and her current affair with a pilot, although the airline she worked for had a no-fraternizing policy.

She glanced back at Gloria and smiled. "I'm fine. I just have a lot to think about, and it would help if I asked you a few questions."

Gloria raised a brow. "What about?"

"You and Eric."

Gloria leaned back in her chair. "What about us?"

Shana took a sip of her wine. "What made you decide to break the rules and get involved when you know what the outcome will be if you're discovered?"

Gloria didn't say anything for a moment and then said, "I wanted to be with him—both physically and mentally. Things started out on a physical level. We were two divorcés who wanted to get wild, butt-naked and stay independent. But then we discovered we liked each other beyond the sex, and two years later it's still beyond the sex…although the sex is still off the charts, mind you."

Shana smiled, figuring it was. She'd seen Eric sneak in and out of Gloria's house many times. "Doesn't the sneaking around bother you?"

A smile slowly faded from Gloria's face. "Sometimes it does, but then I remember I have more than most women right now. I have a man in my life I admire, a man who wants me as much as I want him, a man who understands there are times I don't want to be crowded, but then knows there are going to be times when I don't want to get out of bed as long as he'll stay in it with me."

Shana took a sip of her wine. "Sounds like a woman in love."

Gloria shrugged. "I prefer thinking of myself as a woman who knows what she wants and is gutsy enough to go after it." She paused and then asked, "Is there a reason why you're interested in our hot and heavy affair?"

Shana smiled. The subtle lifting of her friend's eyebrow conveyed that she expected an answer. "What if I told you I was recently in the position?"

"You're having an affair?" Gloria asked, leaning forward as if it was paramount not to miss one word of Shana's answer.

"No, but I did do something with a male client that I should not have. You know my rules."

Gloria smiled. "You mean you actually slept with him?"

"I wouldn't say we slept, but the gist of your question still leans toward an answer of yes."

"Damn," Gloria said, slumping back against her chair. "And you are such a stickler for your rules."

"I guess I have to blame it on the hormones and the fact he's so damn gorgeous. I was attracted to him from the first. I tried to ignore it but couldn't."

Gloria frowned. "Why place the blame on anything? You're a grown-ass woman who can do what you want to do. You made the rules, and you can certainly break them. That's not how it is with Eric and me. We didn't make any rules."

Shana began nibbling on her bottom lip. "But I shouldn't break them. He's a client, for heaven's sake. If things don't work out, it can be messy."

"Says who? It's not like you're going to be working for him forever. How much longer will he be a client?"

Shana shrugged. "I don't know. Probably no more than another month or so."

Gloria slapped a palm to her thigh. "There you have it. Unless you get too attached, the affair will end in a month. But just think of what you'll be getting until then. Unless after making out with him, you've decided he's not worth it."

Shana didn't say anything for a minute and then, "Oh, he was worth it, and I don't regret what we did. But I told him it couldn't happen again and asked that he promise that it wouldn't."

"Did he?"

"Said he couldn't do that."

Gloria smiled. "Good for him. Some things you

can't always control, Shana. A strong sexual attraction is one of them."

Shana stood and began pacing. "But that's just it. I don't want to be attracted to him, sexually or otherwise. But I know I will as long as I work for him. I told him if he couldn't promise, I would have to end our business relationship."

"You'd go that far?"

Shana drew in a deep breath. "I don't have a choice."

"Yes, you do. If you want to be with him, Shana, you have a choice."

Shana shook her head. "That's just it. I don't know what I want. I wanted him yesterday, but I want to think it was hormones working overtime and nothing more."

"And what if it's more?"

Shana stopped her pacing. "It's not more. I told you about Jonathan."

"Yes, but not all men are the same. I found that out, and maybe with this guy you'll find that out, as well."

Shana came back to her chair and sat down. "I have to make a decision by Monday."

Gloria nodded. "Good luck, but can I give you some advice?"

"Yes."

"I know you. You like having total control of your life and everything in it. But every once in a while, it's okay to let go, lose control and forgo the norm."

Shana drew in a deep breath. "There will be a price to pay."

A smile tipped the corners of Gloria's mouth. "Maybe.

Maybe not. But only you can determine if that price, if there is one, is worth it."

Mona's heart was racing overtime as she glanced over to where Ben was sitting. She couldn't see him— at least not clearly—but she felt him. His very presence was radiating emotions through her.

Her talking watch had announced the time just seconds before he'd rung the doorbell earlier that evening. Using what she had come to know as her "magic wand," she had slowly walked to the door. After verifying it was him, she had opened the door and allowed him into her world.

"Did you enjoy the pizza tonight, Mona?"

An easy smile spread across her lips. "Yes, thank you. I thought your daughter would be joining us tonight."

He chuckled. "She was invited but she made other plans. She'll be sorry she missed this." He had been glad Shana hadn't come, since he'd wanted Mona to himself tonight. When she had opened the door, he had stood there and looked at her up and down, appreciating what he saw. She was wearing a beautiful printed sundress with a pair of cute sandals. Her hair was curly and crowned her face.

She had explained that her hand wand, which had been developed by students at the college, was magical. It filed in its memory every outfit she had in her closet and a description of each. All she had to do was scan her wand over an outfit and it told her just what outfit it was as well as the color and a description. Special tags had been sewn into the backs of her dresses to make them easier to put on correctly. Then the handheld wand replaced the cane and could detect any obstruction in her path. He'd found everything she told him fascinating.

"I had a good time tonight," she said softly. "It's been a while since I've been out."

"You mean out on a date?"

"Yes."

He took a sip of his tea and watched her take a sip of hers. She had explained how she could locate everything on the table in front of her. All he had to do was tell her the location once. "When was the last time you went to the beach?"

"Oh, goodness. Years."

"Would you go to the beach with me next weekend?"

He could tell his question had thrown her. "You want me to go to the beach with you?"

"Yes. I want you to walk with me barefoot in the sand, let the waves wiggle between our toes as we listen to the sound of the ocean."

He watched as she slowly smiled, knowing that description had been tempting. "I don't know, Ben. I don't want to be a bother."

"You won't be. In case you haven't figured it out already, I enjoy being with you."

After several moments of silence, Mona said, "You might think so now, but—"

"And I'll think so later." He cleared his throat. "But there is that one thing...."

She bunched up her forehead. "What one thing?"

"That you might not like *my* company."

He watched the way her smile brightened her face,

and she tipped that same face toward him. "Trust me, that's not the case."

"Great. Then it's settled. We'll do the beach next week."

Her head lowered for a minute, and then she lifted her gaze to him. "Thanks. I appreciate you."

"No," he said, reaching out and taking her hand in his. "I appreciate you."

Sunday afternoon, and Shana wasn't any closer to making a decision than she had been two days ago. Although Gloria had given her food for thought, it was food she wasn't quite ready to digest.

Jules had called and they talked, but her sister was the last person who needed to know what she'd done with Jace. Her sister had been full of questions about their father's date with Mona last night. Jules hadn't been happy to know it was past noon already and Shana hadn't even called their father to get any scoop. That meant Jules would have to be the nosy one.

It wasn't that Shana hadn't wondered how her father's pizza night had gone, but she had a lot on her mind. Like her father had told her the last time they talked, when it came to Mona Underwood, he could take care of himself and didn't need her or Jules in his business. Maybe it was time Jules heard the same thing from their father herself.

Shana stretched as she came from the kitchen after enjoying a late breakfast. It had been past midnight by the time Gloria had left. One thing was for certain, Shana had slept like a baby every night since having sex with Jace. Sensuous shivers ran through her at the memory. One minute she was standing there in front of him, and the next she was spread out on her desk, naked, legs spread open with him planted fully inside of her. She wished she didn't think about it so much or how much satisfaction she'd gotten from it, but so far she couldn't stop remembering.

Shana bit her bottom lip, thinking time was winding down. If she planned to walk away, she needed to have other crisis management companies that she could recommend to Granger Aeronautics. But a part of her didn't want to do that. Granger was a puzzle that she wanted to figure out. Why did Jace have to be difficult? Why couldn't he just promise to keep his hands and mouth to himself and make sure what had happened Friday night didn't happen again?

Moving to the living room, she grabbed the remote off the table and was about to settle down on the sofa when she heard the doorbell. Thinking it was Gloria, she moved to the door. She stopped dead in her tracks when she looked through the decorative glass in her front door and saw it wasn't Gloria.

It was Jace Granger.

What was he doing here? She wasn't aware he had her home address. Gritting her teeth, she opened the door, ignoring the afternoon sunlight spilling on him that made him look even sexier in his jeans and shirt. "Jace, what are you doing here?"

He placed his hands in his pockets. "I'd like to talk to you. I'm hoping you can spare me a few minutes."

She was about to tell him that no, she didn't have a few minutes to spare, when she thought better of it. Maybe they should talk today when they were both in control and she wasn't glowing from the aftereffects of the best sex she'd ever had in her life.

"All right, come in."

She backed up and he followed, closing the door behind him.

Chapter Nineteen

She led him through the foyer and into her living room. He quickly glanced around, admiring her decor. The bright, bold colors would have clashed in any other woman's place, but they suited her. The room was spacious and lived-in. Not untidy, but it felt like somewhere you could get comfortable without being told to get your feet off the table or not to slouch on the couch. The huge rug in front of her fireplace would be perfect to lie down on and chill.

He really liked her sofa. It was big and fluffy-looking and had huge pillows you could get lost in. It faced a big-screen television, around sixty-inches he guessed, and he could imagine watching the Super Bowl on it with a beer in his hand. And then there was a brick fireplace, bigger than most, and he could see it emitting enough heat to warm the entire home.

His gaze traveled to the huge portrait hanging on one of her walls. It was one of her, another female and an older man. It wasn't hard to guess it was a family portrait of her, her sister and her father. The three resembled each other, particularly around the nose and mouth.

He turned to her, saw her brooding expression and decided to ignore it for the time being. "Nice place, Shana."

"Thanks," she said, settling into one of the deep cushions on her sofa. "But thanks to you, I've broken another rule. Clients are not invited to my home."

"I wasn't invited." Nor had she offered him a seat, so he continued to stand.

She stared up at him. "No, you weren't invited, so why are you here? And how did you know where I live?"

He returned her stare and wished he didn't have flashes of how she'd looked spread out on her desk— eyes dilated, cheeks flushed, lips damp and a womanly scent that had the ability to bring a man to his knees. That image had burned itself into his brain and wouldn't go away.

Even now, she looked damn good in denim shorts that complemented the curvaceous swell of her hips and a tank top that fit perfectly over firm breasts. This was the first time he had seen her wearing anything other than a business suit, and she looked just as beautiful. She also looked good wearing nothing at all, which is how his mind was fixed on remembering her. At that moment, although he wished otherwise, physical desire was shooting through him from all angles.

Shana suddenly broke eye contact with him, and he knew why. There was no denying the sexual chemistry blatantly stirring the air between them.

"Look, Jace," she said, easing to her feet. "I really

don't care how you found out where I live, but I think you should leave."

He drew in a deep breath and took a step back. He should leave as she suggested, but first he had to make his case. "Are you going to let this attraction between us stop you from doing the right thing with Granger, Shana?"

"Are you?" she fired back.

Jace swore under his breath, and for the next few moments said nothing. Then when he was sure he had himself together, he said with staid calm, "That day I met you at Vannon's, you were with me all the way, and you understood what needed to be done at Granger. And I know you've come across things in those reports that you're questioning, because I sure am. Now is not the time for you to walk away because we can't put a lid on this sexual chemistry between us, Shana."

"For all you know, I could already be involved with someone," she snapped.

A muscle ticked in his jaw. "Are you?"

Shana thought she could easily lie to him but decided to be evasive instead. "What do you think?"

His burning eyes kept locked to hers. "I don't think you would have done what you did with me if you were involved with someone else. I have no reason to question your character."

She was glad to hear that. "No, I'm not involved with anyone and haven't been seriously for about two years now." She paused a moment and then asked, "So what do you suggest we do about this attraction? Pretend it doesn't exist? We tried it, and that didn't work,

Jace." She drew in a frustrated breath. "I let you take me on a desk, damn it."

Shana's saying it made more images flash through Jace's mind, and from the look in her eyes, those same images had flashed through hers, as well. "Can I ask you something?"

"What?" Shana was trying not to be angry at him, because what had happened Friday was just as much her fault as it was his. He hadn't forced her into doing what she did.

"If things were different and we'd met under normal circumstances, would you be fighting this thing between us?"

She weighed his question and gave him an honest answer. "No."

"Then why are you doing so now?"

A frown settled on her features. "Because you are my client and my rule is not to—"

"I know your rule," he interrupted to say. "And I respect it. But considering everything, I think you need to reconsider and make us an exception."

"Why?"

"Because I want you, and I believe that you want me. And there's no reason not to explore what's there."

Shana shook her head. He'd said it like that should settle it and there shouldn't be any discussion on the matter. Now was her chance to deny what he'd said, but she couldn't. "You had me, Jace, and I had you," she said in frustration.

"Yes, and if you thought what we did in your office would be the end of it, then we wouldn't be having this discussion. But we both know it's not. If anything, I want you more than ever."

And heaven help her, she wanted him just as much. What was there about Jace Granger that had her juices flowing? And why did she constantly think of making love to him again...and again? The attraction between them was too amazing and way too downright powerful. She'd never come across anything like this before in her life. She'd been attracted to Jonathan from the first, but nothing like this. It had been months before he'd gotten as close to her as Jace had in four weeks, and nothing had been as spontaneous as her ripping her clothes off and making out in a professional setting.

Shana eased back down on the sofa, feeling as if her back was against the wall. "You could end this by promising to—"

"I told you I can't, Shana. I would be giving you my word with no intention of keeping it."

She held his gaze for a moment and then asked stubbornly, "Would it be so hard, Jace?"

"It would be impossible, Shana."

Silence settled between them for a long moment, and then Shana broke it by saying, "So, I'll ask again. Other than my ending my contract and walking away, what do you suggest? I assume you're here because you have an idea that you want me to consider."

He was glad they were moving from avoidance to acceptance and could now work on a solution. "You might not like my suggestion, Shana, but I think it will work."

"What is it?"

"I suggest we become involved."

He was right...she didn't like it. "Are you out of your mind?"

Jace shrugged his massive shoulders. "That's the only alternative we have."

"No," she said in a firmer tone. "My professional role at Granger would be jeopardized and no longer effective, especially if your employees get wind of it. I can just hear all the whispering behind our backs. We need to retain our business relationship in front of everyone."

"I agree, which is why I propose to keep the involvement between us. No one has to know, since there's no reason to flaunt it. What we do during our off time is our business. While in the office, we'll concentrate on the business at hand. Granger Aeronautics. But after hours, we can do just what we please."

Her eyes shot up in surprise. "You want to engage in a secret affair?"

"No, that's not what I want. But because of your rule, which you refuse to break, if we want to be together, we don't have a choice."

No, they didn't…if they wanted to be together. He was speaking as if it was a foregone conclusion that they did. He didn't know her, not really, yet he had the ability to read her so well, and she wasn't sure just how she felt about that. She and Jonathan had been together for almost eight months before she found out the truth about him. She wished she'd read his motives in pursuing her. It would have saved her a lot of heartache.

She stood and began pacing, considering what Jace had suggested. It would be so unlike her to consider doing such a thing, engaging in a secret affair with a man. Definitely a novelty. But already she'd done the far-fetched with him. Something that was so unlike her. And what was most surprising was that she had totally enjoyed it. Didn't have an ounce of remorse in any bone in her body when God knows she probably should.

Besides, his suggestion wasn't far from what she had questioned Gloria about last night. Eric and Gloria had resolved that if that was the only way they could be together, then they were willing to meet in secret. It had been almost two years now, and their hidden affair didn't seem to bother either of them. And Shana would be lying to herself if she didn't admit that such an idea had crossed her own mind.

She stopped and turned to Jace. He was watching her, and a part of her resented that he'd had the courage to suggest such a thing to her when she would never have done so with him.

"It's not my fault that you're such a beautiful woman, Shana," he said.

She didn't want his compliment, but that didn't stop her breath from catching in her throat. "It's not about you and me, Jace. It's about Granger Aeronautics and figuring out just who's trying to destroy it."

While she was saying those words, she knew it went beyond that. She was asking him to control emotions when she doubted she could control herself. And it was hard, almost too difficult, not to consider what he was suggesting when he was standing in front of her looking so breathtakingly handsome. Jace Granger had that air about him, one that could set any female's sensual side rocketing and her pulse leaping.

Even now, her heart was beating hard and her nipples were throbbing. And when he lowered his gaze from her eyes to the front of her shirt, she knew he was well aware that her breasts were taut and aroused.

She could feel their fullness and a tingling sensation in the engorged tips.

"I'll let you know my decision in a week," she said, moving around him toward the door to let him out. She needed to get him out of there. They were like a ticking time bomb, about to explode from all the sexual chemistry in the air.

Jace reached out and snagged Shana's hand. As far as he was concerned, she could make her decision right here and now. He doubted he could endure another sleepless night. He'd expected her to snatch her hand back, but she didn't. Instead, she met his gaze. "Why are you doing this to me?" she asked in a frustrated tone.

"And why are you doing this to me?" he countered. "Do you think I was looking for this? Or that I wanted it? Your mind isn't the only one that should be focused."

"Then maybe it will be best if I end our business association," she said in annoyance.

"No, it wouldn't be best, because I still wouldn't be able to focus even if you weren't there. I would still be able to breathe in your scent, and sensual visions of you would still play around in my head. I've never been unable to resist a woman, Shana, but you're a temptation I can't seem to shake. I've never wanted a woman as deeply as I want you."

Oh, God. Why would he say something like that? And why did hearing him say it give her so much pleasure? Arouse her even more? And his hand on hers was causing an onslaught of sensations to erupt within her which were magnified by the intense look in his eyes.

And then silently, softly, his hand began moving,

slowly up and down her arm, feathering her flesh and causing shivers to discharge within her. Suddenly, her breaths began coming in shallow gasps while an intense need settled deep between her legs.

She'd never been shy when it came to going after what she wanted, so why was she hesitating now? He had made it clear that he wanted her, and maybe it was time she made it clear she did want him, as well. They could work out specifics about how they intended to handle their unorthodox, intense attraction later.

"Okay, I'll give you my decision now," she said, easing closer to him.

"What is it?" he asked as his breath rushed from his lungs.

"What do you think?" she responded, lifting the hand that held hers to her lips and pressing a kiss in his palm. And then she began kissing her way up his arm. Jace drew in a deep breath when he felt her damp tongue make a circular motion near his shoulder. Blood began pumping through his body at an alarming rate of speed.

"Shana?" he murmured, barely able to get her name past his lips.

She tilted her head to look up at him while her fingers stroked his upper arm in a sensual motion. "Yes?"

"Give me your answer."

He watched as a thoughtful smile eased onto her lips. And then she leaned up and kissed him lightly on the cheek. Her breath was hot and close to his neck. "My answer is whatever you want it to be. I feel easy today. How do you feel?"

His mouth broke into a sensuous smile. He couldn't help it. She had just opened the door to many opportunities, and he was ready for them all. "I feel like touching you all over, kissing you, stroking you and tasting every single spot on your body," he said huskily, moving closer to her.

Shana's reaction to his words was instantaneous. A tremulous smile spread across her lips at the feel of her body responding to primitive desire. She slowly began backing up to the stairs. When she reached the first step, she stopped and said, "I know what you can do with me spread out on a desk. Now let me see what you can do with me in a bed."

She turned and moved up the stairs, taking her time with her hips swaying with every step.

Chapter Twenty

Jace stopped dead in Shana's bedroom doorway. If he had any doubt she was into bright colors, it was more evident in here. Splashes of bright yellow covered the walls, and vivid lime-green curtains adorned her windows. Her bedspread seemed to be a rainbow coalition with solid-colored pillows of red, green, blue and orange. He slid his gaze from the pillows to where she stood beside the bed. She'd already removed her blouse and was removing her bra.

"May I join this party?" he asked, moving from the doorway to stand in the middle of the room.

She glanced over at him and her smile had a spark of eroticism. "By all means. You're the guest of honor." She then tossed her bra to him.

He couldn't help but chuckle when he caught it. Black lace. He was seeing another side of Shana, one he liked. It seemed that once she'd made up her mind about moving ahead with their affair, she was jumping in with both feet. She might have regrets tomorrow, but none were showing now. He hadn't known what to expect when she came to the door, wasn't sure she would let him in. Now he was in her bedroom, watching her undress.

"You're slow. Having second thoughts?"

He glanced over at her at the same time she was easing her shorts down her thighs. Seeing her had his body responding, hardening. He was propelled into action and quickly began removing his clothes.

"Beat you."

She was there, naked, right in front of him before he could remove his pants. He couldn't help stopping what he was doing to reach out and knead the twin globes, liking how they felt in his hands when he gently squeezed. He thought her breasts were beautiful, and the lusciousness of them taunted him.

He heard the catch of her breath as the tips of his fingers gently caressed her nipples, loving the turgid texture. When she laid her hands flat on his chest and leaned into him, he left her breasts to snake his arms around her back to give her support when it seemed her knees had weakened.

"Let me get you in that bed before I make love to you right here, standing up."

When she raised her brows inquiringly, he smiled and said, "Yes, it's possible, trust me." And then he swept her into his arms and walked the short distance to the bed and placed her on it.

He took a step back to unclip the cell phone from his belt to place it on her nightstand next to the bed before he undid the belt. He tossed it into an empty chair. He glanced over at her, saw her watching when he slid his pants and briefs down his legs.

"I missed this part the last time," she explained. "I was too busy taking off my own clothes."

Jace sat on the edge of the bed to remove his socks and could feel her fingertips tracing up and down the swell of his back. It was as if she was intent on discovering the feel of his flesh. He closed his eyes when she scooted up on her knees and began massaging his shoulders. The sensations of her hands on his skin were causing his muscles beneath her fingers to flex in need. And then he moaned deep in his throat when she pressed her chest against his back and deliberately rubbed her breasts against him.

What was she doing to him? And why? As if she read his mind, she wrapped her arms around his neck and hugged him closer and whispered in his ear, "Our affair isn't meant to last forever, and I want to savor it for as long as I can." And when her tongue began licking around his ear, leaving damp imprints in its wake, he couldn't take any more and felt a powerful need to be inside of her.

Shifting his body, he reached behind him, pulled her around to him and lifted her into his lap to face him. Her shapely and curvy legs automatically straddled his waist, then she tilted her hips back at an angle so those same legs could touch the crown of his back.

He would figure out how she'd managed to do that later. The only thing he cared about was that the position presented endless opportunities, and he knew which one he intended to take advantage of first.

Jace held her gaze as he lifted her thighs, aiming his engorged erection straight toward her. He groaned as he slid inside of her heated warmth, burying himself deep, as far as he could possibly go. She moaned, as well, and the look on her face at that moment was priceless. He was able to see the degree of pleasure that flared into her eyes.

He could have made love to her right there in this position, but she deserved a bed this time, and he hadn't been able to wait a minute longer. Shivers ran through him at the feel of her inner muscles clenching him, holding him tight within her. "Okay, this is how we're going to do it," he said, slowly easing to his feet with her legs still wrapped solidly around him.

"I'm going to ease us both down on the bed, all right?"

Instead of answering, she just nodded. He turned slightly, and without disconnecting their bodies, he lowered her to the bed. As soon as her back touched the coverlet, he realized that once again, the thought of a condom hadn't crossed his mind.

"Still taking the pill, right?" he asked, his breaths forced from his lungs in short, uneven rasps while looking down at her.

She held his gaze as his body straddled hers. "Every day."

He was glad, because he loved the feel of being skin-to-skin with her, and he was definitely feeling it. The way her muscles contracted around him had him writhing inside. But he wasn't ready to let go without her being there with him. Jace glanced down at how enticing her breasts looked, and like a magnet, his lips were drawn to her nipples that seemed ripe just for his mouth.

Shana sucked in a deep mouthful of air when the warm tip of Jace's tongue made circular motions around her nipples before going in for the kill, opening his mouth wide and sucking one in between parted lips. She was filled with a heady rush of pleasure when he began sucking on her nipples with ardent greed. An unadulterated pleasure that spread through every part of her body, especially that part connected to his. She felt him buried deep within her, and although she knew this was nothing more than great sex, an appeasement of testosterones and hormones they'd given in to, she somehow felt more.

She heard herself moan with each suck and lick to her breasts as sensations began to overtake her, and she couldn't help but reach out and cradle his head to her, holding him there. He was devouring her breasts in a way they'd never been consumed before, and she couldn't just lie there. She began moving, and when she did, so did he.

She felt the beginning of his hard thrusts as he moved inside of her with sure, firm strokes. She became overwhelmed, engulfed and swept away by passion of the most intense kind. Each thrust went deeper and grew bolder, and when his mouth left her breasts to take control of her mouth, she groaned. This is what made her enter into an affair that she knew wouldn't go anywhere. Two days ago, she had gotten a taste of Jace, and now she was unashamedly hooked.

He was ravaging her mouth and pounding relentlessly into her simultaneously, nearly driving her over an edge, then jerking her back only to drive her over and over again. Farther and farther, deeper and deeper, he continued thrusting so unerringly between her legs.

"Jace!"

He suddenly broke off the kiss to stare down at her, and the heated gaze in his eyes was filled with intense need, want and desire. In a surprising move, he drew out of her then thrust back in, harder and deeper. It was then that something within her broke. Erupting and tearing into her, sending sensations exploding, her mind reeling and her muscles contracting even more, holding captive the engorged shaft whipping her insides into one delicious orgasm.

Jace increased the rhythm, deepened his thrust, and Shana lifted up her hips when he came pounding down. When she screamed out his name, his body bucked in response. The feel of her insides flooded with his release sent shivers of pleasure through her body, and she tightened her legs around him.

"Shana!"

He groaned out her name, and Shana's inner muscles contracted, claiming him in a way she thought she would never claim a man. Her flesh continued to pulsate even when he collapsed against her. She wasn't sure how long they lay there, trying to get their breathing under control. But at some point, she recalled the moment he scooped her body closer to his side with their legs entwined.

Gathering as much energy as she could, she turned her head and stared into the face close to hers. She couldn't help but smile at him.

"What's that smile for?" he asked huskily, wrapping his arms tighter around her.

"For giving me something I needed," she whispered. And she was not ashamed to admit it. Far from it. She was never one not to give credit where credit was due.

"My pleasure, and I will give you just that... pleasure...any time you want it," he said, brushing a few tendrils back from her face.

Shana felt her heart tighten, and she forced from her mind the idea that this was more than sex, because it wasn't. This was sex and nothing else. But there was something about his offer, his sensual proposition, that had crazy thoughts running around in her head. "I'll remember that."

She was beginning to feel sleepy, although dusk was just settling in outside. It was past her dinnertime. She had planned to go out and grab something at one of the many restaurants located in the strip mall a couple of miles away. But now all she wanted to do was sleep.

As if he knew what she needed, he tucked her head under his chin and curled his arms around her. "Sleep."

With satisfaction flowing in every part of her body, she drew in a deep breath, inhaled his scent and then closed her eyes to sleep.

Jace gazed down at the woman who slept in his arms. He no longer questioned the strange phenomenon between them, simply accepted it. There had to be a reason she had this pull on him. He just didn't know what it was. However, he was certain there was one; otherwise, he wouldn't be here, in her bed on a Sunday evening when he had a briefcase of papers he still needed to read. But at this moment, those papers were the last thing on his mind. The only thing he wanted to do was think about Shana and remember how much he had enjoyed making love to her just now.

And he had enjoyed it. Probably too damn much.

His ex-wife should have taught him a lesson about letting a pretty face and a hot body rule his mind. But this was the furthest thing from his thoughts. He wanted to believe Shana was different, but all he would be doing was making assumptions since there was a lot about her he didn't know. Did it matter? Especially when their relationship would only be short and physical. It shouldn't matter; however, there was a lot about her he wanted to know. Instead of keeping things impersonal, he wanted to get personal. If that wasn't affecting his frame of mind, he didn't know what was.

He glanced over at the clock on her nightstand. It was getting late, and neither of them had eaten anything for hours. Not only would they need something to eat, they needed to talk, to set up a plan of action, a strategy. Not about Granger Aeronautics but about them. He figured that during work hours they would be business associates and nothing more. But at other times, they would be lovers.

She shifted in his arms, and he didn't have to wait long for her eyes to open. She looked up at him. At first, she seemed disoriented, and then her eyes filled with clarity. She pressed her lips together, her mouth lush, and studied his face. He felt the tension leave her body seconds before she spoke in a soft voice. "Hi."

"Hi. You're beautiful when you sleep."

And she had slept naked in his arms. Her breathing had been soft and even, and for some reason he had derived pleasure just lying there and listening to it while inhaling her scent. The air surrounding them was filled with her fragrance mingled with the aroma of sex. He liked the combined smell.

"I don't know about that," she said, smiling. "My sister wouldn't agree. She claims I don't snore but that I make sounds in my sleep. Do I?"

"None that I heard. She was probably teasing you."

"Knowing Jules, I wouldn't be surprised."

He lifted a brow. "Jules?"

"Short for Juliet. She got tired of the Romeo and Juliet jokes and decided to shorten it in junior high school."

She pulled herself up in bed and glanced over at the clock. "It's almost eight. I can't believe I slept that long."

He kept his arms around her. "Are you hungry? If so, we can order in."

She quickly looked up at him. "Aren't you leaving?"

Was that her way of saying she wanted him gone? "Hadn't planned on it until we talked."

Her brows drew together in a questioning frown. "Talk about what?"

"How we're going to handle our affair."

Shana's lips pressed together as she held Jace's gaze, and then she said, "There's no need for discussion. It's not that serious."

"It is to me."

She saw the way his jaw had tensed and knew she'd pushed a wrong button. "Look, Jace. I'm the one who made the rules and the one who agreed to break them. If you're worried that I will not act professional at Granger and corner you somewhere to rip your shirt off or something, you don't have anything to concern yourself with. No matter how I might have acted in this bed, I know how to control myself."

A smile touched Jace's lips as he was thinking she had it all wrong. He was not concerned with her self-control but his own. "And what if I feel the urge to corner you somewhere and rip off your shirt?"

"You wouldn't."

"Don't be too sure of that."

She studied his features and saw the sensual gleam in his eyes and the lustful look to his lips. Maybe they did need to talk. "I would think the way we conduct ourselves would be self-explanatory."

"Like it was the other night?"

He did have a point. "Okay. If you need to hear it verbally, then here goes. During office hours, we will conduct ourselves in a professional way and not give any clue that we're involved."

"For how long?"

Her eyebrows rose. "What do you mean for how long? For the time we're in the office."

"I was asking how long will the affair last?"

Her lips parted in surprise, only because she hadn't thought of a timetable. "Until this craziness between us wears off."

"What if it doesn't?"

She would think he was pulling her leg with all these questions if she hadn't seen the seriousness in his face. "It will."

She sounded so sure of that, and Jace decided not to push the issue. The bottom line was that they had an understanding. Hands off at Granger...but after hours had no such restrictions. "Okay, we're straight. I know my limitations and will abide by them."

"So will I," she said. "Let's shake on it."

She extended her hand to him, and he glanced down at it for a minute before taking it into the warmth of his. But instead of shaking it, he used it to tug her into his arms.

Leaning down, Jace captured her lips and immediately felt a warmth flow from her and straight into him. He was compelled to tighten his arms around her and deepen the kiss. And when he heard her moan, he deepened it still, discovering it was hard to get enough of her.

He wasn't sure just how this affair with her would work out, but he was looking forward to finding out.

Chapter Twenty-One

"**G**ood morning, Mr. Granger."

Dalton returned the smile to the woman entering his office carrying a stack of folders. He remembered her well. She was the receptionist from downstairs. He'd been quite taken with her his first day at Granger. He had wanted her for his private secretary, but Jace had been a killjoy and given his stamp of disapproval.

"Good morning. You're Brandy, right?" Her dress was short and showed off a pair of gorgeous legs and a shapely backside.

"Yes, I'm Brandy. Melissa needed assistance today, and here I am," she said, her smile widening.

"Yes, here you are," he replied, scanning her up and down as she crossed the room to place the stack of folders on his desk. The one thing he appreciated was a woman with round, firm breasts, and she definitely owned a nice pair. A surge of dangerous heat spread through his body.

"Is there anything else you want, Mr. Granger?"

Dalton couldn't help running his tongue across his bottom lip upon hearing that question while remaining focused on her chest. Brandy was definitely a hot number, but an involvement with her would ensure an ass-kicking from Jace. But that didn't mean he couldn't test the waters to see how far she was willing to go, just in case he decided to forget about Jace and yield to temptation.

"No, there's nothing else at the moment, but I might think of something later," he said, leaning back in his chair and shifting his gaze back to her face.

"Just let me know. I aim to please," she said with a flirty toss of her head, sending luxurious auburn curls twirling around her head.

Dalton wasn't a fool. He could definitely read between those lines. "That's good to hear. How long have you worked for Granger?"

"This is my third year. I came right out of college."

He lifted a brow. Most of the employees with college degrees had supervisory or management positions. She was the company's receptionist. "You have a degree?"

"No, I quit school in my second year. I found the place boring."

So had he. He'd only gone to class and kept his grades up because it was required to be on the football team.

"We're a Granger family," she said, breaking into his thoughts. "Both my parents used to work here."

"Did they?"

"Yes. Mom went back to school for a nursing degree. She works at Virginia General. Dad divorced Mom eight years ago, quit the company and then moved to Texas."

He was about to ask her something he shouldn't…

like what plans she had for tonight…when there was a knock on his office door. "Come in."

Jace walked in, and when his brother's gaze lit on Brandy, who'd gotten comfortable enough to prop her curvy ass on Dalton's desk, a frown settled on Jace's features. And when she kept sitting there as if her butt were glued to the spot, Jace said, "I believe Melissa is looking for you, Miss Booker. She has plenty for you to do."

It was then that she eased off the desk. Dalton followed her every movement and appreciated his twenty-twenty vision.

"Yes, sir." She turned to Dalton. "Will you need me for anything else, Mr. Granger?"

Dalton smiled. He would just love to give her an earful of ideas. However, none were decent enough to say in front of his straitlaced brother. "No, that will be all." And then he watched as she sashayed her delectable backside past Jace and right out of his office.

Dalton shifted his gaze to his brother. "Do I have to remind you that I'm a grown-ass man who doesn't need you for a watchdog?"

Jace walked to the middle of the room with his arms folded across his chest and his feet braced apart. "Yes, go ahead and remind me."

Dalton's face split into a sudden smile. "You're crazy, you do know that, right?"

"Not until you told me just now. I thought I was perfectly sane. And I know you can take care of yourself, Dalton, but when it comes to Granger, we have to draw a fine line on certain things."

"You don't say?" Dalton said, picking up a pencil and toying with it while looking at his brother with shrewd eyes. "Does that apply to you, as well? Don't know if Hannah mentioned it, but I dropped by last night."

Jace moved to sit down in the chair across from Dalton's desk. "And?"

"And you weren't home."

Jace shrugged. "Not a crime that I went out for the evening."

"No," Dalton said with a mocking grin. "But I know for a fact you never made it back home. At least, you hadn't arrived when I left this morning."

Jace's face registered surprise. "You were there?"

"Yes. I arrived late yesterday afternoon and decided to stay the night."

Dalton figured there was no need to tell him he'd known he could count on leftovers since Hannah was known to prepare a feast for Sunday dinner. She hadn't disappointed, but Jace was nowhere to be found and hadn't told Hannah where he was going. Dalton figured Jace would return at a decent hour and had hung around, caught a ball game on television and eventually dozed off. When he'd awakened, it was past midnight, so he'd decided to stay for the night. He'd gotten up around six this morning to return to his place, and Jace still hadn't come home.

"Surely, you're not questioning my comings and goings, Dalton."

"No more than you're questioning mine. But I am curious who you spent so much time with. One-night stands are my specialty, not yours."

Jace held his brother's stare. "Do you know that for certain?"

Dalton's gaze was sharp and assessing. "No, I discovered that, in this life, nothing is for certain. Do you want to know what I think?"

"Not really."

"I'll tell you anyway, and since you don't kiss and tell any more than I do, you don't have to confirm anything. I think you were with your wonder-woman."

Jace frowned. "Your thinking is wrong."

Dalton didn't think so, mainly because his older brother couldn't lie very well. He had the word *cover-up* written all over his face. But Dalton would leave it alone for now. "Okay, my mistake. I just hope whoever the lady was that she was worth your missing Hannah's delicious dinner. She wasn't too happy with you, and was glad I dropped by so dinner wouldn't go to waste. I even brought some in for lunch today."

Jace nodded. "You came into the office early. Why?"

Dalton chuckled. "Definitely not for the same reason you were late. I happened to notice your wonder-girl was late, as well."

"Was she?"

"Yes. Makes you wonder."

Jace stood. "Don't be a pain in the ass, Dalton."

"Okay. Then let's agree on something. You stay out of my business, and I'll stay out of yours." Dalton stood and extended his hand to his brother. "Deal?"

Dalton didn't miss the scalding look in his brother's eyes when he reluctantly shook his hand. "Deal." Jace glowered at him for a minute and then turned and walked out of the office.

Dalton couldn't help the smile that touched his lips. He'd never been certain just what kind of hold, if any, Jace's ex had on him after the divorce. But he had a feeling his brother was finally shaking free of the woman Dalton had long ago nicknamed Evil Eve.

Even if the woman Jace was being elusive about was wonder-woman, Dalton was damn glad about it.

A few moments later, Jace stood at the window with his hands in his pockets as he looked out. Frustrated. Disgusted. Dalton was too damn smart for his own good. His brother had pretty much figured things out before he and Shana could get through day one. Although Jace had not admitted to anything, Dalton pretty much thought he was onto something. Hopefully, their handshake would keep Dalton's mouth shut and his assumptions to himself.

And Jace would have to admit his own fault in day one getting off to a suspicious start. He hadn't intended to spend the night with Shana, but one lovemaking session had led to another and another and then another. By the time they'd gotten out of bed, it was past midnight and they were starving. He had driven her to a fast-food place that stayed open twenty-four hours. They had gone through the drive-through for burgers, fries and shakes and had taken them back to her place. After they had consumed their food, Shana had walked him to the door. But it had been the hot and heavy good-night kiss that had driven him to sweep her off her feet, into his arms and back up the stairs to her bedroom.

After a night of marathon sex, they had overslept. He hadn't left her house until after seven, rushing to Sutton Hills, dashing past Hannah with an apologetic look on his face in an attempt to shower, get dressed and out the door in an hour. He would have made it had

Caden not called for an update. That conversation had cost him a good twenty minutes. He'd arrived at the office a half hour behind Shana. No one had noticed... except for Dalton.

Jace turned when the intercom on his desk went off. Moving away from the window, he pushed the button. "Yes, Melissa?"

"This is Brandy. Melissa had a dentist appointment."

Jace rolled his eyes. "Okay, Brandy, you buzzed me."

"Yes, sir. Your wife is on line two."

A muscle in Jace's jaw began to tick. "I don't have a wife."

"That's what I thought, but the lady says differently."

Jace settled in the chair behind his desk. "Put the lady on."

He drew in a deep breath, wondering what the hell his vain and shallow ex wanted this time.

"Jace?"

"What do you want, Eve?"

"I need money."

Jace leaned back in his chair. "And your point in calling me?"

"For a loan, and I promise to pay you back."

He chuckled. He knew any money he gave her wouldn't be paid back. "And what happens if I don't give you a loan? You'll have to get a job, right?"

"Surely you don't expect me to do that. I'm a Granger."

"In name only, and I wish you'd ditch it. We've been divorced three years now. You're free to marry again."

"But I won't remarry. You have my true heart."

"Whatever." Because he'd had such a fantastic night and the aftereffects still had him in a good mood, he asked, "How much do you need?"

There was a pause. She was probably picking her jaw up off the floor. "You're going to loan it to me?"

"How much, Eve?" He could visualize dollar signs clanking like slot machines in her head.

"Ten thousand."

She was pushing it now. Taking advantage of his kindness. "I'll give you five."

"Give? I don't have to pay it back?"

He rolled his eyes. "Can you?"

"No."

"Then why did you ask for a loan?"

She didn't say anything, and he preferred that she didn't anyway. She needed to stop while she was ahead. "You'll have the money in forty-eight hours. What's your bank?"

He jotted down the information as quickly as she rattled it off. He figured she wanted to hurry up and get him off the phone before he changed his mind.

"Why?"

He raised a brow. "Why what?"

"Why are you being so nice?"

He thought that was an odd question. He wasn't being nice, just tolerant.

"The reason I'm tolerating your call is because you've caught me in a good mood."

"And why are you in a good mood?"

He turned to glance over at the solid door that separated him from Shana. "I have my reasons."

"I owe you."

"No, you don't, and make it last, because you'll never get another penny out of me. No matter how good a mood I'm in. Goodbye, Eve." He then hung up the phone.

Bruce Townsend flipped his briefcase closed and glanced over at Shana. "You did the right thing to call me when you did. You were right. Someone tried hacking into this computer system."

Shana frowned. "Did they succeed?"

A slow, sinister smile curved the corners of Bruce's lips. "Not on my watch. I built this baby to last and to keep your secrets."

She figured as much. Bruce worked for both her and Jules. The man was a computer genius and the mastermind behind Greta. Whenever she worked from inside any corporation, she would install her own network for security purposes. In all her five years, this was the first time anyone had tried hacking into the system.

"Can you identify the hackers?"

"Not yet, but I can tell you it was someone from within this building."

Shana gave him a nod. She'd figured as much.

"They're probably in a quandary as to why they couldn't succeed and have figured out you're not on the same server. Chances are, they'll be more determined than ever to discover what you're trying to hide."

She hoped so and looked forward to the person or persons being exposed. She needed to call Kent. He was doing a thorough investigation of a number of employees of interest, and she needed to see how he was coming along.

"So what did you do?" she asked. Bruce was known

to have a briefcase of toys, both software and hardware specifically created to combat computer espionage.

"Installed an additional security device. And just so you know, I ran an open scan of this room and found a bug."

Shana leaned forward in her chair and was convinced her face lost some of its color. Had someone been spying on her? But most important, had the bug been in place Friday evening during her meeting with Jace and Dalton? Then another question slammed into her mind, an alarming possibility. What about during her sexual romp in this office with Jace later?

"I need to know when—and I mean exactly when—the bug was activated, Bruce."

He glanced over at her, apparently hearing the panic in her voice. "When I get back to the office, I can—"

"No. If there's a way you can find that out now, I want to know."

He gave her a curious stare, longer than she liked, before nodding. "All right. It won't take me but a second." He reopened his briefcase and took out some handheld device that resembled a transistor radio.

She nervously began clicking her pen and would not have realized she was doing so if Bruce hadn't stopped what he was doing and glanced over at her.

"What?"

He smiled. "Don't you want to take a break or something?"

Shana stopped clicking her pen. "Sorry." Moving away from her desk, she walked over to the window to appreciate the view, trying to stand in place instead of pacing. What if there was a video of what she and Jace had been doing in here? She'd never found herself in such a situation. But then, she'd never encountered a man quite like Jace before.

Goose bumps ran up and down her arms when she thought about everything they'd done last night. Fervent passion. And he had stirred it relentlessly in his kisses and the way he had stroked her body into orgasm after orgasm. Sending pleasurable contractions all through her womb and in every cell in her body. She had gasped, begged, and when he'd delivered, she had screamed countless times.

His hard thrusts would make her body fragment into an endless flow of climaxes whenever she was skin-to-skin with him. Sheathing his engorged penis within her, so ecstatically deep, had made her feel incredibly womanly. Then there was the way her body would expand for him, the feel of her inner muscles tightening around him, clenching him possessively, while she was slung into a whirlwind of red-hot heat and embraced another orgasm. Then another. And another.

And if that hadn't been enough, she had awakened this morning with his hands between her legs, caressing her clitoris into an aroused state and compelling her to want him all over again. His every thrust had promised her everything, and more than once she was certain she would die of pleasure.

"Got it!"

She turned quickly as Bruce moved away from the computer. "Well?"

He glanced at her and smiled. "Well what?"

She narrowed her eyes at him. "Now is not the time to play with me."

"I gather that and can't help wondering why, Shana?

What has you so uptight? Why is it so important to know when the cameras began rolling?"

Only Bruce, who was not only an associate but a close friend to her and Jules, could push the issue by asking her that. "Because it does. So tell me."

He studied her features for a while longer before picking up the ink pen she had been clicking furiously just moments ago. "This here is the culprit."

She stared at the pen. "You're kidding, right?" she asked, moving back to her desk.

"No. In fact it's rather a sophisticated piece of spyware with the way it operates. See this part here that makes the pen light up?"

She moved closer to see what he was pointing out to her. "Yes."

"This is the major cell. When activated, it emits airwaves that cover an area one hundred feet in diameter. Then at a certain specified time, the airwaves are imprisoned and transported to be viewed later. It's capable of capturing both video and sound."

The thought of a specialized ink pen being able to do all that was amazing. She swallowed and then nervously gnawed on her bottom lip. "So when was it activated?"

"At exactly eight this morning, Eastern Standard Time."

"And not before?" she asked, needing to make certain.

"And not before," Bruce confirmed.

"You're sure?" She recalled having that same pen from day one, as part of the supplies provided to her when she'd moved into this office. She had liked the bronze color and the sleek design and had begun using it exclusively.

"Yes, I'm positive that's the date and time," Bruce responded, eyeing her speculatively.

Relief rushed through her, and she drew in a thankful breath. "I've had that pen since my first day here and enjoy writing with it. Why wasn't it activated before today?"

Bruce shrugged. "Probably because the individual didn't feel there was anything to spy on before this morning. It wasn't by accident this pen was given to you, Shana. Who stocked your office?"

Shana recalled a number of people had but mostly Jace's administrative assistant, Melissa. And Jace mentioned he'd done a few things in here, as well. She didn't say anything for a minute and then she said, "I still don't understand how the person knew this is the pen I would use."

"It didn't have to be the pen you would use all the time. It could have been the one that sat on your desk in this pen and pencil holder with a number of others," Bruce said. "The only thing that would have stopped it from working was if you'd stuck the pen in your drawer. Otherwise, when activated, it had free rein to video this entire office twenty-four hours a day. That meant the person who put this in here would have overheard any and all conversations as well as been privy to any private meetings held in here."

She thought about what he said for a minute. "I don't understand. I read the reports. Granger Aeronautics has a state-of-the-art security system that is able to detect any foreign software brought into this building. It detected the one you installed in here and asked Jace about it. Why wasn't it able to pick up on this piece of spyware?"

"Because this cell is highly advanced, designed to be used for remote electronic surveillance. It's something similar to what is now being tested in police investigations, namely by the FBI, CIA and Homeland Security. It's a new kind of wiretap that not only transmits sound but provides a pretty clear video to go along with it."

He paused a moment and then said, "This concerns me, Shana. Whoever put this in here is in the big boys' league, because acquiring this kind of spyware isn't cheap. It's advanced and costly. That tells me the person is interested in what you're doing and what you're finding out. They are spending money to keep tabs on you, and it makes me wonder why. But then, when it comes to industrial espionage, this sort of thing doesn't surprise me."

Shana nodded. It shouldn't surprise her, either, but this only added to the puzzle. And it was a puzzle she was determined to solve. "I'm calling Jace in here," she said, picking up the phone, feeling irritated as well as anxious while dialing the direct number to his office. "He needs to be advised as to what's going on."

Chapter Twenty-Two

Shana watched Jace's reaction to what Bruce was telling him, explaining things in detail the same way he had done with her. Jace was listening attentively, taking it all in, and since she'd been as intimate with him as she had over the past seventy-two hours, she could read the signs.

He was pissed.

But his professionalism as well as his control wouldn't reveal on the outside just how he was steaming on the inside. Every so often, he would ask Bruce a question, and she should not have been surprised by Jace's vast knowledge of industrial espionage. From her research on him, she knew he'd worked for the state of California and recalled that he had assisted the California Bureau of Investigations—the CBI—in nabbing a sophisticated group involved with human trafficking that had used a major corporation as a front to do so. The authorities had used spyware to bring the corporation down.

Jace shifted in his seat, and her eyes shifted as well, moving from his fierce features to the suit he was wearing. Nice. Expensive. *GQ*. He carried himself with the ease of a man born to lead. His brothers were right. He was a true leader, and she could see him working alongside his father and grandfather had things turned out differently.

"Well, that's about it, Jace," Bruce was saying. "Do you have any more questions?"

"Yes," Jace said, standing and moving toward the window. He paused a moment and glanced out before turning back to them. "What about my office and those belonging to my brothers? Could spyware be planted there, as well?"

"Possibly. I can check them out before I leave."

"I would like for you to do that." He moved back over to stand by Shana's desk and picked up the pen, studied it and then said, "So someone wants to play hardball. We figured there was a traitor among us, and now we know just how far they will go."

He moved his gaze from the pen to her, and Shana could feel the heat in his eyes. Earlier, he had been aware of each and every time she moved in her chair. His gaze would shift from Bruce to her, and a shiver would pass through her whenever he captured her within his scope…like now. It took a lot to contain her composure whenever she became the center of his attention. And she felt herself being drawn more and more to him.

Bruce cleared his throat, and both she and Jace glanced over at him. He smiled and said, "I'll get started on those other offices once you give me the okay, Jace."

Jace nodded. "Martin Fillmore heads my security team, and I want to make him aware of what's going on." He turned to Shana, smiled, and as if he'd read her thoughts, he said, "And I know everyone is a suspect until we find out who's behind this. I will move forward on that premise and handle Fillmore and everyone else accordingly."

Shana nodded, glad he saw the value in doing that. "When will Caden be returning?" she asked.

"Not until next Monday." He then turned to Bruce. "And I want you to work with Shana to put my own security safety net in place. In other words, I want a watchdog to monitor the watchdog. Understand?"

"Completely. And I hope you're aware that whoever is behind this will know they've been discovered. And since this is possibly an inside job...working with others on the outside...they will begin covering their tracks."

A muscle in Jace's jaw began to twitch. "That may be the case, but I'm determined to find out who's behind this."

"This is real James Bond stuff," Dalton said, smiling as he eased into the chair across from Jace's desk. "I was disappointed they didn't find anything in my office. I'm offended someone doesn't think I know anything."

Jace fought back a smile. "You don't."

"The hell you say," Dalton said, straightening up in his chair. "I've been reading all that crap just like you and Caden. Shit. I haven't read so much boring stuff since college. Just don't try being a smart-ass and throw an exam at me."

Jace chuckled. "I won't, but there are certain departments I'm assigning you to monitor. For starters,

Security." He was glad that Bruce had reported there weren't any security breaches in the other offices. And as requested, the watchdog was now being monitored. Bruce even suggested they check Jace's father's office, although no one had used the office in over fifteen years and it was normally kept locked. No breach in security was found in Shep's office, either.

Dalton nodded, and Jace could see from the expression on his face that he was well aware, like everyone else, that Security was an important department here at Granger Aeronautics. And in light of what Bruce had uncovered, it was even more so. Hopefully, this would keep Dalton busy and out of Brandy Booker's pants.

A smile spread across Dalton's lips. "Yeah, I saw how Martin Fillmore was sweating. The crap came down on his watch, and it didn't make him look good. Like he'd been sleeping on the job."

"I want you to stay on top of things, Dalton," Jace said, tossing his pen down on the desk. He was about to hold a meeting with his other executives and had to sit there and pretend that perhaps one of them wasn't behind it. That one of them didn't have ulterior motives for wanting the company to fail.

"And you're sure it was an inside job?" Dalton asked, breaking into his thoughts.

"Looks that way. Someone put that pen in Shana's office, and it's been there from day one."

Dalton nodded. "Melissa set up her office, right?"

"Yes, with a little help from Brandy Booker." He saw the lifting of Dalton's eyes when he was remembering the way Brandy had looked that morning. For good measure, Jace then added, "But there were also a number of people in and out, including a couple of our technicians installing the computer software, a few guys from maintenance who assisted in moving furniture around and the guy cleaning the carpet."

"Basically everyone is a suspect," Dalton said thoughtfully.

Jace smiled. "No, not everybody. You're not."

Although it wasn't a laughing matter, Dalton couldn't help but do so. "Like I said, man, you're crazy. But I appreciate the vote of confidence."

"And I appreciate you and Caden having my back."

There was silence for a minute, and then Dalton asked, "When is he returning? I hate to admit it, but I miss him. Funny how over the years, the three of us have never been in each other's pockets, yet now that we're back together, it seems as if that's how it's supposed to be."

Jace was surprised to hear Dalton say that. "Does that mean there's no more wanderlust in your blood?"

"I didn't say that. All I'm saying is that I like being around you guys for now. It might be a different story next week when either of you pisses me off about something."

Jace stood and glanced at his watch. He had a meeting to get to. He then glanced over at Dalton. "What are your plans for later?"

"I'm heading to that joint on the corner. Food's great, and the female company is even better. You ought to join me."

"I think I will."

Dalton lifted a brow as he stood, as well. "You mean you don't plan to spend another night away from home?"

"Remember our deal, Dalton," Jace replied sternly.

"You stay out of my business, and I'll stay out of yours."

"All right, already. Jeez. But I can't help worrying about you."

Jace chuckled as he slid into his jacket. "For what reason?"

"You haven't been in the game for a while, and you might not know how it works. Things have changed since before the time you married Eve. You might be a little rusty, out of your element."

Jace inwardly laughed at the absurdity of his baby brother thinking that he could give Jace pointers when it came to women. "I think I know how to handle my business, Dalton."

"I hope so. I don't want your ineptness to give me a bad name. I have a reputation to protect."

Jace rolled his eyes as he headed to the door. "I'll keep that in mind."

Dalton followed. "Make sure that you do."

Shana glanced across the kitchen table at her father. She had left Granger a little early today to drop by here since she hadn't talked to him all weekend. And if she got one more call from Jules pushing her to find out as much as she could about their father's Saturday-night date, Shana would scream. So here she was, wishing she'd gone home and straight to bed. If anyone needed to catch up on at least eight hours or more of sleep, she did.

Jace had been in a meeting when she'd left, and she figured he wouldn't drop by her place anyway. No need to wear out a good thing on either of their parts...

although the thought of making love to him again sent pleasurable shivers down her spine.

"So what do you want to know, Shana?"

She blinked at her father's question that pulled her out of her reverie. "I haven't asked anything."

Ben chuckled. "But you will. That's why you're here, right?"

She felt a little offended. "You act like I don't come by during the week."

"You do, but never on Mondays."

He had a point there. But only because she usually visited on the weekend. However, this past weekend, that hadn't been the case. She'd known he had a date for Saturday night and had decided not to get underfoot. Besides, her mind had been filled with memories of all the action that had taken place in her office Friday night.

She had meant to drop by on Sunday, or even call at least. But a late night with Gloria had made her sleep late, and then unexpectedly, Jace had arrived. And once she'd given him access to her bedroom, she had forgotten about everything else for the next ten hours or so.

"Mona was disappointed that you didn't join us."

Shana raised her brow. "I wasn't asked."

He chuckled. "Yes, I know."

Shana couldn't help but smile. "So you wanted Mona to yourself. How did it go?"

"I took her to Kal's Pizza, and we had a great time. She looked great, and I enjoyed her company. I'm taking her to the beach on Saturday."

Shana took a sip of her tea. "Don't plan on letting any grass grow under her feet, uh?"

"Not a single blade. So now you can go tell your sister that I made it through the date all in one piece."

Shana put her cup down. "Surely you can understand why it's taking a while for both Jules and me to get a grip on this, Dad. You've never dated before."

"Yes, I did. I dated plenty of times while the two of you were growing up. I'd just never met a woman I cared enough about to bring home for you girls to meet. There are women you hang out with…for fun… and there are those you know you want to have a lasting relationship with."

Hang out with for fun. Shana couldn't help but think about what her father said. In other words, women a man just wanted to sleep with. Was that how Jace saw her?

"So what did you do this weekend? I had expected my phone to be ringing off the hook starting Sunday morning."

"I slept late. Gloria and I took in a movie Saturday night and were up until almost five in the morning just talking. Because she's been assigned to international flights, I don't get to see her as much as I used to, and we had a lot of catching up to do. Girl talk and all that."

"And from that car—a beauty of a white Lexus— that was parked outside your condo yesterday afternoon, I take it you had company later?"

Shana almost choked on the tea she'd just sipped. She stared at her father. "You came by my place yesterday?"

"Yes, but when I saw you had company, I decided not to stop."

"What time was that?" she asked.

"Around six."

Shana nodded. She and Jace had made it up to the bedroom by then and were making out like bandits, going into their third round. "You still could have stopped," she said to be nice, knowing it was a good thing he hadn't. It would have been very awkward all the way around. She was a grown woman, old enough to do what she pleased, but still. Your daddy was your daddy.

"I hadn't heard from you and was worried," he added, breaking into her thoughts. "Like I said, I'd expected my phone to start ringing off the hook before I got out of bed, and when it didn't happen, I was concerned."

"Thanks for your concern, but I was fine." Her father would never know just how fine she had been. Jace had brought out the sexual greed in her, and she had gotten her fill in ways she'd never imagined.

"So when is Jules coming home?" Ben asked.

"Didn't you talk to her yesterday?" Shana asked.

"Not for long. She had an important call come through. You know how she is with her work. I worry that you girls don't get out more and date."

Shana could feel it coming on, that talk he would have with her and Jules on occasion. The one when he told them in so many words that he was looking forward to a grandbaby to bounce on his knee and a son-in-law to watch the games with.

"I can't speak for Jules, but I'm busy, Dad. This new case is going to take more of my time than I imagined it would. Just today, I found spyware in my office."

He nodded. "It's an aeronautics company, right?"

"Yes. Marcel is working on it. I've given him everything, and I've made him aware of this new development. He didn't seem surprised."

"Why would he be? Granger would be ripe for trade-secret violations, considering the competition for government contracts that's going on. It's gotten to be a war between the strongest and the fittest. Some companies believe being devious and underhanded is the way to go."

Enough for people to resort to corporate and industrial theft, Shana thought. But she didn't want to think about all of what Bruce had discovered or what Marcel was doing with the information she'd supplied to him. Until she'd contacted him today, she hadn't heard from him in a while. But then, that's the way the feds worked while building their case. Marcel would contact her when he felt the time was right.

Deciding to get back on the subject of Ben and Mona, she asked, "So which beach are you taking Mona to?"

He shrugged. "Don't know yet. I want to make it a full day."

"Although it might take her out of her comfort zone?"

"Especially so. I want to become her comfort zone."

Shana paused with her teacup to her lips, thinking that her father had said something very powerful. There was no doubt in her mind that he intended to move ahead in this affair with Mona, and it would be serious. "Why didn't you?" she asked.

He looked over at her. "Why didn't I what?"

"Bring home those dates. There had to be some lady at one time who caught your eye."

"Like I said, they were fun times. I honestly never met a woman who I thought could replace your mother."

"Now you feel that Mona can?" she inquired quietly.

He shook his head. "No, because there's no one who can ever replace your mother. It's not about re-placement, Shana. It's about addition, and there is a difference."

Her father's words weighed heavily on Shana's mind hours later when she was getting ready for bed. It was early, but considering her activities of the night before, she had no problem not watching television or reading her book but looked forward to crawling be-tween the covers and getting some much-needed sleep.

She had come downstairs to turn off the lights and set the alarm when the doorbell rang. She knew it wasn't Gloria, since she'd left on an international flight to China earlier in the day.

The porch light was still on, and as she moved to-ward the door, she stopped when she saw who was standing there in front of it.

Jace.

Chapter Twenty-Three

Shana opened the door. There was no need to ask why he was there. She had become one of those women her father had described, a woman a man could have fun with. Why did such a thought bother her? It shouldn't really, when she should see him only as a man she could have fun with. She didn't want a serious relationship with anyone any more than Jace did.

She stepped back and let him inside, and he closed and locked the door behind him. Before she could say anything, he rushed to ask, "When I got out of my meeting, they said you left the office early. You never leave early. Is anything wrong?" He reached out and pushed a wayward curl back from her face. She figured he probably assumed she was ill or something since she had on her pj's.

"No, I'm fine. I hadn't visited my father all weekend and wanted to see him."

"Oh. And you're dressed for bed already. I should have called first. I had decided to call you when I got home, but halfway there, I turned around and headed back this way. I wanted to see you."

Jace drew in a deep breath. All of what he'd just said was the truth. He had joined Dalton for dinner, and when Dalton had invited two women to join them for drinks afterward, Jace knew it was time for him to split. The women had been nice enough, but there was no interest on his part. There was none of the gut-stirring attraction and desire he'd felt for Shana from the start. He had been on his way home, halfway there, when the need to see her again had tugged inside of him so badly that it became an ache. He'd then made a U-turn and come here.

Jace was well aware of the brief amount of sleep they'd both gotten the night before and figured Shana needed her rest; that was fine. All he wanted to do was hold her in his arms for a while. "You were about to go to bed?"

"Yes."

"Come on, then, and let me tuck you in before I leave."

Shana quirked her eyebrows questioningly. "Tuck me in?"

"Yes, and then I'll leave."

This I got to see, Shana thought. No man had ever tucked her into bed without staying the night. "Okay."

He took her hand, and she thought he would walk her up the stairs. She gasped when he swept her off her feet and into his arms. "I can walk, Jace," she said, looking up at him.

"Why do so when you don't have to?" was his reply.

He took the stairs with ease while holding her, and Shana felt cuddled firmly in his strong arms. When they reached the bedroom, he set her down beside the bed. He then began removing his jacket. After placing it across the wingback chair in her room, he pushed back the bedcovers and then glanced over at her. "In."

Like a dutiful child, she moved to crawl between the covers, and then he kicked off his shoes and joined her on the bed, stretching out his legs. "I want to hold you until you doze off to sleep."

She nodded and, filled with an emotion she tried and failed to push back, she eased toward him, and he held her in his arms with her head pressed against his chest. She could inhale his masculine scent and could hear the steady beat of his heart. For some reason, she was comforted by the sound. His arms were wrapped around her, and she thought that she could lie in his arms like this forever.

She glanced up at him, parted her lips to say something…what, she wasn't sure…and instead she tipped her mouth up for a kiss she desperately wanted. He lowered his head and complied.

The stroke of his tongue against hers was soothing, passionate, and her body responded by stretching upward for more. And he delivered, deepening the kiss, intensifying those strokes, and she heard herself moaning out her pleasure.

He broke off the kiss, and his breath seared across her parted lips when he whispered, "Don't tempt me, Shana. Go to sleep."

Drawing in a deep, satisfying breath with the taste of him still embedded on her tongue, she settled back down in bed and he wrapped his arms around her again. Held against him moments later, she heard it…a steady hum…and realized what he was doing. Not only was he holding her, but he was humming her to sleep, as well. She recognized the tune, *Twinkle, Twinkle, Little Star.* She smiled as she closed her eyes, and that was the last thing she remembered.

Jace stopped humming and glanced down when he heard the steadiness of Shana's breathing. She had fallen asleep. A part of him had felt guilty most of the day knowing he had robbed her of sleep Sunday night. Hopefully, this would make up for it.

Carefully, he eased away from her and smiled when she whispered his name in her sleep. He couldn't resist leaning over and placing a tender kiss on her lips. Then, covering her up completely, he moved away from the bed, slid back into his shoes and put on his jacket again. He glanced back over at her one final time before turning out the lights and quietly moving downstairs.

A part of him knew he should not have come here, but then another part knew he had no other choice. Shana had gotten under his skin from day one, and although he'd tried, there was no eradicating her. This affair they'd agreed to would eventually run its course. This fierce attraction and desire would one day be a thing of the past. They were merely enjoying each other for now. It was about sex and nothing more.

If all those things were true, then why did he feel possessiveness toward her that he hadn't felt for a woman in a long time? He'd felt possessive toward Eve, but then he'd had every right to do so since she was his wife. But no other woman had stirred such need for exclusivity and selfishness where she was concerned.

He recalled the first time he'd met Bruce, that first

day the man had come to install her computer. Jealousy had eaten at Jace as he observed the man's easy and carefree relationship with Shana. It was a relationship he didn't have with her and couldn't have with her. Now things were different. He had the relationship he wanted, so why wasn't it enough?

He armed her security system and quickly opened the door, locking it behind him. As he walked to his car, he couldn't help but recall how good it felt holding her while she dozed off to sleep. He'd liked the feel of her in his arms, experiencing something apart from deep intimacy...although he damn well liked doing that.

Being inside her body was like a high he'd never felt before. He didn't just feel passion, he felt feverish passion. He was discovering there was a difference between the two. And whenever he thrust in and out of her, a need that bordered on madness would take over him, driving him to satisfy a greed that controlled everything within him at that particular moment.

Moments later, he was back on the interstate again and headed toward home. Damn, but he missed her already and had to talk himself out of making yet another U-turn and going back. She needed her rest, and he needed his. Besides, if he slept away from home two nights in a row, Hannah would start thinking things. It was Hannah's ardent desire that one of them finally settle down and fill Sutton Hills with the patter of little feet.

Hannah had never liked Eve; she thought Eve was too selfish for her own good and, like Jace's grandfather, felt he could do better. Now he was convinced he could, as well. So why did his thoughts automatically come back to Shana?

Hell, other than being off the charts in bed, what did he know about her? He knew she had a father and a sister and that she got along great with her staff, some of whom he had met. He knew where she lived and that she liked her hamburgers well-done and was in love with strawberry shakes.

But there was more, and a part of him wanted to know all there was. He released a deep sigh, satisfied with his goal of finding out. For the moment, he wouldn't question why he felt the need; he would just accept that he did.

Dalton walked into his condo while stripping off his tie. Tonight had been fun and the woman enjoyable. She was disappointed they had gone to her place instead of his. But she soon got over it. She'd wanted him to stay the night, and he'd turned her down. A one-night stand was just that, a one-night stand. There was no need to get greedy.

He headed for his bedroom to take a shower. Then he would call Victoria. He hadn't talked to her but twice since he'd been here. She was involved with Wimbledon, and he knew how hectic her schedule was these days. And he'd seen her several times in the paper being escorted to and from events by Sir Isaac Muldrow.

Dalton had met the man and thought he was nice enough, but probably a little too old for Victoria's taste. But he thought Muldrow was just the man Victoria needed. He was as rich as she was, and he was well-respected in European circles.

A short while later, after taking his shower and slipping into a pair of briefs—which was the only thing
he wore to bed—he lay back against the pillows and
placed a call to Victoria.

He liked his condo and liked Holly, the cute young
woman who'd come to decorate the place, even better.
Holly was playing hard to get, but get her he would
eventually. He'd missed a call from her tonight, which
meant she was softening. He would make it a point to
return her call tomorrow.

"Hello?"

Victoria sounded wide-awake, which made him remember the time difference. It was daytime in England
and Tuesday already. "Miss me?"

"Dalton! Glad to hear your voice. I was beginning
to think you'd forgotten about me."

"Never. How are things going? I see Wimbledon
went off without a hitch."

"Yes, and I'm so glad about it. We're still recover-
ing from all the work we did during last year's Olym-
pics. So tell me, how are things going with your being
a corporate executive? Is it simply boring, darling?"

He had to admit it wasn't as bad as he thought it
would be, but then there was nothing better than making money doing nothing, which is what he'd done
for the past year. "It's okay, not as bad as I thought it
would be. I'm learning a lot. Staying busy."

"But not too busy to keep your hands off the
women?" she asked, laughing.

"I'll never be too busy for that." That's what he liked
about his relationship with Victoria. She knew him
like he knew her. They enjoyed each other in bed, but

they were also friends. There was no possessiveness, jealousy or control. It was what it was.

They talked for a little while longer, and he was determined not to bring up her ex if she didn't. She didn't, so he hoped she was still getting over the bastard. "I thought about taking a trip to the States to see you. I haven't been to America in years."

He smiled. "Then come. I'd love to see you."

She chuckled. "But your brothers might not. I believe they think I'm a bad influence or something."

"Who gives a crap what they think? We're friends and nothing more. Friends with benefits."

"Yes, but maybe it's time for you to look for more with another woman. I've been thinking about that." She paused a moment and then said, "I've been seeing a lot of Sir Isaac."

"I know."

"You do?" she asked, sounding surprised. "How?"

"We get the papers here, Victoria, and I'm also interested in what's happening over there. I take it that you like him."

"Yes. He reminds me of an older you."

He smiled. "An older me isn't so bad, is it?"

"No. I like him, Dalton."

"And if he's smart, he would like you, as well."

He didn't have to see the smile he knew had touched her lips. "Father said the same thing."

"Stuart and I think alike. I consider that a compliment."

She didn't say anything for a moment and then said, "I have decisions to make, Dalton. If I decide to marry Muldrow, that means ending things between us. Muldrow wouldn't want me to retain our close friendship."

In other words, Dalton thought, the man wouldn't want Dalton fucking his wife. "I can't blame him. We will always be friends, you know that. Just not bed pals. I can handle that. Can you?"

"Not sure at the moment, Dalton. You're more than my bed pal. You've become my security blanket. You make me have confidence in myself."

He tightened his hand on the phone, hearing the lack of self-assurance in her voice. "You will always have my support like I know I'll always have yours, Victoria. You are a beautiful woman who deserves a man like Muldrow. He will make you happy."

"I truly believe that he will. But there's a lot to think about. I'll let you know what I decide."

"All right."

"Okay, I have to run. Good night, Dalton."

He smiled. "And a very good day to you, my lady."

As he hung up the phone, he had a feeling she wouldn't be "his" lady too much longer.

Chapter Twenty-Four

"Hmm," Jace agreed, licking his lips. "Now, this is a great sandwich. I didn't know there was a sandwich shop around here." He had walked into his brother's office during the lunch hour to find Dalton sitting at his desk with a spread in front of him. Dalton had invited him to pull up a chair and offered him half his sandwich. It was simply delicious.

"There's not a sandwich shop around here," Dalton said, wiping his mouth and then grabbing a bag of chips.

Jace lifted a brow. "Then where did you get all this?"

"From Hannah."

Jace stared at his brother for a long moment and then he asked, "You have Hannah preparing your lunch?"

"She offered."

"Yeah, I bet," Jace said, rolling his eyes.

"Honest. I called to thank her for the leftovers that I brought in yesterday, and she offered to prepare lunch for me this week. I didn't want to hurt her feelings by declining."

"Sure. Turning her down would have killed you."

Dalton smiled over at his brother. "You're jealous. Admit it, you're jealous."

Jace frowned. "I'm not jealous."

"Yes, you are. You were the firstborn, and Hannah just doted on you right and left. You were her favorite. Now you're sharing the spot, and that's eating at you," Dalton accused.

"It's not!"

"You're a liar. It is."

"Boys. Boys. Do I have to take a strap to you guys? I can't leave you alone for a week before you're acting like uncivilized heathens."

Dalton and Jace jerked their heads around to find Caden leaning lazily in the doorway. Jace was out of his chair, and Dalton followed suit. "What are you doing here? We weren't looking for you to get back until next week."

"I know," Caden said, smiling and taking a good look at his brothers to see if there were any scars he needed to check out. "But I had a couple of free days and decided I was tired of living out of a hotel room."

"Why bitch about it now when you've been doing it for years?" Dalton countered.

Instead of answering, Caden glanced over at Jace. "Hold me back before I smash his face in."

"Stand in line. Wait your turn," Jace said, fighting back a smile. "You want to smash his face, and I prefer kicking his ass."

"Need I remind the both of you that I'm younger

and more physically fit?" Dalton asked. "If anyone is about to get whipped, it's not going to be me."

Caden chuckled. "I choose to differ. I suggest we go to the place on the corner, have a few drinks and the both of you can bring me up to date on what's going on."

"Sounds like a good plan to me," Dalton said, moving to grab his jacket.

"Same here," Jace said, about to leave Dalton's office to go to his own to grab his jacket.

"Oh, and I forgot to correct you guys on something," Caden said.

"What?" Dalton asked as he paused, straightening his tie.

Caden smiled and then said, "Neither of you is Hannah's favorite, because I am. Always have been and always will be."

"Working late tonight, I see."

Shana's heart skipped at the sound of the deep, throaty voice. She glanced to her side and saw Jace standing in the doorway that connected her office to his. She'd noticed the door a number of times and used to get distracted wondering what he was doing on the other side of it. Until now, neither had opened it.

She had seen him earlier today in a departmental meeting, and she had sat across a table from him trying not to remember how he'd held her in his arms the night before and hummed her to sleep. But every time he would glance over at her, she could actually feel the heat from his eyes.

"But not for too much longer. I thought you had left for today."

"Caden flew home for a couple of days, and Dalton and I left to spend time with him at McQueen's. They decided to leave there and go play a game of tennis to prove who is the fittest."

She leaned back in her chair. "And you decided to come back here?"

"Yes, I decided to come back here. Told them I'd hook up with them later." He came inside her office and closed the connecting door behind him. "What are you reading?"

"The last report I gave you. Marcel just called. He didn't provide any details but wants to meet with us Monday, around eleven. Will you be available then? And I think he wants to include your brothers in this meeting." Even from across the room, the whiff of his cologne had the ability to stir her.

Jace nodded. "Shouldn't be a problem. Caden will be leaving day after tomorrow, but he'll be back Sunday night, and I'll make sure Dalton is here."

He paused by her side and said in a low, husky tone, "I hope you slept well last night."

She couldn't help smiling up at him. "I did, and I have you to thank."

He nodded as he held her gaze and then said in an even lower voice, "You can thank me by going away with me this weekend."

She lifted a brow. "Away?"

"Yes. I know a place a few hours away from here. I'm going there this weekend and would love for you to come with me."

She paused a moment and then asked, "It's not the beach, is it?"

"No, it's a cabin in the mountains near Shenandoah. Why?"

"My father is taking a friend to the beach, and I wouldn't want to run into them."

"You won't. We'll leave early Saturday morning and return late Sunday afternoon. So will you go with me?"

Shana didn't say anything for a minute, and as she held his gaze, she was exposed to all the desire she saw there. And it was desire she couldn't combat, because she knew it was a mirror of her own. There was no sense denying it or denying the pleasure she knew would await her this weekend if she went with him. "Yes, I'll go away with you this weekend."

Caden looked up at the sky. It was a beautiful June night, and he was glad to be home, even if it was for only a few days. He had needed to split from his band for a while. Rena had gotten into a near altercation with a fan, and it could have gotten ugly if he and Roscoe hadn't been there to intervene. He had warned her for the last time, and it was time to make changes. He had already advised Grover, the group's manager, that after this week, they needed to start looking for another guitarist.

"I wondered where you'd gone."

He glanced around when Jace stepped out onto the porch. "Yes, I thought I'd breathe in Virginia's air while I could."

Jace came to stand beside his brother. "It's a beautiful night."

"Yes, it is, and it reminds me of why I've always loved Sutton Hills. It has the mountains, lakes, streams and plenty of land. I think it's the most beautiful place on earth. But things were never the same after Mom died. And although Granddad did the best he could, he could never replace Dad. Someone turned our world upside down, Jace, and after fifteen years, they are still walking around free, while Dad is sitting in jail paying time for a crime he didn't commit. And I don't understand why he doesn't want us to hire a private investigator to help set him free. Who is he protecting?"

Jace sighed deeply, grateful that he wasn't the only one left with the feeling that their father was protecting someone. During their visit with him a few weeks back, the subject had come up of their grandfather's other deathbed request. To prove their father's innocence. Shep had been adamant about not reopening the case. Why?

Evidently feeling the need to change the subject, Caden then asked, "So what's going on with you and wonder-woman?"

Jace jerked his head around and met Caden's stare. "You can't believe everything Dalton tells you."

Caden chuckled as he leaned against a post. "That's just it. Dalton isn't telling me anything. Any other time, he's known to have loose lips, but he's keeping them sealed for some reason."

About time, Jace thought. "If Dalton didn't mention anything, why are you asking?"

"Because I'm not as dumb as you evidently think

I am. Remember that incident with you beating on that vending machine while taking out all your sexual frustration? Trust me, I know the feeling, and I know who's the reason."

"Do you?"

"Yes."

"What if I said you're wrong?"

Caden smiled easily. "You have the prerogative to tell me anything you want. And I have that same prerogative to take what you say with a grain of salt if I choose to do so."

"Then I plead the fifth."

Caden threw his head back and laughed. It felt good to be home.

"And you're really going out of town with him?"

Shana glanced over at Jules, who'd arrived in town that day. Shana was glad to see her sister, and after catching her up on what was going on with their father, she proceeded to come clean and let her in on what was going on with her, as well. By nature, Jules was curious, which was why she was perfect for what she did. She also had the ability to read a person like a book and knew immediately when someone was lying about something or trying to be evasive. That was one of the reasons Shana had decided not to waste her time doing either.

"Yes."

For the next few seconds, Jules just stared at her. Finally, Shana had enough and asked what her problem was. Jules's entire face spread into a smile when she said, "You like being in control. I've never known

you to relinquish that control to a man." She saw Shana
about to refute what she'd said, so she threw up her
hand to stop her.

"No, Shana. Listen to what I'm saying for a second
before you get all pissed and flustered. Sometimes letting go of control is a good thing, as long as the man
is worthy. Evidently, you think Jace Granger is. I wish
I could find a man I thought was so worthy."

"It's purely a physical thing, Jules."

Her sister chuckled. "Hey, I'd take that, too. Like
I said, the man would have to be worthy on all ac-
counts."

Shana sipped her tea as she thought about what her
sister had said. Was Jace worthy? She knew the answer
without thinking too hard about the question. Yes, he
was. If she'd had any doubt, it was removed from her
mind the night he held her in his arms and hummed
her to sleep after settling on a kiss and nothing more.
Any other man would have had her blindfolded and
handcuffed to the bed for a night of fun without caring how exhausted she was. But not Jace.

"You know this is a bummer, don't you?" Jules
asked.

"What?"

"My first weekend back and both you and Dad are
deserting me."

Shana gave her sister a pity look. "If you're trying
to make me feel bad, don't waste your time. If the shoe
was on the other foot—"

"I'd wear it proudly, keep stepping high and not
give you a backward glance."

"I figured as much." Shana chuckled. She loved her

sister and would do anything for her, and she knew it was the same for Jules. When their mother died, all they had was each other…and their dad. He had been their rock, their tower of strength. Their hero.

"Speaking of shoes, you know what I think I'm going to do this weekend, Shana?"

"I'm almost afraid to ask."

Jules gave her that mischievous grin that had gotten them in trouble more than once during their lifetimes. "Pull out my favorite pair of stilettos, find my shortest dress and go barhopping."

"Will you be looking for anyone in particular?" Shana asked.

"Yes, it's a new case I'm working on. Some low-life who's turning one-night stands into movie night on the internet."

"You're kidding!"

"Wish I was. He uses a different alias with each woman and takes them to a different hotel each time. Unfortunately, they aren't aware the entire thing is being filmed until the DVD shows up somewhere and they are recognized."

"What an asshole," Shana said angrily.

"Yes, those are my feelings. Four women joined forces to become my clients after the police claimed lack of manpower due to budget cuts as the reason they haven't brought him in. He's known to hang out at different bars looking for his next easy conquest. I got a good description of him. He's drop-dead gorgeous and uses his looks to get women to drop their panties and their guard."

"Sounds interesting. I hope you catch him, and please take care of yourself."

Jules gave Shana a cheeky grin. "Don't I always?"

Chapter Twenty-Five

"I want to see through your eyes, Ben. Tell me what you see."

Ben glanced across the blanket at Mona. They had arrived at the beach around ten, early enough to claim a section of the beach before the lunchtime crowd arrived. The spot was perfect and shaded by the shadows of endless hotels, restaurants and cafés spread out along the oceanfront.

He reached out and captured her hand in his. "It will be my pleasure." For the next ten minutes, he spoke, letting her see through his eyes. He saw how her smile widened when he told her about the teens playing volleyball in the sand not far away, about the colorful Jet Skis and the beautiful clouds overhead.

"And last but not least," he said, tightening his hand on hers, "I see this beautiful woman who is wearing a beautiful yellow sundress that goes perfectly with her golden-brown eyes. Then there's her hair that frames such a gorgeous face that can light up my whole world with her smile. And a pair of lips that I've been tempted to taste from the first, because she has to be the most beautiful woman I know."

"Oh, Ben," Mona said, wiping at the tears forming in her eyes. "You shouldn't say such things," she whispered brokenly.

"I should, and I will, Mona, because I plan to pursue you the way a man pursues a woman he wants in his life." And he wanted her in his life. He felt he'd gotten to know her over the past months. He had watched her when she hadn't known he'd been doing so. He'd talked to her, held pleasant conversations with her. He admired her.

He loved her.

"But you don't know me, and what you do know is what you can see. You're a wonderful man who needs a woman—"

"Like you," he finished. "Like you," he repeated. He leaned over and kissed her trembling lips.

"I want my eyesight back, Ben. I don't want you to be a blur in my eyes. I want to see the man who's cared enough to reach out and accept me as I am. I want to see the man who has made me feel special."

"You are special, and you will see again, sweetheart. I believe you will. Those flashes of light are something positive. Your doctor's appointment this week confirmed that. But if you don't ever see again, then that's okay, too, because I'll be here regardless. I'll be by your side. Always."

Ben knew what he was saying, the commitment he was pledging, and meant each and every word. He was getting used to telling Mona to watch her step, used to telling her where things were and being her eyes.

He felt it wasn't an inconvenience but an honor. Not a burden but a privilege.

"You ready to take a walk on the beach?" he asked, pushing tendrils of hair back from her face.

"Yes."

He reached down and unhooked her sandals, brushing his hands against her ankles. He heard her sharp intake of breath. He smiled. Sight wasn't needed when it came to chemistry between two people. Especially when that chemistry was fueled by feelings and emotions.

Ben helped her up and tenderly continued holding her hand as they began walking underneath the brightness of the sun. It was a beautiful day, and they would enjoy it.

"Look around. Make yourself at home."

Gripping her overnight bag in her hand, Shana stepped into the living room and glanced around. She wasn't sure what she would find after traveling several miles past the entrance to Shenandoah National Park and then driving another hour through miles and miles of wilderness as they made their way up the Blue Ridge Mountains. According to Jace, he'd called ahead to tell the caretaker he would be arriving and to have the cabin ready.

As Shana glanced around, her thoughts, the same ones she'd had when they'd pulled up to the cabin, were confirmed. This was not the cabin she thought she would find. Instead, it looked more like a beautiful château in the mountains. It had two stories with the second floor overlooking the first. The walls were made of stained wood and the downstairs was spacious, with an open concept. The kitchen belonged to someone who loved to cook and the dining area to someone with a big family. The living room was enormous, with a huge fireplace on one solid wall and a wide-screen television on the other. Rugs scattered about on the floor gave the place a lived-in look, while the silk plants that looked almost real added foliage that wasn't grown in this area. The greenery enhanced the inside scenery to complement the outside. What she liked most was that the entire back wall was made of glass and provided a panoramic view of Streater Lake and the rest of the Blue Ridge Mountains.

"So what do you think?" Jace asked, joining her after closing the door behind him with the heel of his boot. His arms were full of grocery bags. They'd made a stop at one of the general stores at the foot of the mountain. He claimed he could cook, and she was dying to see if he was telling the truth. She had no problem admitting that cooking wasn't her specialty.

"I think it's beautiful. How long have you had it?" she asked, setting her bag on the sofa.

She tried not to notice how sexy he looked in a T-shirt, scruffy jeans and battered boots. He'd arrived at her place bright and early at seven, and when she'd opened the door, her heart had gone pitter-pat. He'd been smiling, and as soon as he'd stepped inside her house, he had pulled her into his arms and kissed her. If she hadn't been wide-awake before, that kiss had definitely done it.

"I've had it for a couple of years now. My family owned one about four miles east of here," he said, moving toward the kitchen. "After Mom died and Dad was sent away, no one wanted to come here, so Grand-dad sold it."

He placed the bags on the counter. "Dad used to take us camping a lot, and I've always liked being close to nature. I heard about this place going up for sale and grabbed it. This is only my third time coming here."

She joined him in the kitchen, and without asking if he needed help, she assisted in going through the bags and putting items away. Although the kitchen was large, it seemed they would occasionally bump into each other, making the simmering sparks inside of her flare even more.

It had felt odd pushing a grocery cart around in the store while he filled it. It had felt as if they were a married couple. He had teased her about her lack of knowledge when it came to spices and couldn't believe the one time she had cooked spaghetti, the sauce hadn't been homemade.

They put away the items quickly, and then he gave her a tour of the place. She saw the bedroom where they would spend the night and thought the view of the lake and mountains was spectacular. The bed faced a huge window, and she could imagine waking up to see the sun rise each morning.

"You want to take a walk?" Jace asked when they walked back down the stairs to the living room. "I'd like to show you a favorite place of mine."

"All right."

Taking her hand, he led her out the back door and down a wooded path. "This is what sold me on this place," he said, opening a wrought iron gate and then leading her through thick foliage. They hadn't gone far before they reached a clearing and glanced down at the meadow below. It was simply breathtaking. Covered in all kinds of wildflowers, and in the center of it all was a huge geyser with water gushing upward toward the sky.

"It's not a part of my property, but as long as I can view it from here whenever I want, I feel that it is. I've even built this bench," he said, easing down on it.

Shana wondered what thoughts had plagued him so much that he needed this place, a place of peace and solitude, to escape to. He'd had a lot of unhappiness in his life. It had to have been hard going through what he and his brothers had. He hadn't just lost one parent; in a way, he'd lost two.

She joined him on the bench, and for a minute, neither said anything as they looked down at the meadow below. She'd never been one who liked the outdoors but had to admit that this was something she could get used to. Grassy green slopes covered in wildflowers of every color in the rainbow. She couldn't imagine anyone not being able to see such beauty, and her thoughts shifted to Mona.

"What was that deep sigh about?"

Shana glanced over at Jace. She hadn't been aware she'd made it. "I was thinking about Mona, the woman my father has fallen in love with." There. She'd said it, and in saying it, she was basically accepting it. The verdict was still out for Jules, but Shana was convinced. She had seen their father on Monday and saw the way his face lit up whenever he mentioned Mona's name. Yes, Ben Bradford was definitely in love.

"What about her?"

"She's blind as a result of an auto accident a few years ago. The doctors think her sight might come back, but there aren't any guarantees. But it wouldn't matter to Dad one way or the other. He loves her and will take her with sight or blind. Now, that's true love."

"True love," he scoffed. "Is there such a thing?"

Evidently, you don't think so, Shana surmised. "My father believes there is. Says he's been in love twice in his life. With Mom and now Mona."

"What about you? Have you ever been in love?"

She was surprised by his question and immediately thought of Jonathan. "Yes, at one time I thought I was in love."

He lifted a brow. "Thought?"

"Yes. I was intentionally swept off my feet, treated like a queen and led to believe I was the woman of his dreams," she said bitterly.

He'd hung on her every word. "And?"

"And…it was a deliberate setup, and I was too taken with him to know it. I didn't read the signs until it was almost too late."

He didn't say anything, and when she felt his arms circle around her, she moved closer into his embrace. "What happened?" he asked softly.

She started to say she didn't want to talk about it, that he didn't need to know what a fool she'd been. But Jace had of way of getting to her at every angle. He was the perfect lover, and when it came to caring for others, he could be the most unselfish person she'd met in a long time. She watched him with his brothers and his employees. She'd heard how he spoke lovingly of his grandfather and the housekeeper who had been in his family since before he was born. But still, her past personal life was none of his business. On the other hand, maybe she should tell him so he'd know that she would never be any man's fool again. But then she was susceptible to falling in love and truly believed she was close to the mark with him. Now, that was something he would never know.

"Jonathan and I met at a party and were immediately taken with each other. Not so much on a physical level as it was on an intellectual level. He engaged me in a conversation about Aristotle, and I was a goner."

At his questioning look, she explained, "I'm a fan of Greek mythology and philosophy. We dated for about nine months, and then I found out the truth. It was a setup, and I was part of this well-orchestrated, diabolical plan. One of my clients was an oil tycoon and had me on retainer for a year. Jonathan's job was to get close to me and obtain information to feed to his client, who happened to be my client's biggest competitor."

"How did you find out?"

She could hear the anger in his voice. "I didn't. Kent did, and Bruce came to me with the proof. Jonathan's intent was to have evidence to use against me in case I found out what he was doing and broke things off. Then he would resort to blackmail. Lucky for me, Bruce wiped out every piece of electronic data Jonathan thought he had on me as well as my client."

"Good for Bruce. Where is the asshole now?"

"Don't know. He moved away from Boston months before I did. My involvement with him was a valuable lesson only to take affairs at face value."

She didn't say anything else for a minute, and then it was her time to be inquisitive. "You were married once, so I assume you've been in love."

Yes, she could assume that, Jace thought. But it hadn't taken long to realize his marriage to Eve had been a mistake. However, he was a man who knew how to deal with whatever hand he was dealt, and with Eve, God knows he tried. But as far as he was concerned, Eve had betrayed him in the worst possible way, and he doubted he could ever forgive her for it.

But there was no way he could tell Shana that he'd never been in love because for a short while he had… or at least he'd thought so. "Yes, I've been in love."

"What happened?"

He knew she had every right to ask him that. After all, he'd dug into her business by asking her. Besides, he could wrap up what happened with him and Eve in one sentence. "I discovered love wasn't all it was cracked up to be, and therefore, I won't ever indulge in such madness again."

There. They understood each other, he thought. He understood what drove her, and she now knew what didn't drive him. Their affair was about the physical and nothing else.

"Ready to go back?" he asked, tightening his arms around her.

She lifted her face toward him. "Not if you're going to make me help you in the kitchen."

"You really don't like handling pots and pans?"

She chuckled. "Not unless I'm forced to. Jules likes to cook, and while we were growing up, I let her knock herself out."

He gently brushed his knuckles against her cheek. "One favor deserves another. If I give you a pass, it's only because I want you well rested for later."

Shana knew exactly what he was talking about. She turned around and wrapped her arms around his neck, leaned up and placed a kiss on his lips. "That's a deal."

* * *

"Dinner was wonderful, Jace," Shana said later that evening as she helped him clear off the table.

And it hadn't been just the meal he'd prepared without any assistance from her. Over dinner, he was a wonderful conversationalist. Charming. At times amusing. And at others tempting as sin. He looked like he needed a shave, and he wore the scruffy look well. Too well, since it added to his sexiness.

When she began helping him load the dishes in the sink, he placed his hand on hers. "I got this. Why don't you go upstairs and run our bathwater?" he suggested.

"Our bathwater?" she asked, raising a brow.

He leaned down and kissed the tip of her nose. "Yes, our bathwater. I'll be up when I finish in here."

She fought back a smile at the same time as she narrowed her gaze at him. "Surely you're not going to hold me to that silly deal we made earlier today."

He chuckled. "On the contrary. I can clearly recall that while I was doing all the cooking, you were in the living room with your feet propped up on the sofa, reading some book on your iPad."

She couldn't deny what he said was true, so she chuckled and headed toward the stairs.

"Shana?"

She turned around. "Yes?"

The smile in his eyes lit a sensuous flame within her. "I'm glad you enjoyed dinner."

She drew in a deep breath, nodded and all but rushed up the stairs.

Jace walked into his bedroom and stopped short. The room was dark, and kerosene lanterns were lit and placed in several spots around the room. He kept the lanterns in case there was ever a loss of power. But it seemed Shana had decided to use them for something else, and he had to admit they bathed the room in a soft, luminous glow.

"Your bath awaits you, Jace."

He blinked. Shana materialized from heaven knows where, and what really had him mesmerized was that she was stark naked. She had a beautiful body, and automatically his gaze roamed all over her, taking in every inch of her. There was such a profound femininity about her that it had his gut churning.

"Jace?"

He swallowed. "Yes?"

"Come on," she said, taking his hand and pulling him toward the bathroom.

After pulling himself together, thoughts of all the possibilities with the naked woman leading him made his manhood throb, and he went willingly. There was no doubt in his mind that she would keep her end of the deal. And he couldn't wait.

Stepping into the bathroom, he saw the bathtub was full of bubbly water and the scent of jasmine filled the air. "Now for your clothes." She leaned up to whisper close to his ear. Doing so made a breast brush against his arm, and he fought back a moan.

For the next few minutes, he stood there, smiling like a ninny, while she stripped him of his clothing. The only time he assisted was when she had a difficult time easing his zipper down past his engorged erection.

In no time at all, he was standing there as naked as she was. When he extended his arm for her, she quickly moved out of his reach. "Not yet. Get in the tub, Jace."

He chuckled before easing his long legs over the edge of the huge, freestanding tub to settle his body comfortably in place in the warm, bubbly water. "You're going to join me, right?" he asked.

"Eventually. You fed me well today here, and I told you how much I enjoyed it. Now I want you to enjoy this," she said, crouching down on her knees beside the tub. "I'm about to give you a bath that you won't forget for a long time."

Jace watched how she slowly slid the washcloth through the warm water before gliding it across his skin. First she worked his chest, causing a tingling sensation in his nipples before moving over his shoulders.

Then she moved down his body, circling the cloth around his navel before moving toward his groin. That's when she replaced the cloth with her hands. He was more than conscious of every stroke of her fingers on him, her hand curling around his engorged penis, the same penis he planned on plunging deep inside her later.

He drew in a sharp breath when she began stroking him in a way he'd never been stroked before, and he stared into her eyes, saw the heated desire burning in them and knew the blaze was as hot as in his own. His body felt as if it was in turbulent ecstasy, and he fought back a moan. A tingling rush of pleasure moved from the soles of his feet all the way up to the top of his head.

And while she continued to prove the skills of her hands, she leaned in close and kissed his lips. He thought it would be a light brush of her lips across his, but when she parted her lips over his, she used her tongue to fuel more desire within him. He kissed her back with wanton barbarity that channeled a feverish rush, invading his body, as their tongues continued to duel.

Convinced he needed more, specifically the feel of wet flesh against wet flesh, he reached out and pulled her into the tub on top of him, not caring how much water splashed out of the tub in the process. She pulled back and stared at him in stunned disbelief. He merely shrugged a wet shoulder and smiled when he settled her between his thighs facing him.

"I wanted to bathe you," she said in a perturbed tone with a pout on her lips.

He leaned in and kissed those pouty lips, deepening the kiss, all with one deep plunge of his tongue. He enjoyed kissing her, figured he could make a field day of it and probably would have if she hadn't shifted and pressed her womanly core right smack against his hard erection. Immediately, he craved the feel of being planted deep inside of her.

Hot lust razzed his brain, and he lifted her hips at the perfect angle to ease through her heated flesh and become intimate with her. She moaned and threw her head back as he plunged forward, holding her hips steady to receive all of him. When he was convinced he was buried to the hilt, he placed a kiss on the smoothness of her neck and whispered, "Ride me, baby. I need you to ride me hard."

He didn't care that later he would be mopping the floor. All he cared about was the way she was making him feel as she lifted her hips off him to come towering back down again and began riding him the way she'd done in his dreams plenty of times. Even better, because this was the real thing. "That's it, baby. Take it all," he whispered brokenly.

And she was taking it. He could feel it in every part of his body. Her inner muscles were molding to his erection, generating more fire and heat each time she rode him hard. And he pushed her on by caressing the nipples of her breasts and trailing circular motions on her back.

Jace shifted his body slightly to capture the budded tips in his mouth while she continued to ride him hard. This was hot passion that was driving the lower part of his body to act as a spring with her movements.

Then he felt it, the slow stirring that starts in your bones before exploding to all parts of your body and ambushing your mind with breathtaking intensity. She was riding him. Boy, was she riding him. He felt every muscle in his body respond, and he instinctively lifted his hips to meet her downward plunge.

"Shana!"

Needing his mouth to be locked on hers, he went back for her lips, crushing down on hers and easing his tongue inside and stroking hers with wild abandonment and greed he felt in every pore.

And then she broke off the kiss to scream his name. The raw passion he heard in her voice was too much. Grabbing a fistful of her hair, he brought her mouth back down to him, and his tongue claimed hers once again as another orgasm rammed through him and his response almost toppled them over the tub.

It was a while before the kiss ended and he slowly stood and got out of the tub, helped her out and toweled them both dry. He then swept her off her feet into his arms. She curled her body close to his and licked his shoulder before lightly biting into his skin.

"Let's finish this in bed, shall we?" he asked.

She tightened her arms around his neck. "We'll finish this wherever you like."

Chapter Twenty-Six

It was nice when a man had the pick of any woman he wanted, Dalton thought, glancing around the night-club. Women of every shape, size and color. He was one who definitely believed that variety was the spice of life. Already, he'd been hit on more times tonight than he could count, yet he hadn't selected the woman whose bed he would spend time in tonight. It wasn't eleven o'clock yet, so he had plenty of time.

He couldn't help but be amused at how hard they were vying for his attention. Feminine heads had turned the minute he'd walked in wearing an expensive pair of linen trousers, a designer jacket and leather shoes. It never ceased to amaze him how far some women would go to pursue a man they thought had money. Knowing most of them were gold diggers didn't bother him. He knew how to handle them. He only parted with his money when he got good and ready to do so.

"Would you like another drink, Mr. Granger?"

He rolled his eyes. "Drop the Mr. Granger shit, Percy," he said to his waiter. "I'm Dalton, remember?"

Percy chuckled. "Yes, I remember. Just following the rules on how to address the customer."

"Then you're allowed to break them tonight while serving this table."

He and Percy Johnson had never been close friends while attending the same high school, but they had played on the same football teams since middle school. Percy had been a damn good quarterback in senior high school and had gotten a scholarship to attend South Carolina University. He surprised everyone and turned it down when his girlfriend got pregnant, doing the honorable thing by staying here and getting married.

This was the third time Dalton had come here, and each time, Percy had waited on his table. Dalton wondered if this was his full-time job or if it was a second gig. He decided to find out.

"You married Trina Morgan, right?" he asked, knowing he had.

"Yes, Trina and I married right out of high school. Still married. It's been almost ten years now with three kids."

Dalton nodded. "Congratulations. Not every couple lasts that long." He leaned back in his chair. "So, what's been going on? I moved back to town a month ago."

"I know. I read about you and your brothers in the paper. Sorry about your grandfather."

"Thanks. So is this your primary gig?"

"No, part-time. I work full-time at the Cullum Meat Plant as a forklift operator," Percy said, refilling Dalton's glass. "Been there since I got married. I got my college degree last year. Took me a few years, but I got it."

"Congratulations again," Dalton said, glad for Percy. "It could not have been easy doing so while raising a family."

"Thanks, and no, it wasn't easy. I figured with my degree that I would move up within my company, you know, move from working inside the plant to working inside behind a desk. My degree is in Computer Technology. I graduated top of my class, but so far, no such luck. I'm hoping to find something that pays enough to quit this job. Percy Jr. is at the age where he wants to play ball, and it's hard getting to his games when I have to work at night."

Dalton nodded. Suddenly, an idea came into his head. "How would you like working at Granger Aeronautics?"

Percy's eyes lit up. "Oh, boy, would I? I applied a couple of times and never got an interview."

"You just did," Dalton said, standing and fishing a business card out of his wallet. "Give this to the person in Human Resources and tell them to call me."

Percy's lips broke into a huge smile. "Thanks, Dalton. I don't know what to say."

"There's nothing to say. You said something to me one day years ago that I'll never forget. And to this day, I appreciate it."

Percy frowned, racking his brain to remember, so Dalton decided to help him out. "It was the day I returned to school after my father's trial ended."

Then as if a light went off in his head, Percy blinked. "Oh, that."

"Yes, that," Dalton said. "You didn't even know my dad, yet you acted as if you believed in his innocence when some of my closest friends who knew him didn't."

Percy shrugged. "I didn't know your dad personally. But I'd seen him once or twice after the game when he came to pick you up from practice. He always seemed like a cool dude, and I just couldn't imagine him doing what the law said he did."

Percy then looked down at the business card in his hand before staring back up at Dalton. "You don't know how much this means, man. It doesn't matter if I start off in maintenance. I bet the starting salary for a low-end position at Granger is double what I'm making working both jobs. Thanks, and I'll do a good job."

"I know you will."

He watched as Percy hurried off to serve another table, and something about what he'd just done made him feel good inside. His brothers and grandfather had been right. In life, everything had come easy for him, and he never thought about where it came from or the hard work someone had to do to get it.

Okay, he would admit he'd grown up selfish and spoiled. And he wouldn't change overnight about feeling entitled when it came to certain things. Like women, he thought, glancing around the room looking at the number of them looking his way, trying to decide when to make their move. He'd already turned a few down tonight, but it was getting late, and he needed to decide on one and soon.

He was about to take another sip of his drink when he glanced at the entrance. *Holy shit.* Just when he'd given up and figured he would have to settle, in walks a woman wearing a pair of stilettos on long gorgeous legs that went all the way under a dress that was way too short to be considered decent.

And he liked it.

When she paused in the doorway and glanced around, he bet the penis of every male in the place got hard. Lordy, she was hot. And when she began walking toward an empty table, his erection began throbbing like it was about to explode. She had that seductive walk in those shoes down to an art form. And he could just imagine getting some of that.

His lips curved into an I-want-you smile. This was the woman he was going home with tonight.

Jules settled in at the table feeling tired and frustrated. This was the third club she'd been to tonight and still no luck in finding Mr. Asshole. But she had run into a couple of his cousins, she thought, remembering the two men who'd tried coming on to her at the last club and wouldn't take no for an answer. She ended up kneeing both really hard in the balls before they understood she was not a woman to be manhandled. Now one of her knees felt sore, her feet hurt and she…

She looked up when a glass of wine was placed in front of her, and a man slid into the seat opposite her. She blinked. Okay, it wasn't Mr. Asshole Number

One, the man she had spent most of the night looking for, but she wondered if she'd run into another cousin.

"And what is this?" she asked, frowning down at the drink.

The man smiled at her, and she tried keeping her insides from quivering. He was definitely a cutie. "Your drink. I ordered it for you. You look thirsty."

"Do I?"

"Yes."

He had a pair of gorgeous eyes, light brown in color, and he smelled good. Just as good as he looked. If she didn't have another club to hit tonight, she would hang around and get to know him. But she had a job to do. Besides, he was kind of pushy, and she didn't like pushy men.

"Thanks for the drink, but no thanks. I order my own. Do I look stupid?"

Her question seemed to take him aback a little, but he quickly recovered. "No, you look highly intelligent."

"In that case, then you should know that an intelligent woman would never accept a drink from a stranger. For all I know, you could have loaded that drink with Ecstasy."

He chuckled. "I wouldn't do that."

"I don't know you well enough to agree," she said.

Dalton licked his lips, deciding he liked her. She had a mouth on her, but he could definitely put that mouth to other uses than talking. "Okay then, order your own drink."

"I will." She then got the attention of a waitress.

"Yes, may I help you?" the waitress asked.

Before Jules could open her mouth, the stranger cut in. "The lady doesn't want that drink. Give her another and put it on my tab."

Jules opened her mouth to tell the man she could pay for her own drink, but then she changed her mind. She had no problem with a man buying her a drink. She would enjoy it, and then she would leave to go to that next club. And she hoped Mr. Asshole was there.

She gave the waitress her order and glanced up to find the stranger staring at her. "So, what's your name?" he asked

Jules wished his voice didn't sound so sexy. "You don't need to know my name, and I don't need to know yours."

"Why would you think that?"

When the waitress set the drink in front of her, Jules took a sip and sighed deeply. She needed that. "Because I came here looking for a man."

A smile spread across Dalton's lips. "The last time I looked I had all the necessary parts."

Jules rolled her eyes. "A particular man," she clarified. "You aren't him, so I plan on enjoying this drink and then moving on."

"If your guy stood you up, then…"

"Then nothing. Look. Don't waste your time hitting on me. I'm not interested."

"You're not?"

"No."

Dalton's face split into a wide grin. Maybe he should be offended, but instead he was amused. This woman with the short, barely there dress and long, gorgeous legs had not only piqued his interest, she had all kinds of fantasies floating around in his head. Like the one of her naked, stretched out with him over her. He would pour the drink she was sipping over her body then proceed to lick it off her.

"Thanks for the drink. I needed it," she said, standing up.

He was snapped out of his sensuous reverie. "Where are you going?"

She gave him a pointed stare. "That's none of your business. Again, thanks for the drink." She then headed for the door.

"Wait!"

She turned back to him. "Yes?"

"What if I want to see you again?"

The smile that touched her lips was just as provocative as her shoes, dress and legs. "Find me." She turned around and strutted her cute, curvy ass out the door.

He sat there a moment, then threw his head back and laughed. *Find her?* Shit. Dalton Granger never ran behind any woman. Nor had he ever pursued one or hunted one down, and he wasn't about to start now. Suddenly, that fantasy he'd had earlier flashed through his mind, and his penis began throbbing again. He was out of his seat in a flash and walked quickly out the door. He glanced around the parking lot as a car drove off.

"Damn!" Had he been quick enough, he would have at least gotten her license plate number.

Find me.

He leaned against a column and frowned. He'd never been one to pursue a woman, but he had no problem pursuing a challenge. "Lady, I don't know who you are, but I will find you," he mumbled before turning and going back inside.

Chapter Twenty-Seven

"What do you have for us, Marcel?" Shana asked the man sitting across from her, with Jace and his brothers looking on.

The five of them were assembled in Jace's office. She'd spent a wonderful weekend with Jace, and now it was time to get to work. Back to finishing what she'd been hired to do.

Marcel was in his late fifties and had been an agent for over fifteen years. He'd been married for twenty years and was the father of triplets who would be entering college in the fall. Like Shana's father, Marcel had been a dedicated cop and was even more so as a federal agent. This wasn't the first case he'd become involved in because of her, and as long as people thought it was okay not to do the right thing, she knew it wouldn't be the last.

He leaned back in his chair. "I'm sure you noticed Ms. Swanson did not come in today."

Jace raised a brow. "Yes, Melissa isn't here, and according to Ms. Booker, she hasn't called in."

"And she won't be," Marcel said casually. "At six

this morning, federal agents knocked on the doors of two of your current employees and one former— Melissa Swanson, Cal Arrington and Titus Freeman. Swanson and Arrington were taken in for questioning, but Freeman's whereabouts are unknown at the moment. An alert is out for his arrest."

"Christ!" Dalton exclaimed, shaking his head. "I figured something in the milk wasn't clean with Freeman, and I'm not surprised at Arrington. He seemed like an annoying fart. But Melissa Swanson? She was so kind. Making sure I ate lunch and—"

"She was Freeman's lover," Marcel interrupted. "And has been for more than a year. He's the one who convinced your grandfather to promote her as his personal assistant. Of course, he had ulterior motives in doing so. She reported back to him whatever he wanted to know."

"And she admitted to that?" Jace asked quietly. Like Dalton, he'd liked the woman, thought she was efficient with not only how the executive offices ran but with always being solicitous of their needs, as well.

"Not to everything, but we had evidence she couldn't refute thanks to the work of my undercover agents and Shana's man Kent." He glanced over at Shana and smiled. "Kent's report was pretty thorough."

She smiled back. "Always is."

She glanced over at Jace. He was staring at her, and she saw the tightness in his jaw. Was he upset that she hadn't shared her suspicions about Melissa with him? Would he understand that she had made the decision not to say anything until she was certain?

"Just what has she admitted to?" Jace asked, switching his gaze from Shana to Marcel.

"Basically those two things about her and Freeman being lovers and his being responsible for her becoming Richard Granger's personal assistant. However, she swears she had nothing to do with bugging Shana's office."

He paused a minute and then said, "Arrington denied everything. Called his attorney, but since we'd obtained a search warrant, we had confiscated evidence before his attorney arrived."

"What sort of evidence?" Caden wanted to know.

"Various airplane designs that belong to this company. It seems he was selling those designs to Barnes Aerospace. We have a search warrant for their premises, as well, and the search is taking place as we speak."

"Where do you think Freeman is?" Shana asked.

"Not sure, but his photograph is out there in case he decides to leave town or the country."

Pushing away from his desk, Jace stood and walked over to the window and gazed out. Shana knew he was upset and rightly so. Those who'd been arrested were employees his grandfather had trusted.

He turned back to them, shaking his head. "I just don't get it. Freeman was bright, intelligent and excited about taking Granger to the next level. That's the main reason Granddad made him second-in-command. If my brothers and I hadn't decided to stay, he could have run the company whatever way he saw fit. He was CEO, and we would not have interfered."

"But that's just it," Marcel said somberly. "The three of you did decide to stay, which messed up his plans."

"And just what were his plans?" Caden asked.

"That under his leadership, Barnes would have initiated a merger, one he would have agreed to. According to Swanson, a deal had been made, a fellow's agreement, so to speak, between Freeman and the people over at Barnes months ago, before your grandfather's death. His job was to convince your grandfather to go along with it. In doing so, your grandfather might have become suspicious."

Jace sighed. He was almost certain Richard had.

"And it seems that he might have deliberately set the company up to fail so your grandfather had no choice," Marcel added. "That's where Arrington came in." He paused a second then said, "I know this is not good news to have to deal with on a Monday, or any other day for that matter."

"No, it's not," Jace agreed.

"And just so you know, there might be others involved, others willing to take cash under the table for the company's failure. We're trying to develop a paper trail. Swanson is telling all now, trying to paint herself as a woman taken advantage of. Right now, Arrington's refusing to say anything. We believe Freeman is the mastermind, but I can't guarantee we've gotten him and all his troops. Hopefully, someone will want to make a plea deal."

"So, in other words, until this case is completely solved, we have to continue not to trust anyone," Shana reiterated.

Dalton stood. "Shit. I need a drink. All this spy, knife-in-the-back stuff is too much for my blood," he said, heading for the door.

"It's early, but I think I'm going to have that drink with him," Caden said, following Dalton out the door.

Marcel stood and chuckled as he rubbed a tired hand down his face. "I think your brothers have the right idea with that drink, but some of us still have work to do, and I have a feeling this case is far from over."

He headed for the door. Before opening it, he turned and said to Shana and Jace, "I'll keep the two of you informed of anything I think you need to know." He then left.

Jace glanced over at Shana. "I need to call a meeting of my executives immediately to let everyone know what's going on before they get wind of it in the media."

Shana nodded. "There's something else you might want to do, as well."

At the lifting of his brow, she added, "Get prepared to hold a press conference."

Several hours later, Jace sat at his desk with his head thrown back. This had been one hell of a day. It was amazing the difference a few hours made. He had awakened that morning after such a wonderful weekend feeling on top of the world. Never had a day started off so right to end up so wrong.

He felt tired, drained. Although he'd felt the same way several times over the weekend, at least he could claim during those times the exhaustion had been pleasurable and enjoyable. This time, it was not. He had been on the job a little more than a month, and already he'd been thrown in the line of fire. He was glad both the meeting with his management staff and the press conference had gone well.

"Granddad, I hope you know what the hell you were doing by asking Caden, Dalton and me to make that promise," he muttered quietly to himself. Luckily, his brothers had returned from McQueen's in time to make appearances at both meetings. It felt good having them by his side.

And then there was Shana.

Although she hadn't interfered with what his public relations department was being paid to do, she had been there, on the sidelines, positioning herself where he could see her and know she was there to offer support.

He took a moment to close his eyes, needing just for a little while to go back in time. And he knew just what he wanted to revisit. This past weekend and the cabin in the mountains with Shana. Beginning with the bath they'd taken together…although they'd had sex in the tub more than they'd bathed.

And then, after drying them both off, he'd carried her to the bed. Then they had made love again, several times, before finally calling it a night and drifting off to sleep in each other's arms. More than once during the night, she would shift in sleep, awaken him. He would tighten his arms around her and draw her body more snugly against him.

Sunday morning, he had opened his eyes to find her already awake and staring over at him. He wasn't privy to what thoughts were going through her mind, but he knew what thoughts immediately began flowing through his.

He'd reached out and stroked his fingers through

her hair before raising his mouth to hers. Her lips parted sweetly, and he thrust his tongue between them, greedy for her taste. But that hadn't been enough.

Jace had left her mouth and began kissing her neck, lower still to her breasts, where he enjoyed a feast with her nipples, sucking wildly. And while she moaned and groaned through the sensations, his tongue tunneled lower still. Easing her legs apart and lifting her hips, he settled his mouth on her womanly core, reacquainting his tongue with her taste there. His mouth feasted on her sensitized flesh, nibbled on her clit and lapped her sweet nectar.

He had licked her into one orgasm and then another, certain that even today the taste of her lingered on his tongue. And when she had been on the brink of sexual delirium, pressed close to a third orgasm, she had begged him to take her. And he'd done just that.

He'd made love to her enough times to know she liked being taken hard, and he'd had no problem delivering. They eventually sexed themselves to sleep again, and by the time they'd awakened, it had been close to noon.

They'd had every intention of coming back to town before six but ended up barely making it back before midnight. He'd been tempted to spend the night but figured she needed her rest, what little she would get before her alarm awakened her at six. Besides, Caden was due back in town Sunday evening. Luckily for Jace, his brother had arrived and retired to bed by the time he'd gotten in. Just as well, as Jace was certain Shana's scent was all over him.

Jace opened his eyes. Remembering what had taken place this weekend between him and Shana sent heated lust flowing through him. Now was not the time and not the place to get a case of horniness. He'd messed up once about that and couldn't do so again.

But it was hard, knowing she was there, right next door. Dalton and Caden had left hours ago, and so had Brandy Booker. She seemed really taken aback, genuinely hurt and let down by Melissa's duplicity. She wasn't the only one.

Jace stood and stretched his body and then tried talking himself into sitting back down and couldn't. He glanced over at the connecting door, stared at it for a long moment. The next thing he knew, he was walking toward it.

Shana glanced up and saw Jace standing in the doorway where their offices connected and wondered how long he'd been standing there. She stared at him, saw the heat in his gaze. The desire.

"Working late again, I see," he said in a deep, husky timbre, breaking the silence between them and moving from the door to stand in front of her desk.

She gave him a slow once-over and thought, as she always did, that Jace Granger was good on the eyes. No matter what he put on his body, he wore it well. But then, although his shirt and pants looked nice, she also enjoyed seeing him wear nothing at all. Those were the times in bed that she would curl into the curve of his naked body while hearing his heartbeat throb against her ear.

"Yes," she said. "Thought I'd try my hand at putting together pieces of this puzzle since there still seem to be links missing." A small smile touched her voice. "Vidal was in the office and stopped by. He gave me a pep talk. By the time he left, he had me believing I'll have this thing figured out in no time."

"And you will."

She wasn't so sure. Marcel had called them earlier to report that Melissa had retained an attorney who advised her not to provide any additional information without a plea deal, and Cal Arrington still wasn't talking. Freeman remained nowhere to be found.

"You handled the media well during that press conference," she decided to say, wondering when he would make his move on her.

There was no doubt in her mind that he would. The sexual chemistry flowing between them was potent, stimulating and was filling the air with an electrical charge she could feel. The thought of him acting on the strong attraction between them didn't bother her like it once did. Mainly because she was tired of fooling herself about what she wanted. An affair with no future was probably not the best thing for her, but at the moment, when it came to Jace, it was all she wanted.

Now she was fooling herself again. She did want more but knew more was highly unlikely with him. He'd made that pretty clear this weekend. He was not a true love believer and a forever kind of guy. Then why had she allowed herself to fall in love with him? That was another admission she could make. If there was any doubt in her mind, it was eradicated yesterday when she'd arrived home from their weekend trip.

For her, it hadn't been just about sex. It had been about getting to know the man who'd captured her heart. They talked a lot about things that mattered to them. She'd told him about her mother and how her mother's death had affected her, and he'd opened up and told her about his mother's death and his father's subsequent trial. He went into how his so-called friends had deserted him and his brothers and how Dalton and his grandfather would occasionally butt heads because the two were so strong-willed. She had gotten to know Jace Granger the man and truly appreciated the person he was.

"Thanks. I think the press conference went pretty well myself." He gave her a tired smile, which still managed to send goose bumps trailing across her skin. "A few minutes ago, I was sitting in my office thinking about this weekend."

"Any particular part?" she asked, tightening her thighs together at any mention of this weekend. Need was radiating from the soft core of her body, causing sensations to flow between her legs.

"Yes, all of it."

A smile touched her lips. *Good answer.* But she was fishing for more. She wanted to hear him say it. Claim it. "So, there wasn't anything in particular that stood out more than the rest?"

She saw a glint of passion shroud his eyes. "Now that you mention it, there is something that stands out."

"What?"

"The sex."

She wanted him to break it down even further. "What about the sex?"

He stared at her. "It was great. Off the charts. Pretty damn remarkable. And..."

She held his gaze, lifted a brow. "And what?"

"And I want more. I want you. Now."

Jace knew he had a lot of nerve saying that to her. He knew her rules about an office affair and had agreed to avoid one, which is why they had decided on this secret affair in the first place—one that was in its third week. Yet here he was, in the office, horny as hell and asking for the one thing he knew better than to ask for. It wasn't her fault he desired her more than he had any woman, including his ex-wife, or that his penis was throbbing mercilessly. With him standing in front of her desk, she might be a witness to it.

He opened his mouth to apologize, to ask her to forget what he said, when she surprised him by saying, "I want you, too. Now. But not on the desk again. That day Bruce did a security scan of your father's office, I noticed a sitting room with a sofa. Let's use that."

Surprise lit his gaze, and he wondered why she would be so accommodating, but decided not to question his good fortune. A smooth smile overtook his features and he said in a throaty voice, "Come with me, baby."

She stood, came around her desk. He took her hand in his, and together they crossed the room to the door that connected her office to his father's.

He unlocked it, and they went inside and locked it behind them.

Chapter Twenty-Eight

"Mercy," Jace muttered before closing his eyes and placing a hand over his face, convinced he would never move again. Never had making love to a woman been so damn draining. His blood was pounding like he was about to take his last breath. He was convinced there was no way he wasn't paralyzed from the penis up. No man in his right mind stayed hard this long. There had to be a law against this much intimacy with a woman. If there was, they might as well handcuff him, put him in shackles, toss him in jail and throw away the key. He was guilty as sin.

And speaking of sin…

He dropped his hand, opened his eyes and looked down. Shana was beneath him, passed out with her limbs entwined with his, and in a position where the tip of one dark nipple pressed against his cheek. Tempted to go another round and giving in to it, he slightly moved his head, opened his mouth and sucked the delicious morsel between his lips at the same time his hand lowered to gently caress her stomach.

He heard that first moan moments later, which was

followed by a close second. Then instinctively, she arched her body at just the right angle so he could slide inside of her, while inwardly calling himself one greedy ass. When he'd gone deep, he didn't move, he just wanted to lie there a second to savor the feel of being skin-to-skin, flesh-to-flesh with her again.

But she wasn't having any of that. She slowly opened her eyes and reached out, grabbed his head and pulled his mouth away from her breasts to her mouth, sliding her tongue between his already-wet lips. And then she proceeded to kiss him in a way that had him moving, had him pumping, thrusting and taking her hard.

She wrapped her legs around him tight, locked him inside her, where he had no choice but to go in and out. And he did, whipping moans repeatedly out of her. He liked the sexual sounds filling the air—her moans, skin slapping against skin and the creaking of the sofa getting one hell of a workout.

Suddenly, an orgasm rammed through him, nearly knocking him backward. He felt his release shoot far and deep into her womb, and for a second, he thought of his semen targeting one of those eggs and quickly forced the thought from his mind. A couple engaged in an affair didn't have sex for babies. They had sex for pleasure. And this was pleasure of the richest kind. When she screamed his name and spasms began moving through her body, he knew she had gotten her pleasure, as well.

"I can't find my panties," Shana said, looking everywhere, around the sofa, beneath the cushions and by the table.

She shot an accusing glance over at Jace, who had just slid into his pants. "You sure you don't have them?"

His lips eased into a smile as he reached for his shirt to put it on. "Now, why would I take your panties?"

She shrugged. "I don't know. I heard some men get a kick out of doing that sort of thing. They see it as a trophy of a conquest."

He chuckled, possibly seeing Dalton doing some crap like that. "Trust me...that's not me."

Still naked, Shana eased down on her knees to reach her hand under the sofa to feel around and then she looked at Jace and frowned. "That's odd."

He was buttoning his shirt. "What is?"

"This sofa has a secret compartment."

His brow furrowed. "A secret compartment?"

"Yes."

"You sure?"

"See for yourself."

He moved to her as she stood, and with little effort, he pushed the sofa over on its side. And sure enough, the entire bottom had opened to reveal a neat-looking trunk. Shana had never seen anything like it.

"I must have activated it somehow when my hand was fumbling around."

He nodded and then handed her the missing panties. "Here you go."

"You did have them!" she accused, sliding into them.

"No, they were stuck inside my shirt. I wasn't aware of it until I put my shirt on."

"Then why didn't you say anything?"

His mouth curved into a smile. "I liked seeing you naked on all fours. It gave me plenty of ideas."

Shana rolled her eyes as she slid into her skirt while glancing back at the sofa. "Why do you think this sofa has a secret compartment?"

Jace drew in a deep breath. "I'm not sure, but I'm going to find out."

Turning his attention back to the secret compartment, he slid open a drawer and raised a brow when he saw a file folder. "Umm, what do we have here?"

Taking the folder, he put the sofa back on its legs and then sat down. Shana, who had finished dressing, dropped down beside him. "What is it, Jace, and who does that file belong to?"

"Evidently, my father," he said, opening it up. He read the first document, and Shana felt him tense beside her. "What is it?"

He glanced up at her. "This is a letter from a Ms. Yolanda Greene dated almost sixteen years ago. And she was writing my dad to inform him, just in case he didn't know, that my mother was having an affair with her husband."

Jace then opened the packet of pictures, and several fell out. They were pictures of his mother with another man…in several intimate poses. Jace shoved them back in the packet and then handed them to Shana.

She looked at them and knew how it must feel for a son to see such photos of his mother. "She was beautiful," she said, which was the truth. Her sons had her light brown eyes and long lashes.

"I always thought so," Jace said softly. "Until now." He drew in a deep breath.

Shana didn't know what to say to that. This was

one situation she couldn't offer any advice on. But she would be here if he needed her. Shoving the photographs back in the packet she asked, "Do you know them? The Greenes?"

Jace nodded. "Yes, I know them. Michael Greene worked for Granger for years. Then my father fired him. I never knew why."

"And when was that?" she asked.

"Two months before my mother was killed."

Shana nodded. "May I read that?" she asked, indicating the letter.

Jace nodded and handed it to her. Moments later, she lifted her head. "This woman is threatening your mother, all but saying she would come to a not-so-nice end if your mother didn't leave her husband alone. Was this presented as evidence in your father's defense?"

Jace shook his head. "I don't think so. This is the first time I'm hearing about any of this. Michael and Yolanda Greene weren't at my grandfather's funeral, but Ivan Greene was."

Shana lifted a brow. "Ivan Greene, the same one who's running for mayor?"

"Yes, same family. Ivan is the oldest son. He's ten years older than I am. They also have two daughters my age."

Shana handed the letter back to him and looked up when he cursed. "And just to think the prosecution's case was built on the premise that my father was the one having an affair and killed my mother during a heated argument because she wouldn't give him a divorce. They never came up with the mystery woman. All they had were these receipts to several hotels signed by an S. Granger. It's hard to believe no one ever thought to assume the *S* could stand for Sylvia instead of Sheppard."

"Why didn't your father say something to clear his name? And to cast doubt from him to Yolanda Greene? All it would have taken was reasonable doubt in the jurors' minds."

Jace stood, tucking the file under his arm. "Not sure, but I'm going to find out. And the only person who can answer that question is my father. It's too late to make that call tonight, but I plan to do so first thing in the morning."

Dalton pushed the covers back and eased out of bed. What the hell was wrong with him? With all the bullshit that had gone down at Granger today, you would think that crap would be occupying his mind, making it difficult to sleep. But the thoughts plaguing him had nothing to do with Granger but with that woman in the bar Saturday night.

At first, he'd made up his mind to find her, but then by the time he'd awakened Sunday morning, pissed that his desire for her had ruined the rest of his evening at that club, he'd thought WTF, he was not going to find her and to hell with her.

But last night and now tonight, he was tormented with visions of her in those stilettos and that barely there dress. And his visions hadn't stopped there. Now he was dreaming about making love to her to the point that it almost seemed real.

Walking into his kitchen, he felt for the first time ever that his condo was small, cramped, tight. He wasn't used to being so confined. He needed to get away for a while and knew Jace wouldn't like it if he did. Caden wouldn't like it, either. Now wasn't a good time with all the craziness that was going down. Besides, he was in charge of the Security Department, and Jace was depending on him to stay on top of things.

Opening the refrigerator, he grabbed a beer bottle, then popped the top. He needed to stay focused on Granger and not on some woman whose body he wanted with a passion. Taking a deep swig of beer, he felt the cold liquid as it trickled down to his stomach and wished it could cool off his pecker, as well.

Knowing that wasn't possible, he finished off the beer and headed back to bed, hoping he could get some sleep this time around.

"Caden, there's someone here to see you."

Caden glanced at his watch before turning around to Hannah. "It's after ten. Who is it?"

"Shiloh Timmons."

He muttered an expletive deep in his throat. "Send her out here, Hannah."

He turned back to stare up at the stars. This was to be his peaceful moment, which was something he needed after all the stuff that had gone down at Granger today. But now Shiloh had invaded it.

He picked up her scent before she spoke a word behind him. "Hello, Caden."

He turned around. It was then that he drew in a sharp breath. The moonlight combined with the porch lanterns hit her at an angle that made her look even more beautiful than she was. He immediately hardened his heart at such a stunning picture of exquisiteness.

"What do you want, Shiloh?"

"We need to talk, Caden."

He shook his head. "I don't want to hear anything you have to say."

"But I need to tell you why I—"

He threw up his hand. "No. I don't want to hear it. It was years ago. Doesn't matter now."

"It does matter, Caden. I can't let you hate me any longer."

He chuckled derisively. "You don't have a choice." He paused a moment and then said, "I believed in you. I trusted you, and I loved you. Damn it, Shiloh, I waited for you to show up. Waited days in a damn hotel room in Vegas. But you never came, and then I saw those pictures and knew why. There were pictures of you half-naked lying on a private beach someplace with one of those rich businessmen your father was trying to woo."

"No! That wasn't—"

"Frankly, I don't want to hear it," he interrupted crossly. "You mean nothing to me now. In fact, I can't stand the sight of you."

He saw the tears forming in her eyes but hardened his heart against any reaction to them. He wanted to hurt her the same way she had hurt him. She had not only torn out his heart, but her deceit had trampled it.

He stood there, emotionless, and stared at her, wanting her to see he'd meant everything he'd said. Moments later, she turned and walked off the porch and into the house to leave.

He turned back around, staring up at the sky. But instead of feeling peace, he felt pain.

Jace put in the call to his father first thing the next morning before leaving for the office. The warden promised he would allow Shep to call him back within the hour. His cell phone rang within twenty minutes. "Hello?"

"Jace, what's wrong? Warden Smallwood said for me to call you. Said it was extremely important."

Jace had already spoken to his father yesterday to let him know about Freeman and the others involved in the trade-secret scandal. He had awakened to see it dominating the local news with photographs of Swanson, Arrington and Freeman flashing across the screen. And just in case the good people of Charlottesville had forgotten, a photograph of his father—taken fifteen years ago—had flashed across it, as well, reminding everyone that the former CEO of Granger Aeronautics was presently in prison, serving time for killing his wife.

Jace drew in a deep breath. "I was in your office yesterday, Dad. I found the secret compartment embedded in the sofa. I saw the file." He paused a minute and then asked, "Why didn't you tell the authorities it was Mom having an affair and not you?"

Sheppard tightened his hand on the phone and closed his eyes. He'd never wanted his sons to know. They loved their mother, thought the world of her and...

"Dad, please tell me why. That could have possibly cleared you."

"Or strengthened the prosecution's claim of a motive. They would have claimed I killed Sylvia out of jealous rage. It wasn't worth taking the chance. She was the mother of my sons, and I refused to let her name be dragged through the mud just to clear me, when there was no guarantee that it would have."

"But you had that letter from Yolanda Greene, threatening to do Mom bodily harm."

"Yes, and Yolanda came to see me while I was out on bail. She was nervous and scared that I would turn it over to the authorities and she would be implicated. But she had an ironclad alibi. Both she and Michael did. The week your mother was killed, they had taken a cruise together, trying to repair their marriage. They were thousands of miles away from Charlottesville, so neither of them could have been involved."

Jace's jaw tightened. "Are you certain of that? She could have been lying."

"Yes, I'm certain. Dad checked out their story. They were trying to save their marriage, and I didn't see the need to let the world know about Michael's and your mother's indiscretions."

Jace inwardly cursed. His father was too much a man of honor, caring for others when no one cared a crap about him. Someone was willing to let him take the rap for something he didn't do. He tried to make his father see reason. "If it wasn't one of the Greenes, then it was someone else. Maybe Ms. Greene hired someone to do it and—"

"Maybe you've been watching too many episodes of *NCIS*."

Jace frowned. "Dad, I'm serious."

"So am I. Don't you think that at the time I weighed all my options? I made my decision about what I was and was not going to tell the authorities. The jury reached a verdict of guilty. Let it go."

Now it was Jace's hand that tightened on the phone. "No, Dad. I can't let it go. You're sitting in jail while the person who killed my mother is out here, walking around footloose and fancy-free. Enough is enough. Whether you want us to do so or not, your sons are going to prove your innocence."

"No! The three of you need to make a combined, concentrated effort to save the company."

Jace's temper flared. "Do you think we care more for the company than we do for you?"

Shep heard the torment in Jace's voice and knew he had to do something to keep his sons from snooping around. He needed to keep them safe. Taking a deep breath, he said, "Would you leave it alone if I were to confess that I did kill your mother?"

Jace flinched. "No! Because I wouldn't believe you. And it would make me even more determined to uncover just who you're trying to protect."

"Damn it, Jace, I'm trying to protect the three of you. Besides the affair, your mother was involved in something else. I'm not sure what, but I believe it was enough to get her killed."

Jace went still for a second. Then he recovered enough to ask, "Involved in what?"

"I have no idea."

He had a feeling his father did have an idea but just wasn't saying. "All right, I have to go. We'll keep in touch. Goodbye, Dad."

"Wait! Jace, promise me you'll let this go and that you won't say anything to your brothers about what you found out about your mother."

Jace ran a frustrated hand down his face. He immediately thought about Dalton and how he would handle learning something like that. He worshipped the ground Sylvia Granger walked on and thought she could do no wrong. "I can't make you that promise,

Dad. All I can say is that I won't tell them anytime soon, not until I wrap my head around a few things. But at some point, they need to know, and if you won't tell them, I will."

"Jace, listen to me."

"No, Dad, you need to listen to me. Nobody's perfect, and I never thought Mom was. But I can't see me letting my father rot in prison for something he didn't do. You might be willing to be the sacrificial lamb for some cold-blooded killer, but I refuse to let you do this any longer. Like I said, I'll keep in touch. Goodbye, Dad."

Shep cursed when he heard the click on the other end and knew that even while in prison, he had to do whatever he could to protect his sons.

Chapter Twenty-Nine

Shana lifted her head from looking down at the document and drew in a deep breath. Why was she feeling so nauseated? She hoped she wasn't coming down with something else. She had finished taking the antibiotics her doctor had prescribed for her a couple of weeks ago and had been feeling just fine until this morning.

Now was not the time to start feeling under the weather. She had a lot to do today, and she'd promised Jules she would meet her for lunch at noon. Standing, she decided to grab a pack of crackers from the vending machine. She had hoped to have heard from Jace by now. She knew he would be late coming into the office after he'd had that phone conversation with his father. She couldn't wait to find out how it went.

She left her office and rounded the corner to head toward the break room when she stopped. Standing in front of Brandy's desk was a woman who looked to be a model from the profile she presented. Tall, with a mass of luxurious black hair flowing down her shoulders, she was the perfect shape, size and height and was wearing an outfit that appeared designed just for her body. The dress looked fabulous on her. Even her shoes were perfect for the dress, and it was evident they cost a lot. Whoever the woman was, she had money and wore "classy" as if she rightly deserved the title.

Brandy glanced Shana's way, saw her, and with what Shana read as a relieved smile on her face, she said quickly to the woman, "Like I said, none of the Grangers have arrived yet, but I expect them soon. But here's Ms. Bradford. She works very closely with Mr. Jace Granger, and perhaps she can tell you more than I can as to when to expect him."

The woman turned quickly and cut Shana a sharp glance while letting her eyes roam up and down her in displeasure. "And who are you?" the woman asked as if she had every right to know.

Shana gazed back, looking into what she thought was a perfect face to go along with everything else that was perfect about this woman. The one thing Shana immediately disliked was the woman's attitude. She recognized downright snootiness when she heard it. And she was sure the woman's eyes had been used for intimidation more than once, but she would soon discover that, when it came to Shana, those tactics didn't work.

Walking over toward the woman, Shana extended her hand. "I'm Shana Bradford. And you are?"

Before answering, the woman moved her gaze up and down Shana once more, and without accepting Shana's hand, she lifted her chin, looked Shana in the eye with a smirk on her face and said, "I'm Eve Granger. Jace's wife."

Shana suddenly felt dizzy and thought she would

fall flat on her face when a sharp, loud voice behind her reeled her in and kept her standing.

"Ex-wife!"

Shana recognized Jace's voice and turned to see the three Granger brothers, standing tall, each looking incredibly handsome with their feet braced apart, standing side by side with fierce expressions on their faces.

"Jace, I just had to come." The woman rushed over to Jace and threw her arms around him in a display of dramatics that Shana found astounding.

Shana watched Jace stiffen, refusing to return the embrace. In fact, his arms remained stiffly by his side. Dalton rolled his eyes, and Caden remained expressionless.

Jace pried the woman's arms from around him and stepped back. "What are you doing here, Eve?" And from his biting tone, it was obvious he wasn't glad to see her.

"Oh, Jace, I told you. I just had to come. I couldn't let you go through this alone."

"What are we? Chopped liver? Last we looked, he wasn't alone," Dalton snapped.

Ignoring Dalton, Eve tilted her head up to gaze into Jace's face. "The media is reporting about those horrid people who tried to ruin your company and betray you."

"Betrayal is something you know a lot about, isn't it?" Jace said with a hard tone.

"Oh, Jace," the woman moaned as tears appeared in her eyes. "How can you be so unforgiving?"

Dalton chuckled, clapped his hands together and said, "Will someone please give this woman an Oscar?"

Just as quickly as the fake tears had started, they

dried up when Eve snapped her head around and glared at Dalton. Jace threw his brother a warning glance before turning his attention back to Eve. "We'll talk privately in my office." Taking her arm, he ushered her inside his office and slammed the door shut behind him.

"Evil Eve strikes again," Dalton said, shaking his head. He laughed all the way to his office and closed the door behind him.

Caden walked over to Shana. "My ex-sister-in-law can be quite a character at times."

Shana glanced at the closed door. "Apparently."

"I wouldn't worry about her if I were you," he said softly.

Shana raised a brow. "And why should I worry about her?"

Caden shrugged. "No reason, I guess." He then walked off.

Shana glanced over at Brandy, who pretended to look busy. Drawing in a deep breath, Shana walked away to grab those crackers from the vending machine, and a part of her wished for once she could be a fly on the wall in Jace's office.

"Please, Jace, be reasonable," Eve implored.

Jace frowned from behind his desk. "The fact that I'm allowing you any of my time shows what a reasonable man I can be. There's no way in hell you can stay at Sutton Hills for a week."

"But I need a place to stay. I told you that I had to leave Los Angeles for a while."

"Because some woman thinks you're involved with

her husband and hired a couple of goons to teach you a lesson."

"Yes. Someone tried running me off the road a few days ago, my tires were slashed and my front door was egged."

Jace had never heard anything so ridiculous. In fact, it was too ridiculous for even her to have made up. "Why didn't you report it to the police?"

"I did, but they didn't have enough proof to link it to that jealous bitch."

"And what good will being here one week do?"

She nervously wrung her hands together. "It will give Maurice time to convince his wife that nothing is going on between us and that we're just business associates."

"Why not go to your parents, Eve?"

"I can't do that. I'm not on good terms with them."

He wondered what the reason for their tiff was this time. "Fine, stay a week, but not at Sutton Hills." He could just imagine Hannah's reaction if she did. Eve had worn out her welcome with Hannah the last time when Eve complained they treated Hannah more like a family member than the servant she was.

"I'll put you up at a hotel. Long Meadows. And I want you gone in a week," Jace said, standing to put on his jacket. He figured that Long Meadows would be to her liking since it was five-star.

"I will give the hotel permission to kick you out on your behind if you're not checked out by Tuesday morning. And just so you don't get any crazy ideas, I'm just paying for your hotel room. You are to cover your own incidentals." He could just see her ordering a diamond tennis bracelet from one of the hotel's jewelry stores and adding it to the hotel bill.

"I can't believe you don't trust me."

"Believe it. I'll call Long Meadows and make the arrangements." Jace shoved his hands into his pockets, hoping he wasn't making a mistake. He had a feeling there was more to her story than she claimed, but he had too many more important issues to worry about…like Freeman's whereabouts for instance. He'd meant what he told Eve. After Tuesday she was on her own and her best bet would be on a plane back to California.

"Thanks, Jace. If there's any way I can repay you, then—"

"There's not, and you can't," he broke in to say. "However, what you can do is stop telling people you're my wife, because you're not."

She frowned. "You're replacing me already? I saw the way Ms. Bradford was looking at you."

Jace rolled his eyes. She hadn't seen a thing but was merely fishing. "First of all, you don't have a place in my life to be replaced, Eve, and Ms. Bradford doesn't concern you. In fact, nothing about me or this business concerns you."

He looked at his watch. "I have a meeting, and you're not welcome to stay in my office. I'll call a car to take you over to the hotel. I suggest you go downstairs to the lobby and wait for it."

He straightened his tie. "Come on and I'll walk you down." And while he was down there he planned to give security firm orders not to let her back in the building again.

* * *

"I like her."

Shana glanced up from her toast and looked at her sister. "Who?" The two of them were enjoying lunch at a restaurant inside Long Meadows Hotel. They were known to have a wonderful lunch menu.

"Dad's Mona. I met her Sunday morning. After spending a day on the beach with her on Saturday, he invited her to join us for breakfast at the Pancake House. He picked her up, and I met them there. I swear if I didn't know she was blind, I could have been fooled. She is so independent. Once Dad told her where everything in front of her was located, she was on her own."

Jules took a sip of her iced tea and then continued, "At first, I was nervous, thinking she was going to knock something over, but she didn't. And then we got into a discussion of politics, and can you believe we have the same views about a lot of things?"

"That's scary."

"Oh, hush," Jules said, chuckling. "And why are you eating just a piece of toast and drinking water?" She grinned. "If you're tight on money, I could loan you a few dollars."

Shana rolled her eyes. "I woke up this morning not feeling well. I ate a few crackers earlier, and I'm feeling better, but I don't want to risk feeling nauseated again. So tell me, did you find that guy last weekend?"

Jules smiled. "Yes! You should have seen his expression when I handcuffed him to the hotel bed. He thought I was about to get kinky with him. Imagine his surprise when the police showed up and arrested his naked ass and hauled him off to jail."

"If he was taking the women to a hotel, how was he able to pull things off?" Shana asked, biting into her toast.

"He would reserve the room in advance, have it set up the way he wanted it with the hidden cameras, and then when he got them to the hotel, he made it seem as if they were checking in for the first time. They were clueless that he'd already been there to get things ready. The police found everything, including the camera and footage he hadn't put out on the internet yet."

"Umm, sounds like you had a productive weekend."

"I did." A smile ruffled her lips when she said, "I also met this real cute guy at one of the clubs, but since I was working undercover, I couldn't give him the time of day." She then told Shana what happened Saturday night at that club and the mission she'd given the stranger.

"So he's supposed to find you?" Shana asked.

"If he wants to see me again," Jules replied, grinning. "If he does find me, it means he was truly interested. If not, it means he just wanted another notch on his bedpost. But I hope he finds me. He was such a hottie with the most gorgeous pair of brown eyes."

Jules took another sip of her iced tea. "So how was your weekend with Jace Granger?"

Shana drew in a deep breath as memories washed over her. "It was absolutely fantastic." She paused a moment and said softly, truthfully, "I think I've fallen in love with him, Jules. In fact, I know I have."

Jules stared at her. "Goodness! Well, I hope he's worth your love, Shana."

Shana thought about the scene that had unfolded that morning in the office when his ex-wife had shown up. It was obvious that Jace had been upset about it, and she detected some animosity between the ex and his brothers. But still…Eve Granger was a beautiful woman, too beautiful for her own good. Shana could see a man doubting the wisdom of letting such a woman go.

"I believe he's worth it," Shana said easily.

Before leaving the office, she had checked in with Brandy to let her know she was leaving for lunch. Brandy mentioned Jace was in a meeting and his ex-wife had left, escorted out of the office by Jace himself. Shana hoped he would meet with her at some point to tell her about the conversation he'd had with his father.

Her brow furrowed when she recalled that Shelton Fields, the guy who'd been second-in-command under Arrington, had been at Brandy's desk. As soon as she'd approached, he'd walked off rather quickly. She wondered what that was about. When she got back to the office, she would go back over Kent's report on the man.

Jules didn't say anything but continued to look at Shana and the toast she was nibbling on. She remembered a friend of hers having similar symptoms last year. She wondered. "You know there could be another reason why you woke up nauseated this morning."

Shana glanced over at Jules as she took another sip of her water. "What reason is that?"

"You could be pregnant."

Shana choked on her water and began coughing, causing a number of people to look over at their table. "Don't say that," Shana warned, leaning over the table and whispering in a snappish tone. "There's no way I can be pregnant, because I'm on the pill."

"Yes, but you were on antibiotics recently. Did you make sure you were doubly protected?"

It was probably quite evident from the "oops" look on Shana's face that she hadn't.

Jules lifted a brow. "Umm, looks like Dad has fallen in love and will find out he's getting a grandchild in the same year."

"Don't say that! You're wrong!"

"Am I? There's a quick way to find out. The gift shop. I bet they sell pregnancy kits. We can find out the truth in no time."

Shana lifted a brow. "We?"

"Yes," Jules said, grinning from ear to ear. "If I'm going to be an aunt, I want to know about it. I can't wait to see the look on Dad's face when we tell him."

Shana rolled her eyes. "I'm sure he would appreciate hearing about a wedding first, Jules."

Jules continued grinning. "Not my problem. It's yours and Jace Granger's. So hurry up and finish eating. We have a pregnancy kit to buy."

Chapter Thirty

Jace pressed the intercom button.

"Yes, Mr. Granger?"

"Ms. Booker, I just tried calling Ms. Bradford's office, and she didn't answer."

"She left for lunch a while ago."

"Lunch?" Jace's brow furrowed. Shana never left the office for lunch.

"Yes, sir. She mentioned something about meeting with her sister for lunch."

"Oh. All right."

He was a little disappointed, because he'd wanted to see her, talk to her, so he could tell her about his conversation with his father. And then he wanted to kiss her, hold her and make plans with her for later tonight. He couldn't help smiling each time he thought about what they'd done in his father's office. Shana was simply amazing. She trusted him. She listened to him. And he felt that she understood him.

And there was so much about her that he admired. She had worked for Granger well over a month, and he was witness to her strong work ethic. Already, he could see improvements in several of his departments based on her recommendations. And because of her and the people she employed, he knew that three of his employees had meant the company no good. And there could be more. Jace was convinced she would expose them, as well.

And that same woman could be the most sensuous female on legs. She could turn a man's bedroom into a pleasurable haven. At the moment, he was feeling thoroughly satisfied.

Then he remembered his ex-wife.

The last person he had expected to see today was Eve. But by the time he had gotten her out of his hair, he had attended two meetings and hadn't seen Shana. And that was the crux of his problem. He wanted to see her. Badly.

There was a knock on his door, and he glanced up, hoping it was Shana returning from lunch. "Come in."

When Caden appeared in the doorway, he said in a disappointed tone, "Oh, it's you."

Caden chuckled. "Yes, it's me. I hope you weren't hoping it was Eve returning."

Jace frowned. "Funny. I'm still trying to get over the fact that she'll be in town for a week."

"A week?"

"Yes." He then conveyed to Caden the same ridiculous story Eve had given him.

"Well, at least she's not setting foot on Sutton Hills," Caden said, sliding into the chair across from Jace's desk. "Your ex-wife doesn't know the meaning of being gracious, and I don't want Hannah upset about anything."

"Neither do I."

"And while I'm on a roll with complaints, why did you put Dalton in charge of Security? Now he thinks he's James Bond. I guess he talked you into putting that damn tracker on your phone."

Jace chuckled. "Yes, but it only works if I turn it on. It's on during the day just in case he randomly checks it, but when I leave here, I disable it."

He leaned back in his chair. "The only reason I placed him over the Security Department was I knew it would challenge his mind. Make him feel useful. And I needed someone to have another pair of ears and eyes focused on what's going on."

"Okay," Caden said, understanding now that it had been explained.

Jace studied his brother. "So, how are things going since you've been back, Caden?"

"Okay, I guess. I'm still reeling about what that FBI agent told us yesterday. Got any updates?"

"Not since late yesterday," Jace said. "Last report is that Melissa is holding out for a plea deal and Arrington still isn't talking. And I have no word yet on Freeman's whereabouts."

Jace didn't say anything else for a few minutes, and he could tell his brother had gotten lost in his thoughts since he was sitting there and studying the floor. "I understand you had a visitor last night, Caden."

Caden raised his head and met Jace's gaze. There was no need to wonder how Jace knew. Hannah. She'd always liked Shiloh. "Yes. Shiloh dropped by."

Jace nodded. "Is there something going on that I don't know about? And if it's none of my business, just say so."

"Like you've all but told me what's going on with

you and Shana is none of mine," Caden couldn't help countering. Then he chuckled and said, "Don't get uptight, Jace. I don't have a problem answering your question. There isn't anything going on with Shiloh and me. At least not now."

"But there had been?" Jace asked quietly.

"Yes. We ran into each other again a few years ago. Four to be exact. She showed up one night at one of my concerts. I was glad to see her. It had been years since I'd seen her. We got together after the concert, and it was as if we'd never parted. It was so easy to pick up our friendship. She came to several more concerts after that, and then I realized how much I loved her…and that I'd always loved her. She claimed she felt the same way and wanted to be with me."

Caden paused for a minute and then continued, "We made plans. She had graduated from college and was no longer under her father's thumb, or so she claimed. So we set a date to marry in Vegas. We hadn't planned to tell anyone about it until after the deed was done."

"What happened?" Jace asked, hearing the pain in his brother's voice.

"She never showed up. I stayed in that hotel room for three days waiting on her. I didn't get a phone call or any message from her. I tried calling her cell phone and discovered the number had been changed. I called her parents' house, and the old man blasted me out for calling and said Shiloh was on vacation somewhere. I didn't believe him, and the next day I got a special delivery package. Inside was a newspaper clipping of Shiloh on the beach with another man. From what the article said, the guy was a business client of her father's. I never heard from her or saw her again until Granddad's funeral."

Jace drew in a deep breath. "I'm sorry."

"I'm not. I found out the truth about her. She came by last night saying she needed to explain what happened four years ago, but I didn't want to hear it. It was four years too late."

Jace leaned back in his chair. What his brother said explained a lot of things. Now he knew...and understood. He checked his watch. He hadn't had lunch yet because he was hoping to get a chance to talk to Shana. "Have you eaten lunch yet?"

"No. Dalton and I were leaving to grab something at McQueen's. We've both agreed there has been too much action for us these last two days. Yesterday it was the FBI, and today it was Eve. I don't want any shockers tomorrow."

Jace stood and reached for his jacket. "Neither do I. And I think I'll join you guys for lunch."

Eve came down the escalator, smiling as she glanced around. Jace knew her taste and had put her in a gorgeous hotel for a week. And her suite was simply to die for. She knew he was paying a lot for her comfort and wouldn't be doing so if he didn't still care about her well-being. He hadn't been happy to see her, but she planned on changing that.

When it came to men, she knew how to work them. And she intended to work Jace. No doubt he would put up some resistance, but once she got him in bed and showed him what he was missing, he would come around. And if a baby was what he wanted, she would give him one. The thought of gaining a few pounds didn't bother her like it once did. Besides, she would have Sutton Hills, and he would get the kid he'd always wanted. And the first thing she would do was fire that heifer Hannah. That old hag would never take care of a baby of hers.

Her thoughts shifted back to Jace. He had looked good sitting behind that desk, which is where she'd always wanted him to be. Of course, he would be upset with her when she didn't leave in a week, but Jace was a man of honor and would not kick her out of this hotel like he threatened to do. Besides, Jace had been a free man for close to three years now. If he'd wanted to replace her, he would have done so, which meant he still loved her, whether he admitted it or not. She hadn't been the first woman ever to get an abortion, and she wouldn't be the last. So he needed to get over it.

She frowned when she saw two women walking toward the gift shop. She recognized one immediately. Shana Bradford. Regardless of what Jace had said, Eve had picked up on vibes. More from the woman than from Jace, who'd been too busy frowning at her. Maybe it was time she and Ms. Bradford had a private talk just in case she had any crazy thoughts of getting her hands on Jace.

Moving across the hotel lobby, she watched as the women entered the gift shop and moved toward the section of the store that sold toiletries. Eve followed, deciding it was time for that talk.

"Here we are," Jules said, smiling. "Take your pick."

Shana studied all the packages. There were so many different brands. At first, she'd thought Jules was out of her mind at the thought that she could be pregnant.

But then it hit her that she was a week late. So much had been happening that it had slipped her mind.

"Any one will do," she said, snatching one off the shelf.

"When will you find out?" Jules asked excitedly.

Shana frowned. She wished Jules wouldn't be so giddy at the possibility. "I don't know. Sometime today."

"Call me when you find out, no matter which way it goes. And if you are pregnant, will you tell Jace?"

Shana swallowed. She didn't want to think that far ahead. "Just let me find out one way or another, Jules. I'm probably just coming down with a cold or something."

"We'll see." Her sister then glanced at her watch. "Come on. I'll drop you back off at Granger. I have a two o'clock appointment, and I don't want to be late."

Jules grabbed Shana's arm and dragged her to the cash register, where Shana paid for her purchase. Then they hurriedly left the gift shop. Neither saw the woman who'd been standing in the next aisle deliberately eavesdropping.

Eve drew in a deep breath as she came out of her moment of shock. There was a chance that Shana Bradford could be pregnant with Jace's child! Anger filled every part of her body. If the woman thought she would get her clutches on Jace, then she had another thought coming.

Eve put her hand to her forehead as she felt a tension headache coming on. She needed to keep her cool. She needed to think.

"May I help you, miss?"

She glanced up at the store clerk, a matronly older

woman who was eyeing her as if she thought Eve was a shoplifter or something.

The thought pissed Eve off. "No, you can't help me, so get out of my damn face."

Eve left the gift shop and headed for the bank of elevators. She needed to go back up to her hotel room and come up with a plan.

"Is Jace out of his meeting?" Shana asked Brandy when she returned from lunch.

"Yes, but he left for lunch with his brothers a half hour ago. He indicated he would be returning in an hour since he has a three o'clock meeting."

Shana glanced at her watch. "Okay." She headed to her office. Once inside, she pulled the bag with the pregnancy kit out of her purse. Rubbing her hand over her stomach as she sat down behind her desk, she wondered whether Jules could be right. Was she pregnant?

And if so, would she tell Jace?

Of course you'll tell him, her mind argued. *He has a right to know.* But the one thing she would not do is allow him to feel obligated in any way. She was financially able to raise a child on her own without depending on any man. However, that didn't mean she wouldn't expect him to do right by his child.

But then, the other side of her mind reasoned, *it's a child he didn't ask for and you don't know if he even wants a family. He asked, and you assured him you were on the pill and therefore protected. He might think it was entrapment.*

The thought of him believing such a thing sent chills down her body.

She stood and began pacing. She was probably getting worked up over nothing. Chances were she was fine and that there was a reason she was late and felt nauseated this morning. She would clear things up when she got home and took that test. When it showed it was a false scare, she would drink a glass of wine, shower and go to bed.

She smiled, thinking that sounded like a good plan.

Shana turned at the brisk knock on her door. Before she could call out for the person to come in, Jace opened the door and closed it behind him and locked it. He then braced against the door and stared at her. "I wanted to see you earlier, but I had a meeting."

"I know," she said softly, knowing at that moment how much she loved him. "You're seeing me now."

A smile fanned across his face. "I am, aren't I?"

He strode across the room, and when he reached her, he pulled her into his arms and captured her mouth in his. And it was a kiss that had her feeling weak in the knees from how expertly his tongue was mating with hers, long and greedily.

Her body slid effortlessly closer to his, and he tightened his hold while deepening the kiss. The heat from his body was burning up her senses, stoking her hunger for him and surging her into a mist of desire so thick she couldn't think logically.

So she didn't.

All she wanted to think about and concentrate on were the sensations this kiss was making her feel and how easily her body was responding. Her hands couldn't stay still, and she reached up and caressed the side of his face where their mouths were joined and stroked his warm, smooth skin. She loved him. God, she loved him, and whether or not he loved her back, she never wanted to lose this. Being the woman he wanted.

Moments later, he broke off the kiss and whispered against her moist lips, "I needed that." He refused to release her from his arms.

She smiled up at him. "So did I. What about your father? Did you get a chance to talk to him?"

He nodded. "Yes." He then told her what was said.

She didn't say anything for a minute and then asked, "What do you think your dad meant by saying your mother could have been involved in something?"

"I don't know, baby, but I intend to find out."

Baby. She wondered if it was a slip of the tongue and whether he even realized he'd said it.

He glanced at his watch. "I have a three o'clock meeting, so I need to go. What are you doing later tonight? Around seven?"

She thought of the pregnancy kit and pushed it out of her mind. "Nothing."

"May I drop by?"

"Yes."

He smiled and brushed a kiss across her lips. "Okay, I'll see you then."

She wanted to let it go and couldn't. He hadn't brought up his ex-wife, so she decided to do so. "And how is Eve?"

He turned around before reaching the door and shoved his hands in his pockets. "Right now, Eve's situation is rather complicated. She needed a place to stay for a week, and I'm helping her out."

Shana fought the disappointment that settled around her heart. "A week?"

"Yes. I've put her up in a hotel."

He'd put his ex-wife up in a hotel? "That's very generous of you."

"Yes, it is." He then walked back over to Shana. Pulling her into his arms, he brushed a kiss across her lips. "I'm involved with you now. Don't worry about Eve."

She nodded. "Okay."

She watched as he walked back to the door, unlocked it and then walked out of her office. He hadn't wanted her to worry about Eve. Was it because the woman meant nothing to him anymore? He certainly hadn't acted as if he was glad to see her this morning.

Deciding she would do what he asked and not worry about Eve Granger, Shana moved back to her desk, looking forward to tonight.

Eve glanced at her watch. If she called now, she probably could reach Jace before he left the office. She didn't know what plans he had for tonight, but she intended to change them.

Picking up her cell phone, she called his number and smiled when he answered. "What do you want, Eve?"

Not exactly the greeting she'd hoped for, but she would deal with it. "I'm lonely, Jace. There's nothing to do stuck here at this hotel."

"And I should care why?"

She rolled her eyes. Determined not to be deterred, she said, "Because we once meant something to each other. We—"

"The key word was *once,* Eve. Don't know why you're calling me when there are taxis surrounding the hotel. If you're lonely, get in one and go someplace. There's a movie theater within walking distance."

"You want me to walk someplace?"

"No, I prefer that you get on a plane and return to California."

Eve dropped down on the bed, stunned. Did he really mean that? Could he really hold a grudge this long because of the abortion? In that case, it was a good thing he didn't know the whole truth surrounding it.

"You hate me that much, Jace?" she asked, and for the first time, she realized carrying out her plan might not be as easy as she thought.

Jace rubbed a hand on the back of his neck. Jesus! He didn't need this. Eve hadn't done anything but cause him pain since he'd known her. Why was he even wasting his time talking to her when he needed to be on his way someplace else?

"Look, Eve, I don't hate you. I just don't have any feelings one way or the other. What you did hurt me, killed something inside of me. You destroyed something that was part of me."

"Damn it, Jace, it was my body!"

"And it was *my* child!" He drew in a deep breath. "Look, I have somewhere to go. Goodbye."

"Wait! When will I see you?"

Jace shook his head. The woman just didn't get it. "There's no reason for you to see me, Eve. You needed a place to stay for a week, and I made sure you got one. But please don't think you can take advantage of my kindness. Goodbye." He then clicked off the phone.

Eve was furious, so much in fact she was tempted to throw the phone against the wall. She slowly pulled herself together and quickly made another call. Her temper exploded as soon as the person answered. "You requested that I come here, and I'm here. And if you don't want anyone to find out what you've been doing, you better come up with another plan. Jace is acting like a shithead, and there's a chance Shana Bradford is pregnant."

Chapter Thirty-One

Shana went still, feeling a sense of denial as she stared at the pregnancy test. It was positive, which meant her entire world was now upside down. Instinctively, her hand went to her stomach, and she inhaled a deep breath. She was unsure of a lot of things, but the one thing she knew was that she wanted this baby. She hadn't prepared for one. Hadn't given a thought to having children anytime soon. But fate had determined otherwise, and she was in with both feet.

A short while later, she was sitting on her patio, drinking a glass of springwater instead of the wine she had planned. She glanced at her watch. Jace would be arriving in an hour, and she needed to make decisions. Did she tell him tonight or not?

She shook her head. No, not tonight. She needed to digest the situation herself for a while. Besides, she needed to know how she would handle it. She wasn't sure he even liked kids. Not that it mattered if he didn't. Her decision had been made.

Deciding it was time to go upstairs and take a

shower, she reached for her phone when it rang and wasn't surprised the caller ID indicated it was Jules.

"What, Jules?"

"Hey, don't 'what' me. I want to know if it was a negative or a positive?"

Shana frowned. She wondered if Jules would be in such a happy mood if the shoe was on the other foot. "Not sure I want to divulge something so personal."

"Don't play with me, Shana. 'Fess up."

Shana took a slow sip of her water, deciding to let Jules stew for a minute. When she thought enough time had passed, she said, "Positive."

Jules didn't say anything for a second and then, "Positive?"

"Yes, positive."

Shana held the phone out from her ear when Jules let out an exuberant scream. She couldn't help smiling herself. The thought that she would be a mother was beginning to grow on her. "Will you calm down, Jules?"

"No, I can't calm down. I'm going to be an aunt, and I want the entire world to know."

Shana frowned, deciding it was time to reel her in. "No, you don't. At least not yet. Promise that you're going to seal those lips until I say it's okay to open them."

"Sure, if that's what you want."

"That's what I want. It is still very early, and I need to decide when would be a good time to tell Jace."

"So, you plan to tell him?"

"Yes, of course I do. He has a right to know. It doesn't matter how he feels about it, he has a right to know. How he deals with it afterward is his business."

"I like the way you think. I'm so glad you're my big sister. You would make Mama proud."

Shana smiled, believing so, as well. "Thanks."

"When will you tell him?"

Shana began nibbling on her bottom lip. "He'll be here in an hour, but I don't think tonight is a good time to spring the news. I'll do so this week, but not tonight."

A short while later, Shana had taken her shower and slid into a sundress. She returned downstairs when the doorbell rang. It was Jace. Drawing in a deep breath, she went to the door, opened it and took a step back. She saw the bags in his hands.

"You brought dinner," she said, smiling and leading him to the kitchen.

"Yes, I brought dinner. I haven't eaten and figured you hadn't, either."

He placed the bags on the counter. "I hope you're in the mood for Chinese."

"I am." Now that the nausea had passed, she was in the mood to eat practically anything. "Thanks."

"You're welcome."

He then reached out and pulled her into his arms, captured her lips with his and began feasting on her mouth. Moments later, he reluctantly released her lips and stared down at her without saying anything.

She tilted her head and returned his stare. "Why are you staring at me like that?"

Instead of answering, he reached down, took her hands and laced them together with his. "I just realized something."

She arched a brow. "What?"

He smiled. "I'll tell you later."

* * *

Hours later, close to midnight, Jace eased from the bed and glanced back at a sleeping Shana. Tonight had been wonderful. They'd eaten and made love, and he could be wrong, but it seemed something was different about their lovemaking tonight. Just as hot, but it was as if their relationship had taken another turn.

For him it had.

He mentioned earlier that he would tell her why he had stared at her in the kitchen. Luckily for him, she hadn't brought it up again, because he wasn't ready to let her know he'd fallen in love with her.

He shook his head while sliding into his pants. Wasn't it this past weekend he had told her he didn't believe in true love? At the time, he had been so sure of it, and when he'd seen Eve this morning, her appearance had confirmed it. The bitterness and resentment had all but consumed him, reminded him of why it would be hard for him to fall in love with any woman again. But all it had taken was seeing Shana earlier, kissing her in her office. And then again when he had arrived tonight. She was nothing like Eve. She was not a manipulator. A woman who couldn't be trusted. A woman who felt entitled.

This was Shana, the woman he loved.

"You're leaving?"

He glanced over at the bed as he continued buttoning his shirt. "Yes. If I stay, neither of us will get a good night's sleep."

A smile curved her lips. "That wouldn't bother me."

No, it wouldn't. Whenever she gave herself to him, it was freely, without reservation. With Eve, she'd always used sex as a way to get whatever she wanted.

He walked back over to the bed and leaned down to drop a kiss on her forehead. "You want me to hum you to sleep again?"

Her eyes lit up. "Would you?"

He chuckled. "My pleasure." He then eased back in bed and pulled her into his arms.

"Your clothes are going to get wrinkled."

He glanced down at her a second before getting up again. He stood and began removing his clothes again, knowing they both knew what that meant. Moments later, when he lifted the covers and settled in beside her, pulling her soft and warm body next to his, he captured her mouth, instantly triggering an electrical charge that overtook him. He was sexually aroused all over again.

He broke off the kiss. "I want you," he murmured softly against her lips. He fought back telling her he loved her, as well. That would come another day when he thought she was ready to hear it.

The next day, after she'd gotten to the office, Shana got a call from Marcel. A plea bargain would be reached with Melissa, Arrington was out on bail and Freeman was still nowhere to be found. It was as if he had fallen off the face of the earth.

She'd also gotten a call from Jules to let her know she was at the airport, about to take off for Seattle. She'd gotten a lead on a new missing persons case she'd taken on.

Shana had taken the time to call her dad, and he sounded excited about preparing dinner for Mona. They chatted for a little while before ending the call.

As she tried going over another report Kent had sent her, she couldn't stop thinking about Jace.

He had left her place before dawn this morning, and for her it was a good thing. He hadn't been there to see her throw up. She drew in a deep breath as she nibbled on a saltine. This morning sickness thing was no joke. She glanced at her watch; it was almost noon.

Shana hadn't seen Jace all morning. He'd mentioned last night that he would be doing interviews for a replacement for Cal Arrington. Deciding she would get another pack of crackers from the vending machine, she left her office, and when she turned the corner, she saw Shelton Fields at Brandy's desk again. When she approached, the man gave her a terse greeting before hurriedly walking away.

She looked at Brandy, who couldn't meet her eyes. Instead she picked up a file and began working with it. "Is everything okay, Brandy?"

"Yes, things are fine, Ms. Bradford."

Shana stared at Brandy a minute longer before walking off. Brandy was lying. There was something going on, and Shana was determined to find out what.

"You're certainly in a good mood," Dalton said to Jace as the two of them left the meeting. Caden had stayed behind to make an important phone call to his agent.

Jace smiled over at him. "Yes, I am."

"Does it have anything to do with wonder-woman?"

When the elevator opened, Jace stepped in and Dalton followed. "Have you forgotten about our deal?" Jace asked.

Dalton grinned. "I guess I had."

A few moments later Dalton said, "I got a question for you. A friend of mine is in a quandary."

Jace glanced over at him. "What kind of quandary?"

"He's met a woman and didn't get a chance to find out anything about her, not even her name. He wants to meet her again. What do you suggest he do...if anything?"

Jace chuckled. "Oh, I would do something, especially if it was someone I really wanted to meet and see again. If push came to shove, I would hire a private investigator."

The elevator door swooshed open, and Jace walked off with Dalton right on his heels. "A private investigator?"

"Yes. They're good at finding people."

Dalton smiled. Why hadn't he thought of that?

"Are you going to suggest that to your *friend*?" Jace asked him.

Dalton glanced at Jace, who was looking at him funny. Dalton shrugged. "I don't think he's decided if he wants to find her. He has to think about it some more."

Jace had to smile. "Whatever."

Eve answered her cell phone. "Yes?"

"Everything has been worked out."

She raised her brow. "You've come up with a new plan?"

"Yes, and since your services are no longer needed, you can return to California."

Eve frowned. If he thought he was going to get rid of her that fast, he had another thought coming. "No, I think I'll stick around. This is a nice hotel, and I have it for a week, so I might as well enjoy it."

"Suit yourself."

Eve hung up the phone, thinking that she would suit herself. And then before she left, she would make sure the person who just called made sure she had enough money to tide her over for a while. After all, she knew things he definitely wouldn't want anyone else to know.

Kent looked over the list of names he'd been working with now for more than a month. Three names were marked off. Melissa Swanson, Cal Arrington and Titus Freeman. All were participants in the selling of trade secrets. There were others who looked highly suspect, but he had a feeling there was something he was missing. Sighing deeply, he picked up the phone to call Shana.

"Hello?"

"It's Kent. I need a rundown of those names again. Of everyone who was in your office at some point in time that first day."

"All right. I'll send it over to you now. Just keep in mind that this might not be everyone. Several workers were moving things around in here and hooking stuff up."

"Okay. I'll call you if I find anything," Kent said, then hung up the phone.

Chapter Thirty-Two

Two days later, Shana knew she couldn't put off telling Jace any longer. Her morning sickness wasn't going away, and he had spent the past two nights with her. But again, she was grateful he'd left before morning. What if he decided to stay the entire night without leaving early the next morning? She ran the risk of his being there when she was sick in the mornings. If that happened, she would be forced to tell him what was wrong with her, and she preferred not having to tell him that way.

Drawing in a deep breath, she knocked on the door that connected her office to Jace's. He opened it and smiled down at her. "Hello, beautiful."

She couldn't help returning his smile. "I need to talk to you about something."

"Okay, what is it?"

She shook her head. "It's private. Personal. I'd rather do it at my place. I just wanted to make sure you were coming over again tonight."

He leaned in the doorway. "Yes, as long as you have a welcome mat for me, I'll be there."

She met his gaze. "The welcome mat is there."

He reached out and touched her cheek. His eyes darkened with concern. "You okay?"

She nodded. "Yes, but I'll be better once we've had our talk."

Jace knew that to be true. He had been putting off telling her how he felt and decided tonight he would do it. He wasn't sure what she needed to talk to him about, but they would discuss whatever was on her mind tonight. As well as what was on his.

"Expect me at the usual time, and I'll bring dinner," he said.

"No, it will be my treat this time."

He lifted a brow. "You're cooking?"

She chuckled. "No. I plan to stop and pick something up for us on the way home."

"That won't be an inconvenience for you?"

"No more than it's an inconvenience for you whenever you do it." He'd fed her for the past three nights. Now it was her turn.

"All right, if you're sure it's okay."

"It's okay, Jace. In fact, I want it to be a special evening."

He definitely liked the sound of that. He leaned down and brushed a kiss across her lips. "Then I can't wait."

Jace glanced at his watch. It was a little after six and time for him to call it a day. He looked forward to leaving to head over to Shana's place. He stood to slide into his jacket and lifted a brow when he thought he heard a sound outside his door. As far as he knew, everyone had left for today.

Moving to the door, he opened it and glanced out. He frowned when he saw Shelton Fields at Brandy's desk. "Shelton, is there anything you need?"

The man jerked around nervously. From the expression on Shelton's face, it was apparent he hadn't known Jace was still at the office.

"No, I was just leaving. I needed to place something on Ms. Booker's desk."

Jace nodded as he locked his office door. "I'm about to leave, as well. We can walk out together."

"All right."

Jace made a mental note to read Shana's report on Shelton Fields again first thing in the morning. The last time, there hadn't been any red flags, nothing to give the man a second look, but now that he thought about it, Fields had been acting kind of strange lately. But then, he hadn't been the only one. Once word had gotten out about Melissa, Arrington and Freeman, a number of the other employees were acting like they thought someone suspected them.

"We had nice weather today," Jace said when they stepped in the elevator.

"Yes, it was."

And that was all he said. Jace tossed around in his mind just what he knew about Fields. In his early forties, the man had been hired by Jace's grandfather around seven years ago. He was divorced, and his ex-wife lived somewhere in Oregon. Jace recalled his grandfather mentioning that, after his divorce, Fields had become a ladies' man around the office. But all it had taken was his grandfather letting Fields know he disapproved of such behavior to put a stop to it.

They left the building together and walked out to

the parking lot not saying anything else to each other until they needed to part ways to go to their respective parking spots.

"Have a good evening, Jace," Fields said as he moved in the direction where his car was parked.

"You do the same, Shelton."

Jace continued to his car, thinking of the evening ahead and how he couldn't wait to get to Shana's place. He pulled the keys from his pants pocket to open his car door and that was the last thing he recalled after feeling a needle sting in the back of his neck.

Shana smiled as she looked over at the table she'd set for two. Whenever Jace brought the food, they would eat right out of the carry-out boxes. Tonight, things would be different. She had no idea how he felt about her, but she would tell him he would be a father nonetheless.

She was about to step on the patio and relax a minute when her cell phone rang. It was Kent. "Yes, Kent?"

"Get to your computer. I'm about to send you a report that you need to see."

She glanced at her watch. It was forty minutes past seven. Jace's arrival at her place was always like clockwork. He was late tonight. "Is it something I can look at later?"

"No, I believe it's something you should look at now."

Shana had worked with Kent long enough to know when he was onto something. "All right. Give me a second to boot up my system."

"Okay. I'm hanging on the phone until you do."

Shana walked to the extra bedroom she'd made

into an office and slid into the chair behind the desk. "You're still there, Kent?" she asked as she placed her phone on speaker.

"Yes, I'm still here."

Once the system came up, she immediately pulled the file Kent had sent her. She began reading, and her eyes widened. "Holy cow! How did you find out about this stuff?"

"Doesn't matter. Jace Granger needs to know."

Shana agreed and glanced at her watch again. It wasn't like Jace to be late.

"Hold on, I'm switching to a new line so I can call Jace's cell phone." He should have left the office a good forty-five minutes ago, Shana thought.

She tried Jace's phone and didn't get an answer. Maybe he'd been detained at the office for some reason, so she decided to call his office number. When he didn't answer, she clicked back over to Kent as she nibbled on her bottom lip. Something wasn't right… she could feel it.

"I couldn't reach him on his mobile line, and I even tried his office and couldn't get him. It's not like him not to be accessible," she said.

"Maybe you need to contact his brothers. There's a chance he might be somewhere hanging out with them."

Or his ex-wife, Shana thought, and then forced the thought from her mind. When she saw him at the office, he'd said he was looking forward to tonight. "Okay, I have their numbers. I'll give them a call."

Jace's head was hurting something fierce when he slowly opened his eyes, regaining consciousness. He glanced around, and the first person he saw when he tried focusing his eyes was Titus Freeman.

And as Jace began coming around, he realized that Freeman was bound to his chair with his hands tied behind his back like Jace was. The only difference was that Freeman was also gagged.

"Welcome to my secret hideaway, Jace."

Although it hurt to do so, Jace twisted his head to glance up at the man standing in the doorway. He closed his eyes, certain he was seeing things, but when he reopened them and sharpened his focus as best he could, there was no denying the man standing there with a gun in his hand.

Jace's tongue felt thick, and his mouth felt dry, but he forced the words through his lips. "What's going on?"

Vidal Duncan let out a screeching laugh, one that grated on Jace's skin. The man then placed the gun on a table and sat in a chair. "What's going on is that you messed up my plan, Jace. So this is plan B."

Jace frowned, ignoring the ache in his head. He wasn't sure what Vidal was talking about. Vidal laughed again, then said, "You are so clueless and so damn trusting. A pity. There's so much you don't know, so let me tell you everything before you die."

Jace's body jerked. What was Vidal talking about? What was going on?

"And yes, you'll die. I'm going to make it seem as if Freeman did you in before turning the gun on himself. Nice end to the both of you, don't you think?"

Jace glanced over at Freeman and saw the fear in the man's eyes. Whatever Vidal was involved with, Jace would not let him get away with it. Shana would be

expecting him, and hopefully she would think something was wrong when he didn't show up. And he still
had the tracker on his phone enabled. He had to believe
help would be coming. What he needed to do was to
keep Vidal talking.

"Why, Vidal?" Jace asked in a raspy tone.

He watched as the man filled his glass with wine
and stretched his legs out in front of him. "I guess I
should take the time to tell you since you don't need
to die right away. Besides, you might appreciate my
plan."

Jace doubted it.

Dalton and Caden stepped off the elevator. Dalton
frowned. "I can't believe you came back here for a
stack of papers you need to read tonight."

Caden rolled his eyes as they walked toward his
office. "Stop whining. You could have stayed at Mc-
Queen's."

"I could have, but I didn't." There was no need to
tell Caden that no other woman had interested him
since he'd seen that woman Saturday night at the club.
There had been something about her that continued
to plague his thoughts, although he wished otherwise.
Jace had suggested he hire a private investigator, and
he'd been giving it a lot of thought. Just the idea that he
was considering such a thing was crazy, but there had
been something about her that had pulled him in, and
he wouldn't be satisfied until he found out what it was.

"I noticed Jace's car is still in the parking lot, and I
thought he told us he had someplace to be by seven,"
Caden said, glancing at Jace's closed office door as he
entered his own office. "I wonder why he's being de-

tained." He headed toward his desk and Dalton closed the door behind them and then dropped down in the nearest chair.

Caden's cell phone rang, and he lifted a brow when he saw caller ID. "It's Shana Bradford." He answered the call. "Yes, Shana?"

"I'm trying to locate Jace. There's been a major development, and I need to talk to him immediately."

Caden leaned against his desk. "His car is still here, so I assume he's in his office. Hold on, let me check."

He muted the phone and then glanced over at Dalton as he headed for the door. "Jace never showed up for his seven o'clock appointment." Jace hadn't had to tell them his seven o'clock appointment was with Shana. They weren't dumb.

Dalton followed Caden out of his office to knock on Jace's door. After several knocks, Caden glanced over at Dalton. "He's not here."

Dalton's lips dipped into a frown. "Where would Jace go without his car?"

Caden put his phone on speaker so Dalton could hear his conversation with Shana. "He's not here, Shana."

He could hear her deep sigh. "Is there a chance he visited Eve at the hotel?" she asked.

Caden snorted. "I doubt it."

"We need to make sure, so can you check? If Jace isn't with her, then I'm worried."

"Why are you worried?"

"Because Kent was able to dig up info on another one of your employees, and what he found is disturbing. This person covered his tracks well and has no idea we're onto him. And I have a feeling he'll do anything to make sure he's not found out."

Concern appeared in both Caden's and Dalton's faces. "What employee are we talking about, Shana?" Caden asked.

Shana paused before briefly saying, "Vidal Duncan."

"Well, you see, Jace, my plan started four years ago," Vidal said, sitting down and sipping on a glass of wine as if he had all the time in the world. "With your wife, actually. That year when the two of you came home for Thanksgiving, she approached me asking that I talk to you about returning to Virginia and working alongside Richard. I pretended I was all for it, even promised her I would do what I could."

He chuckled. "Then I asked how badly she wanted me to succeed in doing what she wanted, and she claimed she would do anything. So I had her prove it. We became lovers that night and our affair continued after the two of you returned to California. Nice little piece you were married to. She could become a real freak in the bedroom. And just so you know, that baby she aborted wasn't yours. It was mine, and she did so with my blessing. There was no way we could let her give birth to a kid that might come out looking like me."

A sharp pain sliced across Jace's chest and he drew in a deep breath, not wanting to believe what he was hearing. "No!" he shouted as loud as he could.

Vidal chuckled again. "Having a hard time believing it, huh? I understand. Eve is a rather good actress. I'm going to let you digest that for a minute before I continue."

Chapter Thirty-Three

With cold fear running up her spine, Shana quickly stepped off the elevator at Granger Aeronautics with Marcel at her side. After Caden called her back to confirm that Jace was not with Eve, Shana immediately called Marcel. She had reached him just minutes before he left the FBI office for home.

"Heard anything?" she asked Caden when she headed straight for his office.

"Not a thing." He then glanced over at Marcel. "What do you suggest we do?" Caden just couldn't believe that the man who had been a longtime trusted family friend, someone who was like a godfather to the three of them, was the same person Shana was painting him to be. But she had forwarded him and Dalton the same report her man Kent had given her and the information was pretty damn damaging.

"I already have a couple of my agents scouring the parking lot and checking out Jace's car," Marcel said. "Hopefully, we'll find something. And we have someone keeping an eye on Duncan's home. We don't want to tip him off that he's under suspicion about anything, especially since we don't know for certain that he had anything to do with Jace's disappearance."

Shana shook her head. "I can't believe Vidal is doing this. My suspicions had been focused on Shelton Fields. He's been acting strange lately and hanging around Brandy's desk a lot."

"They're having an affair," Dalton spoke up and said.

Everyone turned to Dalton. "And how do you know?" Caden asked incredulously.

"She told me. That's why we aren't sleeping together," he said as if there was nothing wrong with his having an office affair. "She's already involved with him."

"He's divorced and she's single. Why are they keeping it secret?" Shana inquired and then thought that she of all people was a fine one to ask, considering what she and Jace had been doing.

"They weren't sure how Jace would like it, so they decided to keep it hush-hush."

At that moment, one of the agents who'd been searching the parking lot approached. Marcel looked up. "Yes, Greg?"

"This was found in the parking lot near where Mr. Granger's car is parked," he said, lifting a see-through baggie that contained a syringe.

Marcel frowned. "Get it to the lab immediately. I have a feeling it was used on Jace."

Eve nervously paced back and forth in her hotel room. Jace was missing? What on earth was Vidal doing? Was he certain no one would suspect him? Or her?

Caden had called, questioning Jace's whereabouts, and she had made sure he believed she hadn't seen or talked to Jace in a couple of days. There was no way she would get pulled into anything.

She had tried calling Vidal, and he wouldn't answer. So she would sit here and wait and hope like hell he wouldn't do anything stupid.

"Your ex-wife keeps calling me," Vidal mumbled, placing his cell phone next to where he'd set the gun on the table. "I guess people are looking for you, and someone called her to see if the two of you were together. That's funny."

He then took a sip of his drink and said, "Now to take up where I left off. You didn't take the bait and return to Virginia like Eve wanted. Then you found out about the abortion and kicked poor Eve to the curb. In the meantime, your grandfather began suspecting that someone was selling trade secrets. He wanted to bring Ms. Bradford on board to find the guilty persons. Unfortunately, he died before doing so."

"Why would you encourage me to hire Shana knowing her reputation for success?" Jace asked. "Weren't you afraid she would find out what you were doing?"

Vidal chuckled. "No. I had covered my tracks too well. Besides, I wasn't into trade secrets. I was growing money."

"Embezzling," Jace said with disgust.

"Yes," Vidal said smiling. "So I decided to throw you a bone. Let your girl go after Freeman here and his group and not give any thought to what I was up to. Remember, I was the trusted company attorney. I was considered part of the family."

Jace didn't say anything as everything Vidal said sank in. He hated to admit it, but the man was right. Vidal had worked for the Grangers for years. He was like part of the family. They'd never given a thought to his being involved in anything shady.

"I'm going to let you absorb that bit into your mind while I take a few more sips of my drink here."

The lab verified that the syringe had been used recently to inject a drug known for rendering a person unconscious. Everyone was in Caden's office listening to the update Marcel was providing when suddenly Dalton said, "Holy shit! I'd almost forgotten."

Everyone glanced over at him. "Forgotten what, Dalton?" Caden asked.

"The tracker. I had Security place a tracker on Jace's phone."

"But he said he wouldn't let you track him after hours," Caden said, running a tired hand across the back of his neck. "He probably turned it off."

"But what if he forgot or didn't have time to do so?" Dalton asked, moving to the door. "The guys in Security are still here. I'm going to see if there's a chance they can pinpoint Jace's location."

"Imagine my joy when the FBI focused their investigation on Freeman and his group," Vidal was saying. "That just made my day, and things were working in my favor…until you began getting chummy with Ms. Bradford. I happened to be there one night when the two of you walked out together. And then I deliberately drove by her condo another night, and your car was parked outside."

He shifted in his chair and continued. "I figured she had done what I needed her to do, and I wanted her to move on. A relationship with you wasn't in my plan, because she could start snooping again later. That's when I called Eve. I paid her a lot of money to fly to Charlottesville and break things up. She was certain once you saw her again you'd forget all about Ms. Bradford. But you didn't bite. And then all hell broke loose when Eve overheard that conversation Ms. Bradford had with her sister the other day at Long Meadows. Ms. Bradford told her sister that she thought she was pregnant with your child."

The lashes that shadowed Jace's eyes flew up at the same time he was hit full force in the gut. *Shana thought she was pregnant? Was that what she had to tell him tonight?* The thought that she was pregnant with his child sent shivers of happiness through him even when these could possibly be his last breaths.

"That's when I knew I had to come up with plan B," Vidal continued. "So, this is how it will work. Everyone is looking for Freeman. When they find you with a bullet in your gut and that same gun used by Freeman to put a hole in his own head, everyone will assume that Freeman, in despair over how things went down with you finding out what he'd done and the authorities tracking him down like some kind of animal, killed you and then himself. Caden and Dalton will be totally heartbroken and distraught. It's bad enough to have a father in jail, but now to have a brother dead? That will be too much for them. They will be overwrought with grief, and being the close family friend that I am, I will advise them to live the lives they've always wanted to live. I'll encourage Dalton to return to Europe and Caden to his music. I'll recommend that they agree to a merger with Barnes Aerospace. Of course they will take my advice, since they will feel you were killed because of Granger Aeronautics and would want to wash their hands of the company."

Jace couldn't believe what he was hearing. "You think you have everything figured out, don't you?"

Vidal answered, "Yes." He stood. "Now for what I have to do. And I wouldn't advise you or Freeman to give me any problems. I will carry this out, and then I'm going to go and take care of Eve. She's become a liability."

"You'll never get away with this," Jace growled.

"Of course you'd think that. You keep that thought in your mind while I put this bullet through your head."

Vidal reached for his gun, and the moment he did so, a shot rang out, hitting him in the arm. Federal agents burst through the door, and within seconds, he was overpowered and taken into custody.

An agent rushed over to Jace and another to Freeman to untie them from the chairs. Freeman was handcuffed and taken into custody, as well. Jace smiled when he saw Marcel. "Boy, am I glad to see you guys."

Marcel chuckled. "I'm sure you are. While Freeman was sitting by the window in plain view, one of my agents, a sharpshooter, has had Vidal within his scope all the while. That made him an easy target and as soon as he picked up that gun, we took action." Marcel then smiled and added, "You have your brother to thank for putting that tracker on your phone. Unlike other trackers that merely provide a fifty-mile radius, the one you have pinpoints your location precisely. It definitely made finding you easier."

"I'll be sure to thank Dalton. He can be a pain in the ass at times, but I think I'll keep him."

"You better," Dalton said, grinning as he and Caden walked through the door. "I'm beginning to like this spy stuff."

"Jace!"

Shana then burst through the door and ran straight into Jace's arms. A flood of heat and love encompassed him when he lowered his head to kiss her, not caring that they had an audience. She curled her arms around his neck and slid into his body. She felt right in his arms.

Suddenly, he broke off the kiss, and Shana found herself being steered to a corner of the room for privacy.

"Don't go too far, Jace," Marcel called out. "We'll need you to give a statement."

Jace nodded before glancing down at Shana. "I am so glad to see you," he whispered.

"And I'm glad to see you, too. I've never been so scared in my life. I never thought Vidal could be so..."

"Evil," he finished for her. "Neither did I."

Jace shook his head sadly. "And just to think he's a man I'd considered trustworthy. He worked for Granddad for years. He was there for us when Dad went to prison and when Granddad died...or so we thought. He's admitted to skimming off Granger for years."

He didn't say anything for a minute and then he reached out and placed his hand on her stomach. "Are you pregnant?"

Shana's mouth dropped open. "Why would you think—"

"Eve."

She was almost too stunned to speak. "Eve?"

"Yes. She overheard a conversation you and your sister had at Long Meadows."

Shana's head began spinning. "I don't understand."

"I'll explain Eve's part in all of this later. But please answer me. Do you think you're pregnant? Do you know for certain?"

Shana drew in a deep breath. This was not how she had planned to tell him, but since he was asking, she would. "Yes. I found out Tuesday when I took a home pregnancy test. That's what I wanted to tell you tonight. And I *was* on the pill like I told you. But the antibiotics I was taking affected their potency. I'm sorry."

Jace pulled her into his arms. "Don't apologize, baby. I love children and always wanted some of my own. The reason I divorced Eve was because I came home from a business trip early to discover she'd had an abortion. For three years, I've been heartbroken over what she did."

He paused for a moment and then added, "And tonight Vidal had the gall to tell me it was his baby. *His* baby. He and Eve had an affair, and she had the abortion with his blessing."

The shock of what Jace had just said almost made Shana's heart hurt. She couldn't say anything, and stood there speechless. And then she couldn't stop the tears that formed in her eyes. How could any woman deceive him that way? Jace was such a beautiful, kind and honorable man.

"Don't cry, sweetheart," he said, reaching up and using the pad of his thumb to wipe away her tears. "Nothing Eve can do will ever hurt me again. Only you can do that, because I love you."

Talk about another shocker. This one almost brought

Shana to her knees. He tightened his arms around her. And just in case she didn't get it, Jace said. "I love you, and I want you, and I want our child."

His words filled her with joy, and she felt totally elated. "And I love you, too, Jace. I love you so much."

Jace kissed her again. There was no doubt in his mind that she was the woman meant for him. The woman who had his heart and his love. The woman who was having his baby.

He took her hand as his lips curved into a smile. "Come on, sweetheart. I need to give Marcel that statement, and then we're leaving. We have a future to plan."

Later that night, Shana lay in Jace's arms. His statement had been given at police headquarters, and they'd both been there when Eve was brought in for questioning. There was nothing the woman could say, since Jace knew the truth.

"When do I get to meet your dad and sister?" he asked her, smiling.

"You get to meet Dad this weekend, but Jules left for Seattle this morning, and no telling when she'll return. She's working on a new case."

He lifted a brow. "A new case?"

"Yes, she's a private investigator and owns her own company."

"Is she any good?"

"The best. But then, I would say that because I'm biased."

Jace didn't say anything for a minute then said, "I want to marry you, Shana. Not just because I don't want my child born out of wedlock, but because I love you, and I want you to have my name."

Shana felt her heart expand with happiness. "You sure?"

"I haven't been so sure about anything in my life. So, will you marry me?"

She threw her arms around his neck and held his gaze that was so full of love and a mirror of her own. "Yes, I'll marry you."

Emotions ripped through Jace. Since returning to Virginia, he felt as if he'd gained more than any person had a right to claim: a company that had always been his legacy; the kind of relationship with his brothers that he'd always wanted; a beautiful fiancée and a child on the way.

He couldn't wait to tell his father, and Jace was determined that his son or daughter would get to know Sheppard Granger as a free man, and not a man behind bars for a crime he didn't commit. He, Caden and Dalton would move heaven and earth to make that happen.

He bent his head and captured Shana's lips with his. This was only the beginning.

* * * * *

Coming in June 2014,
Caden Granger's story titled,
A SON'S PROMISE

ROMANCE.
FAMILY.
PASSION.
ADVENTURE.
TRUE LOVE.

A MADARIS BRIDE FOR CHRISTMAS

NEW YORK TIMES BESTSELLING AUTHOR

BRENDA JACKSON

Her 100th novel!
Get ready to celebrate on October 29.

H HARLEQUIN®
™ www.Harlequin.com

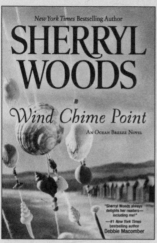

#1 *New York Times* Bestselling Author
ROBYN CARR

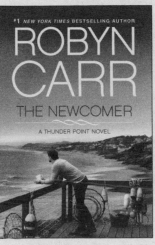

Single dad and Thunder Point's deputy sheriff "Mac" McCain has worked hard to keep everyone safe and happy. Now he's found his own happiness with Gina James. The longtime friends have always shared the challenges and rewards of raising their adolescent daughters. With an unexpected romance growing between them, they're feeling like love-struck teenagers themselves.

But just when things are really taking off, their lives are suddenly thrown into chaos. When Mac's long-lost—and not missed—ex-wife shows up in town, drama takes on a whole new meaning. They're wondering if their new feelings for each other can withstand the pressure…but they are not going down without a fight.

On sale June 25 wherever books are sold.

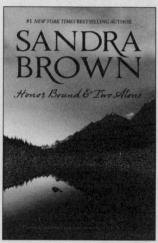

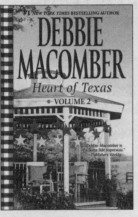

REQUEST YOUR FREE BOOKS!

2 FREE NOVELS
FROM THE ROMANCE COLLECTION
PLUS 2 FREE GIFTS!

YES! Please send me 2 FREE novels from the Romance Collection and my 2 FREE gifts (gifts are worth about $10). After receiving them, if I don't wish to receive any more books, I can return the shipping statement marked "cancel." If I don't cancel, I will receive 4 brand-new novels every month and be billed just $6.24 per book in the U.S. or $6.74 per book in Canada. That's a savings of at least 22% off the cover price. It's quite a bargain! Shipping and handling is just 50¢ per book in the U.S. and 75¢ per book in Canada.* I understand that accepting the 2 free books and gifts places me under no obligation to buy anything. I can always return a shipment and cancel at any time. Even if I never buy another book, the two free books and gifts are mine to keep forever.

194/394 MDN F4XY

Name _____ (PLEASE PRINT) _____

Address _____ Apt. # _____

City _____ State/Prov. _____ Zip/Postal Code _____

Signature (if under 18, a parent or guardian must sign)

Mail to the **Harlequin® Reader Service:**
IN U.S.A.: P.O. Box 1867, Buffalo, NY 14240-1867
IN CANADA: P.O. Box 609, Fort Erie, Ontario L2A 5X3

Want to try two free books from another line?
Call 1-800-873-8635 or visit www.ReaderService.com.

* Terms and prices subject to change without notice. Prices do not include applicable taxes. Sales tax applicable in N.Y. Canadian residents will be charged applicable taxes. Offer not valid in Quebec. This offer is limited to one order per household. Not valid for current subscribers to the Romance Collection or the Romance/Suspense Collection. All orders subject to credit approval. Credit or debit balances in a customer's account(s) may be offset by any other outstanding balance owed by or to the customer. Please allow 4 to 6 weeks for delivery. Offer available while quantities last.

Your Privacy—The Harlequin® Reader Service is committed to protecting your privacy. Our Privacy Policy is available online at www.ReaderService.com or upon request from the Harlequin Reader Service.

We make a portion of our mailing list available to reputable third parties that offer products we believe may interest you. If you prefer that we not exchange your name with third parties, or if you wish to clarify or modify your communication preferences, please visit us at www.ReaderService.com/consumerschoice or write to us at Harlequin Reader Service Preference Service, P.O. Box 9062, Buffalo, NY 14269. Include your complete name and address.

ROM13R

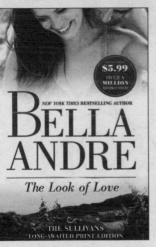